RUBY JEAN COTTLE

BLACK RIVER

**SIMON &
SCHUSTER**

London · New York · Amsterdam/Antwerp · Sydney/Melbourne · Toronto · New Delhi

First published in Great Britain in 2026 by Simon & Schuster UK Ltd.

First published in Australia in 2025 by Atria Books Australia,
an imprint of Simon & Schuster (Australia) Pty Limited
Level 4, 32 York St, Sydney NSW 2000

Text copyright © 2025 Ruby Jean Cottle

This book is copyright under the Berne Convention.
No reproduction without permission.
All rights reserved.

The right of Ruby Jean Cottle to be identified as the author and illustrator
of this work has been asserted by them in accordance with sections 77
and 78 of the Copyright, Designs and Patents Act, 1988.

1 3 5 7 9 10 8 6 4 2

Simon & Schuster UK Ltd
1st Floor, 222 Gray's Inn Road
London WC1X 8HB

For more than 100 years, Simon & Schuster has championed authors and the stories they create. By respecting the copyright of an author's intellectual property, you enable Simon & Schuster and the author to continue publishing exceptional books for years to come. We thank you for supporting the author's copyright by purchasing an authorized edition of this book. No amount of this book may be reproduced or stored in any format, nor may it be uploaded to any website, database, language-learning model, or other repository, retrieval, or artificial intelligence system without express permission. All rights reserved. Inquiries may be directed to Simon & Schuster, 222 Gray's Inn Road, London WC1X 8HB or RightsMailbox@simonandschuster.co.uk

www.simonandschuster.co.uk
www.simonandschuster.com.au
www.simonandschuster.co.in

The authorised representative in the EEA is Simon & Schuster Netherlands BV, Herculesplein 96,
3584 AA Utrecht, Netherlands. info@simonandschuster.nl

Simon & Schuster Australia, Sydney
Simon & Schuster India, New Delhi

A CIP catalogue record for this book
is available from the British Library.

PB ISBN 9781398553323
eBook ISBN 9781398553347
eAudio ISBN 9781398553330

This book is a work of fiction. Names, characters, places and incidents are either the product of the author's imagination or are used fictitiously. Any resemblance to actual people living or dead, events or locales is entirely coincidental.

Printed and Bound in the UK using 100% Renewable
Electricity at CPI Group (UK) Ltd

Praise for *Black River*

'There's something haunting about *Black River* – the kind of story with chilling twists, a slow-burn romance, and just the right amount of bite. It pulls you into its eerie depths and doesn't let you go – *Black River* is dark, intoxicating, and impossible to put down. More please!'
Courtney Peppernell, author of *Pillow Thoughts*

'Atmospheric and suspenseful, this classic YA paranormal tale combines genres skillfully and delivers a brooding monster story that's part family drama, part thriller, part romance and all bite.'
Lisa Tirreno, author of *Prince of Fortune*

'*Black River* is a smart, sensual, deeply atmospheric debut, brimming with immersive world-building, compelling characters, and all the right kinds of tension. The mystery at its heart keeps you guessing right to the last page, where it becomes clear this is only the beginning of Dusty's story. I sank my teeth in and barely came up for air.'
Emma Lord, author of *Anomaly*

'Part fantasy, part astute coming of age story, *Black River* brilliantly depicts the angst of adolescence, along with its burgeoning – and sometimes terrifying – power. Like its dynamic heroine Dusty, the prose brims with vitality; I felt every moment of her transformation as if I were right there on the mountain with her. It's not often that I wish for a do-over of my teenage years, but the world of *Black River* was so evocative, I found myself envying Dusty's unfurling connection to the natural world, and to her own formidable nature. I need to know what happens next!'
Jacqueline Bublitz, author of *Before You Knew My Name*

'My teenage self felt a real connection to book-loving Dusty and the tender, sisterly love she shares with Opi. I felt emotionally invested in Dusty's story, and the high-stakes plot kept me riveted to the page. Ruby's storytelling keeps things hot with a spicy romance and original with turns into the mystical. *Black River* is an impressive debut, and I'm looking forward to part two.'
Becca Fitzpatrick, author of *Hush, Hush*

Ruby Jean Cottle is a writer from Sydney, Australia. Growing up, Ruby spent childhood summers in upstate New York, where her passion for writing blossomed as her imagination ran wild in the mountains and forests far from her home. After studying art history at university, Ruby found herself on a winding career path in fashion, digital media and creative direction. After becoming a mother, she decided to return to her first love: writing stories.

For you.
Then, now and somewhere along the road.

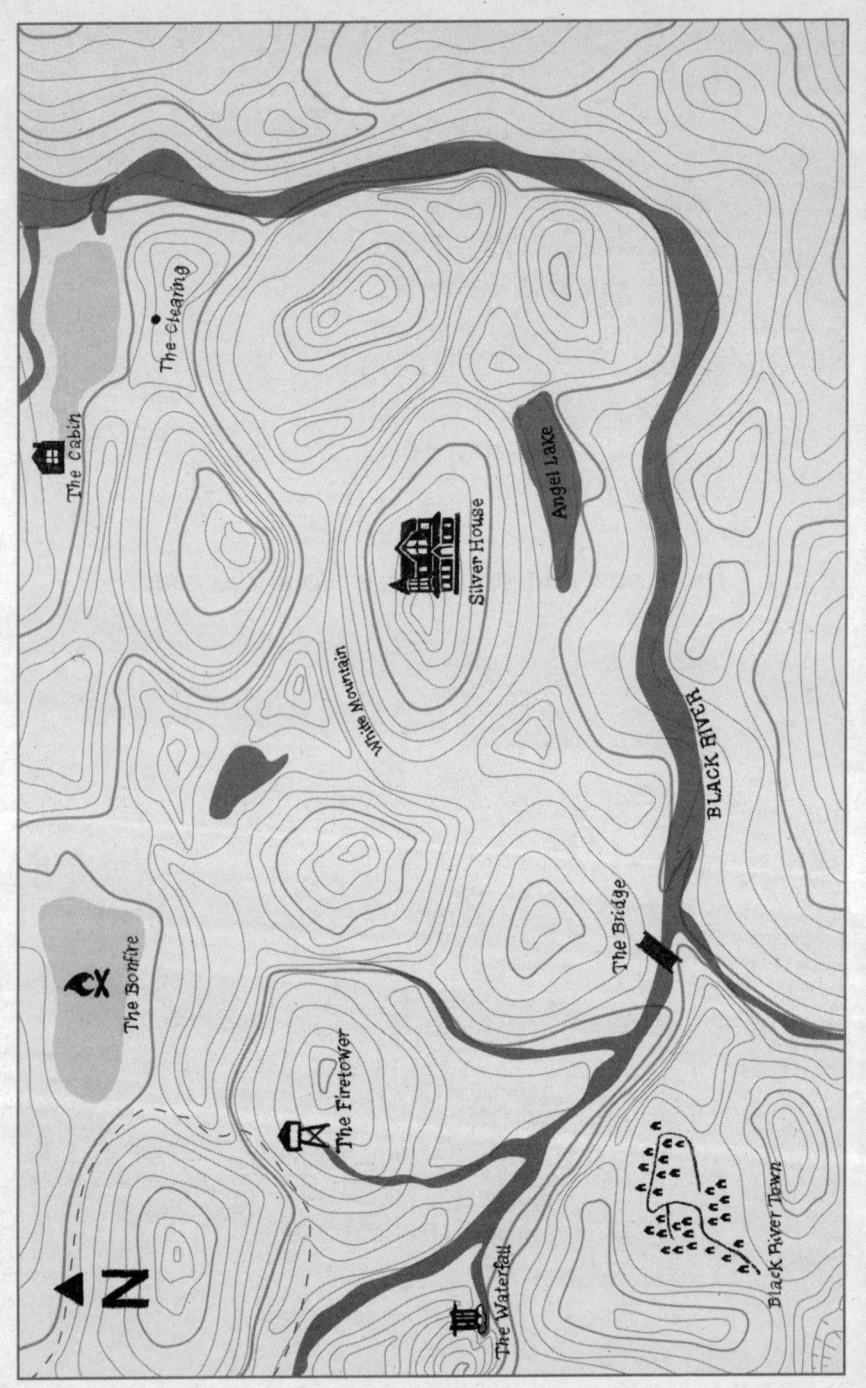

Prologue

The light of the bonfire distorts the crowd. A collective gasp still lingers.

She can feel her heartbeat everywhere.

At first, she doesn't understand what it is her body wants—what it is that's happened that could incite an urge unlike anything she's ever conceived of. But as she looks around, she sees him staring, transfixed.

His eyes are a mirror of what she feels.

He steps forward and tilts his head. Arms grab at him, trying to stop him. He shakes them off like they're nothing but ash.

Without thinking, she walks through the cluster of people, fighting the call of the metallic smell that seems to consume the air. Blood. She bites down on the pressure building in her teeth and steps directly in front of him, blocking his line of sight. His gaze still fixed beyond her, he tries to push her aside. She doesn't move. Instead, she grabs his arm and leans in close to whisper in his ear.

"I know what you're feeling. I feel it too."

He pulls back and his eyes meet hers, searching.

She can see he's scared.

"We shouldn't be here, feeling like this. We need to go," she says with more force, holding out her hand. "Now."

He looks down at her hand then takes hold of it. She pulls, and they run into the darkness.

PART I

1
The Trees

Soft sunlight warms Dusty's face. The chime of birdsong pings against her window and the shifting light whispers that it's her favorite time of year. Early summer.

For a second, something a little like optimism courses through her sleepy body.

Her arm escapes the warmth of her blankets, reaching for the cold phone on her bedside table. Squinting, she can see that she's just in time. Five fifty-eight. Two minutes before her alarm is set to go off. She swipes it off, grateful to avoid the jarring trill.

Sitting up, she rubs her eyes open. Green leaves cover the giant beech tree outside her window and their gilded shadows dance in the alcove of her bed.

Beyond the tree, Dusty can see southward down the steep slope of White Mountain, past a shimmering blue lake, all the way to the base of the valley where Black River flows. Somewhere beyond that, hidden by trees, is her hometown, named after the river, and the Adirondack Mountains, looming in every direction.

On top of her comforter there's a black, soft-cover Moleskine notebook. Beside it is an open book lying face down. She must have fallen asleep reading it sometime late last night, lost in a world of spells, dragons and romance. Her dad would have turned her light out at some point, like he always does.

The temptation to stay in bed and read is almost overwhelming—safe in the house that grounds her, her head in a book that sets her free.

But today is a school day, and Dusty has a life to face.

She picks up the book, carefully folds the corner of the last page she remembers reading, then neatly places it on top of the pile beside her bed. She reaches to the window and shimmies it open. A cool breeze sighs through the gap and she lets out a quick breath like she's flicking a switch—an attempt at turning off emotions that have roamed her body for years. Feelings that ache unless kept in check. Sometimes it works. Sometimes it doesn't.

She makes her bed before heading over to a big old chest of drawers—inherited, like almost everything else in this house, from her grandparents, who had inherited it from their parents and so on—and exchanges her t-shirt and boxers for a fresh t-shirt and some well-worn Levi's that she buttons up tight around the curves of her hips.

The hall outside her bedroom is dim and quiet. Several closed doors lead to mostly unused rooms, but her sister's door is open. There's a staircase at each end of the hall. One leads downstairs and the other leads up to her dad's room. The tattered Persian rug feels soft under Dusty's feet as she crosses it to the bathroom.

She splashes water on her face, brushes her teeth and looks at her reflection just long enough to decide that today isn't going to be the day she starts making more of an effort. Her long, wavy brown hair is neat enough, with layered bangs that she trims herself every few weeks framing fair skin and hazel eyes. Freckles are sprinkled across her nose and her cheeks are still rosy from sleep. Already uncomfortable with the girl in the reflection, she looks away and returns to her room to stuff her laptop and notebook into a backpack, along with a book for good measure.

As she descends the creaky, wide wooden staircase, sunshine flickers through the downstairs windows, motes floating in golden beams. Besides a few simple touch-ups, the Victorian house remains mostly as it was when her ancestors built it.

It's a large, open-plan space painted creamy white, with two living areas, a dining area and the kitchen all connected by wide archways complete with intricate wooden detailing, and broad floorboards that still show the twisting life-lines of trees felled right here on the mountain. High ceilings, large rugs and two enormous fireplaces make the space feel even bigger. The furniture is scuffed and a little worn, the walls adorned with Silver family history.

But Dusty braces herself as she moves through the rooms, and as she glances at the near-empty shelves behind the sofa, she remembers what they'd looked like when they were packed with her mom's art books. They'd brought so much color to the room, especially at this time of day when their spines were drenched in sunlight. The memory cuts through Dusty's chest like a blade and that familiar feeling hits. That unprovoked sense that something terrible could happen at any moment. As if it's written in her bones.

She hates her body for experiencing everything so viscerally.

Realizing her fists are clenched, she shakes out her hands then releases another quick breath to turn her feelings off. But the breath only makes her gasp for another, then another, as her chest tightens. On the sideboard beside her she notices that a rectangular dish is askew. She straightens it so it aligns with the table's edge and the tension inside her dissipates, just a little.

A cabinet bangs in the kitchen and the kettle begins to hum. Her dad will have left for work by now, which means Opi's getting breakfast ready. Dusty tries to slow her breath, and sure enough, as she rounds the archway to the kitchen, her sister is there, plucking freshly cut herbs from vases and jars that cover the countertops like bouquets in a flower shop.

"Oh good! You're up!" Opi smiles over her shoulder before breezing past to whisk the kettle from the stove. She pours the steaming water into a glass teapot full of fresh leaves then looks closely at Dusty. "Everything okay?"

Dusty nods and attempts a smile.

"Did one of your book boyfriends die?" Opi asks, completely sincere.

Dusty looks at her sister flatly as Opi twists a strand of her long, golden-brown hair around a finger, concerned. "Want to talk about it?" Opi asks, stepping closer.

Dusty shakes her head as she steps back, then sits down at the dining table.

"You know it's okay to vent your feelings?" Opi says. "If not to me, then to Mali. Or dad," she adds encouragingly.

Dusty reaches into her bag and takes out her notebook and a pen. Flicking to an empty page, she begins to draw inky-black curved shapes with dots and lines inside them. The pressure of the pen on the paper is like a funnel—a controlled outlet for the storm inside her.

Opi watches as she continues, "You can't just *avoid*—"

"I don't *avoid*. I manage," Dusty interrupts, exasperated.

"Potato-potahto."

Dusty can't help the smile tugging at her cheeks as she continues to draw.

"You know what you need?" Opi prompts, her voice the epitome of optimism.

"Coffee?" Dusty looks up to catch Opi rolling her eyes.

"No. Some time outside."

"We're about to go outside. We have school. Remember?"

"I mean *outside* outside. We live on a mountain. In the middle of a forest. *Remember*?"

"Fine. We can have breakfast on the porch."

"Actually," Opi says, her eyebrows rising with her voice. "I was thinking . . ."

Dusty's eyes narrow, skeptical.

"It's already June third. You know what that means, right?" Excitement shimmers in Opi's eyes.

"That there's less than four weeks of school before summer vacation?"

Opi sighs. "It means that it's the end of morel season! If we wait until the weekend we might miss out—"

"So go with Theo after school."

"I don't want to go with Theo."

"He's your best friend—"

"I want to go with you," Opi says firmly. "You used to love it out there. You were so happy—"

"That was before—" But Dusty stops herself from saying more. The last thing she wants is to upset her sister. She sighs. "So you're saying you want to forage for mushrooms before school?"

Opi nods, grinning.

Dusty glances at the clock. Six-twenty.

"We don't have to leave until seven-fifteen," Opi pleads, hopeful. "I know you hate being late, but it will only take half an hour. Max. Plenty of time to sauté them up in some butter when we get back," she tempts, her eyebrows raised as if the allure is undeniable. "Dad got fresh bread yesterday . . ."

"I don't want to be rushed, Op," Dusty groans. "I wanted to make coffee, read my book . . ." She looks around. "If you go, I can get the kitchen ready for you when you get back."

"I already made you *tea*," Opi says, pouring the yellow-tinged infusion into two flasks. "And I want to go with *you*." Opi disappears for a moment, returning with both of their walking boots. "Let's go." She smiles as she opens the kitchen door and steps onto the porch.

Dusty remains seated, determined not to follow. She looks down at her pen, the tip still pressed into the notebook. Black ink pools on the page and a vision of Opi tripping and hitting her head on a jagged rock invades Dusty's mind, forcing her to stand.

She sucks in a breath, trying to shake the irrational thought as she grabs the flasks and follows Opi onto the porch.

"You do know I'm your *big* sister, don't you?" Dusty asks, barely a trace of anxiety in her voice. "Shouldn't that make me *your* boss?"

"Firstly, you're not even eighteen months older than me," Opi says, as they both tug on their boots at the top of the stairs. "Secondly, if you were the boss, we'd just sit around and read all day and miss out on all of *this*." She gestures beyond the porch, as if life is as clear cut as blue sky and sunshine.

"*This* exists in books too," Dusty teases, ignoring the crisp scent of dew-covered pines. "The difference is you get to see it through someone else's eyes. And there are witches and warriors and fairies there too."

Opi frowns. "Why would you want to be someone else?"

Dusty shrugs. "I'm not like you. I don't have what you have with your herbs and this garden." She looks out over the grassy slope, covered by a plush tangle of vegetables, fruits and herbs. "*You* know where your puzzle piece fits, but I . . . I'm seventeen and should at least have a vague idea of what I want to do. And no, don't say writing. I'm no good at that. I just feel . . . like nothing jumps out at me. Like there's nothing that feels like *me*."

Opi's big brown eyes are curious and watchful. The golden highlights in her brown hair glisten in the sunshine like she's wearing a crown. "But . . . you're the best."

Opi's sincerity is felt like a lump in Dusty's throat which she immediately tries to swallow. "That's impossible," she says matter-of-factly. "Because you are." She stands, boots on, ready to go.

Opi joins her. She's dressed in a knee-length, floral print dress, camo-green bomber jacket and white socks that sprout a ruffle out the top of her boots. Opi—or Ophelia, but only her teachers call her that—has a sense of self-confidence that Dusty is always in awe of.

"What?" Opi asks, catching Dusty's assessing gaze.

"You look cute today." She smiles.

Opi grins. She drapes an empty satchel over her shoulder and hands Dusty one of her own, along with her tea. "Even if you don't drink it, it'll warm up your hands."

Dusty rolls her eyes. "Only because you're a little weirdo and tea's your love language." She takes a sip. It's undeniably comforting. "Let's go."

There are trails that lead into the forest in all directions around their property, including north to the mountain's summit, but Opi leads the way south, down through her garden to where the cultivated plants are met by wild ones. There's a narrow track visible through the understory, worn down by their ancestors year after year, and the sisters enter there, enveloped by a thick canopy of trees.

"Remember," Dusty warns. "Fifteen minutes down, fifteen minutes back."

"I know!" Opi calls.

Although not as expert as her sister, Dusty is far from a stranger to these woods. She recognizes the different plants—giant spruce, hemlock and cherry trees, their bases cushioned by clusters of hobblebush, elderberry, dogwood and honeysuckle—and registers landmarks as they pass through. It's a force of habit their dad drilled into them from a young age. The price for being allowed to run wild here. A precaution against getting lost.

"The vastness of this forest could swallow you whole," Dusty says.

"Huh?" Opi doesn't bother looking back.

"Dad said that once."

"Oh," Opi murmurs, distracted by something in the canopy.

"How long has it been since you did this with him?"

Opi shrugs. "I don't know."

"Maybe if we both get jobs over summer, he can ease up with work a little."

"At least he loves it though," Opi says. "He basically gets to do *this* for a living. Plus, I don't mind being left to our own devices." She looks back conspiratorially.

"Mhmm," Dusty says. "Just look at how badass we are . . . foraging for mushrooms on a school day." She winks at her sister, trying to cover how painful it is for her to be out here—how much it reminds her of their childhood. Of what they had, and what they lost.

Opi chuckles as she slows, scanning the forest floor. "We have to be close," she murmurs.

Desperate to hurry this along, Dusty begins to look too. "Come on," she says, placing her flask on the trail and breaking off the path. Opi does the same.

They tread slowly and carefully as they look for signs, trying not to trample too heavily on the mosaic of living organisms underfoot. Leaves rustle, not far, and they look up to see a white-tailed deer trotting away from them. Within seconds it's hidden by the collage of green.

"It's okay," Dusty calls after it. "She's a pescatarian!"

Opi rolls her eyes. She's never eaten red meat, even as a young child, which in Dusty's opinion, is just another reason to admire Opi's self-assuredness, considering they come from a long tradition of hunting what you eat. "It's lucky it's not hunting season," Opi adds before continuing forward.

Always aware of the direction of the trail, they scan the ground, peeling back decaying leaves and branches that might be hiding the mushrooms underneath. The smell of earth is rich and heady.

"We can't go much further, Op," Dusty says as she crouches beside an enormous old ash tree. Brushing aside some moss and pine needles, she sees the crest of a brown honeycomb-like structure that's attached to a creamy stalk. She plucks it from the ground. "Found one!" she yells, surprised by her excitement.

"For real?" Opi shouts, running over. "Are you sure!?"

Dusty inspects the mushroom, noticing where the cap meets the stem. The sides of the cap are attached to the stipe at the bottom. A good sign. She breaks it apart. It's completely hollow, as it should be. It's a good size too, about the length of her palm. "Yep. Look, there's more."

It's like a treasure hunt. At first glance, they look like pinecones strewn among the leaves, but the more they focus, the true morels stand out. Gathering the mushrooms delicately, the sisters are careful not to harvest too many.

"Shake them gently before you put them in your bag," Opi reminds Dusty, who rolls her eyes as if it's obvious. It was one of the first things their grandmother taught them about foraging—so that loose spores can make their way to the ground and return as more mushrooms next year.

The terrain becomes denser as they duck under low-hanging branches and climb over long-fallen trees.

"Last one then we head back, okay?" Dusty calls. She bends down to gather a particularly big morel. "Okay?" she calls again. Frustrated to be the only one in a rush, she stands and turns.

But Opi isn't there.

"Op?" she calls. She can't see her sister, but the distinct feeling that someone—or something—is close by is disorienting. She turns quickly, scanning for another deer, but there's nothing but plant life waving in the breeze.

Dusty listens, aware of the slim chance that black bears could be around. She stills herself, waiting for a snap or a deep grunt. There's nothing.

Telling herself Opi must have headed back to the trail, Dusty starts to retrace her steps. She's surprised to see a dozen or so pink lady's slipper orchids she hadn't noticed before. They only bloom for a few weeks this time of year. Bobbing on their leafless stalks, they'll probably come and go without another soul ever seeing them. The thought draws a shiver across her skin.

She continues, looking for her sister and the trail, but she doesn't recognize anything around her. There are trees she swears she hadn't come past. They grow in front of a huge boulder that casts dark shadows.

A sinking feeling begins to weigh heavy in the pit of Dusty's stomach and a hot rush of adrenaline runs through her veins.

"Opi," she tries, but her voice falters.

She spins, staggering as she searches for any sign of where she is. *This doesn't make sense*, she thinks. *Where is Opi? Where am I?* Her heart is starting to thud against her ribs. Then suddenly, she comes to a stop.

A tingling prickle creeps over the back of her neck.

Complete silence has befallen the forest. There isn't even a whisper of wind. The air is thick and still.

And even though all she can see are the twisting trees and shadows of plant life, somehow she knows that something is definitely here with her. Watching her.

Paralyzed by the feeling, Dusty realizes she's holding her breath. Using every ounce of her willpower she tries to suck in air as she places her fingers to her ears, trying to convince herself that her hearing is deceiving her. The low thud of her heart fills her head as she feels her blood coursing hard, her pulse points throbbing. She tries to call out for Opi again, but fear has settled into the back of her throat, trapping any words, choking her.

She tries to swallow.

Whatever is watching her is just beyond sight, hidden by the trees.

Run, a primal part of her whispers.

She obeys.

Clambering over logs and bushes, scraping past shrubs and under branches, it feels like the forest is swallowing her up, sucking her in deeper and deeper. Her vision blurs from the overwhelming sense of panic as if she's about to pass out, but just as darkness begins to take her, she emerges into open grass and a sun-drenched lake stretches before her.

Dusty doesn't stop running until she reaches the lake's bank. Her heartbeat pounds in her head until the sound of water lapping against the rocks slowly overtakes it. She drops her hands to her knees, her head slumped, gasping for breath.

"Dusty!"

She looks up. Opi is running toward her from further down the tree line. She's flooded with relief.

It's only now that she notices the sounds of the forest have returned.

"Are you okay?" Dusty asks, panting, as Opi reaches her.

Opi nods as she tries to catch her breath.

"Where are we?" Dusty asks.

Opi scans their surroundings. It's clear that whatever it was that had scared Dusty had scared her too. Viscerally. She shakes her head in disbelief. "Angel Lake," she says.

Dusty is confused. "We couldn't—" But then she notices a grove of paper birch trees on the other side of the lake. "Is . . . is that the trail back to our house? Over there?" She points to where distinctive white bark stands out like a beacon in the sunshine.

The sisters stare in silence.

"But to get here would take—"

"An hour and a half. At least."

"It felt like minutes . . ." Opi whispers.

"I wish I'd brought my phone," Dusty curses.

"That would be a first."

Dusty manages to smile. "Or a watch."

A breeze swirls overhead, drawing Dusty's attention to the clammy sweat covering her body. She turns to her little sister. "Are you sure you're okay?"

"What *was* that, Dust? You were right in front of me. Then you weren't. And I swear something was there, close, but I couldn't see it."

"Me too," Dusty says as she turns to peer into the shadowy forest. "Maybe a bear? But then everything went quiet . . ." Her voice trails off.

Opi is looking around like she doesn't trust what she's seeing. "How did we get *here*?"

"I couldn't see you," Dusty manages, guilt clenching in her stomach. "I know I should've waited for you, looked for you, but I couldn't help it." She shakes her head. "I needed to run. I swear it was only for a few minutes." She looks out toward the paper birch trees on the other side of the lake as if they hold the answer. White Mountain rises up behind them. Toward the top, she can just make out their house among the trees. She sighs. "I think we're gonna be late for school."

They hug the edge of the lake to the other side where the birch trees wait to usher them home. Heading back into the woods and onto the trail, they stick close together as Dusty tries to rationalize what just happened.

"Do you think . . ." Opi says quietly, as if she doesn't want her voice to make them heard. "Everything in the forest is interconnected, right? So it makes sense that if one thing went silent, others would too."

"Maybe," Dusty says softly. "But have you ever known a bear to scare crickets quiet?"

Opi doesn't answer.

As they walk, Dusty catches glimpses of her sister's eyes darting around. She can't remember a time Opi was ever scared in the forest. Or lost. She can't believe she almost let her come out here on her own. For once, Dusty is grateful for her intrusive thoughts.

She opens her mouth to say something about the inexplicable jump in time and place but bites down on her words.

As they ascend the steep trail the thud of Dusty's heart pumps faster with her breath. She tries to focus on the sound of her footsteps crunching on the ground, as if they'll leave the fear behind her, but the anxious nausea remains.

They walk in silence for what feels like a lifetime until they're closer to the place they'd started foraging. There's a fork in the trail. Both routes lead home.

"This way," Dusty says, leading them along the way they hadn't come.

"But we left our flasks . . ." Opi says.

"Forget about them," Dusty dismisses. She slides an arm around her sister's waist and they continue together along the alternate trail. The promise of home quickens their pace.

They finally emerge from the trees into their garden. Bees and butterflies flit around them and the house is still covered in dappled sunlight. Dusty feels a pinch on her arm. It's a mosquito. She swats it, leaving a smear of blood on her skin.

She rushes up the back steps, Opi following close, and bursts into the kitchen to look at the time.

Eight-fifteen.

She tries to do the math.

To get to the other side of Angel Lake and back should have taken over three hours. Plus the time they stopped to forage. So it should be nine-thirty, at least. A chill sweeps over her, reminding her of the sweat soaking her clothes.

"That adds up," Opi says.

"Excuse me?"

"As in . . . that's how long it felt." Opi shrugs. "Twenty minutes or so before . . . we ran. And then an hour and a half from the other side of the lake."

Dusty's brow furrows. "None of that adds up. You see that, right?" Her voice is harsher than she intends.

Opi's eyes glimmer with a sheen of tears.

"Sorry," Dusty manages. "I'm just . . . that freaked me out. We must have gotten lost. Or turned around." She sighs, softening. "Come on, let's get changed and go. We're already late, and they'll call Dad soon."

Opi nods, offering a faint smile before she heads upstairs.

Still standing in front of the clock, Dusty looks out the window to the trees.

She can't shake the feeling that something's still out there, waiting in the shadows.

2
Her Periphery

For most of the twenty-five-minute drive to school, they weave through the serpentine roads lining the mountains and the curving, tumbling flow of Black River. The sound of Laura Veirs' guitar fills the old Jeep as Dusty replays what happened in the forest over and over in her mind, trying to make sense of it. As they enter a narrow stretch of road where the surrounding trees meet, the sudden shadowy darkness draws up that disorienting fear she still doesn't understand. The car swerves as she takes a corner too fast. The tires screech loudly, sending crows flying from something roadside they'd been scavenging. She can feel Opi looking at her, but she doesn't say anything.

They enter the outskirts of Black River through an eighty-foot-long bridge that towers over a bend in the river. Only one car can pass at a time from either direction, but you hardly ever need to wait before crossing. There isn't much traffic around Black River. Dusty normally finds something comforting in the way the shingled roof and latticed walls envelop the car in near-darkness as they bob over the wide wooden planks. But today she speeds up toward the light on the other side.

They pass by modest wooden houses, paint peeling off their pastel facades, before stopping at one of the few traffic lights in town, the indicator clicking. Dusty rolls down the windows and she can almost taste the long, wide-open days of summer ahead of her. But a tang of apprehension sours her mouth.

A horn beeps loudly behind them, snapping Dusty out of her head. She looks up at the now-green light, but before she can shift into drive, a big white pick-up accelerates around them and into the gas station across the road.

Dusty mutters, "Arrogant, impatient—"

"He must be late for school too," Opi offers.

Dusty snorts. "Rules don't apply when you're the only famous person in town."

"What's he famous for again?" Opi asks. "Other than the way he looks, I mean."

Dusty can recognize that Eli Blake is objectively dreamy. Tall and athletic, his high cheekbones are balanced by a sculpted jawline and mesmerizing emerald-green eyes. He has coppery hair that's always cropped short in a buzz cut, and as far as Dusty can tell, his self-confidence is unparalleled. She knows all of this without having ever actually interacted with him. Because for Dusty, Eli Blake mostly exists within her phone. In fact, he's a big part of the reason she hates the thing—one of the many glittery mirages that make her feel like she doesn't fit into this world. Like she doesn't understand her own peers, as if she's some sort of alien for preferring to be private. For preferring to be on her own. But still, there have been one too many nights that she's found herself swiping onto one of Eli's videos.

It doesn't help knowing he lives so close to her, just down the road on White Mountain.

As she turns the corner, Dusty tries not to look in his direction or at his sleepy eyes lit up by the morning sun. "He's just a BMX bro with a big following on TikTok," she dismisses.

In the heart of Black River, they pass the grander houses and buildings—double, even triple-story Colonial and Victorian structures fronted by trees so substantial you almost don't notice the telephone poles overhead. Then, three churches among a dozen storefronts that all lead to a large triangular town green complete with a gazebo surrounded by shady trees.

In the dead of winter, Black River can feel like the end of the world. But this morning, with leaves fluttering in the wind and flowers bursting from their beds, Dusty thinks it looks rather pretty. It's a relief to be here for once, away from that presence on the mountain.

They pull into the full parking lot of Black River High at eight forty-five—almost an hour late—slamming their doors and slinging on their backpacks as they rush inside. This is where Dusty and Opi's lives diverge, separated by friends and classes, and their world becomes bigger than their life at home.

Dusty runs down the main corridor toward her biology class, surrounded by the standard mush of beige tiled walls, white paneled ceilings marked by leak stains and speckled gray linoleum floors drenched by fluorescent lighting. In contrast, rows of bright red metallic lockers line the walls.

It's not that Dusty doesn't like school. In fact, she's a straight-A student. But her aversion to crowds, and attention, has made her step back from school life to the point that if she were graded on it, she'd get a D for participation.

The classroom door is closed. Through the small glass window, Dusty can see the rows of students facing the front of the room, laptops open, and her empty desk toward the back. She can hear the muffled voice of Mrs. Thompson explaining something to the class. *I'll just slip in*, she tells herself. *No one will notice*. She grips the handle and takes a slow breath in and out before stepping inside.

"Dusty!" Mrs. Thompson announces with a clear, bright voice.

Every face in the room turns to look.

"Sorry," Dusty says sheepishly. "Car trouble."

Mrs. Thompson smiles, apparently unfazed, and returns to the presentation projected at the front of the room.

Dusty moves to her desk, trying to avoid eye contact with anyone still watching her. She slots in between JD, who gives her a friendly nod, and Mali, her best friend and one of the very few people who counts as an exception to Dusty's preference for solitude. As she slides into her seat, she realizes Mali is staring at her like she's waiting for an explanation.

"Later," Dusty mouths.

Mali winks, her usual warmth ever-present on her face, before resuming her note-taking. Dusty takes out her laptop, making sure it's aligned perfectly with her desk, then looks to the screen at the front of the room, which features a graphic of a double-helix whirling around itself.

"DNA appeared on earth around four billion years ago," Mrs. Thompson continues, "but how it came into existence is still unknown. It has mutated and replicated, leading to the millions of plant and animal species all around us. Us included!" She clicks through to a slide featuring a young girl walking through a forest and Dusty pushes away the memory of what happened only an hour ago. "We share at least fifty percent of our genes with plants, and despite human differences, we're all actually ninety-nine point nine percent identical." The sound of fingers tapping against keyboards skims the room as a new slide with the solar system appears. "If you were able to stretch out the DNA contained in your own body, it would reach one hundred and twenty-five billion miles from where you sit right now. You could wrap it around the Earth five million times."

Dusty fights the urge to take out her notebook and translate the concept into lines and shapes. Something she can hold onto. But she wouldn't risk it so close to others. Someone might see.

"DNA is the code that writes our physical form," Mrs. Thompson is saying, "but only two percent of it actually means anything." She skips to the next slide. "So, let's get into the nitty-gritty. DNA is stored in chromosomes, which—"

"What does the other ninety-eight percent do?" Dusty is unaware that she's the one speaking until heads turn in her direction. Again. She feels her cheeks flush and the residual adrenaline from earlier at war with the tight hold she usually has on herself.

"*Great* question," says Mrs. Thompson. "Only two percent of our DNA contains instructions, or coding, that are used to create proteins in our cells. The rest is known as junk DNA. It refers to the regions of DNA that are unimportant. Noncoding." She clicks to the next slide. "As I was saying—"

"Sorry, I don't understand." *What the fuck?* Dusty asks herself as her flush deepens. She's never spoken up this much. She normally just googles her questions after class.

Mrs. Thompson waits for Dusty to continue.

"I mean . . . what do you mean by junk?" She doesn't know why it's bothering her so much.

"I don't know about you," JD says, "but my junk's pretty important to me."

Chuckles resound around the room and JD smirks contentedly.

Mrs. Thompson sighs. "Thank you, Jake." She turns back to Dusty. "A hangover of evolution?" she offers. "Take the appendix. Or wisdom teeth. We don't need those anymore."

Dusty nods slowly and Mrs. Thompson turns to continue her lesson, clicking to the next slide.

"Mrs. Thompson?" a voice says from the back row. It's gravelly, like it's the first time he's spoken all day.

Their teacher looks up, surprise registering on her face. "Yes, Will?"

Dusty doesn't bother to turn around, even though half the class does.

"I don't mean to interrupt," he says, his voice smoother. "But I think researchers are starting to explore the fact that junk DNA might . . . not be junk." Now everyone in the room is looking at him, including Dusty, who notices how empty his desk is. No laptop, no notebook, just his phone. She wonders why Mrs. Thompson hasn't said anything about it, or if it's always like that. She vaguely remembers hearing that he transferred here a few months ago, but that's all she knows about him.

His tall, lean figure shifts in his chair. He glances at Dusty, dark eyes shadowed by the almost-black hair that falls messily over his forehead. He rakes it back before he continues. "Something about it actually controlling genes and how they express themselves."

"Thank you, Will, I'll look into that," Mrs. Thompson says, smiling softly. "May I continue with my lesson now?"

Will gives a subtle nod, and everyone turns back to their screens.

Dusty glances back at him one more time, just catching his eyes on her before he leans back in his chair and looks out the window.

For the rest of the class, she can't shake the awareness of him in her periphery.

"Babe, wait up!" Mali calls, catching up to Dusty as she makes her way into the hall after class. "You alright?" she asks, looking at Dusty's hands. They're gripping the straps of her backpack too tightly.

"Sorry, yeah. Just one of those mornings."

"Car all good now?"

"Huh?"

"You had car trouble . . ."

"Oh, yeah. All good." Dusty glances at Mali, who's still studying her like she knows something's up. Dusty slows to a stop, meeting Mali's gaze. "Really," she says, raising her eyebrows. They remain in a standoff until Dusty finally cracks a smile. It's impossible not to soften around her best friend.

"This weekend, you're coming out for once, okay?" Mali says, grabbing Dusty's shoulders and shaking them playfully. "It's time you let go a little. Maybe you'll even give in to your crush."

"What crush?" Dusty asks, defensive.

After he'd spoken and looked at her for a breath too long, Will had distracted Dusty. She doesn't know why. She doesn't even think she's heard him speak before. But something about him had gnawed at her, his presence hard to shake. At least it had kept her mind away from the fact that something more than a little strange happened in the forest this morning.

But whatever it was that had made her so aware of him, it's definitely not a crush.

"I've seen you looking. Don't pretend you don't."

Dusty's confused. "I . . . I don't—"

"Wanna take a ride on the back of my BMX?" Mali says in a deep voice. She flicks her long, dark-brown twist braids off her shoulder and bats her almond-shaped eyes that pop against her dark skin.

Dusty blinks.

Eli. Mali's talking about Eli.

"What?" Mali baits. "You don't like my sexy, cool voice?" Then, in her normal voice, "I bet he smells good after going hard on all those dirty jumps."

"I don't know when you decided that I'm obsessed with Eli, because I'm obviously not, so drop it already."

"Mmhmm, sure." Mali nods, her mouth twisting to cover her smile.

Dusty rolls her eyes, also trying not to smile. "You're just desperate for me to have a crush on *anyone*. Isn't Eli a bit obvious?"

"Please," Mali says. "If *I* were into dudes, he'd be my number one pick. *For sure*. Anyway, I just wanna see you have some fun. And it would be convenient, living so close to him and all . . . There's going to be a bonfire on Sat—"

"I don't need a guy to have fun," Dusty cuts in. "I have plenty of fun on my own."

They look at each other with raised eyebrows before bursting into laughter.

But as they keep walking, Dusty tries not to think about the truth—that the idea of intimacy, even with herself, is something she chooses to ignore. It would put her at risk of feeling, which she strongly dislikes, because for Dusty, feeling *anything*, emotionally or physically, is like standing on the edge of a cliff looking down. The anticipation of falling hums through her with a wince, making her stomach flip and her muscles seize. So she tries to step outside of herself, dissociate, as if she's an impartial observer.

Books are the only exception. When she's lost in a story, the love and romance of it can completely sweep her away. She feels it all—the tug at her heart, the bubbles popping deep in her stomach, the soft melting down her spine. But when she puts the book down and her perspective shifts out of a character's and back into her own, all she can bear is numbness.

As an extra precaution, she has her notebook. A place to lay down any residual emotions, transforming them into something clean and simple. Secrets expressed through a code of her own. She let Mali flick through the pages once, but even her best friend couldn't decipher any meaning.

"Seriously, girl," Mali continues. "You know it's not healthy to be cooped up at home every weekend. You're seventeen!"

"Parties are your fun, not mine."

"Fine. But that doesn't mean you won't regret never coming to *any* when you're old and gray. Or at least finding someone to pine over!"

Dusty rolls her eyes, not saying out loud that pining over someone is her worst nightmare.

Dusty looks down at the tray she's just been handed. Neatly separated into sections is a burger with cheese, a pink iced donut, one broccoli floret and a carton of milk. It's a surprisingly colorful offering compared to what they're normally served, and Dusty realizes she's starving.

At her usual table, Mali, Amber and JD are already sitting down. It's been pretty much the same group since elementary school. Mali had sat down next to Dusty on their first day, proclaiming that Dusty's hair was a mess and that she'd be happy to do it for her. By the end of lunch, Dusty wore two neat braids complete with beaded ties that Mali had taken out of her own hair. Amber lives around the corner from Mali, always has, so she came with the territory. JD had joined the group in the sixth grade, when he'd moved to White Mountain from the city and met Dusty on the bus. They'd barely spoken, but when he'd sat down at their table later that day, and every day after, that was that.

But even after so many years, Dusty has never felt particularly close with Amber or JD. Not in that effortless way that Mali is with them. Last year Dusty heard Amber ask Mali why Dusty bothers sitting with them at all. Dusty hadn't been offended, despite Amber's slightly bitter tone, because the reality is that Dusty has to resist the urge to find somewhere quiet to read or draw almost every day. But as someone who spends so much time alone at home, there's a part of her that's afraid that if she doesn't force herself to be around people, she might fade away completely. That she might disappear into her thoughts, lost in the murky darkness until she no longer exists at all.

As she sits down at the table, they're in a heated discussion about a true crime show that came out on Netflix last night.

"It's so obvious she did it," JD groans, one AirPod blaring something electronic into his ear.

"As if!" Amber exclaims. Her thick, almost-black loose curls framing an expressive, olive-skinned face, clearly outraged. "In what world is the woman the killer?! It's *always* a dude."

JD feigns offense. "Excuse me, not all *dudes* are villains."

"I'm with Amber on this one." Mali laughs. "Statistically, it's got to be the boyfriend."

"Nah, women are just sneakier," JD says, shaking his head. "They can get away with more."

"Right, like you know anything about women," Amber deadpans.

Dusty is looking down at Amber's tray of food. Untouched. It's not the first time she's noticed this. When she looks up, her eyes meet Amber's. Amber smiles, but there's an iciness to it. Mali once said that she thinks Amber's prickly edge toward Dusty stems from the fact that they're both straight A students. Dusty doesn't know if it's competitiveness or resentment, but she does her best to not overstep with Amber.

"Babe?" Mali says to Dusty, apparently for the second time. "Are you coming to the bonfire on Saturday?"

"What bonfire?"

JD and Amber laugh.

"At Matt Miller's place—" Mali starts to say.

"He and Eli built a track there last summer," JD offers, chewing on his burger.

Amber huffs a laugh. "You say that like you've been out there to hang with them."

JD's expression turns sour. "Don't worry, I'm well aware that I'm only invited because they want you girls there."

As JD picks at the icing of his donut, Dusty remembers that Eli, Matt and their friends gave JD a hard time in the past. In their defense, when JD had first arrived in Black River his bragging about New York City had been pretty incessant. Other kids would pepper him with questions, and it was clear he loved the attention, but when he started complaining about how boring it was here in comparison, Eli and his friends reveled in taking him down with a harsh comment or two.

"Maybe you can play some of your music?" Amber offers JD, her tone more gentle this time. "I heard there'll be some insane speakers or something . . ."

JD's face lights up like Amber has just given him the world.

"So you'll come?" Mali says to Dusty.

The group look at Dusty expectantly, as if she's supposed to be thrilled by the idea.

"Yeah, I might," she finally says.

Mali isn't convinced. "It'll be fun . . ." JD and Amber start talking and Mali adds more quietly, "I know it's not your thing, but if there's *one* party to come to this year, it's this one. Let's make some memories? *For me?*" she pleads.

Dusty glances over at the table where Eli, Matt and their friends are laughing and talking. They're all angled slightly toward Eli, as if he's their center of gravity. He reaches over and swipes a donut from his friend Jesse's tray, taking a huge bite as he grins at Jesse, his eyes sparkling with mischief. Jesse throws a piece of broccoli at Eli's cheek and they all laugh even louder.

Dusty sighs and leans close to Mali, not wanting to disappoint her. "Fine. I'll come."

Mali raises an eyebrow.

"I promise," Dusty adds.

What's the worst that could happen?

After school, Dusty and Opi agree not to tell their dad, Chris, about getting lost—which is what they've convinced themselves happened that morning. Not only would he be disappointed that they'd been careless, he'd feel guilty that he wasn't out there with them.

Chris is an environmental conservation officer. It's his job to protect the local environment from illegal activity, lead search and rescue operations and enforce laws around hunting and fishing. The work takes him far and wide, so he clocks a lot of overtime, even on holidays and weekends. But today he gets home at five, carrying groceries under one arm and a cooler in the other. Dusty is tidying the kitchen when he walks in.

"Hey, sweetheart." His smile is tender but it's clear he's tired.

His standard-issue dark green uniform hangs from his wiry frame, anchored by black boots and a black firearm holster around his waist. His hair is dark like Dusty's, but flecked with silver, and his eyes are brown and kind. Just like Opi's. He doesn't smile as much as he used to, but when he does it lights up a room.

"Fresh trout," he says, unloading the cooler and groceries on the counter.

"Fishing on the job?" Dusty asks as she peeks in at the speckled scales.

"When in Rome. Just gonna shower then I'll get dinner going. Meanwhile, you prep the fish?"

"Do I have to?"

"You do if you don't want to eat guts for dinner." He smiles one of his brighter smiles, and there it is, making Dusty's heart swell. She quickly breaks eye contact and looks down at his boots.

"Opi will kill you if she sees you wearing those inside," she says.

He turns to head back to the entranceway. "One day. I'll remember one day."

By the time he's ready to cook, the fish has been perfectly cleaned and gutted and Dusty is on the sofa that faces into the kitchen, reading a thick, new fantasy novel. Her feet are propped up on the coffee table and she's doing a decent job of ignoring the empty shelves behind her. The ones that hold too many echoes of the past.

She looks up at her dad as he begins to cook. It still amazes her how confident he is in there now. Until Dusty was eight, her grandparents,

Chris's parents, had lived here too. The kitchen had been her grandmother's domain, her grandfather's the vegetable garden outside. They'd died close together, one after the other, but as always, Dusty tries not to think about that. After they were gone, Dusty's mom, Sarah, did the majority of the cooking, then for the past five years Chris has stepped up. He didn't have a choice.

Opi was the one to resurrect the garden when her dad had given her some seeds for her twelfth birthday. Before that, it had been left untouched.

Dusty's phone pings.

Mali
In the spirit of making memories . . .
come to the diner tonight?

Dusty
What's with everyone wanting to do stuff on a Tuesday?

Mali
Pleaseeee 🙏
It'll just be me and Amber
Maybe JD

So everyone, Dusty smiles to herself.

Dusty
Can't, Dad's already cooking

Mali
So come for dessert 🍦

"Who's that?" Opi asks, leaning over the back of the sofa, peering at Dusty's screen.

"None of your business."

"Touchy!"

"It's Mali. She wants to hang out."

"Tonight?"

"Yep. I told her no."

"You should go," Opi says, her eyes suddenly full of concern.

"Don't look at me like I'm an invalid."

"I'm not! I'm looking at you like it might not be such a bad thing to have some fun."

"Have you been talking to Mali?"

"Maybe." Opi grins, then heads into the kitchen.

Dusty rolls her eyes and tosses her phone to the other end of the sofa before following her sister.

They set the table together, one of the daily rituals Dusty had assigned them in the wake of their mother's absence—conscious of making life a little easier for their dad.

Opi disappears outside for a minute, returning with a small posey of chamomile flowers that she puts in a vase at the center of the table.

"Dig in," Chris says, placing a large oval dish down. The trout is covered in fresh herbs and slices of lemon, and there's a salad of leafy greens, cucumbers, and sweet onions, all from Opi's garden.

Up close, under the low-hanging light of their dining room, Dusty notices the deepening lines and wrinkles on her dad's face. It reminds her how much time has passed without her mom, and she wonders if he'll ever be ready to meet someone, or if he prefers to be on his own now, just like her.

"So, how was your day?" he asks.

Opi opens her mouth to answer but Dusty cuts in. "Good," she says, a little too loudly. "We found a ton of morel mushrooms this morning."

"I wondered where those came from. Where'd you find them?"

"Down the mountain a little," Dusty says, nonchalant.

"We went out before school. It was my idea," Opi explains. "I was worried they'd be gone by the weekend."

Chris nods, thoughtful. "Be careful out there, okay? And I don't want you going out on your own, Op. Take Dusty, or me, or Theo."

Dusty and Opi look at each other, surprised by their dad's words. He's never had a problem with them going out into the forest before. If anything, he's been trying to encourage Dusty to do more of it for years.

"Why?" Dusty asks.

He shakes his head. "No reason."

"I'll cook them for breakfast tomorrow," Opi adds, trying to lighten the mood again.

"Can't wait," he says, relaxing.

They finish their dinner without another word. Long silences have become normal between the three of them. Dusty appreciates a comfortable silence, but with their dad, it feels like there's a giant elephant standing next to them, terrified of being seen.

When the dishes are done, Opi begins prepping some sort of herbal infusion and their dad makes his way to the TV to watch *Alone*. Dusty grabs her phone and book and finally retreats upstairs.

Her mind is already wandering into the story when she reaches the landing. The hallway is completely dark. She reaches for the wall, her fingers skimming the cool surface in search of the switch, when a bright light flashes in the corner of her eye.

By the time she turns to look, everything is dark again, but she's certain it came through the open doorway of what used to be her grandfather's study.

She swallows, waiting as the uneasiness she'd felt that morning in the forest makes its way inside her home. But the hall remains dark.

With a sharp intake of breath, she flicks on the light. Everything is as it should be.

Still, she makes her way across the Persian rug, her heart beating faster than she'd like. Standing in the doorway, she glances around the study, still full of her grandfather's belongings. She makes her way past a large desk backed by bookshelves full of leather and cloth-bound hardcovers, then around the worn-in leather armchair until she reaches the window.

Peering outside, Dusty is again face-to-face with darkness. The window faces north, the direction of the summit. As her eyes adjust, she traces the almost-black mountain until she can just make out the peak above, surrounded by sparkling stars.

With no houses above theirs on this side of the mountain, there aren't any street lights that way. *So where did the light come from?* she wonders.

She's already questioning if she'd imagined it.

3
Flowers Need Bees

A shrieking sound wakes Dusty from a deep sleep. The incessant noise sends her into an instant panic as she rummages around for her phone. There's a clunk on the floor and she lunges out of bed to turn off the alarm.

Cool air pricks her bare legs, which feel unusually warm. It takes a few minutes for her brain to switch on and realize that it's Wednesday morning.

Her book is on the floor beside her phone, half of its pages crumpled and creased.

Last night, after closing the door to her grandfather's study, she'd showered then gotten straight into bed to read. She doesn't remember how long it was before she'd fallen asleep.

After smoothing the book out she makes her bed as a dull headache mingles with her usual apprehension to go to school. She gets dressed in jeans and a loose white t-shirt, then shuffles to the bathroom to splash her face with cold water. With the tap still running, she glances into the wood-framed mirror above the sink and does a double take. She looks just like her mother, apart from her hair. Her mother's had been lighter, like Opi's.

Inspecting herself more closely, she notices that the whites of her eyes are slightly bloodshot, and the skin underneath is darkened by a faint, purplish hue. Her cheeks are devoid of color.

It must have been a late one, she thinks.

For a second she considers digging around for the concealer she bought before Mali's birthday dinner months ago, but she can't be bothered. Instead, she pinches her cheeks to bring some life back to the surface. Her hair is in a tangle and as she combs her fingers through it she notices a dry leaf caught in a knot. She plucks the leaf out, baffled, then wonders if it was from yesterday when they'd gotten lost.

Her headache swells, cutting into her thoughts. She pulls her hair into a messy bun and secures it with a black scrunchie. Ready(ish) to face the day.

In the kitchen, Opi stands over the well-worn chopping board that's covered in a mound of cut-up apples, celery, parsley, ginger and lemons.

"Juice?" Opi offers brightly as she registers her sister.

"No, thanks."

"What's left of the mushrooms are on the stove. I had to stop Dad from finishing them."

"Thanks," Dusty manages. "I'm not that hungry." She drops into a chair and burrows her head into the crook of her elbow on the table.

"How was the diner?" Opi asks.

"Huh?" Dusty mumbles into her arm.

"The diner. With Mali. Last night?"

Dusty furrows her eyebrows, confused.

"I went into your room around midnight. You weren't in your bed . . . or the bathroom."

Dusty blinks. "What do you mean?"

Opi pushes a celery stalk into the noisy juicer, raising her voice to reply. "Don't worry, I won't tell Dad! I was feeling weird after yesterday but went back to bed and watched *The Buccaneers* until I fell asleep. What time did you get home?"

Dusty shakes her head, yelling over the loud juicer, "I didn't go anywhere! I went straight to bed!"

The juicer goes silent.

Lowering her voice, Dusty adds, "I showered right after dinner, read, then went to sleep . . ." Her voice trails off.

Opi turns and sees Dusty's face properly for the first time. "You look exhausted!" she says, trying not to grimace. "Maybe you were sleepwalking? I didn't check downstairs."

Dusty is thoughtful, fighting off the subtle dread that's scraping under her skin even more than usual.

"Sorry, I should have—"

"You're right," Dusty cuts in. "Sleepwalking. I must have been sleepwalking." She huffs a half-hearted laugh. "Thought I'd grown out of it." But as she begins to refold a cloth napkin that was left on the table, a shiver crawls up her spine at the idea of having no control over her body or her consciousness. She'd gone through a stage of sleepwalking a few years ago. Her dad told her later that he'd often find her standing at the front door like she was about to leave or she was waiting for someone. He said he'd locked her bedroom door for a while to keep her safe but stopped because Opi always wanted to climb into bed with her sister.

Eventually, the sleepwalking happened less and less, until it stopped entirely.

Until now, apparently.

Dusty remembers the leaf in her hair and her stomach drops as she pictures herself wandering outside in the dark, on her own and unaware.

Realizing she can't possibly fold the napkin any neater, she puts it down and rubs her aching eyes, pushing all feeling away, and looks up at her sister reassuringly. "Lucky I didn't break any eggs this time."

The sisters laugh at the memory. Their dad had shown them the mess the next morning and they'd howled with laughter at the thought of Dusty trying to cook in her sleep. They'd found tiny pieces of eggshell around the kitchen for weeks. It somehow made all the other nights seem less frightening.

When it's time to leave for school, Dusty sits on a wooden bench at the front door and starts to pull on her socks. She stops, noticing that the soles of her bare feet are caked with dirt. There are small leaves and blades of grass stuck in between her toes.

She stares.

"Let's go!" Opi trills as she breezes out the door. Her voice feels like knives piercing the crown of Dusty's head, then as if to torture her further, her phone pings loudly.

It's a message.

JD
Power's out. My car's stuck in
the garage. Can I get a ride?

Dusty sighs, struggling to summon energy for the day ahead. She brushes off her feet, slides into her socks and sneakers and trudges outside.

Squinting through the changing light, Dusty has to use every bit of brainpower to concentrate. There are thirty-two houses spread out along White Mountain Road, which wraps its way around the slopes like lights upon a Christmas tree. From what you can glimpse through the varying fences, gates and trees, every one is different. Big, small, old and new, each house is separated by forest so dense you could easily forget you have neighbors until you come or go. Most are set back from the road, with long driveways winding up or down.

The Silver house is the oldest on the mountain. Her great-great-grandparents settled here to oversee a nearby logging operation, and they were the ones to clear the road up to their house. It was no more than a trail wide enough for horse and carriage then.

In contrast, JD's house is the newest. Dusty remembers when it was built, when she was in the sixth grade. They'd knocked down an old wooden hunter's shack and brought in cranes and equipment that dwarfed the giant trees surrounding it. She still hasn't been inside—none of their friends have.

The first time Dusty met JD she'd been waiting at the bus stop at the bottom of the mountain, wiping away tears. Her mom had been gone for two weeks and it was Dusty's first day going back to school. She'd insisted on getting the bus so her dad could focus on Opi, who wouldn't leave his side.

Through her tear-blurred vision, she hadn't noticed the boy who had appeared until he was standing right beside her. He had spiked-up brown hair and was wearing a bright blue SpongeBob t-shirt, and instead of ignoring her, he'd told a terrible knock-knock joke that somehow managed to make her laugh.

Later, when he'd waltzed over and sat down at their table at lunch, he'd ignored the surprise on Mali and Amber's faces and started chatting away like they were all old friends. He never said a word about Dusty crying, and she'd been grateful for it. It helped maintain the wall she was building around herself—the one that's now a fortress that only Mali and Opi are able to climb over, sometimes.

Now, even though Dusty still has a soft spot for JD, she feels like all she really knows about him is that he's obsessed with music and that he has a knack for rubbing people up the wrong way.

As Dusty and Opi pull onto the smooth stone driveway, JD is waiting in front of a tall gate that's armed with security cameras and a high-tech intercom. Dusty tries to catch a glimpse of the house beyond as JD pulls out his headphones and shuffles to the car, but it's far back, out of sight. Given the security, she supposes it's filled with all the expensive things they brought with them from the city.

JD is wearing a yellow Pikachu t-shirt with thick, black canvas cargo pants, pink socks and green Crocs. His peroxided hair is stuffed into a black beanie that sits high on his head.

"Morning!" Opi says cheerily, turning to smile at JD as he climbs into the back seat.

Dusty watches in the rear-view mirror as he awkwardly nods at Opi then quickly looks away. Opi turns back to the front, glancing at Dusty.

"So your power's out?" Dusty asks, beginning to reverse back onto the road.

"Yeah. Woke up this morning and everything was off. Couldn't even get the generator working. Dad was so pissed."

Heading down the road, Dusty begins to feel slightly nauseous. She grips the wheel tight, trying to focus. "What does your dad do again?"

"A bunch of stuff. Consulting, I guess."

"You guys used to live in Manhattan, right?" Opi asks.

"Yup."

"Do you miss it?"

"Nope."

Dusty's surprised to hear this, given how often he used to talk about his life in the city.

"What about you guys?" he asks, changing the subject. "Was your power out too?"

"No," Opi says. "Our place was fine."

"Great. Now Dad will definitely blame me."

"Why?" Opi asks, concerned.

"I set up all this new equipment last night . . . music production stuff . . . it's stupid."

Dusty glances up at the mirror. JD is biting his lip, frowning. She's noticed that he's often like this in a smaller group. Quiet. Awkward. But given an audience like a room full of students, he's loud and confident, sometimes to the point of being obnoxious.

"That doesn't sound stupid," Opi offers.

"Yeah, that's cool you want to do that," Dusty adds.

JD shrugs, making it clear he doesn't want to talk about it, and they settle into silence as they fly along the road into town.

There are only a dozen or so cars in the parking lot when they arrive at school, and Dusty glances at the time on the dashboard. They're a little early.

"I've gotta pee," JD says as he opens the door. "Thanks for the ride. See you in homeroom."

He's gone before Dusty can reply.

Theo, Opi's best friend, is waiting at the main entrance, so Dusty tells her sister to go ahead without her too.

Sitting alone in the car, Dusty turns up the air conditioning to cool down. She feels flustered, her head still throbbing. She scrunches her eyes closed and is hit by a flash of a feeling. It's a sensation she can't grasp, like when you wake from a dream that you can't remember, but you know it's still there, tucked somewhere out of reach.

There's a loud tap on the window.

Dusty jumps.

Mali's face is pressed close to the glass, her hands cupped around her eyes. "'Sup, cutie?" she smiles, her voice dulled by the glass.

"Sorry I didn't come last night," Dusty says as she gets out and they begin to make their way inside.

Mali waves a hand. "I didn't actually think you would," she says, then bumps her shoulder into Dusty's.

The thud is unexpectedly hard. Dusty winces.

"Are you okay?" Mali asks, studying her friend. "No offense, but you look—"

"Like crap?" Dusty asks, squinting at the fluorescent lights as they enter the building. She stumbles, light-headed.

Mali holds her by the arm, concerned.

"I'm fine. I think I . . . I didn't sleep well last night. And I haven't eaten yet."

"Here." Mali rummages around in her backpack. She pulls out an apple and hands it to her friend.

Dusty looks down at the piece of fruit, her stomach churning. "Thanks. I'll have it when we sit down."

They reach their homeroom and Dusty slumps into her usual chair, rubbing her forehead and eyes with her fingers.

JD is already seated, headphones blaring as he taps the desk in time with the tinny, electronic beat. The sound grates on Dusty like Velcro being ripped apart, over and over.

Amber comes in and sits down beside JD. She opens her backpack and pulls out her laptop, a little flustered.

"I thought you said you finished your history paper," Mali says, leaning forward to look at Amber's screen.

"I did. But then I woke up in the night worried it wasn't good enough. I started editing and now it's a complete mess." She turns to Dusty. "Don't tell me, you put about an hour into yours and it's perfect?" Her tone is dry and Dusty feels her slight hostility more sharply than she usually does.

"Hey, easy," Mali says.

Dusty doesn't know how to respond, because telling Amber that it took her three hours, not one, and that she already handed it in, wouldn't help Amber's stress levels. Besides, Amber always gets near-perfect grades anyway.

Amber sighs. "I'm sorry," she says, turning back to her screen. "I just . . . I have to put more effort in than some people."

Mali looks at Dusty, eyebrows raised, then pulls out her own laptop.

As Dusty sits there, trying to get her bearings, she's drawn to the row behind her. Will is there, looking out the window, large blue headphones over his ears, far away from the world around him. She can't tell what he's listening to, but even through the fog of her headache, she wonders.

"Feeling any better?" Mali asks from beside her.

"Not really," Dusty admits. "My head is killing me."

"I'm sorry," Mali says, pouting in sympathy. "But please stay away. I have a track meet on Saturday, and I absolutely cannot get sick." She holds up her fingers to Dusty in a mock cross.

Dusty thinks about going home, but again, the idea of being there alone makes her feel even worse.

Dusty barely makes it through morning classes. It's like her mind is a sieve and everything her teachers say just scatters to the floor, making a pile at her feet.

At lunch the cafeteria seems more crowded than usual, everyone talking over each other in an erratic hum. Dusty's scalp feels tight from the weight of her bun and she pulls at her scrunchie to let her hair fall around her face.

Following the flow of students to collect her tray, the smells of meat and milk and sugar consume the air.

A sophomore strides past, leaving a musky trail of whatever fragrance she's doused herself in as if she's crop-dusting the room.

It's the last straw.

Dusty dumps her tray on the nearest table and hurries out.

Pushing her way through the fire escape doors, she barely has a chance to take in a breath before she slams into someone.

Tumbling down onto her side, she puts out her hands to stop her head from hitting the ground. Her palms feel raw, pushed into the concrete. "Fuck this day," she mumbles under her breath, blinded by the sun as she tries to get up.

"Here," a voice says as a hand grabs her wrist and pulls her up. It's cool against her warm skin.

"Thanks," she offers, embarrassed. "Sorry."

"All good." The voice is smooth and easy.

Dusty draws in a slow breath, realizing who it is.

Will leans back against the wall of the building, closing his eyes to let the sun beam down on his face.

"I'm just . . ." She looks around. "I felt—" She stumbles backward into a metal table.

Will peels one eye open, watching her for a moment. "You do you," he says casually, then closes his eye again.

Dusty walks over to the next table and sits down, facing the sunshine. The fresh air brings a sense of relief, despite how hot it feels out here.

She opens her bag, hesitating before she glances back at Will, who still has his eyes closed. Assured by his indifference, she takes out her notebook and pen and begins to draw a spiral, marking the black line with small dots at different intervals. The tension between the pen and the thick paper is instantly calming.

"Too much for you in there today?"

Dusty glances back at Will, who still isn't looking at her.

"Too much for me every day," she answers, continuing to draw.

Will lets out a chuckle that she feels all the way down to her toes.

"Do you usually come out here at lunch?" she asks, trying to distract herself. Now that she thinks about it, she can't remember seeing him in the cafeteria since he transferred earlier in the year.

"Yup," he says.

Without moving her pen, Dusty turns her face to him. His eyes are still closed.

It gives Dusty a chance to take him in. He's even taller than she'd realized, wearing a gray t-shirt and green canvas pants, black skate shoes and a camo backpack that's squashed up against the brick wall behind him, cushioning his back. His big headphones rest around his neck and his dark brown hair, longer on top, has almost no warmth to it, even in the sunlight. His skin is fair, but still a shade or two darker than Dusty's.

"Is that a journal?" he asks, his eyes now on her.

Dusty looks away, feeling her cheeks heat. Her first instinct is to be defensive, but the distinct lack of judgment in his tone gives her pause. She lifts the pen off the page but doesn't close the book. "More like a sketchbook. Sort of. Except I don't really sketch." She pauses, waiting for him to say something, but his silence makes words begin to tumble out of her mouth. "The drawings wouldn't look like much to anyone else," she explains. "They're pretty abstract, I guess. Just my way of digesting information." Her heartbeat quickens.

"So, like a map," he says.

She looks at him as he pushes himself off the wall. But he doesn't come closer. There's something so calm about him. Slow and quiet.

"A map to you?" he clarifies.

She's never really thought about it like that, but she likes the way it sounds and nods slowly. "I guess."

The smallest trace of a smile appears across his lips. "Cool," he says. For a moment they just look at each other before he breaks the silence. "Where's your friend?" he asks.

Dusty clears her throat, aware of her headache again. "Mali?"

"Who else?"

"She's not my *only* friend . . ."

That smile returns to Will's face.

"I mean, sure, she kind of is, I guess," Dusty babbles. "Anyway . . . I don't feel great. I just needed some air."

"I was just going," Will says. Looking up at the sky he adds, "It's all yours." But before he goes he slides his backpack off one shoulder, swinging it around to take out a wooden cube with two sides missing and a bunch of hollow tubes tucked into the cavity. He places it on the closest table then takes a white, crumpled envelope out of the bag, empties its contents into his hand, then scatters what looks like seeds around the solitary box hedge planted in a dirt bed beside the wall.

"Okay," Dusty says. "I'll bite."

Will shrugs. "For the bees."

Dusty stares, trying to keep her surprise from reaching her face.

She hasn't presumed much about Will, other than that he's more or less disengaged from everyone and everything, so this interaction has definitely caught her off guard. Again.

Finished with the seeds, he catches Dusty still staring. The faint smile reappears on his face. "Bees need flowers. Flowers need bees," he says as he folds the envelope and stuffs it back into his bag. Picking up the cube, he reaches up to a high ledge behind him and nestles it into the corner where two walls meet. As he lets go, the backs of his fingers graze the rough ledge.

"Shit," he mutters.

When he lifts up his hand, Dusty can see a small graze on his knuckle that's starting to bleed. He brings it to his lips and sucks the blood away.

Dusty's mouth suddenly floods with hot water like she's about to throw up. Her headache throbs, sending a grim tingle into her fingers and toes.

"It's just a scratch," Will says.

Dusty realizes she must look as bad as she feels. "Yeah," she says, waving her hand like it's nothing. She's usually unfazed by blood. "I must be getting sick," she adds.

"Damn," he says, zipping his bag up and pulling it back over his other shoulder. "I'd offer you a ride home, but I don't have a car."

"Thanks. I have mine. I have to wait around for my sister anyway."

He nods, and for a second Dusty wonders if he's hesitant to leave her. "Hope you feel better tomorrow," he says, offering one more subtle smile before he pulls his headphones up over his ears and begins to walk away toward the parking lot.

"See you," Dusty says softly, watching him go.

Dusty doesn't go back inside. She has a double free-period anyway, followed by math, her least favorite subject. Even on a day when she isn't so scattered and distracted, she struggles to engage with numbers and the concepts that bind them. Instead, she waits outside, drawing the same spiral marked by dots, over and over again.

She can't help but glance up at Will's beehouse occasionally, wondering if any bees will ever really come.

When the heat of the day is too much to bear, she retreats to the quiet comfort of her car and blasts the air conditioning. She tries to read but her thoughts jump around, increasingly disorienting, as her headache intensifies. By the time Opi's there, ready to go, fatigue has buried itself so deep into Dusty's bones it's like she's already dreaming. The only thing that keeps her from falling asleep at the wheel is the flashes of adrenaline that hit her the deeper they drive into the forest. The idea of being out here, alone in the night, mingling with the fear she'd felt when they were foraging.

When they head up the incline of their gravel drive, Dusty expects a sense of relief that doesn't come. She tells a concerned Opi that she just needs to rest, and that's what she does.

Crawling into bed, she pulls her comforter up over her head, cocooning herself despite the heat. The darkness feels soft and quiet, but somewhere deep, deep down Dusty can sense it—that somehow, everything has changed.

4
Slow and Steady

Dusty is surrounded by darkness.

She doesn't know where she is or if she's awake, but a warm glow of light comes into focus from among the black. She can't tell if it's right next to her, or miles away. But slowly, it becomes familiar. The outline of a closed door. Her door.

She feels around beside her and her hand brushes against her bedside table. She finds her phone. It's nine pm.

She messages her sister.

Dusty
👋

She's aware of the red dot signaling unread messages, but puts the phone back down, clinging to darkness a little longer.

Allowing her eyes to relax, Dusty realizes that her headache has eased and she actually feels well-rested. More than that, she feels energized. Stretching her legs and arms out from under the sheets, she notices how aware she is of the sensations of her body, tingling and humming. She arches her back and clenches her muscles, then relaxes again.

There's a tap on the door just before it opens. Light from the rest of the house floods through, and Opi tiptoes in with a steaming mug.

"Hey sleeping beauty."

Dusty yawns.

"How are you feeling?"

"Good. Better. Way better."

Chris appears in the doorway. "We were worried, kid."

"Yeah, I *really* needed that nap." She rubs her eyes.

"A nap." He huffs a laugh. "That's an understatement."

Dusty squints, looking between her dad and sister.

"Dust, it's Thursday night," Opi says cautiously. "You slept for, like, twenty-nine hours."

Dusty sits up and crawls across the bed to turn on her lamp, as if a fully lit room will somehow make everything clear.

"Yeah, whatever you had really knocked you out," Chris adds, placing his hand on Dusty's forehead. "You're still hot, but you look a lot better than last night."

"You've been pretty clammy," Opi grimaces. "Really clammy." She sits on the edge of the bed and carefully offers Dusty the mug. "Here. Bone broth. Careful, it's hot."

It's only now that Dusty notices how hungry she is. She takes the mug and lifts it to her lips, but she can't bring herself to take a sip.

Opi watches expectantly, then explains, "I added some holy basil to boost your immunity. Even I'm tempted to drink it!"

"Why can't you?" Chris asks.

Opi looks at him as if he's lost it. "Pescatarian, Dad."

"Pfft. Broth doesn't count."

She rolls her eyes. "You're lucky I see food as medicine, which means I'll always cook what's best for you." She turns to Dusty. "And right now, this is."

"Thanks," Dusty says, putting the mug down on the bedside table. "I'm still a little out of it."

"Don't push it," Chris says, ushering his youngest daughter out. "Rest up as long as you need." Then they slip out into the hallway.

Alone again, Dusty picks up her phone to read her messages. There are *fifteen* from Mali. Finding the brightness overwhelming, she turns off her lamp so her screen remains as a spotlight. The first few are just check-ins to see how she is, the rest are general musings from a day at school, including that Mali's new crush, Kristen King, wasn't there either.

Then Dusty notices texts from an unknown number sent this morning.

Unknown
hope ur feeling better

Then another a few hours later.

Unknown
this is will btw

Dusty presses her lips together, trying to stop herself from smiling. She replies.

Dusty
Better. Save any bees today?

A reply pops up a minute later.

Unknown
probably not
slow and steady

Dusty is smiling now, wondering how he got her number.

She lies back down and an unexpected twinge of yearning courses through her. It's a new sensation, intense. Her brain responds by remembering the way she crashed into him, and how she told him about her notebook. She cringes, her yearning immediately replaced by embarrassment. She tries to flick that mental switch, seeking numbness, but she can't. It's like the option has disappeared completely. She stretches her arms out again, trying to pinpoint what she's feeling, but a wave of heat spreads over her and the blankets suddenly feel stiflingly hot.

She gets up. As she places her feet on the rug beneath her bed, she notices that energy again. A tingle spreads up her legs as the fluffy wool tickles the arches of her soles. She needs to move.

With the room lit only by moonlight, she starts to tidy her room. She neatens the stacks of books so the spines are perfectly aligned, tucks her sheets in so tight you'd think she works at a five-star hotel, then makes sure every item on every surface is in line with the edges and corners, arranging them into size order when she can.

With everything perfectly in place—arguably more so than ever before—she turns to look out the window. The night looks clear and still and she has a sudden urge to go outside.

She pulls on some boxers and goes downstairs.

Opi and Chris look surprised to see her so soon.

"I need some air," she offers, striding past them.

As she opens the kitchen door and steps out onto the porch, the night skims over her skin, filling her lungs and cooling her down inside and out. Insects and frogs chirp like little bells scattered through the darkness, and Dusty wonders how she hasn't noticed how loud they are before now. It feels like forever since she was out here at night. The sounds remind her of a time she'd sat on the porch with her mom, looking up at the stars.

The memory floods her entire body, making every cell ache. Clenching her muscles tight, she turns her back on the night and returns to her room.

But Dusty doesn't go back to sleep.

Her energy simmers as she tries to read one book, then another, but she still can't focus on the words.

Opening her notebook, she presses a pen to the page, marking hundreds of dots that begin to look like constellations. Then a name begins to swirl in her mind, taunting her. *Will.* She fights an urge to write it down. *You don't even know him,* she tells herself. *Get a hold of yourself.*

She slams her notebook closed and stands, pacing back and forth beside her bed.

This is when she realizes how hungry she still is.

Relieved to have something to do, she goes downstairs and opens the fridge. Opi has left dinner for her—chicken, rice, steamed greens and a jar of broth—and the gesture, which is not unusual from her sister, is so caring and sweet that it hurts. Dusty feels her eyes begin to water. She blinks.

What is wrong with me?

She tries to gain control of her emotions, breathing deep, reasoning that her period must be coming soon. And it doesn't help that she's so. Damn. Hungry.

Dusty takes the Tupperware out and opens the lid, but the food smells sour and rank. Her brow furrows. She leans in and sniffs but *everything* about it is wrong. Grimacing, she empties it into the trash. Not wanting to offend Opi, she scrunches up some paper towel and covers the uneaten food.

Back in her room, Dusty picks up her phone and succumbs to the inevitable, endless scroll. Curated life, self-improvement, productivity, news, something to buy, somewhere to go, how to do better, how to *be* better. Her legs twitch, restless.

A not-so-casual search for Will reveals no trace of him. She pulls a pillow over her face, frustrated.

She waits for morning, hyper-aware of her body as her thoughts keep drifting to the forest outside. Through her closed window she could swear she can hear every sound beyond it, shifting and transforming, alive with movement.

A lot can happen in a day and a half. At least according to Mali.

As they enter the school on Friday morning, she barely takes a breath, filling Dusty in on this and that as they make their way to homeroom. Dusty smiles and nods, but is distracted by the unfamiliarity of her surroundings. The lights still seem brighter than they usually do, the lockers a more vibrant red. Or maybe it's the sound, normally muffled by a constant stream of shuffling teenagers, that now seems too sharp, more definite. A locker slams shut, a shoe squeaks on the plastic floor, and a laugh that sounds like it's an inch from her ear bellows from a freshman at the other end of the hall.

As they approach their homeroom, Dusty is already desperate to be somewhere else. Not home, which is equally obscured. Just, anywhere but here. She's so distracted that she's forgotten Will is in her homeroom. He's already at his desk.

He turns his head as Dusty enters, and their eyes lock for a moment. But pushed forward by Mali, Dusty looks away to navigate the tangle of tables, legs and bags.

"Dust?" Mali says.

Dusty turns to her friend, forcing herself to concentrate as she sits down. "Yeah?"

Mali studies her. "You sure you're feeling better?"

"Yeah," Dusty smiles, praying the concealer she put on before she left is doing its job.

She still hasn't eaten.

"JD was home yesterday too," Mali says, poking his shoulder with her pen.

"Yeah, thanks for the cooties, Dusty," JD teases.

"Sorry," she offers, feeling guilty for not staying home when she knew she wasn't feeling well. "What do you think it was?" she asks.

He shrugs. "Just a cold."

"Hey Dusty?" Amber asks from the desk next to JD. "Do you know what the deal was with all those cows outside Remsen?"

"Uh, no. What happened?"

Mali opens a can of soda and Dusty can feel her eardrums vibrate as the loud fizz is unleashed.

"I thought your dad might have been called out, or whatever," Amber says. "I guess the other day these farmers woke up and all their cattle were dead. Dozens of them."

"They weren't just dead," JD adds. "Their eyes, brains, tongues and udders were all gone."

"JD!" Mali protests, putting her drink down in disgust.

"A few of them were also partially skinned," he says. "So messed up."

They all look to Dusty like she might have more information.

She clears her throat, wondering if this is why her dad told Opi not to go into the forest alone. "Dad didn't mention it," she says. "But he wouldn't be involved unless a wild animal did it."

"Do you think it was a person then?" Amber asks.

"I hope not," Dusty manages. "That's awful."

"People are messed up," JD says.

"Guys, please." Mali groans. "It's too early for this, okay?"

"Speaking of mysteries," Amber says to Mali. "Did you watch last night?"

Realizing they're about to talk about a show she hasn't seen, Dusty leans toward JD. "So, are you feeling better now?"

"Huh?" He's already distracted by something on his phone.

"Your cold?"

"Oh, yeah, totally. Just needed to sleep it off."

It isn't long before the bell rings for first period. Making her way out, Dusty looks down at the ground, trying to sort through the assault of sounds and smells around her. But something cuts through it all, distinct. She inhales.

When she looks up, Will is walking directly in front of her.

She breathes in again, and suddenly she can't hear anything over the thud of her own heartbeat.

Disoriented, Dusty tries her usual deep breathing in an attempt to turn it all off. To numb herself to the world around her. To stop feeling.

It doesn't work.

Forcing herself to walk in the opposite direction to Will, she pulls out her phone to check the time. There's a message.

Will
hi

A genuine smile sweeps her face for the first time today.

Dusty
Hey

Slow and steady, she reminds herself.

The smell of rotten food hits her like a sack of bricks. It's lunchtime, and Dusty is hovering near the cafeteria entrance, unable to go inside despite her aching hunger. She watches in disbelief as students make their way to tables, sitting down with their food as if it doesn't smell of death. She concludes that the virus she had must have messed up her sense of smell.

Scanning the room, she sees Opi with Theo and their friends, laughing and eating. A little beyond them, her gaze is drawn to Eli Blake.

He's at his table, surrounded by friends, but there's something different about him today. His jaw is clenched tight, his expression intense, and while his arms are propped up on the table, steady, his knees bounce up and down frantically beneath. In front of him his tray is pushed aside, his food untouched.

"Thirsty girl," Mali teases from beside her, noticing the direction of Dusty's stare.

Dusty turns, thinking, *I'm not thirsty. I'm starving.* But the idea of even trying to eat food makes her stomach ache with anxiety.

Mali's brow furrows. "You still don't look so great, Dust."

Dusty drops her head and rubs her eyes. "I know. I gotta go. Call you later?"

Mali nods sympathetically, kissing the air as Dusty pulls out her phone to tell Opi she's leaving, and she'll pick her up after school.

As she walks away, she realizes she doesn't know where she's going. She can't just sit outside or in the car again. She needs to move. She needs a distraction.

Hesitating for only a second, she sends another message.

Dusty
Want to get out of here?

A half a minute later there's a reply.

Will
yes

5
So Much That It Hurts

"Where to?" Will asks.

Dusty is pulling out of the school lot, trying not to panic over her own impulsiveness. It feels like a stranger is wearing her skin. A bead of sweat drips down her chest and she blasts the air conditioning.

"I don't actually know," she says, gripping the steering wheel tight. "Got any ideas?"

"I'm guessing you don't do this much, do you?"

"You mean leave school with a random guy? No. I don't." She glances over to catch him trying to suppress a smile. He looks different in profile, the angles of his nose and jawline more refined, his mouth soft and subtle.

"Yeah, I didn't take you for a ditcher," he says.

"I'm not ditching. I'm . . . taking a mental health afternoon."

"I didn't know that was a thing. Guess I take a lot of those."

The car feels like it's finally starting to cool down. Dusty breathes, relaxing a little. "What did you take me for then?"

There's a pause. "I've been trying to figure that out since I moved here."

She can feel him looking at her and the heat in her cheeks spreads down her neck.

"Here, turn up ahead," he says, pointing to the left. "I think I know a place."

They head north-west, past Bernie's Diner, then the Bowl-a-Rama, all the way to the parkway. She looks at the time. Twelve-fifteen.

"I have to be back to get my sister by three."

"It's not far," he assures her.

Dusty is relieved not to be making decisions and follows Will's directions onto a dirt road that she's never noticed. She winds the windows down and the breeze whips her hair around her face, making her skin tingle.

As they slow down, the air in the car settles and she catches that smell. Him. She breathes it in.

"Anywhere here," Will says, pointing to a small dirt lot ahead of them.

As they pull up, the hum of crickets fills the car, so loud Dusty can picture the scrapers on their wings being drawn along the underside of one another, creating their sound like a finger running along a comb. The tempo is unusual for this time of year, more like the end of summer, even though it's just beginning.

They step out of the car and onto the dirt ground. There's a small wooden sign that says "Trail" backed by tall trees that sway in the breeze. The land looks relatively flat, compared to the mountain at least. As Will rounds the car to stand beside her, Dusty feels a rush of something . . . excitement, maybe. Relief to be somewhere other than home or school, too. But somewhere underneath, there is fear. She can't put her finger on what it is she's afraid of, but the feeling settles in the pit of her stomach like black tar. She looks at Will and the rest of her body is awash with that dizzying combination of flustered calm. The midday heat hits her and sweat returns to her chest, running under her tank top. She deeply regrets having worn jeans, but jeans are like a uniform for Dusty, even in summer, *so what's different now*? "It's hot for this time of year," she says out loud.

Will smiles broadly, knowingly. "That's why we're here."

Dusty raises her eyebrows and Will nods toward the trail.

The track is shady and narrow, lined by maidenhair ferns that brush against Dusty's legs as she follows him. Beyond them the forest is a mix of northern hardwoods, with old, wide pines, hemlocks, and ash. Will glances back from time to time as Dusty quietly tries to steady her heart rate. It beats more rapidly with every step and as the silence between them lengthens it grows taut, like it might snap. "So what's up with the beehouse thing anyway?" Dusty asks, sounding far more casual than she feels.

Will keeps walking ahead of her, thoughtful, before he answers. "You know there are over a hundred species of native bees around here? They're mostly solitary, so they don't have a hive, but they do need somewhere to rest and lay their eggs. I spend a lot of time outside. Always have. And every year, wherever I am, I notice fewer bees than the year before . . . You'd think out here they'd be fine, but there's all that new farmland up north, and I've seen them spraying pesticides. Anyway, it started out as something to keep my hands busy, but it does feel good to be doing something . . ." He shrugs and lets his words trail off into the wild.

Dusty is speechless, her smile twisting her lips as she tries to suppress it.

Will looks back at her. "What?"

"Nothing," she says. "I just didn't expect you to nerd out on me like that."

"*Nerd out?*" Will repeats.

She sets her smile free. "It's a good thing. You sound like my sister."

"Okay?" he says slowly.

"So, how many beehouses have you made?" Dusty asks.

"A dozen or so, I guess. Probably not enough to make a difference . . ."

"Wow," she says.

"Yeah, it sucks to be a bee these days."

"No." She laughs. "I mean you. You're so quiet at school. Until the other day in class, I don't think you've ever spoken—"

"Like you can talk."

"Fair point. I guess I just assumed you weren't interested."

"In what?" Confusion pulls at his features.

"In all this," she gestures around them.

"What does *all this* have to do with school?"

Dusty smiles, conceding.

"How about you?" Will asks. "Why did you really ditch today?"

"I'm just . . . not myself this week. Figured some time outside might help." She recalls Opi saying that to her before they'd gone foraging, and wonders if her sister had been right. Maybe not feeling like herself is what she needs.

But out here, alone with Will, something is gnawing at her. It's like she's playing with fire and she doesn't know why.

Looking ahead, Dusty tries to stay calm. To be present in the moment, as Opi would say, and not get too into her head. They move up and down over the earth's rocky, rooted contours without saying more. When they come to a stream, Will steps over first, then turns, holding his hand out to help Dusty. She hesitates, but doesn't take it. As she jumps over the stream to join him, she notices his face flush as he drops his hand, then leads her up a gradual slope. He moves confidently over the land. If he hadn't mentioned that he spends a lot of time outside, Dusty would have guessed it.

She hears the waterfall before she sees it.

A shift in the light draws her attention down the other side of the hill, where through the trees there's a rocky pool, its sparkling surface full of movement that bounces a glow through the undergrowth. Relief trickles down her spine, the cool water calling to her.

They quicken their pace, the sound of the cascade that they still can't see drowning out the crickets the closer they get. The trail leads them to two large boulders which they have to squeeze between, their bodies pressed against their ancient weight. When they emerge, the waterfall is before them, just beyond the pool. Its white torrent is drenched in sunlight, tumbling down over hidden rocks.

"What do you think?" Will calls over the sound of the water.

"It's beautiful," she says.

"I've never seen anyone else here." He kicks off his shoes then moves closer to lower his voice. "The second time I came here I followed the stream over there all the way to town without passing a soul. It flows into Black River. All the running water around here does, one way or another."

"I can see Black River from my bedroom," Dusty says absently, gazing at the shadows that shift across the pool's depths. "What about your first time?" she asks.

"Huh?"

"The first time you came here . . ."

"Oh, yeah. I actually found it with my mom."

Dusty smiles, trying not to show the twinge of pain she feels whenever someone mentions their mother. "Are you close?" she asks.

"We are," he says.

Dusty gulps, bracing herself, and sits down to busy herself with her shoelaces.

"But she works a lot," Will continues, sitting down beside her. He reaches out with a long arm, his fair skin glistening with dewy sweat as he picks up a twig to play with. "When we first moved here, a few days before Christmas, she didn't have a job, so we spent the holidays exploring. It wasn't easy in the snow, but it's our tradition when we move to a new town. A way to get our bearings. She works at the diner now."

"Is your dad . . .?"

"Long gone? Sort of."

Dusty swallows.

"What about you?" he asks. "I think I've seen you around with your dad . . ."

Dusty hesitates, dreading these moments when she's forced to face the truth.

"Sorry, we don't have to—"

"No, it's okay," she says. "Actually, my mom left."

Will sighs. "I'm sorry."

She smiles to put him at ease. "It's fine. I'm over it," she says, her emotions bubbling just beneath the surface, closer than she's let them get to her in years.

Will doesn't respond, and when she glances at him, he's studying her, his dark eyes watchful.

She looks away. "I don't know why I said that. I'm not . . . over it. I think about her every day."

"How old were you?" he asks.

"When she left?" She picks up a leaf and begins to tear it along its veins. "Twelve. How about you? With your dad?"

"Around four, so I don't remember him much."

"Do you know what happened?"

Will is quiet.

"Sorry—"

"We had to run away, I guess. From him." He starts to snap the twig into tiny pieces. "We moved from town to town, getting further and further away. Mom tried to make a game of it. But I knew she was scared. She was really young when she had me. Her parents had kicked her out, so we had nowhere to go. I don't think my dad is looking for us anymore, but she keeps moving, so . . ." He shakes his head.

Dusty sighs, her heart wrenching as she turns to look at him.

"What about you?" he deflects. "What happened with your mom?"

Dusty's eyes drift back over the water. "It was different," she manages. "My grandparents, dad's parents, used to live with us, or I guess, we lived with them. My mom's parents died when she was a teenager, so my dad's parents kind of became her new family. She could be sort of . . . distant at times, when I think about it now. Then, when I was eight, my grandma died of cancer, and then my grandpa died a few weeks later. They said it was from a broken heart, if you can believe it. I mean, it was a heart attack, but the doctor said that it's possible . . . to actually die from grief like that. We were all devastated, but after that, my mom started to change." She takes a deep breath as the memories flood back. "She'd be affectionate one day and wouldn't come out of her room the next. But Dad kept me and my sister busy outdoors, teaching us about the forest, letting us run wild there, so we were still . . . happy. Then, one day Mom . . . she was just gone."

Dusty's heart pounds in the wake of her words. Every part of her aches. "It was so surreal," she says. Dusty can feel Will's eyes on her, but she can't meet his gaze. "Sometimes I wish I could see her. Pass her on the street even, like a stranger, just to know she was actually real. That she isn't some figment of my imagination."

She can see Will nodding from the corner of her eye. "I thought I saw my dad once," he says. "At a gas station in the middle of nowhere. It wasn't him, but it made me realize that he's still out there, living his life. I don't miss him, and I knew that the idea of seeing him should have scared me, but . . . it really just kind of gutted me."

Dusty breathes in deep, trying to tame the swell inside of her. But it's all too close to the surface now, and she can feel her pain searching for somewhere to seep out. "Is it bad that sometimes I wish she'd died?" She pauses, relishing the release of such a dark part of herself. "Sometimes I think it would have been easier . . . because it would mean we could talk about her. Remember her. Instead we just pretend she never existed."

"Not at all," Will says, taking her words in. "That makes sense."

"When it was clear she wasn't coming back, or even going to call, my dad tried to explain how complicated she was. That she loved us. I begged him to go look for her, but he said she didn't want to be followed. That she couldn't be around us anymore, and that she needed to be on her own. And I was left using everything I had to try not to . . . hurt. To try not to feel angry. I didn't want to make it worse for my dad, or my sister."

"Your sister must feel the same though, right?"

Dusty shrugs. "It was different for her. She was only ten, so we sheltered her from a lot of it. Drip fed her what was happening. I mean, it was still awful for her, but in the end, I don't think it broke her in the same way it broke me. I still hadn't recovered from my grandparents' deaths. We were really close to them, but my sister was only six then, and a little too young to be so . . . affected by it. Then when Mom left, I was so scared the pain of it would kill me too, just like Grandpa, so I guess I found a way to turn it off. Like my life actually depended on it."

They both stare out at the water, listening to the sound all around. It takes Dusty a few moments to realize how much she's just dumped on him.

"I'm so sorry," she says, standing. "I don't usually talk about . . . That was *way* too much—"

"It wasn't," Will cuts in, rising beside her. He's facing her, as if urging Dusty to look up at him.

When she does, the sincerity in his eyes is completely captivating, and for the first time she can see that they're deep blue. Like the ocean on a stormy day. His hair has fallen over them, casting dark shadows over their depths. He pushes it back then looks up to the sky.

Dusty's heart quickens as she notices his Adam's apple, and his neck, sinewy and strong. She looks back up to find his eyes on her.

She swallows, a rush of energy flooding her whole body as another drop of sweat travels down her back. The heat of the sun beams down, and for a moment Dusty is faint from thirst and hunger.

"Come on," Will says, breaking the spell between them. He takes off his jeans and t-shirt, leaving only his boxers on, and goes to a fallen tree that rests out over the water. He starts to walk along the broad trunk and the distance allows Dusty to notice his body. How his height is accentuated by lean muscles that are revealed as he holds out his arms to balance.

"You coming?" he shouts over the cascade.

Dusty's throat feels dry and scratchy. She needs the water.

She pulls off her jeans, leaving her tank top on over her underwear. She's only ever been swimming with people she knows—her family, Mali, Theo, and once at a lake party. She's never felt as self-conscious as she does now.

She makes her way along the fallen tree. Will keeps his eyes on her face, on her eyes, and her tension relaxes a little.

When she reaches him, Will mouths a countdown, holding up his fingers. "Three . . . Two . . ." but before he's finished Dusty pushes him, sending him crashing into the water.

She covers her grin with her hands as Will comes up for air, breathless from the cold. When he smiles up at her his eyes light up, brighter than ever in the sunshine. He splashes, spraying cold droplets against Dusty's legs. It feels incredible.

She sucks in air and jumps in.

Under the surface it's cool and quiet. Dusty opens her mouth and lets water flow in. The icy cold is instantly soothing, and even though she's still thirsty, it's the best she's felt in days.

The current draws her back up above where Will is treading water, looking up at the sun, and Dusty has the strangest sensation—that it's him, his calm, flowing through the water, wrapping itself around her, cooling her.

One of his legs brushes against hers.

"Sorry," he says.

"Thank you," Dusty whispers. But the sound of the waterfall drowns her words.

"What?" Will asks, swimming closer.

Dusty leans in, cupping her hand around his ear. "Thank you for listening to me, before."

He pulls back so they're face-to-face for a moment. Dusty swallows, knowing that if they weren't in the water the swell of feelings would have overwhelmed her by now, and made her want to run. He shifts to speak into her ear, his hand ice cold against her face. "Thank you for telling me, and for bringing me here with you."

His voice feels like warm honey dripping into her ear.

"You brought me here," Dusty says, louder now.

He pulls back again, a subtle smile reaching his eyes. "Because you wanted to ditch." He flicks some water into her face, keeping his eyes on her.

She laughs, but there's something about the way he looks at her that makes Dusty's breath catch. A rush of heat spreads through her, and she submerges herself underwater, desperate to relax.

She can't believe this guy has quietly sat near her in class for months. *How had I not seen him?* she wonders. It's like he's unfurling before her eyes, shedding some cloak he'd been wearing. Or, she wonders, is it she who's changing? And he's who he's always been.

When she comes back up to the surface, Will's smile is playful and she can't help but mirror it. Their arms brush against each other's and she's struck by how his skin is getting colder, while hers remains hot. Their faces now inches apart, Dusty has a sudden urge to bite down on her lip to stop that chaotic, uncontrollable energy from swelling again. But this close, the heat inside her turns to fire.

She retreats under the water. Again.

Opening her eyes this time, she can see ripples of light bouncing off rocks through the flowing water, and Will as he swims down to her. The sound of the waterfall is soft and gentle down here. Dusty can hear her own heartbeat. She could swear she can hear his too.

Underwater, it's as if they're playing by different rules. Unmasked, allowed to stare a little longer. Not as scared to reach out and touch.

Dusty only realizes she's placing her hand on Will's bare chest as it's happening.

She presses her palm against his skin, feeling the thrum of life inside him. He puts his hand over hers and their fingers intertwine, sending shivers along her arms. Then he pulls, gently tugging her toward him.

Dusty looks at his mouth, wanting it on hers more than she wants her next breath.

But a terrifying jolt rushes up her spine, culminating in her teeth. In a painful instant she's pushing him away, forcing herself back up to the surface, gasping.

Will emerges beside her, sucking air into his lungs. His eyes search Dusty's, trying to understand what's happening between them. "Sorry," he mouths.

Dusty shakes her head, realizing he must be able to see the fear in her eyes. "It's okay," is all she can think to say.

Will slowly nods, then flicks his wet hair back before he swims to the water's edge. Dusty follows and they climb out onto the warm rocks.

Goosebumps cover Will's torso and his lips have turned slightly purple. It's clear that the heat of the sun-soaked rock is a relief for him. For Dusty it's anything but. Without the water, she thinks she might combust.

"How are you not cold?" Will asks, glancing down at her body.

Dusty shrugs, wrapping her arms around her knees. She doesn't know if it's how visible her body is, or the fact that she told Will more about her mom than she's told anyone in years, but Dusty feels exposed.

Out of the corner of her eye she watches him, wondering if the fear she's been feeling is of letting someone in.

Of feeling so much that it hurts.

6

Nothing to Be Afraid of

The only thing Dusty likes about a party is getting ready for it.

It's late Saturday afternoon, the sun making its way back down to the horizon, and she's in the back of her dad's car listening to him instruct Opi as she drives them into town.

"*Easy*," he groans as they take a corner more than a little too hard.

"I've got it!" Opi assures him, glancing in the rear-view at Dusty, who's trying not to laugh.

They jerk to a stop outside Mali's house.

"Good luck," Dusty says dryly, looking at her dad as she gets out. She could swear new grays have appeared since Opi got behind the wheel.

"Let me know if you need a ride home?" Chris asks.

"JD's driving," Dusty says over her shoulder, continuing along the path. "I'll come back with him."

She hears her dad tap the car as they pull away and a vision flashes in her mind—the car swerving off the road, tumbling into the river. "It's not real," she whispers, then stops at Mali's front door, stealing a moment to herself.

She still hasn't eaten anything, despite her hunger growing stronger by the hour. But every time she goes to eat something she's repulsed by the idea. Whatever's wrong with her, it doesn't seem to be affecting her energy, which, if anything, is still in overdrive. So she's been telling herself that her appetite for food will come back in a day or two.

She'd felt particularly ravenous after she left Will yesterday. That, and a torrent of other things. They hadn't spoken much after their swim. Dusty had been too in her head, and later she'd thought that Will was either really good at reading the room and hadn't wanted to push her, or he'd been thinking that she was insane and couldn't wait to get out of there.

When she'd dropped him in town she'd asked if he'd be at the bonfire.

"I didn't think that was your kind of thing," he'd said.

"What makes you say that?"

"I haven't seen you at any parties. I would've noticed you." His eyes had sparkled as he'd looked at her. Like he could see right through her.

It made her even more on edge. "I might see you there then," she'd said.

And they'd left it at that.

Knocking on Mali's door, Dusty's body continues to burn with heat. Under a layer of concealer, purple circles, more pronounced than yesterday, still rim her eyes, and that energy—that current that flows freely, keeping her from sleep, keeping her from sitting still—has her feeling exhilarated.

After greeting Mali's parents, who always welcome her with love and warmth, Dusty makes her way down a dim hallway, into a bedroom with pale lilac walls covered in photos and posters. Mali is standing in front of a giant pile of clothes in an oversized t-shirt. There's a bed somewhere underneath the mess, and Dusty pushes down the urge to tidy. Instead, she smiles at the drama of it all.

"Nothing to wear?" she teases.

Mali turns to her friend. "More like everything to wear. Please help!"

Dusty surveys the wreckage of garments, which includes everything from thick winter coats to crocheted summer dresses. She picks up a black, ankle length, faux-fur coat that stands out among the rest. "I think you can probably rule this one out."

Mali laughs, rolling her eyes at herself. She shoves it back in her closet then starts to dig around in the heap again.

"How was the track meet?" Dusty asks.

Mali glances over her shoulder, shrugging casually. "I set a new PB."

"Of course you did," Dusty grins.

"The best part was . . ." Mali starts as she scoops out a sleeveless golden-brown silk slip dress. "Kristen saw the whole thing." She slips the dress over her head. "Thank God I didn't have to race her. I think she's the only person who could beat me." With the dress on she looks to her friend for approval.

"As if you weren't always going to wear that." Dusty smirks. "It's perfect. And Kristen will be drooling."

Mali turns to a full-length mirror that rests against the wall and runs her hands over her hips. Her expression declares that it's the one. She whips her head around to Dusty, flinging her braids like she's in a hair ad. "But I'm not dressing for *her*. I'm dressing for *me*."

Dusty laughs, nodding. "Sure."

Mali winks. "But *maybe* after tonight I'll have two good reasons to spend summer up on your mountain. We can all hang out together."

Like JD and Eli, Kristen also lives on White Mountain. You wouldn't call it a tight-knit community though. Kristen is a senior, but even if she were in their grade, they wouldn't have much of a reason to spend time together. In middle school, Eli and Kristen had been driven to school by their parents who work in town, while Dusty, Opi and later JD, had gotten the bus. Now they all have cars. Dusty doesn't even know which house is Kristen's. All she knows about her is that she's track-and-field champion and most likely to be valedictorian. She's also extremely beautiful, blonde, blue-eyed and as far as Dusty can tell, excruciatingly nice.

"She is *way* too high-achieving to be my friend," Dusty says. "Neighbors or not. Which means she's perfect for you."

"No joke," Mali says. "She's perfect. Period." She sighs and turns back to the clothes. "Okay my babe. Now for you."

Mali rummages through the options, fabric flying off the bed onto a newly forming heap on the floor.

"Hey . . ." Dusty starts, hesitant. "What do you think about Will?"

"Will who?" She pauses. "Oh, Will, the new guy?"

The randomness of the question is apparent, and Dusty feels a pang of guilt for keeping her recent encounters with him a secret from her best friend. But she also feels cagey, protective of him even. Or maybe it's just that Dusty doesn't understand who he is to her yet.

"I don't know . . ." Mali says, inspecting a mini dress Dusty hopes isn't intended for her. "I don't think I've ever spoken to him. Who's he friends with anyway?"

Dusty shrugs. "He's still pretty new, I don't—"

"This!" Mali squeals. She holds up a dusty-pink silk dress. "Try this."

Dusty obliges and slips it on. It has long sleeves that flute out over her hands, a high neckline and a bias cut reaching just below her knees. It shows every curve of her body.

"Are you *kidding* me?!" Mali exclaims before pretending to faint.

"Is it too dressy?"

"Not with boots."

Dusty looks down at herself. "Are you sure?" She doesn't know about her body being so visible once again, but the silk is cool on her skin and it feels as if the dress somehow acknowledges the shift that's been happening within her.

"I'm *sure* sure. You should just keep it. I thrifted it a year ago and haven't worn it. It's made for you." Mali pulls Dusty's hair out of its messy bun, fluffs out the cascading bangs, then detangles the rest with her fingers so that it hangs long and loose.

Dusty pulls on a pair of black cowboy boots then looks in the mirror. The pale pink silk flatters her fair, olive-toned skin, and she likes the way it only shows a hint of her legs above the boots.

For someone who hasn't slept or eaten in days, she has to admit she looks pretty good.

"Need a bag?" Mali asks.

Dusty shakes her head and slips her phone into the left boot.

The friends take in their reflections side by side.

"It's giving fairycore, and I'm *so* into it," Mali says proudly.

A spectacle of pinks and oranges bounce off scattered clouds before settling into the deep purples and blues of dusk. Mali and Dusty have walked to the parking lot of Bernie's Diner where Amber and JD are waiting for them. It's their ritual before going to a party.

JD is sitting in the front cabin of his giant, brand-new black pickup truck, adjusting the bass and volume of the speakers. Amber is in the back bed sipping on a soda she's most-definitely spiked.

Dusty tries to peer inside the diner, remembering that Will had said his mom works here, but she can't see anything beyond the reflections of the sky.

As she and Mali climb up into the truck, Amber gushes about their outfits. Dusty is relieved that Amber has left her competitive side at school. But it makes her feel guilty for not inviting her to get ready with them. Dusty assumes that Mali kept it to just the two of them to ease Dusty into the night. The thought makes her cringe.

"Let's go, driver!" Amber yells, then offers Dusty her soda. JD's electronic music blares through the rear window as Dusty pretends to sip from the straw, then passes it to Mali.

Matt Miller's property is enormous. After driving through the winding forest roads that divide town and country, JD's truck shoots out from under the trees to where the land is mostly flat and open. There's just enough light left to take it all in—a patchwork of pastures and cropland. Some old trees are scattered along the edge of the road and across the fields, permitted to remain because they serve a purpose like shade or division.

Amber remarks on how pretty it all is, but Dusty isn't used to wide open spaces—unlike the forest around her house, they make her feel like the world could fall apart with no deep roots to hold it all together.

They enter the property through a large wooden gate which has been propped open by a keg with a cheap pink cowboy hat on it. As they turn onto a dirt drive a gust of wind comes down from somewhere distant, sweeping the earth and blowing topsoil into the air. The last light disappears from the sky and JD turns down the music.

Another song is blasting somewhere close by.

The truck's headlights reveal a fence with a hand-written sign that says "Party This Way" and a hand-drawn penis that was once an arrow to guide them.

The music gets louder as the glow of a fire in the middle of a huge, sloped field comes into view. Teenagers are scattered everywhere, their black shadows stretched across the grass. The truck pulls to a stop next to a few dozen others huddled together at the bottom fence.

Dusty jumps down from the back then holds out her hand to help Mali.

"You're so warm!" Mali says, amazed. "I'm already cold." She shivers and hugs herself. "Should've worn the fur."

"Shame there isn't a giant fire to keep you warm," JD says as he lifts Amber down from the pickup, adding a "m'lady" as he places her on the ground.

The group stick together as they make their way up toward the bonfire. The flames draw them close, like they need to pay homage before they're allowed to disperse into the night.

"Is Will coming?" Amber asks quietly, suddenly near enough that no one else can hear. She laughs when she sees the confusion on Dusty's face. "He asked for your number last week."

"Oh," Dusty says, visibly flustered. "I'm not sure."

Amber smiles, and Dusty wonders if she's enjoying watching her squirm just a little too much. "Hope it's okay I gave it to him?"

"Yeah, of course," Dusty says, her throat suddenly dry.

"He was pretty nervous about it. It was cute."

Dusty doesn't know what to say. She's relieved when JD picks up his pace and slides in next to Amber. Dusty slows, watching as they walk ahead of her.

There's a new confidence in JD's body language, and Dusty wonders if she's imagining it, or if Amber seems more interested in what he's saying than she might usually be.

Dusty and Mali find a place to sit down slightly up the slope of the field, but close enough to the fire to people-watch. Dusty knows that Mali is making another accommodation for her, and she's grateful. There's an area close to the fire where half a dozen kegs are on offer, arranged like an altar next to two large speakers that emit a steady thud of bass through the ground. A small crowd is already dancing.

As her eyes get used to the firelight she scans the crowd, telling herself she's not looking for Will, but a strong smell of dirt draws her attention to their right, where the neighboring field has been turned into a BMX track, complete with jump mounds and berms for turning. A smaller fire burns in an old metal drum in the center of the course. Dusty nudges Mali to look as a group at the top of the start ramp chants "shred, shred, shed" to someone in a helmet and full BMX gear. The rider is handed a beer, and as he lifts up his helmet to down it, the flash from a phone reveals that it's Eli. He skulls the beer then smashes the empty can on his helmet, crushing it flat.

Mali grimaces. "He may be cute, but damn, you're right. The boy is a walking stereotype."

Eli pulls his helmet back down and after a loud countdown he speeds off the first ramp toward a jump with three other riders chasing behind. The activity itself, and the bravado that goes with it, doesn't appeal to Dusty in the slightest, but she has to admit: he is impressive. She can't believe the confidence Eli must have in his own body as he launches his bike off the ground, high into the air. The group runs to the finish line where several girls wait, clapping and cheering in excitement. Eli lands the final jump with insane speed and heads straight toward the group like he has no intention of stopping. At the last second, he slides into a burnout that sends a cloud of dust over the girls, making them squeal. As the dust settles, Eli takes off his helmet and brushes a hand over his short hair. His friend Jesse greets him with some secret handshake then hands Eli some clothes. He strips down to his briefs right there, laughing at whatever Jesse's saying.

Dusty and Mali roll their eyes at each other as they turn their attention back to the bonfire. In the crowd, they can see JD talking to Matt.

"I think he's asking to play some of his music," Mali explains. "He was talking about some remix he did yesterday."

They watch as Matt declines JD's offer, and JD walks away, deep in thought. Dusty hopes he's not too disappointed. If he is, he doesn't show it. He returns to Amber, paying close attention to her.

As Dusty does another scan for Will, she sees that Kristen King has arrived. Her blonde hair lights up in the firelight, and Dusty pushes at Mali's back, wordlessly encouraging her to go over.

She watches as Kristen sees Mali approaching. The mutual attraction is obvious, and Dusty is relieved that Kristen isn't hiding it from everyone else. As the only openly gay girl at school, Mali has had a good taste of heartbreak—girls using her for some fun in secret, then ignoring her out in the open.

Dusty remains like this, alone, quietly watching the party around her. She's grateful they're outside and not crammed into some house where it's even more obvious she doesn't fit in. Instead, she relishes the cool earth beneath her. It reminds her of Opi, and how she really might be onto something with the whole "time outside is good for you" thing.

The thud from the speakers is like a heartbeat that steadies the hum within her. Stars twinkle above and Dusty looks up to bask in their silent beauty.

"Good to see you're having fun with all your friends."

Dusty's heart quickens as Will sits down beside her.

"Like you can talk," she answers. "How'd you get here?"

"I walked."

She scans his face to see if he's joking.

The slightest twinkle in his eyes betrays him. "Fine," he concedes. "My mom dropped me on the main road. *Then* I walked."

Dusty stifles a smile. Will chuckles in response and the sound stirs up feelings that make her look away.

With her gaze fixed on the crowd, they sit without speaking, watching the tempo shift as more drinks are consumed and the darkness around them deepens. Amber and JD are still talking, their body language confirming that there *is* something going on between them. Dusty wonders what could have started it. Until tonight Amber was always borderline condescending toward JD, his behavior met with eyerolls and comments like "Don't you have any guys you can hang around with?" or, "Surely the music kids have their own table?"

Mali and Kristen are nearby dancing, getting closer to each other with every passing second. Their bodies are in sync with the rhythm and they look close to kissing when Kristen takes Mali's hand and leads her away into the privacy of the shadows.

Beside Dusty, Will doesn't ask for attention. He's still and silent. But no matter where Dusty looks, her body grows more and more aware of him. The way he smells, sweet and heady, making it hard for her to breathe.

She finally lets herself look down at his legs, then up his torso to his face. His eyes meet hers and they glimmer, reflecting the fire. The rest of the party fades away, ceasing to exist, when Dusty is hit by another wave of that confusing combination of attraction and fear.

There's nothing to be afraid of, she urges herself, her eyes moving over his lips.

Will's mouth spreads into a smile. She feels it in her chest.

"The other day," he says, still looking into her eyes. "When you were asking about DNA . . . You never say much in class either. What made you speak up then?"

She sighs and turns her gaze back up to the stars. "I don't know. I'd had a weird morning. Then all that stuff about how long our DNA would be if you spread it out . . . The idea of it being able to unfurl and reach out into space . . . It was so . . . beautiful. I guess I felt disappointed when such a high percentage of it was minimized like that."

Will doesn't answer and when she looks back at him his eyes are full of emotion, his expression impossible to read.

"What?" she asks, flustered. "What about you? How did you know about junk DNA?"

He smiles, his eyes still drawing her in like a moth to a flame. "I like biology," he says. "I watch a lot of stuff about it online."

"Oh yeah?" she asks. "What else do you watch?"

"A little bit of everything. Documentaries . . . police procedurals . . . a bit of sci-fi. What about you?"

"I watch whatever my sister's watching. Recently that's been every season of *Bridgerton*, for like, the fifth time." She lets out a laugh. "But, more than anything, I read."

His smile is soft as his midnight eyes sweep over her, just for a second, and he asks, "What do you read?"

The intensity of his gaze sends a tingle down her spine. She turns to look at the crowd.

"Where do you keep going?" he asks. "When you pull back like that?"

Dusty swallows, her heart thudding. "It's hard for me to . . . I don't like . . . feeling things."

When he doesn't say anything she turns to look at him. His eyes are watchful, thoughtful. "And I make you feel things?" he asks softly.

She looks away again, reminding herself to breathe. "I read fantasy, mostly," she says, trying to get back to safe ground. "Sometimes historical. Romance, always." She steals a quick glance in his direction, catching him smiling. "What about you? Do you like to read?"

"I listen to audiobooks," he offers.

"That's cool," she says. She has the urge to bite down on something again, and pinches her bottom lip between her teeth. "Not hitting the kegs tonight?" she deflects, forcing herself to face him again.

"Not tonight."

There's a loaded silence as their eyes meet.

"Fuck, Dusty," he whispers, then pushes his face into his hands and sweeps his hair back like he doesn't know what to do with himself.

Shit, Dusty thinks, and blushes at the force of her attraction. She's trying to decide what to say, or do, when raised voices draw her away.

There's a commotion near the fire. Two guys are arguing. One—she thinks his name is Sam—is up in Eli's face. Right away it's clear that the fight is over a girl who's beside them, trying to calm them down, unable to make herself heard. When she tries to get between them they push her aside. Sam grabs Eli's t-shirt, scrunching it tight to pull Eli closer, daring him.

Eli pushes Sam away, so hard that Sam smashes into a group who'd been watching nearby, knocking at least three of them to the ground.

Will and Dusty exchange a look as they get up to see if anyone needs help. When they reach the crowd, Sam is storming toward Eli, and as soon as he's close enough he spits in Eli's face. Eli responds without a thought, punching Sam in the mouth, knocking him back down.

There's a collective gasp.

The sound of Eli's fist against teeth rings in Dusty's ears. The light of the bonfire distorts the crowd and she can feel her heartbeat everywhere. Sam tries to stand, blood streaming from a split lip. Dusty watches as it runs down over his chin and drips onto his t-shirt.

A rush of hot saliva floods her mouth. She swallows.

At first, she doesn't understand what it is her body wants—what it is that's happened that could incite an urge unlike anything she's ever conceived of. A thirst. A hunger.

But staring at the red flowing from Sam's lip, she knows.

It's the blood.

She *wants* the blood.

Her heart thuds against her ribs, so strong it feels like they might break.

She breathes in and out quickly, trying to turn it all off, but for a split second there's a glimmer—a pull she can't explain, to something close. To *someone* close.

It becomes so strong that she can't ignore it.

She looks around, until she finds him. Eli, staring at the blood, transfixed.

His eyes are a mirror of what she feels.

He steps forward and tilts his head. Arms grab at him, trying to stop him from going for Sam again. He shakes them off like they're nothing but ash.

Without thinking, Dusty walks through the cluster of people, fighting the call of the metallic smell that seems to consume the air. She bites down on the building pressure in her teeth and steps directly in front of Eli, blocking his line of sight. His gaze still fixed beyond her, he tries to push her aside. But she doesn't move. Instead, she grabs his arm and leans in close to whisper in his ear.

"I know what you're feeling. I feel it too."

He pulls back and his eyes meet hers, searching.

She can see he's scared.

"We shouldn't be here, feeling like this. We need to go," she says with more force, holding out her hand. "Now."

He looks down at her hand then takes hold of it. She pulls, and they run into the darkness.

PART II

7
Mud and Rock and Dust

Dusty has never run so fast, or so far. She can hear Eli's heartbeat and breath intensifying with hers as they tear through the fields.

Eli never lets go of Dusty's hand. His skin is hot, like hers, and she's surprised that she can keep up with him, that she never tires.

They reach some trees that mark the beginning of a stretch of forest.

"Eli, stop." She pulls, slowing him down.

Even under the trees, Dusty is struck by how well she can see in the darkness. Eli stops beside her, filling his lungs with air. Fragments of moonlight float down through the leaves and onto his stricken face.

"What is happening to me?!" Eli barks. His fists are clenched and Dusty flinches at the anger in his voice.

"I don't know," she says quietly. "But it's happening to me too."

"*What* is happening to you?" His breath is still coming fast and deep.

Dusty tries to think before she speaks. "I felt . . . hunger . . . when I saw . . . Sam." She pauses, letting her words sink in. "I haven't been eating—"

He looks at her sharply. "Since when?"

"Tuesday. Dinner."

He begins to pace, thinking. "Me too."

"Have you been feeling . . . different?" she asks.

"I mean, yeah." He walks over to a log and sits down, burying his face in his hands. "It's been . . . intense. Like everything I feel is *more* than usual. But I don't know why."

"Yeah. Me too."

"It doesn't make sense," he mumbles.

Dusty tries to focus on her breath.

"What's your name again?" he asks, looking up at her.

Dusty rolls her eyes. Eli just stares at her.

"Dusty. Dusty Silver."

"I'm Eli." Then with a trace of a smile he adds, "Eli Blake."

"Yeah, I know." She sits down next to him.

There's a howl in the distance from a coyote, maybe even a wolf.

Eli shakes his head and Dusty can feel his frustration humming between them. "Were you sick too?" he asks, still trying to understand.

"I crashed hard on Wednesday afternoon. My mom couldn't get me out of bed."

"Same. But then I felt better. Well . . . different. Other than a headache, and not sleeping. Or eating . . ." Now she says it out loud she can't believe she hadn't realized that whatever's wrong with her is serious. "Everything smells and tastes disgusting . . ." she continues, dancing around the one thing consuming her mind.

"But the blood . . ." Eli says, his voice gruff and shaky.

Dusty hesitates, then closes her eyes. "I . . . wanted it. I wanted to taste it."

Eli lets out a deep sigh, like he needs to push all the air out of himself at once. "Me too. Not just *taste* it. I wanted to . . ." He stops himself.

"What?" she urges.

He shakes his head.

"Please. Say it. So I know I'm not going insane."

He hesitates, then finally speaks. "I wanted to . . . bite him."

For a moment all the words vanish from within her. She wonders if she's in a nightmare, and all she needs to do is will herself to wake.

"I knew where there was more of it," Eli continues, "flowing under his skin. Every time I think about it I have to stop myself from running back there. It's like I *need* it. It's like I'm a fucking vam—"

"Stop," Dusty says sharply. She stands up to help herself think. "No. This must be a mistake," she mumbles, beginning to pace. "There must be a reason. This is insane." She laughs, shaking her head. "It's a virus, just a virus."

"If it's just a virus then why did we need to run?"

Dusty stops, turning to face him. He's looking up at her, his eyes sad and serious. "I don't know what to do . . ." she says. She knows Eli doesn't have an answer, but she asks him anyway. "What do we do?"

"I can't go back there," Eli says, his voice hard. "Did you see how they looked at me? Like they *knew* something's wrong with me. And what if . . . what if I *had* bitten him. Or worse . . ." His face recoils in anguish.

Dusty tries to think. She remembers that her phone is still tucked into her boot. She takes it out. There's still a signal. But when she goes to call for help the phone feels more useless than ever. "I don't think we should be around people," she finally says. "Until we figure out what's happening. Until we know we aren't . . . dangerous. We can't risk hurting anyone. We can't go home until we know it's safe."

"Shit." Eli runs his hands over his hair, sighing deeply. "I have a little brother. What if I had done something to him? What if—"

"Look, we don't know what we're dealing with, so there's no point spiraling. Maybe it really is just some insane virus and we'll start to feel normal in a few days."

Her words are enough to give them a glimmer of hope. A path forward.

"Totally." Eli nods. "We could stay out here until it blows over. Stick together. Try to figure this out. I know a place. Not far. We camped out there last summer."

Dusty only needs a second to think. "Okay. Let's go."

They walk out of the forest and back to the tree line, which they use as their guide. Dusty messages her dad, telling him she's staying at Mali's, then she messages Mali saying she's with Eli, and that she'll explain later. Then she turns her phone off.

That should placate them for now, she tells herself, almost convinced.

"I haven't been cold at all," she says as it occurs to her again. "Have you?"

"No." Eli pulls at the back of his neck with his hand. "But it is summer."

"I guess it's lucky we don't need camping gear for the night . . . if we don't need sleeping bags for warmth . . . or food to eat . . ." But her words trail away as she realizes that her energy is dwindling. That she's still starving. That sooner or later, they *will* need something to sustain them.

"I guess . . ." Eli says, distracted by whatever he's grappling with in his own head.

They're silent the rest of the way. Dusty has to hold up her dress to get through the tall grass that brushes up against her knees and thighs, pricking her with every step.

Every now and then they see a gleam of light from a house tucked into the darkness. Like a little watchtower, reminding them that they still aren't completely alone, even out here. The thought should be comforting, but tonight Dusty tries to push the rest of the world out of her mind and focus on what's in front of her. But then she thinks of Will, and how she hadn't even looked back at him.

When they reach a stream, Eli says they're close. They follow it back into the forest, letting it lead them uphill as the water runs down in the opposite direction, swirling softly around and under the tree roots that hold the banks. Just as Dusty is about to ask how much further they have to go, they come to a clearing.

The forest floor levels out, forming a carpet of moss. The moon above them is perfectly framed by the opening in the trees, gleaming and luminous, as if it's watching them.

Dusty becomes aware of the heat in her boots making her feet swell, and bends to take them off. The cool, soft moss is a welcome contrast. She wriggles and stretches her toes, basking in the relief.

Eli walks over to a spot darkened by the shadows of some old logs. "This is it." His hands are stuffed in his back pockets, his voice cautious.

What at first seemed quiet, in contrast to the noise of the party, is actually far from it. Creatures of the night are all around, scurrying and swooping. Dusty walks over to Eli and sits on the ground beside him. She can feel his energy, chaotic and fatigued, but also nervous.

"Do you need to use my phone?" she asks gently. "To let your parents know you won't be home tonight?"

He lets out a laugh, pacing above her. "I don't remember the last time I spent a Saturday night at home."

Dusty nods as if she can relate. "I forgot you're the life of the party."

He softens, slightly. "Something like that."

A thought occurs to her. "You were drinking beer earlier."

"Yeah. It was disgusting. I still feel like I might barf."

"Nice. So just keeping up appearances?"

"Something like that," he says again, then looks at her with a sly grin. "Paying close attention, were you?"

"You don't really make it easy to ignore you," she replies dryly.

There's a long pause as Eli looks up at the sky. When he finally looks back down at Dusty he speaks in a whisper. "How did you know?"

They study each other. Strangers. Vulnerable.

She sighs. "Seeing you like that . . . the way you were looking at Sam? It was everything I was feeling."

"But, how were you so in control? How could you think of me, when all I could think about was . . . the blood."

She shakes her head. "I don't know. I guess I've had some practice controlling how I feel. Or at least keeping a lid on it. And . . . it was like I could feel you. Like we were in sync. And then seeing you, the look on your face—it terrified me because I knew that control was slipping away. It has been all week. So I knew I had to leave. That you did too." As she speaks, she's realizing that the fear she'd felt, alone with Will, wasn't just of falling for him. She feared herself, and what she might do to him. "I think it's good we're here," she says. "Away from everyone."

Eli drops his head back, looking at the sky. His breath comes fast. His fists clench.

Dusty thinks she can see a faint mist of color swirling around him. Red and green and orange. But she blinks and it's gone. "Eli . . ."

He ignores her.

"Eli," she repeats. "We need to rest. Can't you feel it? My head is spinning. My whole body feels like it's trembling, trying to tell me something. I need it to stop."

"I can't. I can't sleep—"

"That's okay. Even if we just lie here. We don't really have a choice, because if we don't, we're going to be even hungrier. We're going to keep thinking about the blood." Her voice is sure and calm. "Just rest. We can figure out what we're going to do tomorrow. Or by then, it might have even passed. Okay? Then we can go home."

He relents and sits down beside her.

Awkward, hesitant, they lie down side by side, a few feet between them, on a bed of moss. The earth beneath feels like it's absorbing the chaos inside Dusty, drawing that charge out and burying it deep. Transforming it into mud and rock and dust.

8
First Time

Will lies in bed looking up at the ceiling. His room feels like it's getting smaller by the minute, inching closer, ready to crush him. It's dark and the air is stale. He gets up to turn on the overhead fan which rattles and hums, so he picks up his phone and plays some white noise. A flowing stream.

But the sound reminds him of Dusty. Under the water, just the two of them, her hand reaching out to touch his chest.

He opens his messages and his fingers hover over the letters. But there's nothing to say.

She left with someone else.

On a normal day, it takes a lot for Will to type out a text. Or anything else. His brain just isn't compatible with written words. He doesn't have trouble processing what he can feel, taste, touch and see in shapes and colors—people, places, ideas. But anything visual-verbal, row after row of letters and numbers—they drift around, ever changing, taking all his concentration.

A doctor once called it dyslexia, but the label hasn't helped him much. It's really only caused his mom pain. Guilt too. Before they knew, she'd always talked about what college he'd go to. She dreamed up this life for him, a life she never got to have, only to find out that getting through high school would be difficult enough. Of course, college would be possible if he really wanted it. But deep down he knew he didn't. That was her dream, not his. After his diagnosis, she'd tried to pivot, encouraging him to find something he loves, maybe working with his hands, but he'd already felt like he was letting her down.

So Will has found ways to diminish it. To assure her he's managing just fine, which is true in part. Whenever he starts at a new school they try to provide him with basic resources. Decodable books, programs that help polish the papers he has to hand in. But he knows how he learns best. He has his routine down.

Instead of taking notes, he records the lessons, absorbing what he can, then listening again later to fill in any gaps. And because he's not focused on writing everything down, sometimes he lets his thoughts unfurl, giving himself the time to comb them out.

There are audiobooks and podcasts for almost everything too, which helps, but at this point he's just learning because he likes it. The grades don't matter. He knows he'll have to find another path, another dream. He doesn't quite know what that is yet, but he feels like it's close. Almost within reach.

He'd been thinking about this dream when he'd first noticed Dusty.

It was toward the end of his first week at Black River High. English class. They'd been studying poetry—William Blake's "Auguries of Innocence"—and after class had ended, he'd been behind her as she walked out into the hall where her friend Mali was waiting, and immediately asked her: "How do you think it all started? Consciousness, I mean. Life. Or maybe they're one and the same?"

"Context, Dust," Mali had said. "We've spoken about this."

Dusty's voice carried the weight of her thoughts as she replied, "Well, they say all life began in a primordial soup of bacteria, then evolved randomly. But I mean, surely there's more to it . . . There has to be something else out there, beyond the stars."

The way Dusty spoke, the way her curiosity had made him feel, had sunk under his skin. And there it remained.

Since then, he'd wanted to hear her talk more, to see if her face lit up like her voice did, or if he was lucky, have a chance to stare up at the stars with her. But she always seemed guarded. Unapproachable.

Until this week.

His fingers still hover over his phone.

Did I come on too strong? he wonders. Or had he completely missed something between Dusty and Eli that rendered him meaningless all along?

Back at the party, Matt had yelled out asking if anyone was sober enough to drive Sam home. Will had raised his hand, still stunned, and before he knew it Matt had tossed him some keys and he was driving away from the bonfire, a stranger covered in blood beside him.

He squeezes his eyes shut and his stomach clenches as his mind races over every moment he'd shared with Dusty. How she'd asked if he wanted to leave school with her. The electricity he'd felt. The tension. The ease. The way her cheeks flushed when their eyes met and how he'd finally seen all the shades of green in them, with flecks of golden brown. Like a forest at sunrise.

And tonight, when he couldn't believe he was actually sitting next to her under the stars, she'd been right there. So close. And then she was gone.

Dusty wakes with a jolt, like her body has just saved her subconscious from some imminent danger. Someone flinches beside her. Dusty tries to cling to her dream but it's slipping far away. She has the sense it was important, as if it held a key to a door she can't yet find. But it's already lost, and she shifts into the present.

Beside her is a boy.

The boy is Eli Blake.

She turns to face him. He's already looking at her.

He clears his throat. "I can't believe we actually slept."

"Me too," Dusty admits, still disoriented.

"It's like out here—"

"I could finally be still," she finishes.

The soft ground beneath them holds them in place as Dusty relishes the aftermath of sleep. Relieved that there is, in fact, still an off switch. Low sunlight pierces the tops of the trees to the east, not quite high enough to reach down into the clearing yet.

Dusty feels warm, but that brazen heat is gone, like the fire inside her has dwindled to embers. Her skin, however, is wet all over. She looks down at her dress which has turned a sheer, murky lilac. The fabric feels heavy, stuck to her skin, and her mismatched underwear is clearly visible. She's drenched in morning dew. Both of them are.

Steam rises from the warmth of their bodies.

Dusty sits up.

Eli, just noticing it too, is peeling away the white t-shirt that clings to his torso.

"Guess shelter wouldn't've been so useless after all," he says, sitting up to wring out the hem of his t-shirt onto the moss. He looks Dusty up and down and smiles. It's mischievous, bashful and confident all at once. It's the smile that gives every girl hope, while promising nothing.

"Yeah," she manages, "no shit." She tries not to show how self-conscious she feels. With nowhere to hide she closes her eyes, focusing on the sounds of the morning. So different from last night.

Last night. The second she pictures the blood her eyes open, thirst slapping her in the face. Her heart starts to thud like a bass drum and she wishes the memory was just another invasive thought. A figment of her overactive, anxious imagination. But it wasn't. It was real.

There's a hand on her shoulder and she looks up to find Eli looking down at her. "You okay?" he asks.

The answer is clear.

"I can hear it," he says. "Your heart."

Dusty listens. There's a second thudding, more distant, beating at a slightly slower rhythm to her own. "What else?" she asks, needing to know what he's experiencing.

"I don't know. Smells?" he says, brushing his hand over his buzz-cut. "Everything smells stronger. Especially . . . people." He stops, as if everything he's been feeling the past few days is sinking into the context of last night.

"I think I'm stronger, if that's possible?" Dusty says.

"It isn't, but I am too."

"Have you noticed anything . . . unusual? On the mountain?" Dusty asks, tentative.

"Like the mountain where I live?" He sounds confused.

"Where *we* live."

Eli's eyes widen. "Wait, you live on White Mountain too?"

Dusty nods, amused. She knows he's never paid much attention to her, but this confirms that to him she was, in fact, invisible. Until now.

"Woah." He nods. "Cool."

"So have you noticed anything?"

"Honestly? I'm not home much." He leans back on his arms, looking up at the sky.

She leans back too and the weight of her body on her hands slows everything down, like she's plugged into the moss, slipping into the cracks of the forest. Sunlight finally begins to reach the ground, illuminating a surface more complex than she had realized. The soft, thick moss is dotted with wildflowers and small ferns. They sprawl across the clearing, which is at least forty feet wide, until they reach a scattering of green and brown needles that blur the border of pines and spruce that surround the clearing like a wall.

"How'd you do that?" Eli probes.

"Do what?" she asks, still looking around.

"Slow your heart down like that. And your . . . energy, I guess? I could feel it happening to you . . ." His brow furrows. "And it made me feel it too."

"I didn't do anything. It was all this." Dusty looks around them, trying not to think about how much Opi would love it here.

That playful smile pulls at Eli's mouth. "So you're, like, Nature Girl?"

She lets out a laugh. "Far from it. That's my sister, Opi. And my dad's a game warden, so . . ."

"And you are?"

She shrugs. "I don't know. I read."

He looks at her like she's speaking another language.

"Books," she clarifies, a hint of amusement in her eyes.

"*Oh*, right. I think I've heard of those . . ." He nods slowly, their eyes meeting for a few seconds, reminding them they're strangers.

Dusty notices that her dress is almost completely dry already, from the heat that's beginning to burn in her again, aching with hunger.

"I hope he's okay," Eli says, his voice heavy. "Sam, I mean."

"I'm sure he's fine. It was barely a scratch," she lies. "What happened there, anyway?"

He rubs his face, frustrated. "It was so stupid. I was talking to his girlfriend. Probably giving her more attention than I should. And instead of walking away, I just . . . *couldn't*."

Dusty pictures the crowd and how quickly it all escalated.

"I could have killed him," Eli says.

"But you *didn't*."

"Only because of you."

He turns to face her again, his eyes almost ethereal in the morning light.

"You smell different to everyone else," she says, distracted.

"Okay. Thanks?"

"Good," she says. "But different."

Different to Will.

She's hit with a flash of how Will had looked at her last night, how he'd smelled, and energy surges through her limbs, skittish and electric, swirling around the big, important questions that loom in her mind. *What is happening? Why us? What has made us this way?*

But right now, her thirst, her *need*, is what commands her.

"We're *both* here because we felt that . . . urge . . ." she says, getting up. "So now we just need to figure out what to do about it."

"Yes, captain." He stands, stretching his arms above his head. His t-shirt, which is almost dry, rises, and Dusty glimpses the muscles at the top of his jeans. Her skin flushes at the sight of it.

"Do you think anyone else felt it too?" he asks.

Dusty blinks. When she looks up at him, he winks.

She clears her throat. It hadn't occurred to her, but of course it's possible they're not the only ones. "Not that I saw, or . . . felt," she says. "But I was pretty distracted. I just noticed you . . . and me." They look at each other for another moment. "And I'm still starving." She sighs.

"Speaking of . . . I was thinking," he says, running his hand over his coppery hair again. "Do you hunt?"

"I *can* hunt, but I don't like it. Growing up, Dad was pretty obsessed with us knowing how to be self-sufficient. Why? I really don't think

I could eat—" She stops when she sees that Eli is grinning and the implication sinks in. "Wait. You mean for *blood*?"

"There's a first time for everything."

9

Strangers

With Matt's Ford pickup still outside his house, Will forces himself to get out of bed and return it. He hasn't slept but it's early enough in the day that he figures he'll just walk home from Matt's property. He doesn't have anything else planned anyway.

His mom will be home from her shift soon, so he puts a pot of coffee on for her, showers, throws on some clothes, then checks his phone again.

No new messages.

A fresh knot twists in his stomach.

The low angle of the sun pierces the windscreen as he gets into the car. He looks back at his house in the morning light.

Squeezed amid a row of clones, all painted a weathered white, the house says nothing about who lives inside. The yard, however, is a different story.

Separated by metal fences, on either side of the straight pathways that lead to the front doors, all the other yards contain neglected lawns around eight feet deep, while theirs is filled with wildflowers. His mom had torn out the lawn and replaced it with hundreds of seeds in early spring. She does it wherever they move. A way of leaving a place better than how they'd found it.

It was how Will had noticed the bees, giving him the idea to make them shelters and scatter more seeds where he could. No one, other than his mom, knows that about him.

Not until Dusty.

He blows out a breath then turns the key in the ignition.

The streets are almost empty as he makes his way through town. A tranquil Sunday morning, some folks on their porches with coffees and a paper or phone to read. When he turns onto the road that leads to the Miller property he notices something in the corner of his eye, in the shadowed bank of the road. He slows, checking the rearview mirror.

He begins to reverse as he winds down the window.

"Mali?" he calls out.

Her arms are crossed in front of her and her hair is wrapped around her neck like a scarf keeping her warm. Her golden-brown dress is smudged with dirt and dark stains that look like blood. Scrapes and scratches mark her arms. She tucks her chin to her chest and continues walking, refusing to look up.

Will inches along backwards beside her.

"Mali," he repeats. "It's me, Will, from school. Do you need a ride home?"

She slows, and when she turns to look at him it's clear she's been crying. "Will?" she says, her voice shaky.

"Let me take you home," he says.

She hesitates, looking up at the road as if she's realizing where she is for the first time, then climbs in beside him. Her whole body trembles as she reaches for the seatbelt. Will winds up the window and turns the heat on.

"What happened?" he asks. "Did someone hurt you, Mali?" He takes off his sweater and hands it to her. As she unfurls her arms to pull it on he can see she's clutching her phone.

"My phone died," she says. "Do you have a charger?"

Will looks down at the unfamiliar dashboard then opens the console. "Here," he says, plugging one in for her.

She connects her phone and takes a deep breath, in and out. "My parents must be freaking out," she says.

"Where do you live?"

Mali tells him the name of her street and he pulls onto the main road. They're quiet for a minute before Mali speaks. "Sorry," she says with a forced laugh. "I didn't mean to freak you out. It was a weird night, and my phone died, so I had to walk."

Will nods slowly, aware she's not telling him what really happened. "Nothing to be sorry about," he says.

Mali pulls down the visor and looks at herself in the mirror. Will glances over, noticing a smear of blood on her chin just before she licks her thumb and begins to rub the smear away.

Her phone starts to ping, revived after a night of dormancy. She looks down at the screen, her eyes widening, then turns to Will. Her face is full of confusion when she asks: "Have you seen Dusty?"

Their hunger supersedes the craziness of what they're doing, along with a need to shift their focus from human blood to something vaguely part of their food chain.

Dusty and Eli are crouched beside a fallen log. They've followed a scent trail to an area not far from the clearing, marked by the strong aroma of a pine marten. The smell is completely repulsive, and much stronger than it should be, but it's a start.

"When we see it, I'll catch it, okay?" Eli whispers.

"Why? You think you're faster than me?"

He smiles. "I know I'm faster than you."

"Pfft." Dusty rolls her eyes, trying to cover up her growing nerves. "I bet you don't normally eat what you hunt."

"What? And you do?"

"Of course I do. Or at least, I used to. My grandpa used to say that no one deserves to eat an animal if they can't look it in the eye and hunt it themselves. And even though I haven't done it in a while, every season Dad brings one deer home, and I help him prepare it. It lasts us all winter, maybe longer. Hell of a lot more humane than farmed meat, if you ask me. Not to mention the environmental impact, or the cost."

"Yeah, well, my dad used to give me five dollars for any kill I could bring home. We never ate them, and they were never impressive enough to make the game wall . . . Didn't stop me from wanting to impress the prick. So I got good at it." He pauses. "I thought you were Book Girl, not Nature Girl?"

"I guess I *was* Nature Girl. Now I'm Book Girl."

They hear movement, followed by a flash of distinctive tawny brown and buffy orange fur. The creature scurries across the log, getting closer, and in a movement faster than anything Dusty has seen in real life, Eli lunges for it.

Their hearts pound, stunned, as Eli stands there holding the squirming animal out in front of him. Its bushy tail swirls around as it tries to free itself.

"Ow." Eli winces as it scratches at his hands. But his grip is strong and he begins to smile. "It's kind of cute," he says. "It could be our baby."

Dusty doesn't respond.

"Because of its brown and red coat. Like our hair," he explains innocently.

"I got it," she says, unamused.

The pine marten continues to squirm and screech, beginning to draw blood from the scratches.

"What now?" Eli asks, a hint of panic in his voice.

Dusty hates seeing the animal in fear. She can hear its heart pumping blood through its veins. Without thinking she whisks it from Eli's grip and in a swift movement, she snaps its neck.

Eli stares in shock.

Dusty cradles the animal close to her face and whispers, "I'm sorry, little one. Thank you for giving your life to us."

"I don't think he can hear you," Eli whispers.

Dusty looks at him flatly. "*She* still deserves our respect."

Eli sighs. "You're right . . . sorry." He looks down at his scratched hand. "Fuck," he adds, clearly rattled.

"I thought you were a hunter," Dusty teases.

"I *am* a hunter. But I'm normal and I usually hunt with a gun. So by the time I get to the animal, it's already dead."

Dusty holds the pine marten upside down by its feet. "Shit. I wish we had a knife," she says.

Eli reaches into his jeans and pulls a small pocket knife out.

"Of course you carry a knife."

"My dad gave it to me for my thirteenth birthday," he explains, handing it to her. "He told me that a man always carries a knife. That it's important . . . in case of emergencies. But outside of hunting, I've only ever used it for stupid shit."

"Like carving your initials on a tree?" Dusty teases.

Eli shrugs. "Or poking a hole in a beer can."

Dusty waits a moment, then slits the animal's neck with a steady hand.

Blood begins to stream from the wound.

"Shit, Dusty," Eli says with a twinkle of respect in his eyes.

But as red drips on the forest floor, the enormity of what they're about to do is clear on both of their faces.

Dusty drops the knife to the ground and holds out her hand, letting the rich liquid drip into her palm as her mouth begins to water.

Eli does the same, and together, they lick the blood from their hands. Their tentative expressions deflate into disappointment.

Dusty's head begins to shake back and forth in disbelief as she places the pine marten on the ground. "I can't believe . . . what are we doing?" She wipes her hands on the moss, trying to ignore the self-loathing that's coursing through her.

"It's wasn't as bad as how real food has tasted," Eli says.

When Dusty looks up at him, she isn't surprised to see that the color has drained from his face. She imagines she looks the same.

"What a waste," she says, staring down at the animal, guilt and sadness grumbling around her still-hungry stomach.

"I can't believe we just did that," Eli says.

"I know. Something wasn't right. And I don't just mean because we killed a fucking animal and drank its blood." She tries to breathe, her sanity hanging on by a thread.

The sounds of the forest feel like some sort of timer, counting the seconds until one of them thinks of something useful to say. Then the image of blood dripping from Sam's lip fills Dusty's mind, and the way she'd sensed it in his veins.

"I can't believe I'm about to say this," she says. "But maybe it needs to be . . . flowing, like . . . from something that's still alive."

"Fuck, Dusty. That's dark."

"Oh, I'm sorry if I refuse to believe that for whatever *insane* reason it's just human blood we want. Or should we go back into town and see? Maybe go to the doctor and ask what they think?"

Eli turns and kicks the fallen log, sending splinters of wood flying. There's blood on his chin. "I can't think, I'm so hungry." The frustration in his voice is palpable. "What if this isn't something we can wait out?" he asks. "What if it's forever?"

"It can't be . . ." Dusty shakes her head. "It won't be." Shifting back into survival mode, she begins to push her emotions somewhere deep, so all she feels is hunger. "But for now," she says, "let's try again. This time we won't kill it."

Mali reaches out to turn off the heat. Her mouth is dry, and when she glances at Will, she remembers that he's practically a stranger. But here they are, on their way to Dusty's house after one of the worst nights of Mali's life, and for some reason his presence is comforting her.

Driving along the familiar roads to the mountain, Mali tries to make sense of what's going on. Will has told her what happened at the bonfire, and if she hadn't just read a message from Dusty herself, saying she's with Eli, she would never have believed him.

Instead of going home, Mali had called her parents, who'd been worried out of their minds all night. Her dad had driven around town looking for her after he'd woken up Chris, who said Dusty wasn't home either. They were furious. She'd apologized profusely, telling them she was fine, which isn't true, and that she'd just stayed at Amber's. She'd said she thought she'd messaged them to let them know but her phone hadn't been working. Also not true.

She feels terrible, but her confusion about Dusty is a welcome distraction from everything else. From what really happened. So she tells herself that going to see Chris and Opi and offering them her help is best for everyone. And maybe Dusty will be home by the time they get there.

Eli Blake? Her head spins.

She doesn't know whether to be proud of Dusty or worried. A hookup is one thing, but to not go home . . . She looks at her phone again to check when Opi's latest message came through. Only half an hour ago.

Opi
Mali?? Please let me know
you're both okay.

Mali
> I'm fine. I'm sure Dusty is too.
> I'm on my way to your place now.

Mali tries Dusty's phone again. It's off.

Her mind runs through all possible scenarios, then, out loud, she concludes, "Her phone must have died too. She might have just fallen asleep somewhere, with Eli."

She looks to Will as if he can confirm this, but his expression is tense and he says nothing.

"That must be it," she tries to convince herself. But she knows Chris and Opi must be going insane. If it were anyone else, she wouldn't think twice. But this just isn't Dusty. And her own experience last night lingers heavily, her uneasiness impossible to shake.

Mali's chest tightens as she remembers getting ready for the party. How she'd twisted Dusty's arm to come in the first place. She says a silent prayer, begging for Dusty to be okay.

Then it clicks that Will had said he'd been sitting with Dusty before the fight broke out.

"So you were with Dusty? Before she went to help Eli?"

"I was."

Mali gives Will a sideways look, sensing there's more to it than that. Then she remembers that Dusty had mentioned Will while they were getting ready. "She asked about you. Before the party," she says absently.

Will doesn't answer, so Mali just directs him to Dusty's house.

Their next animal is a squirrel. Dusty takes the lead, stalking and capturing their tiny prey as it searches through a bed of pine needles. Holding it in her hands, her hunger stirs at the thought of what courses inside it.

"Ladies first," Eli says.

"Should we use the knife?" Dusty asks, grimacing at the thought of causing the squirrel pain.

"Is that what your . . . urges . . . are telling you to use?"

She shakes her head and slides her tongue along the bottom of her top teeth. "I don't think they're sharp enough."

Eli shrugs. "You're stronger than you used to be, right?"

She nods.

"You can do it then."

"I don't think I can."

Eli sighs. "There's only one way to find out." He snatches the animal from Dusty and bites hard into its neck.

It squeals. Dusty would be horrified if she wasn't so incredibly starving.

She watches as Eli holds the squirrel in front of his face like he's biting into a burger. She half expects him to recoil, but his face sinks further into its soft fur and the muscles around his eyes relax. The animal stops squirming.

When Eli pulls away his head falls back and he looks up at the blue sky, white clouds skimming the high atmosphere. A drop of blood runs down his cheek from the corner of his mouth.

Dusty waits, speechless.

Dropping the animal to the ground, Eli finally looks at her. "Better," he says. "Way, way better."

She grimaces. "I thought we were going to try not to kill it."

"Try first, judge later." He spits out some fur and holds his hands up in front of him, stretching his fingers out then clenching them into fists, then back again. "Yo, you have to try that."

And so she does.

They don't have to wait long for another squirrel to come along. It's in a tree, running along a branch when Eli jumps up and grabs it by the tail. His movements are faster this time, even more sure of himself. He hands it to Dusty with anticipation.

Her hunger surges.

The switch that controls her common sense flicks off and she knows exactly the right place to bite. Right on its chest where she can sense the blood flow is strongest.

She doesn't have the capacity to hesitate. Its fur is unpleasant on her mouth and hard to penetrate. It tickles her nostrils and feels dry on her tongue. But when her teeth meet skin she bears down and they plunge in smoothly.

Blood gushes, filling Dusty's mouth before running down her throat.

The feeling of pressure in her jaw and teeth is amazing. Satisfying.

But within seconds, there's nothing left to drink.

She looks to Eli, the only person in the world who knows what she's experiencing.

His eyes say it all. They're *wild* in every sense of the word.

The opposing sensations of satiation and dissatisfaction hum through her, lighting up every cell in her body. She wants more. Needs more. "I knew I was hungry . . ." she says, beginning to laugh. "But I didn't know I was *that* hungry."

Eli starts to laugh too, spurring Dusty on until they're hysterical. Then the laughter turns to tears, and Dusty feels like her heart is breaking. As if she's mourning something inherent, without quite understanding what she's lost.

As they head up the gravel driveway, Will can't believe his eyes. Up ahead there's a huge, white, gingerbread house. Dusty's house.

"I know," Mali says. "It's like something out of a fairytale."

Will had assumed that Dusty lived somewhere nicer than he did, but he'd never expected this.

His eyes travel up the three-story home with asymmetrical, steeply pitched gabled roofs and a turret tucked into one corner, then back down to the wrap-around porch complete with a swing seat. To the left of the house—north, Will thinks—the mountain continues to rise, lush and green. To the right it descends, and he remembers Dusty saying she could see Black River from her room. He wonders which window that is.

As they pull up at the steps the front door bursts open and Dusty's sister runs toward them.

"Dusty?!" she yells, but looking past the reflections on the windows her optimism sinks.

The second Mali gets out, the girl wraps her arms around her. Will notices how rigid Mali is at first, then how she softens the tighter Dusty's sister holds her.

A man comes out onto the porch, his face a mix of anger and relief. But when he sees that Dusty isn't here his expression reveals worry and fatigue. He stuffs his hands into his pockets as if to stop them from shaking. "You know where she is?" he asks.

Both father and daughter are looking at Mali.

She hesitates. "She said she's with Eli Blake."

Will doesn't know if he should get out or stay in the car. He feels like an imposter who's inserted himself into something private.

But Mali forces his hand.

"This is Will," she says, waiting for him to get out. "He was with Dusty, before she . . . left the party."

Will raises a hand in an awkward greeting.

10

Far From It

It's a strange thing, to meet the predator inside you. Like she's always been there, dormant, waiting for something to stir her awake. And you may think you know what it's like, to hunt or fish for your food, to take a life. But you really don't know. There are still processes and preparations that come before sustenance touches your lips—a knife in your hand, a dish, a table—creating a framework that separates *us* from *them*. Person from animal. Life from death. Shaping what it means to be human.

But Dusty can see now—there is no partition between a true predator and its prey.

As she walks back to the clearing, her entire perspective is shifting. The mechanisms and assumptions of reality, previously subconscious, are as clear as day while simultaneously bending into something new. Nourished by the blood she has just consumed, hungry for more.

Even the forest feels different. Its whispers remind her of the complex balance that allows for life, and that her place in this world is different now. It makes her body rumble.

She's almost relieved when a sharp, familiar pang of anxiety hits her. All those questions about what is happening still looming inside of her, looking for somewhere to settle. But when she tries to draw them up into her head, she can't. Her body won't let her. It keeps them down, coursing through her.

Dusty can only assume that Eli is experiencing something similar, but when she looks over, it's clear that he's processing in a very different way. Stirred up and charged, he drops to the ground to do push-ups. He sees a tree and jumps up to swing from its branches.

She wants to ask him if he's okay, but she can't bring herself to speak.

They just caught an animal and drank its blood. And she's already ready for another.

The stream that runs beside the clearing sparkles in the sunshine, reflecting light up into the trees that bounce thousands of shades of green and yellow all around. Dusty looks down at her hands. Her short, unpainted nails are caked with dirt, and there's the deep brown-red of dried blood between her fingers and in the creases of her palms. Her dress is filthy, her bare feet are too. She imagines that her face is much the same.

She bends down, reaching into the water, and begins to wash her hands, then her face. At first she doesn't notice that Eli is beside her, scrubbing himself clean.

He stops.

"What *are* we?" he asks, his voice so soft it doesn't sound like him.

Sunlight dances across his face, revealing faint freckles that almost entirely cover his nose, cheeks and forehead. His coppery brows and eyelashes are a striking contrast to those green eyes that glisten above his beautiful features. His clothes are drenched with sweat, clinging to muscles that can only be formed from constant physical movement.

As she holds his gaze, Dusty feels the space between them become dense, like a storm filled with tiny bolts of lightning sparking through a thick fog. She stands, her eyes still locked on his as she tries to make the distinction between *herself* and *her body*, because the two are at odds. She knows she should be horrified by what's happening, about what they've just done, but as Eli stands too, she watches his lips part to draw in a steady breath. He grazes his bottom lip with his tongue then pinches it in his teeth. Dusty's cells vibrate, and her thoughts disappear completely. Her body takes the reins, her muscles resisting at first as she takes a step closer to him. Daring him. Eli's eyes bore into hers, then move down over her body and back up.

Heat radiates from their proximity, burning up everything that is new and terrifying.

Chris sits at the dining table, his hands clasped together like a knot. He'd hoped that Mali would have all the answers, but she hadn't. Just that Dusty hadn't stayed at Mali's, she'd left the party with Eli Blake.

She lied to him.

And the boy, Will, his recollection of events had only left Chris with more questions, but at least he'd been able to describe the direction Dusty and Eli ran in. So he'd thanked them for coming, told Mali to stop putting off going home to her own parents, and watched them drive away.

When the phone had rung in the middle of the night, his first thought was that it might be Sarah. Not that she's called since she left. Instead it was James, Mali's dad, so distressed that Chris couldn't comprehend what he was saying at first. Dusty had messaged to say she was staying at Mali's, and she'd never lied to him before.

Not that he knows of, at least.

Chris had told James he was sure both girls would arrive at one of their houses any minute. But when he'd tried Dusty's phone and found it was off, he'd gone into Opi's room, roused her from sleep, and asked if she knew where her sister was.

She didn't.

Unable to go back to bed, Chris waited downstairs, trying to busy himself by sorting out his tackle box. As he attempted to untangle some line from a lure, he thought about how lucky he was—that he had two, healthy, caring, conscientious girls. He knew he should be home more, but at the end of the day, they ate good food and lived a good life. So far, they'd avoided the stereotypes of teen rebellion, and he wondered if maybe that wasn't such a good thing—if what was happening was Dusty rebelling. If ever since Sarah left Dusty had been working too hard to show him that she was "fine," when really she was still in pain, just like he was.

Of course she was.

When he still hadn't heard from Mali's parents by three am, then five am, then dawn, Chris became increasingly sick with fear and regret. It didn't help that he was still completely shaken by what he'd seen last week when he'd been called out to a farm outside of Remsen.

Never in his life has he seen something like that.

From his car, the dead cows had looked just that—dead. Victims of some kind of disease or infection, maybe even exposure to a toxic plant. But up close, he'd understood the bewildered shock on the faces of almost the entire sheriff's department, who were waiting back on the road, away from the grisly scene.

There were five cows lying in the paddock beside the house. The seven living ones that remained were huddled in the farthest corner, pressed up against the fence. When Chris entered they were skittish, eyes wide and alert. As he approached the dead cows the first thing he noticed was that two looked strangely flattened, their rib cages caved in. But there was no blood in sight. The other three were the ones with missing parts—eyes and udders gone, with only clean incision marks remaining. There were also straight, mechanical cuts in their sides. Chris was later told that those led to other missing organs, varying from animal to animal. Up close, the hairs around the cuts were curled and black. Singed.

There were no tracks around the bodies, or to or from the paddock, human or animal, and for the life of him, Chris couldn't think of a way so much damage could be done without the farmers hearing a thing. They'd been sleeping soundly just yards from the massacre.

It was obvious to Chris that it wasn't the work of any animal, so he'd been relieved that whatever happened there, the problem was out of his hands.

The lack of responsibility hadn't stopped him from losing sleep over it though, or stopped him from shifting his worry to his daughters. He'd debated telling them about what he'd seen, warning them to be careful, but as a parent he walks that fine line between wanting to protect them, and not wanting them to feel fear. Not wanting to admit that even he doesn't know what kind of monsters are out there.

He's always loved the idea of them out in the forest. Exploring. Free. That's how it should be, for as long as it lasts. But after the cattle, he couldn't shake the feeling that his girls still need protecting. That he should be home more. And even though what happened was miles away, on a farm very different to their mountain home, it worried him.

On Thursday he'd called the sheriff to see if they knew more about what happened. They said there had been similar instances all over the country, and in most cases they concluded that it was cult-organized ritual sacrifice. It didn't make Chris feel any better, and Dusty being out of reach just compounded his unease, making it fester into panic.

He called the sheriff's office again, but Dee, the young deputy on night desk-duty, had tried to assure him that Dusty would be home soon. She said that they got calls just like this from parents every weekend, and that just because he was game warden it didn't mean his daughter was any different. Besides, it was too soon for them to do anything.

So he waited.

But now, in the light of day, he's done waiting.

"You stay here, Op," he says as he stands, his chair pushing out from behind him with a croak against the floorboards. "I'm gonna head down to the Blakes'".

"You know them?"

"This is Black River, honey. I went to high school with them. And I've seen their son Eli in town. Can't say I liked the look of him."

Opi opens her mouth to speak, no doubt to lecture him on making assumptions about people, but he holds up a hand to stop her. "Hopefully she's there with him, or his folks might know where they are."

"Dusty would never not come home," Opi says quietly, clutching a pillow to her chest.

He wants to assure her that Dusty's fine, but he can't shake the feeling that she's far from it.

The longer they stand there, the deeper Dusty needs to breath. Still only inches apart, she studies Eli as he studies her. Their bodies are all sensation, all adrenaline, nothing else. Eli moves to close the gap between them, his lips so close to her that she can taste his breath, and with a rush she feels that pang of pressure in her teeth.

Her canine teeth.

She steps back.

Eli is panting, shaking his head. "Sorry," he says, his voice like gravel.

The memory of Will mouthing that very word after she'd pulled away from him in the water makes Dusty dizzy with confusion.

"No," she says, equally breathless. "It's fine. It's been a long, strange day." She's struggling to comprehend how they could have become so distracted. But she tells herself to save the self-disgust for later. It's her teeth that have her immediate attention. She pushes against them with the tip of her finger and feels a tingle that runs all the way up through their roots into her skull. Looking down at her finger, there's a small puncture culminating in a drop of blood. She flashes her teeth at Eli. "Are they sharper?"

He stares at her, still breathing heavily. His face is half dazed, half smiling.

"Eli!" she hurries. "Do my teeth look sharper?"

He leans in close. "They're nice teeth," he says, flirtatious.

"Eli, please."

He looks again. "They look normal, except maybe the bigger ones, on the sides? But not obviously." He touches his own and shudders at the sensation. "Woah."

"Show me yours."

Eli peels back his top lip, and at first glance, they do look normal. But then, she sees, his canines are slightly sharper than average. When he closes his mouth his flirtatiousness has evaporated.

"I didn't really notice them until we were . . . feeding," Dusty says. "And then again when I wanted—"

"To kiss me?" His eyes are serious, staring into hers.

Dusty lets out a slow, steady breath. "I need a minute," she says, sitting down to put her feet in the stream. But the cold flow of water only reminds her of Will again. How good he'd smelled. How steady and calm he is. How much she was starting to like him.

He'd been in danger. He'd been with a monster.

She shudders.

"You know all those books and movies?" Eli asks, his voice tentative. "The ones with . . . people who also need blood . . ."

Dusty hasn't let herself acknowledge any of that yet, but nods.

"You've read those, right?"

She nods again.

"So weren't they all *made* that way by someone else? Someone, like, old as fuck, and they have all these laws and rules, like a secret society? Do you think that's what this is? Like someone *bit* us and made us this way?"

Dusty tries to think over the sound of her thudding heart. "I mean, yeah." She clears her throat. "It's possible. At this point anything's possible. But I don't remember anyone doing anything to me, and I definitely didn't have any marks on my body or anyth—" She stops.

"What?" he asks, anticipation crackling between them.

"On Wednesday morning, when I woke up feeling like crap, before I slept forever . . . My sister told me I hadn't been in my bed the night before. We thought I must have been downstairs, sleepwalking, but I found a leaf in my hair, and then I noticed my feet were dirty. Like I'd been outside."

Eli closes his eyes tight, like he's remembering something. "I was riding all Tuesday afternoon at Matt's track. I went home, around nine maybe. I was tired, but I have trouble sleeping, so I smoked some weed, then went to bed. But on Wednesday morning . . . I woke up outside." He exhales, slow and deep, then opens his eyes. "I was leaning against my front door, with the worst headache I've ever had. I felt like an idiot for being so out of it. Thought I'd smoked too much after riding, and I'd been so hot . . . I've never sleepwalked or anything, but I don't know how else I could've ended up outside. Our front door locks automatically when it closes, so I must've gotten out of bed, gone out, then tried to get back in but couldn't. So I crashed at the door."

Dusty thinks for a moment. "And you didn't notice anything weird before that? In the forest around your house, or anywhere on the mountain?"

"No. I mean, I hadn't been home, so I don't know."

"That Tuesday morning, something really weird happened. My sister, Opi, and I had gone into the forest to forage before school. We took a trail we've taken hundreds of times, but somehow we got lost and separated. And there was this . . . presence . . . it felt like I was being watched, and that something really bad was going to happen. I've never been that scared in my life. So I ran. Like, literally fled, and then I came out of the forest down at Angel Lake. Opi was there. The same thing had happened to her."

They're facing each other now, legs crossed beside the stream. Dusty still plucking at leaves, Eli listening, anxiously bouncing one knee.

"The whole thing only lasted a few minutes," Dusty says, "but the weirdest part was, we somehow ended up on the *other* side of the lake. It should have taken at least an hour from where I thought we'd been." Her hairs prickle on end, like telling the story out loud might invoke that presence again. She shakes her head. "I still can't make sense of it. Later I thought the presence must have been a bear . . . but the time . . . it was so surreal."

Eli is listening, thinking, then his eyes light up with a memory. "My little brother . . . Noah. Before I went to bed on Tuesday night, I could hear my dad yelling at him. I guess he'd wet the bed the night before, and my dad didn't want him doing it again." Eli scoffs. "Like he can help it. He's eleven. Anyway, Dad was saying he should've grown out of it and that Mom shouldn't have to wash his sheets everyday so if he did it again he'd have to wash them himself. Noah was crying, saying it wasn't his fault. He said he thought there was something in his room in the night, and that he was so scared he couldn't call out or get up. Even to go to the bathroom."

They let what they're saying settle around them, as if a bigger picture might come into view.

"Okay," Dusty says, trying to process. "So there was something going on near both of our houses, then on Tuesday night, we *both* left our beds, and with no memory of it we went outside. That's when something must have happened. But we returned home some time before dawn, and that day we felt sick, couldn't eat, then finally crashed in the afternoon and slept for over a day. After that we felt . . . different. And still no interest in food even though we were hungry. Then when we saw blood, we knew that's what we . . . needed." She shakes her head. "We're completely in the dark. And apart from that weird presence, which may not even be linked, or real . . . As far as we know we're on our own."

"Fuck." Eli rubs his head with both hands. "And what? If we don't . . . get better . . . we just stay here forever?"

Dusty can't answer him at first, wondering if that might really be the only plausible option. But it can't be. "We'll have to go home eventually. Besides, people *will* come looking for us," she says, and her stomach drops. "I *know* my dad already is."

They're silent for what could be a minute, or ten, staring into the water. But then, Dusty can feel Eli's eyes on her. Noticing how filthy her dress is, but how the color is still so pretty against her skin. How her dark brown hair is tangled with leaves and fragments of moss. The dark pink of her lips. How much he'd wanted to kiss them.

Wait. She turns to him sharply. Had those been his thoughts, or her own?

"How come I've never seen you at parties before?" he asks, interrupting her confusion. His brow is furrowed, curious.

"I thought you didn't know who I was." Her eyes narrow, skeptical.

"I didn't know your *name*. That doesn't mean I wasn't aware of you."

Sure. She picks up another leaf to rip at. "You never see me at parties because I don't go to many," she answers, matter-of-fact.

"Because . . ."

"I don't know. Group things just aren't for me."

"Group things? Like, groups of people?" He chuckles.

"Yeah. People. I just prefer spending time on my own. Or with someone one-on-one. Things feel clearer that way. In a group people change. They react to each other. And honestly, I always just feel lonely in a crowd. Like everyone's in on something and I can't really grasp what it is."

Eli takes in what she's saying for a minute. "Maybe that's why guys always hang out while we're doing something else."

Dusty looks at him, interested.

"Like, we never just hang around talking. There's always an activity. Fishing, riding, video games, throwing a ball, shooting hoops . . . whatever. When you're doing something else, it doesn't really matter if you don't have much in common. It's a distraction." He lies back in the moss and folds his arms behind his head. "It also doesn't hurt when you're really good at all those things, like me."

Dusty snorts, then lies back next to him.

"That's why I started riding," he adds.

"Because you're good at it?"

"No, because of the bullshit. Kids used to give me a hard time about my hair."

Dusty turns, watching him run his hands over his short hair again. The color suits him so perfectly—coppery-golden-orange-brown—she can't imagine him with anything else. "Why would anyone give you a hard time about your hair?" she asks.

"Were you born under a rock?" Eli rolls his head to face her. "Carrot top, ginger, firecrotch, freckleface. There's literally a day called 'kick a ginger day'."

"What?! No there isn't!"

"Yeah, there is. Even my dad gives me shit about the color. He says how surprised they were when I was born. That my mom must've had an affair with the plumber or whatever. Anyway, it made the idea of doing something you need a helmet for seem pretty sweet. That, and the fact that I'm amazing at it." He laughs but Dusty can feel the hint of pain that lingers.

"I'm sorry. I can't believe you've ever been picked on. Especially for your appearance. Everyone just sees you as . . . perfect. King of the bros."

"Yeah, well . . . the art of distraction. Speaking of, who are your friends anyway?"

Dusty smiles at the pivot. She describes Mali, JD and Amber, trying to articulate the dynamic. She admits that Mali's the only one she really has a close connection with.

"Ohhh *that* crew," he says knowingly.

"What does *that* mean?"

"Your girl Mali, she's gay right?"

Dusty stares at him, unsure how that could be relevant.

"And JD . . . I'm pretty sure he's . . ."

Something about his tone makes Dusty tense up. "What, Eli? He's what?"

"Easy, tiger. It's cool," he adds, more gentle. "It's just not my thing. No offense, though."

Dusty is floored. "No offense?"

"No, I mean, they can do what they want . . . but, ehhh." He holds his hand out and tilts it side to side, like he's on the fence about something.

She sits up. "Are you kidding? Firstly, it's none of your business to even have an opinion on who someone else is attracted to, let alone label them without their consent. Secondly, someone's sexuality doesn't define them. Sure, it's a big part of them, just like the alpha-hetero identity you sling around in everyone's face, but I doubt you would say that that's all you are."

"You *literally* just called me a bro. Because that's what stands out about me to you. And don't pretend you don't judge me for it. How is me calling them gay any different?"

"Oh right, I feel so sad for all the bros who have faced centuries of fear and persecution." A hot flush sweeps through her body, and for the first time in her life, Dusty knows what it's like to want to punch someone.

Eli holds his hands up in surrender. "Sorry. I really didn't mean to offend you . . ." Then he adds, "Are you into girls too or something?"

Dusty's anger is visceral, like it's taken over her. She clenches her fists and stands, then storms across the clearing.

"Dusty!" Eli beckons.

"Don't follow me," she yells, then grabs her phone from her boot and storms into the tree line without looking back.

The Blake house is only four gates down the mountain from theirs, which is almost a mile along the winding road. When Chris reaches the big, mahogany, farmhouse-style gate, banked by impressive, faux stone walls, he winds down the window of his four-by-four and presses the intercom. After a moment the gates begin to open. He realizes there's a small camera just below the button.

The driveway is paved with black granite cobblestone, surrounded by bright green, perfectly mown lawns. Chris wonders how anywhere on the mountain, or anywhere outdoors, can look so tidy. He pulls up at the house which is neat and contemporary, accented with more of that sharp-edged faux stone around the garage and front entranceway. The rest of the house is painted a murky brown that he once heard Dusty describe as "greige." The closest tree to the building is thirty yards away.

Before he's out of his car he sees a woman with blonde hair and a wide, friendly smile coming out the front door to greet him. She's hardly changed since high school, he thinks, and he squints, trying to figure out how that's possible.

"Chris Silver, is that you?" she beams, her voice warm and excited.

From her surprise, he already knows that Dusty isn't here.

"How you doing, Dana?" Chris offers, unable to match her enthusiasm even on an ordinary day.

"Beautiful morning, isn't it?"

"Sure is." He nods politely before cutting to the chase. "Sorry to bother you on a Sunday, but I'm looking for my Dusty."

"Oh?" Her face falters with concern.

"Yeah. She didn't come home last night, and her friends say she left the party at the Millers with your Eli."

There's a slight twitch in the muscles around her mouth, before her smile broadens again. "These kids! Here, you better come inside. I just put on a pot of coffee. Shane's in the gym getting his miles out of the way but he should be done any minute."

The inside of their house is exactly like the outside. Everything looks shiny and new, not a pillow out of place. Chris wonders if they've just finished cleaning, or if it's always like this.

They pass the sitting room which features a wall of taxidermy head-mounts above modern furniture. As a game warden and hunter himself, Chris is used to trophy displays, but personally he's always found the practice wasteful. He hunts for meat, and believes that the only thing you should do with any unutilized parts of an animal is return them to the earth. That's what his father taught him, and what he has taught his girls.

In the large, open plan kitchen, Dana gestures to a row of stools tucked under a massive granite benchtop, then pours Chris a coffee and places it in front of him with a look that is part sympathy, part pity. It's a look that he's received from most of the women in Black River ever since Sarah left.

"So Eli and Dusty! My, my, my," she says brightly.

Chris forces a smile. "Apparently so. The thing is, this is so unlike Dusty, to not come home. Have you heard from Eli?"

"Heavens! Wouldn't that be a miracle?!" She laughs, then adds, "I don't remember the last time he was home on a weekend. And it seems to be a new girl he's with every week . . . But I'm sure it's different with Dusty. Maybe they're just friends!" Even though her mouth is smiling, her eyes are not.

"Maybe . . ." Chris replies. "Either way, you wouldn't mind calling him, would you? See if he might still be with her?"

Just then a tall, broad man bounds through the kitchen door. He's wearing jogging gear and dabbing sweat from his red face and neck with a towel. There isn't a light brown hair out of place on his head and somehow he takes up every bit of space in the room before he's even opened his mouth. "Chris! What a nice surprise." He offers his free hand which is hot and sweaty. "Sorry, man, I didn't know we had company."

"Morning, Shane." Chris nods at the man he's known at arm's length for most of his life.

Shane throws his towel over one shoulder and opens the refrigerator, taking out a bottle of water from a shelf that is dedicated exclusively to water bottles.

"Chris is looking for Dusty," Dana explains. "He says she might be with Eli."

Shane grunts a half-laugh, half-scoff. "Huh." Then he smiles. "Teens will be teens."

"Sure. Anyway, are you able to call him? Just want to know she's safe."

There's an awkward pause.

Chris forces another smile, waiting.

"You betcha," Shane says. He wipes his hands on the towel then picks up his phone and taps the screen. He holds it to his ear then shakes his head. "Sorry man, it's off. Probably out of battery. Too busy partying, you remember what it's like." He's close enough to Chris to jab him in the ribs with his elbow, and all at once Chris remembers why he has never liked Shane.

Loud gunshots boom from a nearby room.

"Noah!" Shane yells almost instantly. "Turn it down or I throw it out!"

The sound of gunfire descends quickly. Chris tries to picture their other son, who he's seen them with around town. He's almost certain he couldn't be older than ten, maybe eleven.

He looks back to Dana and Shane who are smiling at him blankly.

"Okay, well, please, let me know when you hear from him?" He gets up and walks to a whiteboard that hangs from a pantry door and writes his number on it with the small marker at the base.

"Sure thing. But maybe try the Millers?" Dana offers. "Matt's parties can get pretty out of hand, from what I hear. Eli's always talking about all the girls that hang around there too. That BMX track they built is like a magnet for them!"

Chris grits his teeth. "Will do." He turns on his heel and shows himself out.

As he gets into his car, he pictures the Miller's property. He was called out there only a few months back when they'd reported hunters nearby, outside of hunting season. His stomach drops at the scale of the place, and he's grateful Mali brought the boy, Will, to describe the direction Dusty had headed in.

He knows he has a long afternoon, and possibly night, ahead of him, and with one daughter out there, he doesn't like the idea of leaving the other at home, alone.

Sighing, he picks up his phone to message Opi, but it pings before he even has a chance to unlock it.

He reads the message breathlessly.

Dusty

Dad, I know you must be worried,
but I'm okay.
I'm just working through some things
and need some space.
I'll explain when I get home. Soon.
I'm sorry.

Ps. Give Op a hug from me.

He tries calling her immediately, but her phone is already switched off again.

She needs some space? Who does she think she is? She's seventeen.

Anger and frustration thud through him as he sits there in the driveway, reading her message again and again, trying to decide if she sent it herself. It sounds like her, reads like her, but how can he be sure?

He's just decided what he's going to do next when his phone pings again and he jumps, almost dropping it.

Opi

Any news? If she's not at the Blakes'
I think we need to file a police report
then go find her ourselves.

It's exactly what he'd been thinking.

11

The Siren

Dusty is trying to acknowledge the complexity of human beings.

It's something she faces every day in the books she reads, but that doesn't make it any easier to face in reality.

Before her mom left, her dad had always been so affectionate. He'd given his love and warmth so freely. She thinks her mom tried to do the same, but Dusty wonders now if she was giving it at some kind of cost to herself. Forcing it. Then, when her mom was gone, Dusty watched her father change. Dimmed, dulled by a broken heart. But she knew that wasn't all of him. All that was left of him.

She once read that there's a universe inside us all, and she loved that idea. She clung to it. It's like in a book, one line can never reveal a character's entirety. You get pieces of them, page after page, as they evolve and grow. As who they have been is buried by who they'll become—an embodiment of everything around them. Everyone. Every encounter. A mirrored ball reflecting it all.

It would be so much easier if life was black and white. Right and wrong.

But it's not.

And yet here Dusty is, fighting in the forest with Eli Blake about something he said that she's not even sure he meant—and in JD's case, something she's pretty sure is based on a rumor mostly likely started by some of Eli's friends—in the midst of one of the most life-altering experiences they will ever face.

The sky is darkening as she sits on a soft patch of moss, arranging stray leaves into a neat circle around her like they'll somehow order her thoughts. Her fingers itch for a pen to press into her notebook.

Her phone feels lighter now it's turned off again, and at the end of the day she's relieved that she's not alone in this. That Eli is here too, untethered from a reality they're not even close to understanding.

The trace of relief she'd felt after hunting is slipping away as nagging hunger consumes her stomach. She knows they'll have to hunt again tonight, and she dreads the thought as she slowly walks back to the clearing. To Eli.

But before she comes out of the trees, Dusty knows he isn't there. The more sporadic sounds of night are beginning to replace the humming chorus of day, and her ears prick, listening for him. She smells the air, finding only remnants of him.

As she slips her phone back into her boot, there's a shift in the atmosphere. Turning her head, she glimpses a glint of warm yellow light through the trees. At first she thinks it might be a flashlight, but it's too high up and close enough that she'd hear someone's footsteps. The light moves suddenly, shifting to a cool white, then stops a little further away.

Dusty follows it, moving silently down the slope alongside the stream, through the trees. The light remains out of reach, just far enough that she can't make out its source, darting away, then stilling, waiting for her, then darting off again. When she reaches the grassland at the edge of the forest, the light is gone. The fields are empty and the first glimmers of stars are sparkling in the sky. A soft breeze sweeps over the expanse of grasses, rustling them against each other. The sound tingles in her ears and a chill bristles over the back of her neck.

Then, she hears the distinct clang of metal on metal. She closes her eyes.

Another clang, then a clatter. It's faint, but not far, coming from the forest on the other side of the fields.

Dusty runs, holding her dress up so her legs can take full stride, her bare feet flattening the grass beneath them. Her breath is fast but steady.

When she enters the other forest it takes a few moments for her eyes to adjust. It's darker and dryer here, needles whispering underfoot as she makes her way through a maze of white pines and red spruce.

Approaching a dense mass of trees, warm light glows faintly under them, from a source deeper within. When she inhales she can taste Eli's scent. And someone else's too.

She quickens her pace.

Even though her sight is alarmingly sharp, if it weren't for that glow Dusty wouldn't be able to see much around her. Not even the light of the moon or stars can trespass here. She stills herself and listens, then continues until the light glows brighter, and she can hear a heartbeat. Fast and familiar. Then another, steady and strong.

She peers through a gap in the trees.

And there he is. Eli. She sighs with relief.

But then her head tilts.

Frozen in place, Eli is staring toward the light as if he's in a trance.

It's only now that Dusty takes in what's beyond him.

Nestled at the base of a dense grove of pines is a sleek, rectangular structure with three walls made of glass. Warm downlights reveal a modern interior, minimal but luxurious. There are no walls dividing rooms, just areas marked by a perfectly made bed and a sofa that are separated by a suspended wood-burning stove. A deep bathtub sits against the one cement wall at the back, positioned under a low skylight.

A breeze rolls down the hill behind the house, carrying with it a scent that hits Dusty with a thud.

Right there, about fifteen feet away from her, under a carport beside the house, is a man.

He's attaching a bike rack to the back of a huge, black Tesla, tightening a nut to fasten the metal form in place. He's in his late thirties, with dark wavy hair and a five o'clock shadow. He's around Dusty's height—five foot eight—and wears cycling lycras that reveal powerful legs and a robust body. His specialized shoes click against the concrete floor as he moves around. He's drenched with sweat from the ride he must have just returned from.

Dropping the tool into a tray on the ground, he turns to pick up his bike, which rests against one of the posts of the port. The breeze rolls again, sending the smell of him straight to Dusty.

She gasps.

Eli snaps around in her direction.

Their eyes meet in the darkness.

There's movement in the carport and by the time Dusty knows what's happened, the man is standing by the now-open passenger door, pointing a handgun directly at Eli. "What do you want? This is private property," the man warns, his voice deep.

Dusty can hear his heart pounding as he stares at Eli, and she imagines how strange Eli must look to him, staring back through the darkness.

"Kid, I swear, I will shoot you if you don't leave. Right now." The man's voice is steelier than before, his finger on the trigger, ready to squeeze.

"Don't!" Dusty calls.

The man pivots, following her voice with his weapon.

In a movement so quick and so unnatural, Eli is before him, snatching the gun with one hand and pushing him hard in the chest with the other. The man flies backwards with a force so strong his feet leave the ground. There's a loud crack. His head has hit the sharp edge of the car door. Tools scatter as he lands on the concrete floor.

Dusty blinks, praying this is just another intrusive, fearful thought. But then the man raises a hand to the back of his head, disoriented. When he looks at his fingers they're covered in blood.

The breeze swirls, spreading the sweet, metallic scent all around.

Dusty feels her top lip peel up.

Eli kneels down before the man. Staring. Taking him in.

For a moment everything is still and quiet. Then Eli leans closer and breathes him in.

Dusty watches, paralyzed by the strangeness of it all. But the blood, thickening through the sweat soaked hair, is like a siren, calling to her. She isn't aware of her feet moving, and when she thinks about it later, she wonders if she floated over, like something out of a dream.

The man looks between Eli and Dusty, his eyes blinking, his life fading.

It's as if they all know that what's about to happen is inevitable.

And it is.

Eli reaches out and gently touches the man's dark hair. Dusty can feel the warmth of the blood on his fingers. Then, rougher, Eli rakes his fingers through the dark waves and grips them. He lets out a shuddered breath before he tugs the man's head to the side and lunges forward, biting down into his thick, strong neck.

The man's eyes roll back.

Dusty can feel the pulse in her teeth as she watches.

There's a sob that she thinks must have come from the man. But it wasn't him. It was Eli, choking down blood, somewhere between ecstasy and grief. Red streams from the man's neck and Eli's mouth, and Dusty's whole body ignites with a need so strong she feels like her consciousness is being pushed outside of herself.

She is only hunger.

Her body reacts before her mind comprehends what she's doing, and she watches from above as she kneels down beside Eli. Without any more hesitation, she lifts the man's arm and bites down into his wrist.

The blood snaps her back into her own body, and at first she sucks, unsure of how to take such a strong flow. So much of it. But then her throat relaxes and she lets his warmth run down her, lighting up everything it touches. His skin is warm and smooth, and she can taste his salty sweat on her lips. Her eyes close and everything fades. She's above herself again, drifting up into the sky, slipping through the stars, soaring, where everything is clear and perfect.

And she knows that *this* is what she needs. This is what she lives for.

Human life feeding human life.

She can feel wind in her face, and for a moment she has the sense that she's speeding down a mountain road. But as the last of him flows into her, she's pulled back down, into herself.

She opens her eyes and lets go.

They sit there, beside the unmoving man, for what feels like a lifetime.

His body remains, but he is gone.

12

Out of Sight

They stare at the body for what might be hours, frozen in place as the sky shifts above them. Clouds, the moon, the stars and the dense, whispering trees.

Time is rendered meaningless in the face of what they've done, and how this man's blood is affecting their bodies. Changing them.

Then, just as the blackness of night begins to yield to deep purple, one of Dusty's fingers twitches against her thigh. A reminder that this isn't a nightmare. She's awake, and they just killed a man.

When she turns her gaze to Eli, he's already facing her. Dried blood is all around his mouth, and she can feel it around her own too. She can still taste it. When their eyes meet they speak to each other of feelings that words could never express, binding them to one another. Then finally, as if their minds are one, they both know what they have to do.

Slowly, they stand and begin to gather the man by his arms and legs. Smudges of deep red are around his neck and wrist, bruised indents from their front teeth framed by the two puncture wounds of their sharper canines. With Eli in front, carrying the man's ankles under one arm, and Dusty behind, her arms wrapped around the man's chest, his head against her shoulder, they take a step toward the edge of the carport. Dusty can feel the sticky wetness of his blood-soaked hair seeping through her dress.

Neither acknowledge how light he feels. How much stronger they are.

Looking back at the dark blood that remains on the car door, the tools and the concrete ground, Dusty scans for traces of herself and Eli—footprints, handprints—but there are none. They got to him too quickly, and drained him of the rest.

As they carry him away into the trees, the dense layers of pine needles leave no trace of their footsteps. A million questions drift between them. *What does this mean? What does this make us? How did this happen?* But they're too surreal to be acknowledged.

"Should we bury him?" Eli finally asks.

The sound of his voice in the cool, clean morning air is like a lightening bolt of reality. *This is really happening*, Dusty thinks, her body becoming conscious, suddenly aware of the unbound emotions that run rampant through every limb, culminating in a tornado that spins through her core, expands into her chest, contracts through her throat, then spirals at the crown of her head. Frantic, chaotic and scared.

"We could . . ." she answers, trying to control the tremble in her voice, "but someone will come looking for him." She swallows and her words taste like poison. "And because of the blood left back there, they'll start searching the woods. They might even use dogs to track his scent."

"Okay," Eli says. "What, then?"

"Black River," she says, knowing it's their only option. "It's deep enough. We could weigh him down. Find a stretch that's isolated enough . . . far enough . . ."

"I don't even know where the river is," Eli says.

"The stream will lead us there," she says, then repeats Will's words. "It flows into Black River. All the running water around here does, one way or another."

Eli doesn't respond but Dusty thinks she feels the slightest stroke of acknowledgement brush against her consciousness. She doesn't question it. She's too aware of everything else she's experiencing. The heat coursing through her. The ache of emotions she's kept deep inside for too long. The strength. The power. And beyond her, every sound, every movement—sharper, louder. More vibrant in every way.

They get to the open field and begin to cross it, lifting the man's body up so it doesn't brush against the grass.

When they reach the stream just within the tree line, they barely pause before following it in the opposite direction of the clearing.

"We should walk through the shallows," Dusty says absently. "It will mask any trace of us."

Eli says nothing but leads them in until they're trudging through the cold, ankle-deep water. Dusty tries to focus on the sky beyond the canopy above them, noticing the way the lilac gives way to pinks and oranges in the east. But after a while the colors are consumed by dark gray, pillowy clouds, so ominous that she forces herself to look down and focus on her own feet in the water. She doesn't look up until Eli slows to a stop.

They've reached the confluence of the stream and Black River.

A scent on the wind makes them turn their heads at the same moment. Dusty's ears and nose tingle as she searches for the source. She knows it's a bear before she sees it lapping water from the bank upstream. It stops and lifts its head, then begins to huff and snort. Its powerful body sways from side to side as it stares them down. Then, with a final huff, the bear turns and shuffles away into the trees.

"There aren't any tracks or trails nearby?" Eli asks.

"There could be a few," Dusty says. "But I think it's all private farmland out here. Like Matt's place. Some unnamed forest too."

No one else is around, she can feel them both thinking at once.

"Let's go," Eli says, then pulls them forward.

Shifting into the river's depths, Dusty's bare feet grip the riverbed as water swells past their waists and they navigate the rocky banks, strong and powerful. The last remnants of blood wash away from the man as the water engulfs him, and Dusty finally realizes how light he's been to carry. Close to weightless all along.

A mile or two further, they reach a bend where the water darkens and the rocks at their feet tumble like steps into a deep pool. The surface is awash with turbulent flow, hiding what lies beneath. They turn to each other, and Eli nods his head once, an unspoken agreement, and in a synchronized breath they submerge, driving the man's body to the deepest part of the riverbed.

They aren't surprised by how long they can hold their breath as Dusty pins the man down and Eli rolls over rocks bigger than his torso. They weigh him down, burying him until he's part of the river.

Dusty stares through the clear water as Eli pushes off the rocks back up to the surface. She can't move, thinking that she's the one who deserves to be stuck down here. That she's the one who should never return home.

Her heart feels like it's twisting in on itself, so tight it might explode. A hand grips her wrist and tugs her up. She clenches her eyes shut. *I'm sorry. I'm sorry*, she repeats as she rises to the surface of the river. Water floods against her face as she opens her eyes and sucks in her first breath.

There was life before.

This is after.

And nothing will ever be the same again.

Eli's hand moves into hers and pulls her again. She wants to stay, but the swell of emotions inside her is so overwhelming that she relents, letting Eli draw her over to the rocks and out of the water.

At the bank, they turn and look down into the river.

There's nothing to see.

He's gone.

When Eli lets go of her, Dusty can feel her hands shaking, but when she looks down they're completely steady. They're also clean. So is the rest of her, aside from a washed-out brown stain on her pink dress, right where the man's head had rested.

"It's all my fault," Eli says.

Dusty turns, noticing a haze of steam surrounding him.

"All of it," he continues. "If you hadn't run away with me, hadn't helped me—"

"Eli, if I hadn't run away with you, I could have done *that* to someone I love." Her voice is deeper than usual, like her emotions have stretched out her throat. "If I hadn't come here with you . . . that could have been my sister. My dad." *Or Will*, she thinks in disbelief.

"You don't know that," he says, shaking his head. "We only . . . *I* went to him. I don't even know how I knew he was there. I couldn't hear him until I was closer. But he . . . the smell . . . And then when he fell back . . . the blood—"

"You didn't know your own strength," she says, taking his hand in hers and squeezing it tight. "I was the one who gave us away. And I bit him too."

Eli frantically links his fingers in hers. His green eyes are piercing in the gray morning light. Fierce with pain.

"*We* killed an innocent man. And we don't even know his name." A fresh jolt of despair feels like it's ripping her in two. "What if he was a dad, Eli? What if someone is out there, waiting for him? Depending on him?"

"There was no one else at the cabin . . ." Eli says softly. "I couldn't smell anyone, and we could see it was empty."

"That doesn't mean shit, Eli!" She gasps for breath, choking on her self-disgust.

"I know. I know," he says, then looks back at the water. "Should we say something?" he asks. "About him? Like you did with the animals?"

Dusty shakes her head. "I don't think there's anything . . . Nothing will ever make up for . . ." She doesn't bother finishing her sentence. Still looking at Eli, she notices bright colors in the steam surrounding him. They hover and swirl and reach. Alive. Thinking back, they've been around him since they left the carport.

"Let's go," Eli says.

"Where?"

"The clearing."

Dusty looks at him, doubt written all over her face.

"Please. I can't think out here. We need to regroup. We need a plan."

She's too overwhelmed to argue, so they turn their backs on Black River and begin to walk.

Monday mornings are only made worse by a dark, cloud-filled sky. As the Black River High parking lot fills up and yellow buses file in and open their doors, Will is lost in a song as he follows the flow of teenagers inside.

Making his way down the hallway, he tries not to scan every face for Dusty. But as he nears his locker he sees Mali, and his breath catches as he looks around her, bracing himself for awkwardness. But Mali's alone.

She nods and Will pulls his headphones down to rest around his shoulders.

"You haven't heard from her, have you?" she asks. Her eyes are still puffy and sleep-deprived.

Will's heart sinks.

He'd assumed that Dusty had returned home sometime yesterday afternoon, and that letting him know had slipped Mali's mind. "No," he says. "Still nothing?"

Mali sighs. "Nothing. Chris and Opi searched around town for a while, then went out to Matt's property. If there's anyone who'll find her, it's her dad." She shakes her head then rubs her eyes. "This is so unlike her."

Will doesn't know what to say, until he finally asks, "How are you?"

Mali's eyes flash hard at him, and he wonders again what happened to her, before he found her on the edge of the road.

"I wasn't sure you'd be here today," he adds, his tone more hushed. Confidential.

"I'm fine," she says. "I mean, at least I will be when I know my best friend is okay. I couldn't just sit at home all day, and I figured someone here might know something that could help . . ."

The pang of worry he feels for Dusty almost unbearable. "Let me know when you hear something? Just want to know she's safe."

There's a distinctive snap of something heavy treading on the forest floor. Dusty and Eli are almost at the clearing, slowly ascending the slope by the side of the stream. They still themselves to listen. It's hard to focus at first, everything far sounds near, and what's near is layered with a depth that Dusty doesn't understand yet. She closes her eyes to focus, but her sense of smell is just as heightened as her hearing.

A moment later, she smells them. Two people. Close. Familiar.

"No," she whispers, dropping Eli's hand, staring ahead in disbelief.

And there, at the edge of the clearing, are her dad and sister.

"Dust!" Opi calls out, beginning to run toward them.

"Fuck," Eli mutters, turning to face the opposite direction like he can't bear to look at them.

But Dusty's reaction to her sister's need is fundamental. All of the fear and all of the chaos is replaced by a love that soars through her, just for a moment. But then she shakes her head, remembering, and whispers, "I'm not ready. We shouldn't have come back." Then, louder, she yells, "Stop!"

Surprised, Opi slows, still a dozen yards between them.

"Stay over there, okay?" Dusty calls. "Please?"

Opi stares at them, relief shifting to confusion. Chris remains back at the edge of the clearing, studying Dusty and Eli.

Dusty looks down at herself, her bare feet, her dress which is thankfully dry but still stained with brown smears, then at the boy beside her, unable to turn around. She can't even imagine what her dad and sister must think.

She drapes her hair over the stains on her shoulder, as if it will make a difference.

When she looks back at them, Dusty notices a haze of colors that seem to emanate from them. Dark reds, oranges and purples in shades unique to each of them, entwining, reacting, shifting, as if they're alive. Unable to understand it, Dusty shakes her head and squats down, burying her face in her hands. Eli reaches down and touches her head.

"Sweetheart," Chris calls out, tentative. "What's going on?"

"I just need a minute!" she yells.

"Honey—"

"I need a minute!" she growls, shocked by the tone of her own voice and the way her body pulses with anger.

She hears a footstep and snaps her head up to look at her dad.

He lifts his hands in submission but takes another slow step forward to bridge the gap between them. Following his lead, Opi moves to walk toward her sister, but stops in her tracks as Eli turns and glares at her.

Dusty grabs his arm as if to hold him back.

Chris and Opi don't move another muscle, but their eyes continue to scan Dusty, bewildered by the sight of her. It's clear that her bare feet are just as shocking to them as the rest of her appearance.

"What do we do?" Eli whispers.

"Dust, whatever this is . . ." Opi calls out, her voice clear and gentle. "Whatever's happened, we can help you. Dad's not even mad . . ." She looks back at him and he nods once in confirmation.

"You don't understand," Dusty pleads.

"Sweetheart. You need to come home," Chris says, his voice firm now. "You too, son," he says to Eli.

Dusty shakes her head and whispers to Eli, "I needed more time. I don't know what we're supposed to do."

"We could run," he says. "Right now. They'd never catch us."

She's staring ahead at her dad and sister, the emotional pull of them consuming her, clouding every reason she knows she shouldn't go near them.

Eli bends down close. "We could find somewhere further out, somewhere they'll never find us."

Dusty looks him in the eyes, trying to numb herself so she can think. But it's impossible. She feels it all. And the only thing she knows is that she could never leave them. No matter what she is. *Because* of what she is—this version of herself who can't suppress what's inside her.

She cannot, and will not, live without them. Even if living with herself feels impossible.

I'm not Mom.

Breathing deep, she stands. "No matter where we go," she says quietly, "we'll eventually see people. And then what? We need to find a way. We can keep hunting animals . . . on the mountain. And if we do it every day, it will be enough. We can even learn to feed without killing."

Eli watches her, letting her think out loud.

"There aren't many houses on the mountain," she continues. "There aren't many people. And there are plenty of animals." She glances toward her dad and sister. "Smell them. What do you feel?"

Eli pauses, taking in their presence. "I mean, they smell . . . fine. But, not in the way that he . . . I'm not hungry after what we did."

Dusty nods slowly, noticing the same thing for the first time too.

"But do you really want to risk it?" Eli asks. "We still don't really know what we are. *That* could've just been the beginning."

"Eli, I can't leave them. Not without breaking their hearts. Not without breaking mine."

Eli studies Dusty, a curious expression on his face. "You're stubborn, you know that?"

"I know," she whispers, then turns to her dad and Opi, who are still clearly trying to understand the dynamic as she and Eli whisper to each other among the trees. "Okay!" Dusty calls, sounding a little more like herself again. "We'll follow you back. But we need some space for a little bit, alright?"

Chris hesitates, but before he can question them, Opi is nodding in agreement as she backs up to her dad to guide him toward the stream, giving Dusty and Eli the space to follow.

Dusty doesn't miss the way Opi looks at Eli though. It's a shock, to see such hatred coming from her kind brown eyes.

The trail back is even farther than Dusty had realized. She can see why Eli thought they wouldn't be found so soon. Her dad and Opi must have been walking all night.

With every step Dusty notices how different her body feels. Not just her senses, or the emotional overload coursing through her, but the way she moves. The way her bare feet press into the ground, strong and steady, using every muscle and every bone all the way up, making her taller somehow. And the earth beneath her, full of life, like she's aware of every worm, every millipede, a universe of its own. It makes her feel bold. Powerful. But then she's hit with the memory of her teeth sinking into skin. The blood. The faraway place it took her to.

Shame shivers over her, laced with sadness. It seeps into her pores, so heavy she feels like she can't breathe.

"Keep walking," Eli whispers.

Dusty looks at her dad and sister, who are about ten feet ahead, constantly glancing back, concern and confusion written all over their faces. Dusty knows she doesn't have long before they start demanding answers, and that they're only silent now because she asked for space.

It starts to drizzle as they weave in and out of the tree line that surrounds the open fields. Opi and Chris's hiking boots, jeans, hooded jackets and backpacks are a stark contrast to Dusty and Eli. He's still in sneakers, jeans and a thin t-shirt, while Dusty just has her dress and the misty cloud that emanates around their warm bodies in the rain.

She stops and the blood drains from her face.

Her boots. She left them at the clearing, her phone too.

"What's wrong?" Eli asks, studying her.

"Nothing," she dismisses, beginning to walk again. She doesn't want to add to his growing list of worries.

Eli doesn't buy it.

"Everything," she relents, deciding she'll have to go back and get her boots and phone later.

By the time they're near Matt's property it's midafternoon and the sky is dense with pouring rain. Eli is looking out to the BMX track, the exposed earth dark and muddy. Dusty stares at the field where the bonfire had been, fascinated by the streaks of black charcoal that run down from the ashes through the green grass. The place had been so alive when they left it. Music and heat and people everywhere. Now it's overshadowed by death.

She tries not to look at the rise where she'd sat and watched everything with Mali, then with Will.

"This way," Chris calls out. They've reached a fire trail that branches off from one of the fields and Dusty can see her dad's car up ahead. Aware of how close they are to facing the real world again, Dusty's head starts to shake back and forth in protest. *I'm not ready.*

Chris and Opi are already at the car, hovering, pretending they're not watching Dusty and Eli.

Eli's hand slips into Dusty's and he turns to face her. Dusty notices that although the purple under his eyes hadn't been quite as dark as hers, his skin tone is so even now. More than that, he's practically glowing. The whites of his eyes are clear, the green more vibrant, and his cheeks and lips are flushed.

Dusty squeezes his hand.

They let go and slowly walk to either side of the car to get in. As the engine rumbles and they pull away, Dusty keeps picturing the man— still and lifeless at the bottom of Black River, his face buried by stones.

13

A Living, Breathing Lie

Eli gets out of the car without looking back. He'd told Dusty's dad to leave him at the gate to his house and is relieved to have a moment alone before facing his own parents. He doesn't know how they're going to react if he's honest.

It had been hard, painful even, being in that car, in such close proximity to anyone other than Dusty. He'd been acutely aware of what he would've wanted to do to them if they'd been the ones he'd come across, hungry in the dark.

Was that really only last night? he wonders.

It feels like another lifetime. Like he'd been a different person then. Before.

As he listens to their car pulling away behind him, Eli suddenly feels more alone than he's ever felt. He remembers how he'd called Dusty stubborn, but what he'd really meant was that she's so sure of herself. He's never met anyone who knows their own mind like that. So decisive. It's what's gotten him through the nightmare of the past few days, and without her with him now, he's scared he might crumble.

He draws a tense breath in through his nose, then walks up to the intercom and types in the code. The gate moans open and dread sinks into his bones.

His mom is waiting in the front doorway, vacuum in hand, AirPods in, and a knowing smile on her face. She makes a "tsk-tsk-tsk" sound with her tongue and taps her ear to switch the sound off. "Honey, this is a little late past curfew, even for you."

Eli forces himself up the steps. "What curfew?" he manages to joke, then holds his breath as he pecks her on the cheek and slides past her.

"You're lucky I've accepted that you're not going to college next year. But you remember our deal, don't you?"

It's only now that Eli realizes it's Monday, and that he should be at school. His dad must be at work and his brother at school. He relaxes a little, and nods. "Keep my grades up. Get my diploma."

She smiles. "Just one year left to go. *Then* you can go off and be a big BMX star. Honestly, Eli, there's only a few weeks of this school year left. You can do whatever you want over summer. Until then, you still need to play by the rules, okay?"

He nods again. "Is Dad pissed?"

She rolls her eyes. "He should be. But he remembers being seventeen, and God knows he liked to party back then. I swear the man was proud you were with that Silver girl too. Her dad has always annoyed him. He ticketed him once, for hunting out of season." She shakes her head. "It was over a decade ago."

"Oh yeah? How'd he know I was with Dusty?"

"Chris Silver was here yesterday," she says, resuming the vacuuming. She raises her voice; "You'd think his daughter has never left the house he was so worried." She taps her AirPods again and Eli could swear that even over the whirling vacuum he can just make out the voice of the narrator resuming the audiobook.

He turns to the cream carpeted stairs that branch off and up from the shiny granite foyer. They feel different under the strength of his legs. Smaller. Narrower. Like everything else.

As they wind up White Mountain Road, Dusty tucks her knees up in front of her and wraps her arms around herself. She's overwhelmed, not just by what has happened, but by the love she feels for her dad and sister. It courses through her among the chaos of everything else, and within the confines of the car, its closed windows covered in raindrops, that love is suffocating her. Because no matter what she feels for them, they don't know her anymore.

Not the real her. She's not the girl they dropped off at Mali's.

She's a living, breathing lie.

When they pull into the driveway, Dusty can feel her dad watching her through the rear-view mirror. Meeting his gaze, the strange, ever-present colors that cloud him are green and pink. She tries to ignore them and give her dad the most reassuring smile she can muster, but it's only met with a furrowed brow. Small flashes of red and purple spark out in her direction, like they're telling her how he feels.

Chris gets out and goes straight inside the house, leaving his daughters alone together in the parked car.

After a few seconds of silence, Opi breaks it. "Dust, what happened?" She turns around to look back at her sister with worried eyes. When there's no response, she asks again, pleading, "What *happened*?"

Dusty looks down at her dress, pressing the crumpled silk to her knees like it might straighten out the creases.

Opi sighs, then gets out of the car and storms inside.

When Dusty finally follows, the sweet, wet mountain air inundates her with memories. It's like she's returned home after years abroad, and all at once every moment of her childhood, every part of who she was—every part she has spent the past five years trying to forget—is all around her, joining the flood of emotion within. Her grandfather is in the garden, her grandmother's cooking wafting from the kitchen, her mom and Opi laughing as they run up the porch steps.

She clenches her eyes shut, trying suck it all up into her head, to draw it out of her body like she always does, so that *feeling* doesn't consume her. But she can't, and she has no choice but to keep going.

She takes one step toward the house, then another, and she slowly walks up the stairs and onto the porch. The creaking boards groan differently under her bare feet, and when she opens the heavy door it's so light, as if it's been replaced with a cardboard cutout. A reminder that her strength, the one thing she doesn't hate feeling, came from the man. It's not her own. It was stolen.

Inside, Chris is already sitting at the dining table while Opi puts the kettle on in the kitchen.

It's time to talk.

As Dusty takes a seat across from her dad, flashes of what happened come at her like slaps across the face, and with each one she sees herself more and more clearly.

I'm a monster. And they have no idea.

"Dusty—"

"I'm sorry," she interrupts, knowing the words won't be enough.

The last and only time Dusty can remember her dad's face looking like this was when her mom left. She knows it should be adding to her self-loathing, but instead it's making her angry. As if his expression is drawing all the pain to the surface of her skin.

Chris waits.

"I got drunk at the party," she starts, unable to conceal the defensive hostility in her voice. She tries to soften, but her next words come out cold. "It was stupid, but I was in a weird place and just needed to blow off some steam."

Opi slams a jar of dried flowers down onto the counter, but Dusty doesn't look at her.

Chris is tapping his fingers against the wooden table.

"I've been bottling some things in—"

"Whatever you're going through," Chris cuts in, "you *know* you can talk to me. But there is no excuse—"

"When?! You work all the time! You're never home. And then when you are, we're just expected to pretend everything's okay? That we're not in pain every fucking day of our lives?"

Chris's expression doesn't falter, but the colors around him do. Red, purple, blue and black. "Okay," he says, his voice calm. "Let's start from the beginning."

"I already told you. I got drunk at the party. I left with Eli to blow off steam."

"And what about the drugs?" he asks. "What are you on, Dusty? It's okay, you just have to tell me so I can know where to go from here."

Dusty's face twists into an expression of disbelief. "Drugs? Are you serious?"

Chris looks deep into his daughter's eyes then scans her face.

Dusty hasn't looked in a mirror yet, but she'd seen how healthy Eli looked, and despite the dirt, she's guessing she looks better than she looked last week too.

Chris sighs. "I want to believe you. But I wasn't born yesterday."

Opi places a mug of tea in front of each of them and sits down next to her dad. A united front. "What about the fight?" she asks.

Dusty flashes a look at her sister, wondering how she knows.

"Mali came over," Opi explains. "She didn't go home on Saturday night either."

Dusty looks between them, confused.

"We were so worried about you," Opi continues. "Mali brought Will with her so he could tell us what happened at the party. How Eli got into a fight, and then how you just ran off with him."

Shit.

"And whatever you were going through," Chris interjects, anger creeping into his voice, "it doesn't explain what on earth you were doing in the woods for *two* nights with someone you barely know! I don't know what's worse, *that*, or the fact that you didn't even have any gear with you!"

Dusty's temper feels like a volcano about to erupt, and she has no idea how she's going to get through this. She clenches her muscles and her words come out curt and stifled. "I'd been talking to Eli earlier in the night. He's going through some things too. Then, when the fight broke out, I knew he needed to get out of there. So did I. So we went to the clearing to talk."

"That's a lot of talking," Opi says.

"But it still gets cool at night, Dust!" Chris adds, incredulous. "You had nothing, barely anything on and no food. You're not even wearing shoes for Christ's sake!"

Dusty can only meet her father's words with a cold stare.

"Opi told me that she's heard Mali say you have a crush on Eli," he pushes. "Was that what this was about? Getting to spend time with him?"

Dusty turns her glare on her sister, intense heat boiling her body.

Opi looks down at her tea.

"You know better than to let everything you know fly out the window for a boy," Chris adds. "I know you do."

Dusty is cornered, and she realizes that there's only one thing she can say to end this conversation.

"It's Mom, okay?!" she yells, letting some of the pain out into her voice. "I can't stop thinking about her. I've *never* stopped thinking about her. It's too depressing here, pretending all the time. The house used to be full. Now most of the time it's just me and Opi. I feel like shit every day. I miss her. I hate her. And I know it's not your fault, but I just wanted to forget. I *needed* to forget. To get away just for a minute."

She's sickened by the words as they echo through the room—both the truth and a complete manipulation at once.

Chris's eyes move to the table, as do Opi's, and when Dusty follows them she sees that they're looking at her hands. They're gripping the table's edge, her knuckles white. It groans under her pressure. If she grips any harder, she'll crush the wood into pieces.

She lets go, her breath coming hard and fast. "I can't do this right now," she says, throwing her chair back as she stands up.

Walking upstairs she can hear Opi's soft cries, and her dad's gentle voice as he comforts his youngest daughter.

Monster, Dusty repeats to herself. *I'm a fucking monster.*

Dusty sits on her bed, combing out her wet hair as the sound of rain gently taps against her bedroom window. Small leaves ripped from knots fall onto her white sheets as she tries to find comfort in the familiar. This is her happy place after all. But looking back now, she remembers being up here, reading a book or drawing in her notebook. Pretending. Distracting herself from feeling like her heart could sink into the silence of the house.

Now she doesn't think she'll ever experience silence again. And that's not a comfort either.

Sounds from the kitchen below ring like they're all around her—pots and pans and drawers opening as her dad makes dinner, his voice as he speaks to Opi in hushed tones.

"She'll be okay," he says. "One of you was bound to rebel sooner or later. It's healthy to get it all off her chest. Just give her time, alright?"

"But she's so . . . different." Opi sniffs.

"She's your sister. She just needs some time, like she said."

Dusty can't bear to hear it. So she tries to focus on the rain instead, and the sound of the brush against her hair as her thoughts spin through her body. *It's good that they're angry with me. I deserve far worse. Where did Mali spend the night after the party? Why was she with Will? Will was here, in my house. What is Eli doing? What does the dead man's body look like now?*

She places the brush down on her bedside table, making sure it's in line with the edge.

When she'd come upstairs, she'd gone straight into the bathroom to shower. She'd scrunched up the pink silk dress and stuffed it into the washing machine but had stopped when she realized there wasn't any point. It should really be burned. It's evidence, after all. Her insides felt black and disgusting as she'd scrunched the dress into a plastic bag then retreated to her room and placed it in the corner beside her chest of drawers.

She hadn't been able to take her eyes off it as she'd pulled on her baggy sleep t-shirt and a pair of boxers.

She turns to look at the bag now, checking it's still there, and out of the corner of her eye she sees a light out her window. Looking again, it's a car far below, its headlights flashing through gaps in the trees. It reminds her of the light she'd seen in the forest. That flicker through the trees when she'd returned to the clearing and Eli was gone. The way she followed it. Or had it led her?

Getting her laptop out of her backpack, she squints against the blue light as she tries some key words—"light in the forest", "moving light", "light that leads people", "conscious light"—but the internet is chaos. She skims over links to stories of fairies, sprites, airplanes, aliens, ghosts, and more obvious explanations like pranks with flashlights. She sighs and types out the even bigger question—"why do I crave human blood?"—but she stops herself before she hits the return key. *Stupid. So stupid.* More evidence to incriminate her if she's ever linked to the disappearance of the man. She slams the laptop shut and slips it under her bed.

The light in the room is fading as the sun sets somewhere behind the thick gray clouds outside. Unable to face anything more today, Dusty goes to her bedroom door and locks it for the first time. Then, back at her bed, she crawls under the soft covers and pulls them around herself. They're instantly too hot but she doesn't care. She doesn't just want a comfortable cocoon. She wants a prison.

There is something cold and hard scraping against the top of Dusty's head. She opens her eyes, but she's disoriented by the murky, deep gray in front of her. She searches for the stars, but then remembers that she isn't in the clearing. She's home, in her own room.

But something isn't right.

The cold pressure on the crown of her scalp aches, pulling at her hair.

As she adjusts to her surroundings, she realizes that the pressure is actually her bedroom wall. She's flat on her back, facing upwards, head against the wall, but as the ceiling starts to come into focus, it looks like it's moving closer and closer, closing in on her.

Becoming aware of her body, it feels like thousands of tiny, frozen-solid snowflakes are prickling every inch of her skin. She has thrown the covers off and her arms are at her sides, her hands facing upwards next to her hips. But beneath her, where the bed should be, is nothing but cool night air.

When she tries to move, she can't.

Not a finger, not a toe. Immobile. Everything is rigid but her head. And it isn't until she looks to her side that she realizes the ceiling isn't moving down to her. It is she who's moving up to the ceiling.

The crown of her head grinds up the wall, like an anchor, guiding her up.

Dusty is levitating.

She wonders if she's dreaming, but at the same time she knows she's wide awake. And the most surreal part of it all is that she doesn't feel scared. It doesn't feel unnatural. It's like she's a cloud, hovering above, and sooner or later the weight of the world will draw her back down.

She closes her eyes and drifts back to sleep.

14

Together Together

Dusty doesn't sleep for long. She awakes again in darkness, back down on her bed, trying to convince herself that what happened hadn't happened.

But then she remembers—she's living a nightmare already.

She stands up and goes straight to the plastic bag with the stained dress inside. She picks it up, swipes a lighter from beside the candle on her dresser and doesn't bother changing before climbing out her window into the night.

Her feet reach the slanted roof of the porch with ease. The rain has stopped but the sky is still hooded by thick clouds. She's careful not to slip as she peers down through the darkness to the garden beneath. Her room is one story up, but the slope of the mountain makes it a far higher fall on this side of the house. Trying to figure out the best way down, the answer is obvious, and she steps onto a branch of the giant, solid beech tree.

She balances along the branch, unsurprised by how steady she is, as she remembers how her grandfather had predicted she'd one day sneak out this way. Her heart aches at the realization that this is her first time doing it, and how the circumstances are not what he would have had in mind. He'd said it's what he used to do when he was courting her grandmother.

Memories of them, which are imbued in every part of this house, distract her as she makes her way down. When she reaches the ground the air speaks to her of the forest—the breath of every tree, every animal, the wind and all of the microscopic life that binds it together.

She makes her way through the garden then into the trees. She knows the general direction to Eli's house, but with no path to guide her, she moves slowly. Cautiously.

Twigs and leaves crack under her bare feet as she makes her way down. She thinks about the presence she'd felt with Opi, that sense of something watching her, but she doesn't feel it now. Alone, with the night all around her, she feels her heart thud, joining the rhythm of the forest. It almost makes her want to smile. But she doesn't let herself.

Weaving her way around the different properties, she can see the outlines of houses through the night, their windows dark, their inhabitants safely asleep inside, grateful she's still satiated. Then suddenly, she stops. There's something familiar in the air. The scent engulfs her with relief, and she begins to run, faster, down, until she sees him.

Eli is emerging from the forest, his pace quickening as he runs toward Dusty. He doesn't slow until he's right in front of her, and they stand there, facing each other as they catch their breath in the darkness.

"How did you—" they both say at once, then laugh awkwardly.

He looks down at what she's wearing. "Nice boxers," he says, biting down on a smile.

She looks him over too. He's in a white t-shirt and blue-striped boxers. Just like hers. "Snap," she says.

"Thought I'd try out the whole bare feet thing too," he says. "Not bad. But not exactly necessary."

Dusty shrugs.

"So how did you—"

"You first," Dusty says.

"I couldn't fall asleep in my bed," Eli explains. "So I went outside to lie in the yard, like we did in the clearing. I might have slept a little, but it wasn't the same. And I kept thinking about these." He holds up a bag that contains what Dusty assumes are the clothes he'd been wearing when it had all happened. "They're, like, evidence now, I guess."

Dusty holds up her bag. "Same. It feels weird to still have them."

"So, what's your plan?" Eli asks.

"What makes you think I have a plan?"

Even in the dark, Dusty can see his expression, which says, *you obviously do.*

"This way," she relents, and they begin to walk down the mountain.

"How do you think we came out at the same time?" Eli asks.

Dusty shrugs. "Honestly, I don't know how any of this is possible. But it does feel like we're sort of . . ."

"Connected," Eli says, thoughtful. He runs his hand over his hair, a twitch Dusty is coming to know as something he does when he's anxious. "Did you sleep at all?" he asks.

"Yeah, a little," she says. "But when I did . . . I think I levitated."

Eli stops.

"I know," Dusty says, continuing down.

"What do you mean?" Eli asks, catching up to her.

"I mean, I floated up, above my bed, and hovered there."

"What the fuck, Dusty."

"I know."

"We still don't know anything, do we?"

"No. We don't."

Eli groans. "I don't want to grow wings or some shit."

Dusty tries not to laugh. "Don't."

"I'm serious," he says.

"I know," she sighs. "We don't know anything."

They look around at the night.

"Did you see a light?" Dusty asks. "Before you . . . went to the man?"

"A light?" Eli shakes his head. "No. I just . . . felt a sort of pull, I guess. Then I heard him. His tools. Why? Did you?"

"I don't know," Dusty says. "I thought I did. But it's all so surreal now . . ." She doesn't finish her sentence, and they're quiet for a while.

They curve their way back around to the other side of the mountain, then down toward Angel Lake. There are fewer houses on this descent, and they meet up with a trail not far from where Dusty had been with Opi last week. She feels distinctly unafraid. Everything that's happened seems to have drowned out the fear she'd felt that day, and more than that, she can't think of what she could possibly be afraid of anymore. Now that she's the one who ought to be feared.

"What did you say to your family?" Dusty asks.

"What do you mean?"

Her brow furrows. "About where we were for two nights."

"They didn't really ask. What about you?"

"Oh, I basically just made them feel like shit so they'd stop questioning me."

"Nice," Eli says. "At least they care."

Dusty's stomach flips at the thought of facing them again when the sun rises.

When they come to the edge of the lake, Dusty leads them along the bank for a minute or two, then they turn under a grove of aspens where there's a grassy clearing just beyond. At its center is a dark circle of stones that contains the ashen remains of thousands of fires, tended over decades by the inhabitants of the mountain.

Again, Dusty is awash with memories of being here with her dad, mom, Opi and her grandparents. Visions consume her, vivid and green in the sunshine, a peaceful spot where a day of swimming and fishing would turn into a cookout, then a night of stories around the fire. With her grandparents around all the time, the distance creeping between her mom and their family was less obvious. Looking back now, Dusty can see her, quietly sitting, staring out at the lake, or into the fire, in a world of her own.

Dusty blinks the memories away.

She clears her throat. "It's a good place to burn something," she says. "No one would think twice about fresh ashes being here. Plus, I don't think any flames could be seen from the houses above." She looks at Eli, who's staring at the firepit. Soft swirling reds and oranges flow around him. "Eli?" she asks.

"Dusty," he says.

"Can you see . . . colors? Around me?"

"Colors?"

"Yeah," she says, still distracted by them. "Everyone has a kind of haze of color around them now. You don't see it?"

Eli shakes his head. "No."

"At first I thought they were sort of random, but after seeing how they changed when I was with my dad and Opi, I think they reflect feelings. Or energy. Or both. They sort of twist and reach out sometimes. And they pull at me a little, the closer they get."

Eli looks impressed. "Did you ever see anything like that before?"

"No, never." She veers her attention through the colors to Eli's face. "What about you? Is there anything else that's new for you?"

He laughs. "I mean, apart from everything? Not really. It's mostly physical. I feel like a superhero or something. Like I could do *anything* . . ." His voice trails off with sadness, and Dusty knows he's thinking about the man.

They gather some sticks and dry leaves, then Dusty pulls out the lighter and holds it to the tinder. Flames catch instantly.

Eli reaches up to a low-hanging branch of one of the aspens and snaps it off the trunk as if it's a twig. He breaks it against his knee before throwing several decent sized pieces on top of the fire. Dusty heads a little further into the trees and does the same with a branch of birch. She remembers her dad saying it burns hot.

They toss the bags with their clothes inside on the fire, which lights up blue and yellow as it melts the plastic, then orange as the flames incinerate their clothes and Eli's shoes. They both block their noses from the smells as they stand close, watching every bit burn.

Before they go, they splash handfuls of lake water on the dying flames. It already looks as it had when they'd arrived. Black and cold.

They walk back up the mountain in silence, and by time they're at the point where Eli will branch off to return home, the sky is just starting to lighten.

"Think you'll go to school today?" Dusty asks.

"Yeah. I promised my mom. You?"

"Yeah. I don't think I have a choice."

"What're we going to do?" Eli asks, his voice cracking with uncertainty.

Dusty thinks, trying to picture herself around all those people.

"And I don't just mean if we get . . . hungry," Eli adds. "Or the sensory-fucking-overload. I mean, people are going to be talking. About us."

Dusty hadn't thought about it, but of course they will be. Half the juniors and seniors saw them run away from the bonfire. Together. "Us," she echoes.

"I don't know what I should say to my friends. All their questions. The only thing that would shut them up is if I said . . ."

"What?" Dusty asks.

Eli runs his hand over his hair, then sighs. "I think it's easiest if we just say we're like . . . together now."

"What do you mean *together now*?"

"I mean *together* together. Like, dating."

"Oh . . ." Dusty says, her heart beating a little faster.

"It'll buy us some time to be alone, away from everyone else," he says, a little defensive. "So we can talk and whatever. Plus, at night . . . when we need to start hunting again . . ."

"Yeah," Dusty says, clearing her throat. "That makes sense."

But her thoughts are already on her dad and Opi. Dusty hadn't missed the way they'd looked at Eli—like the whole thing was all his fault. And then she pictures Will, and the way he'd made her feel in the water, only days ago.

When Will had gotten the message from Mali telling him Dusty was home and safe, he'd been relieved. But as his phone sat beside him and no more messages appeared, no explanation from Dusty herself, the idea of *tomorrow* had loomed too large to let him get much sleep.

It also made her feelings for him perfectly clear.

He knew he'd most likely have to see her in homeroom in the morning, and the thought left him aching with dread.

Just after three am, he heard his mom come home from a late shift. Knowing she'd crash into a deep sleep, he waited, then got up to get the house ready for the day. He put on a load of laundry, unstacked the dishwasher, showered and fed himself, then put on a pot of coffee for his mom to wake up to.

It's just after five when he heads out the front door.

Standing in the small front yard, his backpack slung over one shoulder, he tries to decide which route he should take out of the half-dozen or so that will eventually lead him to school. Will likes walking, always has, especially when the streets are quiet. He knows that everyone at school would think it's weird, but that's the beauty of doing it so early. None of them will know.

He pulls his headphones over his ears and finds the song he wants—"Centurion" by Sluice.

The streetlights on his road are so bright that he can't see the sky until he turns the corner. The lights are more dispersed here, on the road that leads south, past the old feed mill and into town, and now he can see that there aren't any stars above, just clouds, and right beneath them, mountains in every direction.

He slips his hand into his pocket, feeling for the small compass he always keeps there, and for a second he imagines turning north and heading where it's mostly wilderness. Getting lost. He'd found the compass on a trail a few years back when they'd been living somewhere in Ohio. He liked how it felt in his hand, light but useful. Practical. He barely ever uses it, of course, but still, he likes to carry it with him. Likes knowing he can keep himself on the right path.

Before they'd moved to Black River, Will had thought that after school he'd travel. Not to cities, but to the wild places of the world, so he could see how big it all really is. But now, he'll sometimes find himself daydreaming about getting a house of his own around here, somewhere with some land around it, maybe even on a mountain.

He wonders where Dusty's mom went when she left. Dusty hadn't said, and it didn't seem like she knew. He pictures his own mom and tries to imagine how different he would be if she'd left him with his dad. But he can't, because she would never. His dad was the opposite to Dusty's, as far as Will could tell, and he definitely didn't live in the world's coolest house either.

He turns to look south in the direction of White Mountain, but he can't make it out among the layers of peaks.

Letting go of the compass, he heads toward town, cutting across some overgrown grass to a path that runs parallel to the road. The fluorescent streetlights reach far enough to light the way, and he takes his time, letting the music drown out his worries.

Slowly, the sun begins to rise.

He follows the path past fields, run-down fences, the lumber mill and a few other old industrial buildings, stopping to look at this or that, until he reaches the grounds of Black River High.

He sits down on one of the metal tables that look out over the sports fields to watch the changing sky. He's noticing that the clouds are parting, letting through glimpses of purple behind orange and pink, when he hears a noise behind him. He turns to look up at the school, the boxy buildings quiet and empty. Just as he's about to look away, there's a flash of movement on the rooftop. Dark and indiscernible.

Will stands to get a better look and is startled to see someone standing up there, looking out over the fields. Will peers, trying to see who it is, and as his eyes adjust, he realizes it's JD, who turns to look directly down at Will.

Will raises his hand to wave but stops himself. There's something about the way JD is looking at him that he can't understand, and he doesn't like it. JD lets out a loud laugh and turns to look behind him. Then, someone else steps to his side, tentative. It's Amber, her long, dark curls moving in the breeze.

As they stare down at him, something tells Will not to move, and not to look away.

There's a sudden bang. Loud and close.

Will stumbles off the table to the bench below, his heart pounding. He turns to see boys in training gear pouring out the changing room doors onto the closest field.

Laughing under his breath, his heart still booming, Will looks back up to the rooftop. But no one's there.

"Don't worry, I let Mali know you're safe," Opi says flatly.

Dusty is in the middle of taking one of the sharper turns on the mountain road into Black River. She swerves slightly as she realizes that she hadn't even thought about letting her best friend know she was home.

"Oh, thanks," she manages. "I haven't turned my phone on yet."

"I know," Opi says curtly.

Dusty pictures her phone, in her boot, at the edge of the clearing, waiting to be found and somehow link her to what they did. She tells herself it's far enough away from the man's cabin, and that she'll go back and get it in the next day or two. *One thing at a time.*

She'd felt a little better after burning her dress, at least. There had been something ritualistic, cathartic, about it, as if some of the tension that was binding her anger and fear had burned with it.

After washing her feet and changing her clothes, she'd sat on the floor of her room, listening to her dad getting up and ready, then Opi. She'd tried to think of an excuse to not go to school, but refusing to go would lead to more questions, so she'd resolved to push through it.

She let the fact that she killed a man over the weekend bury itself among everything else she was feeling, including a growing dread of the day ahead, and stayed in her room until it was time to go.

Downstairs, her dad and sister had already eaten breakfast, and it was clear the moment she saw them that her dad, at least, had softened a little since last night.

"Breakfast?" he offered, hovering between the living room and the front entranceway.

He was scanning Dusty from head to toe, still searching for any signs of harm. When their eyes met, he looked taken aback.

"You look good, sweetheart," he said.

Dusty turned to a mirror, letting herself look for the first time since she got home. Her eyes were clear and wildly bright, her skin looked soft and dewy, her cheeks and lips flushed rosy pink. Her strength was buzzing, running up and down her spine, sending a flickering hum around her body all the way up to the crown of her skull.

She couldn't see any colors around herself and wondered why.

"You sleep okay?" her dad asked.

Dusty turned to him, and her heart almost broke at the uncertainty on his face. She cleared her throat. "Yeah, Dad, I did." She smiled, and watched as his shoulders relaxed, warmth spreading over his face. She could tell that above all, he was just relieved to have her home.

"You're okay to get yourself and your sister to school?"

"Yep. All good."

He nodded, but he didn't seem completely convinced. "I've gotta get to work, okay? Breakfast's in the kitchen. I'll be home by five."

"Thanks."

He'd hovered for another few moments, studying her face before turning to leave.

Dusty couldn't bring herself to go into the kitchen, so she waited on the sofa instead, staring at the books and remotes on the coffee table, all askew, listening as Opi slammed drawers and cupboards in the kitchen, huffing and puffing, clearly still fuming at her older sister.

Dusty tried to convince herself that she could leave the objects be. But as she waited, the thought of them askew, haunting her all day, unable to get home and straighten them up, was so intense that by the time Opi came into the room they were all perfectly neat, laid out in order of size from the corner of the table closest to Dusty.

Opi's eyes flicked between Dusty and the table, before she turned and headed straight out the front door to wait for Dusty in the car.

Opi doesn't put any music on, and the rest of the drive to school is silent.

As they pull into the lot, the sky is filled with enormous, billowing white clouds that hover high up against patches of bright blue sky. Opi gets out of the car before Dusty has the chance to turn off the engine, and she's already near the entrance with Theo as Dusty gets out.

"Are you okay?" Dusty hears Theo ask Opi.

"*I'm* fine. But my sister's a selfish . . . Ugh." She shakes her head, unable to say anything mean even at her angriest.

Theo looks back at Dusty and does a double take when he sees her walking toward them. She raises her hand to him, and he waves back awkwardly before turning to catch up with Opi, who's already inside.

Dusty looks down at herself, at her pale blue tank top with delicate ribbing tucked into her jeans, the fabric so fine that in the light of day she can just make out her bra underneath. It's a warm morning, but it's still uncharacteristically revealing for Dusty. Still, she's glad she decided against a thicker t-shirt because she's already sweating. Her trainers feel tight around her too-hot feet.

Closing her eyes, she inhales deeply. She can smell all of the people around her, so clearly it's like she can see them, aware of their distance from her, their colors, and their feelings.

She opens her eyes, tucks her thumbs under the arms of her backpack, puts her head down and makes her way inside.

PART III

15

A Haze of Blues

Eli's at the other end of the hallway. He's talking to a friend, apparently unaware of almost all the other students whose eyes are darting between him and Dusty, trying to pick up on any sign of what might have happened during their now-notorious exit from the bonfire.

Their whispers make Dusty's hairs stand on end. She has a sudden overwhelming urge to run back to the car. Her heart begins to thud and just as she's about to give in and turn on her heel, she feels Eli's awareness of her. Their eyes meet, and they begin to walk toward each other.

The crowd parts to make way for them.

Face-to-face, Dusty feels their combined warmth surround them like a bubble.

"'Sup?" Eli says, unable to suppress his grin.

"Everyone's looking at us," she says quietly.

He shrugs. "Good." Then he puts his arm around her shoulder and begins to guide her through the hallway as she tries to ignore the murmurs of surprise from people around them. "Your heart's beating so loud it's blocking out all the bullshit," he says, laughing. "Breathe, Dusty. Just breathe."

She lets out the air she's been holding in her lungs and sucks more in, but it tastes like everyone around them.

"I don't know if I can do this," she whispers.

"Neither do I," he says, leaning so close she can feel his breath against her ear. "But we're in this together, okay?"

She turns to look into his eyes, full of sincerity, and relief washes over her. "Okay," she says, letting herself smile as her anxiety dissipates, just a little.

"Where's your homeroom?" he asks.

"2B," she says.

"I'll walk you."

They cross the sea of gaping faces and see Opi and Theo up ahead.

"What's your sister's name again?" Eli whispers.

"Opi."

He looks at Dusty sideways. "What is up with your names?"

"Well, Opi is short for Ophelia, but everyone calls her—"

"Hey Ophelia," Eli says, nodding at Opi.

She glares back. Theo nudges her, and as they pass, they hear him asking her what her problem is.

"*He's* my problem," she says. "Dusty would never have run off like that. Anyone who would make her—"

"I can't imagine anyone making Dusty do anything she didn't want to," Theo replies.

"You didn't see them when we found them."

"Sister hates me. Noted," Eli whispers, without looking back.

"It doesn't help that you used her full name."

Eli doesn't respond, but Dusty can feel him smiling.

They're almost at the end of the hallway, and just as Dusty thinks the worst might be over, she smells him.

They round the corner and there he is.

Surrounded by a haze of blues, Will leans against a locker, his hair falling over his eyes as he stares at the ground, seemingly lost in thought, headphones on. For a second Dusty thinks he might not notice her. But then he looks up, and his eyes move directly to hers. She opens her mouth to say something, but his gaze moves to Eli and his brow furrows. Before Dusty knows what to do, Will looks back down to the ground.

"You okay?" Eli asks.

"No," she says as they slow in front of her homeroom. "But it is what it is, right?"

"It is what it is."

Turning to face each other, they both know they're thinking about the same thing—the stranger, and what they did to him.

"See you at lunch," Eli says.

"See you."

He leans in and kisses her on the cheek, and at the same moment Dusty can feel Will behind her, sparks of red and purple firing among the cool blues.

When Eli pulls back, he winks. "For our cover story," he says. But his eyes sadden as he sees how worried she looks. He squeezes her shoulder then turns and walks away.

Dusty sits at her desk with her eyes closed, listening as each new person enters the room, adding a layer to the low hum of heartbeats and breath that murmurs in her ears. She practices focusing on individual sounds, taking them in then letting them go, turning the volume down on one to amplify another, attaching them to the colors of their source.

Before she opens her eyes, she knows that Mali has arrived, and that she's come in with Will.

Seeing Dusty, Mali gasps and runs over, leaning down to wrap her arms around Dusty's waist. It takes all of Dusty's willpower to try to look relaxed, because closeness to someone else, someone other than Eli, is terrifying. She can hear and feel Mali's blood flowing beneath her skin, where it gushes at full force and where it slows down at the ends of her limbs.

Act natural, Dusty repeats to herself like a mantra, even though she doesn't really know what that means anymore.

"What happened?" Mali asks, holding Dusty's face in her hands and searching her eyes for an explanation.

"I'm so sorry," Dusty says as she reaches up and places a hand on Mali's. "I should've called you last night. I was so tired, I just needed to sleep."

Will slips into his chair two rows over, and even though she doesn't look at him, Dusty can feel his rhythm, more restless than it had been last week, but still calmer and steadier than anyone else in the room.

"Let's go somewhere at lunch," Mali says softly. "To talk. Just the two of us?"

Dusty nods and tries her best to smile.

The next twenty minutes are hell. Dusty has a vague sense of everyone around her, including JD and Amber who have also taken their seats, but it's Will's presence that holds almost all her attention. She constantly has to remind herself that he's just a boy, no different to any other. But it's not true.

She hasn't felt anything close to hunger yet, but this close to him, there's something about the way he smells that sets him apart from everyone else. And without looking at him, she's always aware of the colors around him, and the way he keeps them close, like he's holding them back. It intensifies her urge to go to him, to inhale him.

The second the bell rings she's the first out of her chair and out of the room. She stands in the hall with her back against the cold wall, hugging her backpack as she tries to steady herself. Her peers file out to make their way to first period, including Mali, who heads down the hall without noticing Dusty.

Just as she feels like she's able to move again, Will turns out of the doorway, almost straight into her.

"Shit, sorry," he mumbles.

Through his headphones, Dusty catches a voice saying ". . . all great and precious things are lonely—" But the sound cuts out when Will pulls the headphones down around his neck.

"*East of Eden*," she says softly. She'd recognized the words from the book immediately.

Will's brows draw together, studying her.

Under his gaze, it takes Dusty a second to notice that Will's other hand is wrapped around her forearm. He'd grabbed onto it to stop himself from colliding with her. They look down at the same time, then he quickly lets go, taking a step back.

"Will," she says, momentarily stunned. Her skin still tingles where he touched her.

His dark blue eyes look into hers, waiting, giving nothing away.

"I'm sor—" she starts.

"I'm glad you're okay," he says, his tone unreadable, his expression unreadable.

Dusty looks down at her feet, awkward and ashamed.

When he goes to leave she reaches out for his arm. "Wait . . ." she says. She notices that his blue colors glide down to where her hand grips him, wrapping around her fingers where they tighten over his lean muscles. She can't help imagining what it would be like for his colors to envelop her completely. The thought makes her feel molten. When she looks back up, she can't think of what to say.

His eyes grow impatient, and he gently tugs his arm away from her as he sighs. "What do you want, Dusty?"

"I . . . I'm sorry I left like that . . . the other night."

It's not enough, not even close, and she knows it.

"It is what it is," he says, then turns and walks away.

Dusty enters the cafeteria and scans the crowd.

The confined space full of so many voices is unsurprisingly intense. It reminds her of one of those songs where it's hard to catch the melody, and the clashing, layered bursts happening all at once are jarring and disorienting. For once, Dusty is grateful for the smells from the kitchen, which mask the aroma of the other students and what's inside them. It makes her think about the word "human". If *they* are that, then what is she?

It doesn't take long to find Eli. She'd almost forgotten how much he stands out, standing inches taller than almost everyone else around him. He's surrounded by friends peppering him with questions. Dusty doesn't have to listen to know they're probably asking about her, and why they ran off like that. His friend Jesse puts a hand on his shoulder, and Eli shakes it away as he too scans the room.

Eli's eyes land on Dusty. He tips his chin up in a nod to her, a smile starting to pull at his mouth, and his friends follow his gaze.

As soon as they see Dusty they begin to whoop and cheer, and it's not just their group looking at her now. Almost everyone is watching her and Eli.

Whispers echo around the room, dizzying. She tries to focus, more to steady herself than to hear what they're saying.

A familiar voice cuts through the others. "Maybe now she's with him she'll stop pretending she likes us."

Dusty follows the voice to the table she normally sits at, where Amber is sitting with JD.

JD looks up at Dusty, giving her a subtle smile, then turns to drape his hand over the back of Amber's chair.

Dusty notices that Amber's lunch is untouched, like most days, while all that's on JD's tray is an apple. He must have already eaten the rest.

More whoops and whistles sound from Eli's table as he stands to come to Dusty, when someone speaks right beside her.

"Hey."

Dusty spins to find Mali, holding her tray of food.

"I'll wait for you here," Mali adds. "When you're ready we can go find somewhere quiet?"

"Oh, I'm cool," Dusty says. "I had a big breakfast." She swallows, wondering how long she'll be able to cover up this I-don't-eat-food-anymore thing. She looks back at Eli and gestures toward Mali. Eli slows and nods, understanding.

"Is it just me or did he get better looking?" Mali asks. "We obviously have a lot to talk about." She grins, glancing at Eli before she leads Dusty out and into the hall.

They find an empty classroom and slip inside.

There must have been a music class before lunch, because chairs and music stands are scattered around the room in a vague semi-circle. Mali selects a seat, and Dusty follows, picking one that isn't too close, but with none between them so the distance she's keeping isn't obvious.

The girls look at each other, and Mali finally raises her eyebrows. "So? Are you going to tell me how you're suddenly Eli Blake's girlfriend?"

Dusty pauses, fighting an urge to arrange the mess of chairs and music stands around them into a perfectly symmetrical setup. Instead, she considers if telling Mali the truth is even an option. But it's not just Dusty's secret to tell. It's Eli's too. And until they have a better understanding of *what* is happening to them, it would be careless, selfish even, to bring anyone else in.

"Well . . . After you went off with Kristen," Dusty begins, choosing her words carefully, "Eli and I got talking." She pauses, expecting an inundation of questions and exclamations, but Mali just waits. "It wasn't much," she continues, "but he said that he recognized me from the mountain, and that we should hang out sometime. He gave me the impression that he needed some space from his friends."

Dusty has never lied to Mali. She may have withheld little things here and there, but nothing major. Ever. So every word coming out of her mouth tastes gross and deceitful. Just like lying to her dad and sister.

"So, after, when I was sitting with Will and the fight broke out," she goes on, "I thought I should see if Eli was okay. He said he wasn't, and that he needed to get out of there. So that's what we did."

Mali tilts her head as she looks at Dusty, as if she's trying to figure her out. After a long pause, she breaks the silence. "*Excuse* me, but did Eli Blake pop your cherry, Dusty Silver?!" A smile broadens across her face as a twinkle returns to her eyes.

Dusty's relief is enough to inject some life back into her too. "No!" she says, mock-horrified. But then she remembers the cover story, and adds, "But we may have kissed." She can't help but grin at the expression on Mali's face. Shock and excitement perfectly fused in her features, induced by lies.

"Must have been one hell of a kiss," Mali says. "I swear your voice is deeper. And you look . . . amazing. Have you finally started using moisturizer? Tell me everything." Mali leans forward, ready for the play-by-play.

"Ugh," Dusty groans. "It's such a long story, and it feels stupid now that I know how worried you all were. I told myself my texts were enough." She shakes her head as she remembers. "But also, I thought telling my dad I was staying at yours would buy me some time. Where were *you*?"

Dusty watches as Mali's pink and green colors become cocooned by a stormy gray.

"Oh . . ." Mali says, her throat bobbing as she swallows. "I was with Kristen."

"What happened?" Dusty asks, her concern visible.

Mali sighs. "Nothing. I don't think it's going to work out."

"Oh?"

"Yeah," Mali says, her lips twisting to one side. "Another one bites the dust." The stormy gray darkens, just for a second, before pink and green break through again.

"What're you looking at?" Mali asks, self-consciously adjusting her hair.

"I'm sorry," Dusty says, trying to focus. "And I'm so sorry if I scared you."

"Girl, if you can't be swept away by Eli Blake for some crazy, wilderness romance experience, then there is literally no point to anything."

Dusty smiles, thinking, *It would be nice if it were that simple.*

"But you *will* have to spill the tea, eventually, you know that right?" Mali warns.

"I know," Dusty says, sheepish. "But I'm gonna drip feed it to you."

"Come on!" Mali scoffs. "Just give me one thing. *Please.*"

Dusty thinks. "We slept next to each other, on a bed of moss, under the stars."

Mali smiles at her friend. "I honestly can't think of anything worse, but you do you, baby."

Memories of the clearing sweep through Dusty like a whirlwind.

"So, what are you guys now? To each other? All anyone's been talking about is how Eli was all over you this morning."

"I don't know," Dusty says, honestly. "I guess we're . . . together."

"Wow," Mali says as her brows draw tight. "It's just so crazy because, like, no one saw you guys talking or anything before you left the bonfire."

Dusty can feel her defenses begin to prickle.

"I think that's why I was so worried," Mali continues. "Even though you'd texted. I just didn't see a runaway situation for you two. Like, ever. And you know if I'd seen it coming, I would've pushed you away with him myself." She pauses, then adds, "But what's up with Will? I think he's . . . into you. He didn't say anything, but he was *shook* the morning after the bonfire."

"Oh, yeah?" Dusty tries to sound casual. "How come you were with him anyway?"

Mali folds her arms in front of her and scrunches her shoulders up. "Oh, we just ran into each other in town. I asked him if he'd seen what happened to you. He said you'd been sitting together? I had like a hundred texts from Opi, so I got Will to drive me to your house to tell your dad what he knew."

Dusty stays quiet as she takes this in.

"Dust," Mali says quietly. "We were really worried. I've never seen your dad like that. Or Opi. It was just so . . . out of character for you." Her eyes tell Dusty that she needs more answers, and that they can dance all they want around what happened, but eventually they'll keep coming back to it.

Dusty inhales slow and deep. "I know. But as soon as I was out there, just me and Eli, I realized I've needed to do something out of my comfort zone, out of the ordinary, for a while now."

"Ummm, please don't gaslight me," Mali says. "Have I not been saying that since, like, the beginning of time?"

"I know," Dusty says, realizing it's true. "I should've listened to you. And it was really selfish, running away like that. It was shitty. I really am so, so sorry."

Mali reaches out and takes one of Dusty's hands. Dusty's fingers brush against Mali's cool wrist, grazing over a pulse point. She flinches and it takes all of her focus to not throw Mali's hand away from her like it's a snake.

"Since when do you run so hot?" Mali asks, looking down at their hands.

Dusty forces a smile, then squeezes Mali's hand and lets go, ready to change the subject. "So . . . what's up with JD and Amber? Is that a thing?"

"Oh you noticed?" Mali says sarcastically as she starts picking at her food. She dips a fry into glossy red ketchup and folds it into her mouth.

The idea of eating like that already feels like a distant memory to Dusty.

"I guess they're dating now," Mali says as she chews. "I think it started at the bonfire. It was a big night for everyone, apparently." She pauses and puts her food down as if she's lost her appetite. "They're kind of acting weird about it though. JD's all cocky or something. I guess it's both of their first relationship, so maybe that makes it more intense? I don't know, I *cannot* with the drama."

There's a knock on the door before it opens, and Eli's face appears. "Sorry to interrupt," he says hesitantly.

"That's okay," Mali says, her smile absolutely beaming.

"Eli, you know Mali?" Dusty offers, trying not to let her spiking anxiety get the better of her.

"Hey," Eli says, a dazzling smile flashing on his face as he enters, then stops between the two girls.

"Hey," Mali answers, looking between Dusty and Eli.

As if he's just remembered their lie, he places a hand on Dusty's shoulder and Dusty awkwardly reaches up to hold it, forcing herself to smile up at him as Mali watches.

"Nice to meet you . . . properly," Eli says.

There's a silence that lasts a beat too long.

"You too," Mali says, standing with her tray, as if she can see Dusty's discomfort. "I'm gonna leave you to it," she adds, winking at Dusty as she heads for the door. "But let's hang soon!" she calls. Then she's gone.

16
You Remind Me

Dusty makes it through the last two periods.

Absorbed in the whispers and colors of the people around her, she peers through the fog of her new reality, learning that her body, not just her mind, registers everyone and everything around her. Constantly reactive. As if her cells can hear and see and think too.

As the final bell rings and she follows the crowd through the halls, then outside to the waiting cars and buses, she wonders why Eli can't see the colors too, and if maybe they've always been there, and even though she couldn't see them, she still felt them.

Dusty gets in the car, unwilling to let herself remember who she was before her mom left.

The door swings open and Opi gets in, not sparing Dusty a sideways glance.

As they drive home in silence, Opi's anger seeps from her every pore. The road skirts the river's bank, reminding Dusty of what she's done. Of the man at the bottom of Black River. She suddenly feels like icy water is choking her, filling up her lungs. She swerves, her mind clouded with an image of the man underwater, his eyes flashing open, his arms pulling at rocks, trying to escape.

"Dusty!" Opi yells, and she's back in the car, Opi's hands on the steering wheel trying to make sure they don't run off the road.

"Sorry," she says, breathless, trying to regain control of herself and the car.

By the time she's pulling into their driveway on White Mountain, she knows what she has to do.

"I'm going to walk to Eli's, okay?"

"Dust—" Opi starts, but doesn't finish whatever she was going to say as Dusty drops her backpack on the porch, then heads straight to the garden and down toward the trees.

She takes off her shoes the second she's under the canopy. She hadn't realized how much she'd been craving the earth beneath her feet all day. She stands there, letting the sounds of the forest soak into her, soothing her. She breathes deeply, basking in the beauty around her, the peace, as she wills her mind to go back to that morning. The morning she and Opi got lost. The morning they lost time. The last time she felt like she had a hold of herself.

She remembers the taste of the tea Opi had given her, how cool the early morning air had felt, the comforting warmth of her boots and sweater as they'd set off. She retraces their steps.

When she reaches the spot where they'd found the first morel, a wave of sadness gushes through her stomach. They'd been so excited.

Stepping off the trail, she finds that she can still somehow smell traces of herself and her sister lingering in the forest. She follows the scent, letting her senses lead her deeper and deeper. She's looking for the dense grove of trees that had loomed around her, intensifying her fear and the feeling that something was wrong. But she can't find them, and no feeling of fear manifests.

When their scent dies off completely, she's about to turn around and go back to the trail so she can continue down to Angel Lake, when she notices a black mark on a nearby maple tree.

Moving closer, it becomes clear that it's not just a mark. The entire side of the tree is scorched from about five feet up the trunk and up, the bark black and crumbling. She looks up, noticing the leaves on the same side are brown and withered, while the leaves on the other side remain healthy and green.

Looking around her, there are several other trees with the same scorched scars, as if a fire blazed among them, long flames licking their sides. But there's no other evidence of a fire, no ash, and the understory is perfectly intact. She can see that the marked trees form a near-perfect circle. She bends down, parting the newly unfurled fronds of young Christmas ferns covering the area, to find the floor beneath is blackened and scorched too. She walks around, trying to figure out how far the scorch spreads. It stops a few yards from the trees. She follows the edge of the blackened ground and finds that it too is in a perfect circle, about eight or nine feet in diameter, in the middle of the scorched trees.

Unsure of what to make of it, Dusty walks back to the trail and continues down all the way to Angel Lake to look for more, but there's nothing else like it, and she lands on the right side of the lake this time.

When she finally gives up and makes her way home, her mind whirls with possible explanations. She supposes that some sort of giant, raised firepit could have made the ground beneath it wither from the heat, and singed the trees above. If it had been there long enough.

But Dusty didn't see any fire that morning, or smell one so close to her house after. She didn't see anything. And why would someone bring a firepit there in the first place? Besides, she's pretty sure a portable, eight-foot-wide firepit doesn't exist.

Back in her room, she opens her laptop and searches "scorched earth". Other than it being the name of a military strategy, the information is mostly about forest fires. There is, however, something called "leaf scorch", which is when leaves on one side of a tree appear scorched or burnt or dead. Dusty clicks through to a link, reading furiously. It appears that "leaf scorch" is a common occurrence on maple trees and can be nutrient-related, weather-related, or bacterial. And the trees she had seen were definitely maples.

She sighs, wondering if it could've just been a coincidence.

She looks out her window, down the mountain, waiting for some kind of answer to spring from the trees. But it doesn't, and she looks beyond Angel Lake, her gaze settling at the bottom of the mountain on the distinct line of Black River, flowing through the forest.

At lunchtime on Thursday, Will is outside looking up at the bee shelter he'd left on the awning. He's noticed more activity around it every day, and in the garden bed below, green shoots are already pushing up through the soil. The rain over the weekend would have helped, but the dirt already looks too dry again. He takes a bottle out of his bag and is pouring water into his hand to shake it over the new growth when the emergency exit door swings open.

Will freezes, holding his breath, praying it isn't Dusty.

It isn't.

"What're you doing?" Mali asks, looking at his dripping wet hand.

"What're *you* doing?" he echoes, shaking out what's left onto the shoots then putting the bottle back in his bag.

"You think you're the only one who can dine *alfresco*?" she says, then strides over to the table in front of Will and puts down her lunch tray right next to his. "No wonder you're never inside," she says, sitting down and looking out to the fields. "You're out here every day?"

"Mostly," Will says, taking a seat on the bench next to her.

Mali chuckles.

Will frowns. "What?"

"Nothing. You just remind me of someone, that's all." She picks up her slice of pizza and starts eating. "Sooo . . ." she says, pursing her lips to the side as she chews.

Will raises his eyebrows. "So . . ."

"Is this weird for you?" She looks at him sideways.

"No," he says, letting himself smile as he picks up his own pizza, relaxing into the feeling of the hot sun on his face while he eats.

They finish their food without talking, but as soon as Mali is done, she starts to probe Will with questions—about his mom, his interests and his life before he moved to Black River. He gives her a shorter and lighter version than he'd given Dusty, but Mali seems satisfied enough. He finds her unbridled curiosity refreshing and can see why she and Dusty are friends.

That's the only problem with this, he thinks. He's been trying to not dwell on Dusty all week, but he just can't seem to shake her. He'd been doing fine before she crashed into him out here—now he feels untethered somehow. Like his anchor is skidding along the sand of a shallow sea.

"So why are you really out here?" he asks, squinting into the sun to look at her.

"I just . . ." She sighs. "Dusty isn't sitting in the cafeteria anymore. And I get it. Like, all eyes are on her and Eli right now, which for Dusty is hellish. But I feel weird hiding out with them like some kind of third wheel. Anyway, I've been wanting something like this for her for forever, so it's cool."

"What about your other friends? JD? Amber?"

"I'd be third-wheeling it with them too. They're a couple now, you know? And . . . I don't know . . . It's weird with them. But you seem, sort of, drama-free." She shrugs.

Will smiles, wishing that were true as he studies Mali, still wondering what really happened to her the night of the bonfire. She's so honest about everything else, but that morning it had been obvious something had happened to her, and that she didn't want to talk about it. "What kind of weird?" he asks instead.

Mali rolls her eyes. "Ugh, I don't know how to explain it. But it's like, since JD and Amber started dating, they're in some kind of love bubble. They're not all over each other, or anything like that, it's more like they know some big secret, and it's all knowing looks and giggles." She grimaces. "It's like no one else exists suddenly. And the weirdest part is that they didn't really have any chemistry before last weekend, or at least not that I noticed. But what do I know?"

"I saw them the other morning," Will says. "JD and Amber."

"Yeah?"

"It was kind of . . . odd, actually. They were on the roof, just up there." He points above them. "It was like six am, and . . . I don't know." He shakes his head. "It was probably nothing, but JD looked at me with this smile. I can't explain it, but he kind of creeped me out. And Amber looked sort of . . . lost? Or out of it, maybe?"

Mali thinks for a moment. "What were you doing at school at six am?"

"Ha." He fidgets with his tray. "Sometimes I can't sleep. I walked here early, just . . . hanging, listening to music, watching the sunrise. I don't know . . . waiting for the day."

"Likes sunrise walks." She nods. "Got it."

"Anyway, it just seemed sort of off."

Mali shrugs. "I don't know why they'd be at school so early. Maybe they were just watching the sunrise, like you," she teases. "I'll talk to Amber though, if I can get her alone, that is." She shifts in her seat. "Speaking of drama, what about you? Anyone caught your eye since you started here?"

He can feel himself blushing, but he shakes his head. "Not yet."

He looks up to find Mali watching him, her eyes narrowing knowingly. "Got it," she says. "Mysterious type."

Will smiles, but his thoughts drift to where he doesn't want them, under the water, then under the stars, with Dusty.

Despite how different everything feels for Dusty, the echoes of "normal" are just as unwelcome.

As she stands in the shower, cold water blasting her skin, the strong floral fragrance of her shampoo and conditioner is so sickening that it makes her gag. She has to hold her breath as she washes away another school day.

Tonight she will go out hunting with Eli again. They're not hungry yet so they're trying to practice self-control, but without coming across anything bigger than squirrels and hares, they haven't successfully fed without killing. Dusty keeps reassuring Eli that it's because the animals are too small, but she isn't as confident internally.

Getting out of the shower, she tries not to look at her reflection in the mirror, like always. But, fascinated by the cloud of steam around her body, she can't help herself. She's still cushioned by soft curves, but underneath she thinks she can see stronger, firmer muscles. It's like she's still in her skin, but everything under it is changing.

Her eyes move up to her face, and that's where she always sees her—her mother. Dusty has always known that she looks like her, but the older she gets, it's harder to tell where her own face ends and her mother's begins. Or maybe it's just her memory playing tricks.

The bathroom has always been the place that it's hardest to forget her. Not just because of her reflection, but because it's where Dusty had spent the most time one-on-one with her. Dusty used to sit, curled up in the window seat beside the basin, and watch as her mom got ready in the morning or wound down from her day. She'd brush her long hair back with a comb, tie it into a braid, then take a wet, warm cloth and cover her face with it, letting the steam settle before gently wiping it away. She'd mist herself with rose water, spritzing Dusty too, and finish up by massaging her face with whatever oil was on hand.

She'd told Dusty that it was actually Dusty's grandmother, her mother-in-law, who had taught her how to look after herself. She didn't ever mention her own parents, but said she wished she'd started when she was younger, and that's why she showed Dusty. So she'd be able to start looking after herself too.

She looked so fresh when she was done. Happier than she had before, like she'd reset herself, and all the things that bothered her were miraculously gone. Or so Dusty had thought.

Dusty can't bear the smell of roses anymore.

She looks away from herself and wraps a fresh towel around her body.

When she crosses the hall to her bedroom, her old sanctuary, the space feels almost useless now. She doesn't need it for sleep. It doesn't bring her comfort. Opi hasn't been coming in to watch movies with her, or to curl up beside her after a bad dream. And it's not the fact that Dusty has started locking the door that's stopped her. The piles of books, some Dusty hasn't read yet, others she had thought she'd read again, have gathered dust in just a few days, along with everything else that was once special. She hasn't had to neaten up any of the surfaces. Her things are all still perfectly aligned parallel to corners and edges, because she hasn't touched anything.

After pulling on her boxers and a fresh t-shirt, Dusty sits on her bed to wrap her towel around her hair. But she stops herself, realizing it's already almost dry.

She's staring out the window at the darkening mountains in the distance when she hears footsteps in the hall. It's her dad, she can tell. He must have gotten home while she was in the shower. She hopes he'll bypass her room, but he slows, and then there's a knock.

"Come in," Dusty says cautiously, regretting not having locked the door yet.

It cracks open, just wide enough for his face to pop in. He glances around, making Dusty wonder what he'd expected to find her doing.

"Just saying hey," he says as his eyes scan his daughter. "Have you eaten yet?"

Dusty swallows. "I will later."

"You know you can talk to me. About anything."

Dusty nods, but she's distracted by a feeling, something trying to make itself known. "I know," she says absently.

"Opi tells me that you and Eli are . . . an item now?"

Dusty feels a flash of anger toward her sister. Unwarranted, she knows, but there it is just the same. She nods.

"Do you—" Chris starts but hesitates on his words. "I still don't like that he thought it was okay to hide out in the woods with you for days."

Dusty glares. "I told you, it wasn't his idea. It was mine."

"I know, but when we found you, he was so . . . aggressive, at first. Looking away from us like that, it was—"

"Dad. That was because of me. Trust me, okay?"

Chris sighs. "Just . . . be careful. Get to know him, okay? There's no rush, as much as you think there is. There isn't."

The gravity in his voice makes Dusty wonder if he's speaking from experience.

That tug of a feeling pulls at her again. "I know," she says, distracted, and turns back to face the window.

But right before he closes the door, she catches his reflection in the glass. He's looking at her, concerned, like she's a stranger.

That's when a memory floods her like a monsoon.

She's in the same room, but it's darker outside. Chris's voice calls her name from below, and her body becomes rigid with fear. He calls again, then the floorboards at the bottom of the stairs creak under his weight.

He's coming.

She listens as his footsteps ascend the stairs, slowly, tentatively. The closer he gets she can feel her chest tighten, her heart twisting into knots, fear coating her skin in a clammy sweat.

She's can't remember if she turned the old key to lock the door.

She bunches her knees up and wraps her arms around herself.

The doorknob groans as it rotates, then light floods into the dark room. His eyes meet hers in the window's reflection and she flinches, closing hers tight. But the tears stream down her cheeks anyway. Pure, unending terror.

Dusty blinks, coming back into herself, and out from under the memory.

Sarah. The name he'd been calling was Sarah.

Dusty can't believe it.

"No," she whispers to herself, "no, no, no," as she realizes that it wasn't her own memory. It was her mother's. And she'd been terrified.

Was Mom afraid of Dad? she wonders, her mind racing.

A chill engulfs Dusty, her mother's fear still rippling through her. She lies down on the bed to slow her rapid breathing. *In, two, three, four. Out, two, three, four.*

She tries to picture her dad, the dad she knows and loves. But his warmth and steadiness begin to morph into a cold, flickering duality.

Her mind whirls. Who was the version of him her mother had been so afraid of? Is he still in there, hiding behind a mask? And how does conjuring her mother's memories fit into her new abilities? How does this tie into what she's become?

She gathers up the mountain of emotions that surround her and makes her way down the creaky wooden staircase. Opi and Theo are tidying up after dinner, and Chris is on the sofa watching *Alone*. He's still in his uniform, but his boots are off, his feet crossed on the coffee table.

He looks up at Dusty, surprised to see her at first, then smiles as she slips into the armchair across from him. It's a smile that used to make her feel like everything was going to be okay. Now it has a shadow that's twisted and untrue. He looks back at the TV, but Dusty continues to watch him. She's disassembling him like a puzzle that will need to be put back together and might look completely different in the end.

"Was she scared of you?" Dusty asks softly, still drowning in her thoughts.

"Huh?" Chris says absently.

But before she knows if she wants to repeat herself, a phone rings.

Chris flinches and leans back, struggling to get it out of his front pocket.

"Chris Silver," he answers.

Dusty feels her ears straining to listen to the voice on the other end. It's hard to focus at first, with the TV and sounds from the kitchen, but then, there it is.

". . . blood found at the scene," she catches a male voice saying. "We've got a K-9 unit on its way, but we need you out here too."

"Leaving now," her dad says.

Dusty feels the blood drain from her face as she pictures her boots at the edge of the clearing. *Idiot*, she curses, wondering how she could be so stupid. She thought she'd have more time, and could go back on the weekend.

"I've gotta go," her dad says. "Sorry, sweetheart."

She musters a smile, and he turns to leave.

Dusty waits, listening as he puts his boots back on and holsters up. By the time the front door finally closes, she's already bounding out the back.

17

Long Night

The restless, anxious hum that has been coursing through Dusty's body dials up a notch, and the second she's outside she's running.

She half expects Eli to burst out of the trees beside her as she heads north-west, around the curve of the mountain. She calls to him in her mind, testing the link between them, but by the time she reaches the wilderness where there are no roads, she knows she's alone tonight, and that she can't afford to hesitate. She needs to get to the clearing before the police do.

She's telling herself that even if her belongings are found, they wouldn't have any evidence on them—she hasn't touched them since she touched the man—but understanding scent in the way she does now, and knowing there will be dogs that could link her scent to the cabin, the clearing and the river, she picks up her pace.

Her bare feet pound the cool earth as the forest becomes a blur around her. Leaves whip against her face, pulling at her hair. Her legs stretch and contract, propelling her over logs and rocks.

When she reaches the bank of Black River, she lets the flow of the water guide her. She cuts back into the forest, then through fields, into the trees again, listening for the sound of running water. When she finds the stream she follows it, keeping her pace, fast and unwavering. She doesn't slow down until she enters the clearing.

To her relief, it's quiet and empty. The tranquil sanctuary that had held them to the earth and allowed them to sleep when they had so desperately needed it. Neither she nor Eli had been ready to leave, and being here now is a not-so-gentle reminder of that.

The thick moss feels different under her feet, which have already grown stronger and more calloused in the few days since she was here. It has soaked up the rain from the day they left and still holds it like a sponge, releasing it over Dusty's bare toes as she skirts the tree line. Her chest still heaving, she wonders how long it took her to get here. She looks up at the moon, supposing it was under an hour.

Incredible.

A shout cuts through the night.

Dusty freezes, holding her breath to listen. There's movement in the near distance, less than a mile away. A voice calls out again, a man's, and it's answered by a chorus of loud barks.

Dusty's feet sink into the moss as she remains completely still, her whole body on high alert. The voice calls out again, and another voice answers. It's her dad.

Barks sound in every direction.

Dusty spins, scanning the shadowy tree line for her boots. She runs in the direction she thought she'd left them as she hears a bark, then another, getting closer. Some of the dogs must already be at the edge of the forest, on the other side of the grassland.

Come on, she urges, willing her boots to appear before her as she squints through the darkness.

Rustling and panting breath sounds from the field at the bottom of the slope. She hurries, continuing around the edge of the clearing.

Her heart is sinking, her panic rising, when her eyes stop on a shadow that's darker than the rest.

She moves, her adrenaline commanding more speed from her body than she knew possible. She reaches down and picks up her boots, and she slips her hand inside one. It's empty. When she does the same to the other, her fingers meet the cold hard edge of her phone.

Run.

Dusty bolts back into the forest, trying to get a sense of where the dogs are without tripping over herself. It feels impossible to focus while she's moving, when her own breath and feet and heartbeat resound. There's a bark in the distance, far, in the opposite direction to where they started. But before she has a chance to let herself relax, she hears bounding footfall behind her. She shifts her direction, quickening, but one dog must have caught her scent because it follows. She begins to move so fast she can barely see anything around her, but when she realizes she's running north, toward the stretch of Black River where they left the man, she's forced to slow.

That's the last place on earth she can lead them.

Stumbling to a stop, she trips on a raised root and crashes down hard into the rough trunk of a spruce. Sharp needles fly into the air around her, her skin stinging against the hard bark. As she tries to get up she has the distinct sensation of being watched. She turns, searching through the darkness.

A few dozen yards uphill behind her, on top of a boulder that breaks out through the dense trees, is the dog. It's staring directly at her, lit up by the moonlight as if it's on a stage. Its nose sniffs the air, its features a cross of German shepherd and bloodhound. It's enormous. Still watching her, it bares its teeth in a snarl.

Dusty begins to run again, and a ferocious bark cuts through the night.

"This way!" a voice calls.

"Got it!"

The sound of her dad's voice rings in Dusty's ears.

Opi has had trouble sleeping for the past five years, and she doesn't need a psychologist to tell her that it has everything to do with her mom. It's like an instinct kicked in when she left, forcing Opi to stay alert, to sleep light, to be aware of exactly where her loved ones are, even in the darkest, quietest hours of the night.

To be sure that those who remain haven't gone anywhere.

So the fact that Dusty has been sneaking out every night this week has not gone unnoticed. At first, being angry with her sister had allowed Opi not to care. She understood that there was truth to what Dusty had said about their mom, about how hard it is to be in this house, living with that. She knows it was harder for Dusty, who carried more memories of their grandparents too. But Opi also knows that Dusty would never have been so reckless if it weren't for Eli, and she's deeply disappointed in her sister for losing herself like that, just because a boy, popular or not, is suddenly interested.

But night after night, worry has begun to overtake everything else. She's afraid that every time Dusty leaves, she's losing a little part of herself, becoming someone Opi no longer knows.

Tonight, after Theo went home, Opi had gone up to Dusty's room to offer a truce. But Dusty was already gone. She hadn't even bothered waiting for Opi to fall asleep this time. And with their dad out working, Opi had tried not to let the feeling of abandonment overtake her completely. She'd gotten into bed, watched *Bridgerton*, then clung to bravery as she'd turned off the light and waited for sleep to take her.

She doesn't know if it ever came when she becomes alert again.

Her eyes blink in the darkness, until a dim but familiar rectangle appears. Her bedroom window. It anchors the room, and one by one objects emerge from the night as her vision adjusts. Her wardrobe. Her desk. And a dark figure standing at the foot of her bed.

Opi holds her breath.

She can just make out a head, a torso, and limbs obscured by shadows. The figure doesn't move, and as they face each other all Opi wants is to scream out. But there isn't any point. No one else is home, and she can't move a muscle.

She can only close her eyes, praying that when she opens them again whoever it is will be gone.

She feels her sheet and blankets slowly slide down over her body, disappearing beyond the foot of the bed. Then, without a sense of hands or anything touching her, Opi's is dragged across her mattress, to the end of the bed, toward the figure.

She has felt fear before, but this is something entirely different.

A muffled thump from another room forces her eyes back open.

Her heart pounds as she looks down toward the figure, then around the room, but it's gone.

By the time Dusty can make out her house further up the mountain, she hasn't heard a dog for a long time—but she hasn't slowed down.

As the dog had continued to track her, she'd run so fast that even with her new strength her legs had been shaking. Through thick forest, up and down over rocks and ravines, they'd lost the handler and her dad quickly, but the dog had been relentless, trailing her in the distance. When she'd finally felt she was far enough from the body, she had cut back toward Black River, then swum across the tumbling water to the other side, holding her boots up, her scent trail ending at the water's edge.

She hadn't traversed back until she could see White Mountain.

As she allows herself to slow down, Dusty notices that her bedroom window, which she's certain had been closed, is open.

She hears a thud, then a struggle within. Leaping up onto a low-hanging branch of the beech tree she scales its twists and turns, propelling herself up to her window.

When she bursts inside, she's ready to fight, but in a mess of white fabric, she can smell Eli.

"What the fuck," he curses, trying to free himself.

Dusty climbs down from the bed and untangles him from her sheets. She'd be laughing if she weren't so exhausted.

"Is this some sort of booby trap?" he snaps, trying to compose himself.

"It's a sheet, Eli. I don't know what you've got going on at home, but they go on your bed."

Eli looks at her as he stands, his mouth twisting into a smile. "Why don't you come over and see?"

Dusty rolls her eyes. "What're you doing here?"

"I couldn't . . . feel you," he says. "It was weird. And I was worried. I thought I could sense something up here. But there's nothing."

Dusty sighs. "I went to the clearing."

"*Our* clearing?"

"Yeah. My dad was called out to help with a search party."

"Shit . . . you mean . . . ?"

She nods. "I got there just in time. There were dogs . . ."

He looks confused, but when she holds her boots up it clicks.

"My phone was still there too," she says, finally letting herself feel relieved it's over. "Lucky I went. The dogs could have linked our scent at the cabin to the clearing . . . then my dad would know that we . . . that we're connected to it."

"Why didn't you tell me? I would've gone back any time with you."

"We had enough to worry about. It was stupid, I know. But I also couldn't face going back so soon."

"But your dad . . . he already knew where the clearing was."

"Yeah, but it's far enough away from the cabin, and I led the dog downriver, far from the body. So now without my boots there, there shouldn't be any way to link the scent to us."

He nods slowly, and they're quiet for a long moment.

"Are you okay?" he asks, no doubt noticing how shaken she is.

She nods, still catching her breath. "I heard my dad's voice out there. And one of the dogs chased me for a long time. I felt like a criminal. I *am* a criminal."

Eli lets out a slow breath. "Who does a search in the middle of the night?"

"You'd be surprised . . ." Dusty says. "Dad says those dogs are just as good at night, maybe even better. And there's less risk of hikers or hunters . . ."

"Huh," he nods. "At least you're a pretty good criminal, Dusty Silver." When their eyes meet it's clear that the joke fell flat.

"Speaking of," she says. "We should hunt."

Dusty wants to tell Eli about her mom's memory, but she can't find the words to string together. Walking down the mountain, she still doesn't know what to make of what she saw, what she felt, or what it means about her dad.

Before she and Eli had climbed back out her window, she'd gone to check on Opi. Without opening her door she'd been able to hear her in there, her heart beating, her breath fast, like she was in the middle of an intense dream.

She looks at Eli walking beside her. He's been such a constant the past few days that she's barely had a chance to remember that less than a week ago, he didn't even know her name.

"You said you couldn't *feel* me?" she asks.

Eli glances at her then nods, running his hand over his hair, which is growing out of its buzz cut.

"I tried . . . reaching out to you, while I was running. It would be handy if we knew how this all works."

"Tell me about it. I didn't like . . . It felt weird. Like I could tell you were far away."

Dusty thinks. "At first I thought it was just our instincts, or senses, that have made it so easy to find each other every night. But it's more than that. It's like at the bonfire. I'm tuned into you somehow."

"Exactly," Eli says. He stops walking and turns to face Dusty. "And now, outside of this," he gestures between them, "everything else feels fake. It's like there's only you—"

"And what we've done," she finishes. She notices the way he's looking at her, and she can *feel* the confusing emotions running through him. "Maybe it's a trauma bond," she says.

Eli keeps looking at her, until his shoulders slump and he nods. "Maybe," he says.

When they're close to the bottom of the mountain, a breeze coasts up the slope, bringing with it a scent of something big. Their eyes meet again, before they turn and begin to track it.

They can see the young buck, lit up by moonlight, before he knows they're there. Browsing on hobblebush, he's the perfect creature to test their self-restraint on. His antlers are big enough to grab onto and hold, and he has far more blood flowing inside him than any human.

Excited, Eli steps toward the animal, but when Dusty grabs his wrist and shakes her head, he stops. The deer's ears swivel in the direction of the movement, then he raises his head.

Until this point, Dusty hasn't thought about what they'd do with the body of a larger animal if they couldn't stop themselves from killing it. It's one thing to discard a small squirrel with a human-shaped bite in its neck, covering it with leaves or moss, knowing that scavengers will dispose of it within hours. But a deer is different. It would take time, or a bear to come along and disguise what they'd done.

And even though it isn't hunting season, they can't be sure that someone wouldn't find it and suspect a new kind of predator on the mountain.

And the person they'd call to investigate would be Dusty's dad.

Eli pulls at Dusty, not sure why she's hesitating at first, but as Dusty's thoughts unfold, he understands.

"Let's go," Dusty says. "It's been a long night."

18
Bloodlust

Dusty heard her dad come in at around three am, not long after she'd returned from hunting with Eli. She sat on the floor of her room, listening as he'd showered then gone to bed, and remained there, waiting for morning.

She's desperate to sneak up into his room before school and search for answers. Something. Anything. She can't get her mom's memory out of her head.

By six forty-five he's still asleep. Dusty anxiously waits, her foot bouncing against the floor, checking the time on her laptop every few minutes. She hasn't had the courage to turn on her phone, which is still tucked away in a drawer, dead to the world and all her problems.

By seven-twenty there's still no sign of him rising, and it's time to go. She can hear Opi downstairs, waiting.

When she enters the kitchen, she expects the reception Opi has given her all week—no words, just a drawer slammed shut or an aggressive push on the blender. But that's not what she's met with today.

Opi is sitting at the kitchen table, an untouched pot of tea in front of her, and no food in sight. Dusty opens her mouth to say something, to break their silence, but when Opi looks up at her, she stands and walks out of the room toward the front door.

Dusty thinks that Opi must be just as exhausted by this fight as she is, but when she gets to the car the message is clear: Sam Fender's "Seventeen Going Under" blares through the speakers, Opi's way of saying, *don't even try to talk to me*.

"You know what's funny?" Eli asks, catching up to Dusty in the hall before homeroom.

"What?"

"I don't even have your number."

She can't help but smile as she glances up at him. He puts his arm around her, and Dusty wonders again what they really are to each other now.

She can feel that he's wondering the same thing.

Everyone around them still watches, but the stares aren't lasting quite as long as they had on Tuesday.

She can see Will walking up ahead, listening to music, ignoring everyone around him.

"Who is that?" Eli asks, nodding toward Will.

Dusty can feel her cheeks burn, and Eli slows, studying her.

"He smells different for you, doesn't he?"

"What? No," Dusty says, shaking her head as her heart thuds in her chest.

She doesn't know why she doesn't want Eli to know, but she feels overwhelmingly protective of Will. Like he's her secret. Like he's *hers*.

Eli's eyes are still burning into her, and when she glances back up at him, he's struggling not to smile.

"I don't think I've ever seen you this flustered," he says. She can feel the slight pull of his jealousy reaching out for her, so faint she wonders if it's subconscious.

"Fine." She sighs. "There may have been something . . . developing between us, before the bonfire. But that's over now. Obviously."

"Okay," Eli says, thoughtful. "I'm sorry."

"Don't be," she says. She nudges her body into him, smiling, when they reach the end of the hall.

"See you later?" he asks, but before he leaves, two girls, seniors, Dusty thinks, come out of a room opposite them.

The second they see Eli, Dusty watches as their colors shift into pinky reds that begin to flick and twist, then coil, reaching for him. Their faces give nothing away, but when Eli flashes them a smile, their eyes light up, twinkling flirtatiously at him.

No one says a word as Dusty looks between Eli and the girls, amazed.

It's like she's not even there.

She clears her throat, and Eli turns back to face her.

Like some kind of spell has been broken, the girls walk on.

"Ummm, what was that?" Dusty asks.

Eli chuckles. "I swear, I know this is going to sound conceited, but girls are like, even more into me now."

Dusty stares at him blankly.

"I'm serious!" he says. "And it's not even just girls. I had to stop for gas this morning, and I kid you not, when I went to pay, the woman at the register told me it was on the house."

"No," Dusty says, disbelieving.

"Yeah," he says. "It's like . . . a thing now. Like a superpower."

Dusty rolls her eyes. "But, you obviously insisted on paying . . . right?"

Eli looks down at his feet sheepishly.

"Eli!" she scolds.

"What! This has been brutal. If there are any perks, I'm jumping on them." Before Dusty can say any more on it, he winks then heads in the other direction.

Mali is waiting outside homeroom when Dusty approaches. She hasn't looked up yet, so Dusty has a chance to look at her friend. Mali has always been so energized and open, but there's a vacancy in her stare that's unfamiliar. When she looks up at Dusty she smiles, warm, yes, but there's something missing in it.

"You okay? Want to talk about anything?" Dusty asks, assuming Mali is still disappointed about things not working out with Kristen.

"Nope," Mali says, linking her arm with Dusty's as they walk inside together. "I miss you," Mali says softly.

Dusty feels a fresh wave of guilt. "I'm sorry I've been a bit preoccupied," she manages.

Mali looks at her like it's the understatement of the century.

"I haven't been looking at my phone," Dusty offers. "It's been a big week, and I've been processing some stuff about my mom." She hates herself for saying it, for using it as an excuse, but it's not a lie, at least.

Mali's face is full of concern.

"Happy it's Friday?" Dusty adds, trying to change the subject.

"More than ever," Mali says as they take their seats.

Dusty notices Mali turn and nod at Will, like they're more familiar with each other now.

JD and Amber walk in next, holding hands. They don't break apart until they take their seats, but Dusty watches as their colors reach out in place of their hands, tiny sparks firing as the hues entwine. Amber's—a mix of purples, yellows and pinks—seem to change to match JD's, shifting into darker tones, cushioned by hazy reds and grays.

She's so absorbed in the spectacle that it takes Dusty a moment to notice JD has turned to look at her. Their eyes meet.

"Boo," he whispers.

Dusty draws in a sharp breath. Her cheeks flush from being caught staring.

JD grins, then turns back to face the front of the room.

"Psst," Mali says from the table beside her. "Let's hang this weekend?"

Dusty musters a smile. "Definitely."

"I'll come over tomorrow?"

Dusty nods, her heart wrenching at the look of relief on her best friend's face.

Final period is English, which Dusty has been dreading all day. It used to be her favorite, for many reasons, including the fact that being the last class on a Friday, their teacher, Mr. Martin, is smart enough to know there's only so much a teacher can demand in that time slot. He usually screens a movie or does some kind of creative task that doesn't involve lecturing. And he wouldn't even dream of dropping a pop quiz on them.

The fact that Will is also in the class hadn't been a factor Dusty used to consider, but now it's hard to pretend that this time last week they hadn't both been absent from this very class, together, at the waterfall.

As she enters the room, she's pleading *please be a movie day, please be a movie day*. But her pleading comes to a halt immediately.

Will is already at his usual desk close to the door, and behind the myriad blues surrounding him, pieces of his dark hair are strewn across his forehead, falling in front of dark blue eyes that appear almost black as he glances up at Dusty. Before she has a chance to react, he looks straight back down.

Maybe it's because she's exhausted from last night, maybe it's the memory of how he once looked at her, but as Dusty passes him she lets herself notice the sinewy muscles of his arms, and how he smells better than ever—like wood, fresh air, and something sweet. Something uniquely *him*.

Time feels like it's been set to slow motion as she passes, and the only thing that propels her forward is a shudder of goosebumps that hurries her to her seat.

But even with three rows between them, her awareness remains focused on him. She tries to latch on to something, anything else, but it feels impossible.

Mr. Martin has entered and is saying something to the class, but Dusty is somewhere else. She's remembering what it was like to be alone with Will. How easy he'd been to talk to and the way he'd whispered in her ear. She has a flash of being underwater, her hand on his chest, like they were the only two people on earth, and the feeling spreads all over her body.

In the small part of Dusty's brain still receiving signals from the world, she hears chairs and tables being shuffled together and students moving around the room.

"Number four?" a voice says, close to her.

Will has gotten up and is walking toward her side of the room.

"You're a number four?" the voice repeats.

Dusty blinks and turns her head to look at a girl standing in front of her. Her name is Michelle, and she normally sits at the front of the class. Dusty has several periods with her, but they've never had much to do with one another.

"I think we're in a group together," Michelle says slowly, her tone slightly patronizing as she pulls up a chair to share Dusty's desk.

"Oh, yeah, cool," Dusty manages.

Then to her horror, Will sits down at the now-empty desk next to them. When Dusty forces herself to look at him, he raises his eyebrows at both girls, and shrugs in a gesture that says, *guess we're stuck together.*

Is that a dimple? Dusty wonders, trying to tear her eyes away from the slight indent in his right cheek. It's the side his smile pulls up from, the few times he's given it to her.

If she were alone right now, she'd slap herself in the face. *Pull it together*, she curses.

It's apparently obvious that neither Dusty nor Will had been listening to Mr. Martin, so Michelle explains that the afternoon's assignment is to write a creative, stream-of-consciousness piece that flows from one student's words into another's. They're studying Virginia Woolf this semester, so the task makes sense now that Dusty is actually paying attention.

Michelle, in full team-leader mode, suggests they pick a theme that threads their ideas together, and then they can "break off" to write their individual prose.

"So, any ideas for our theme?" Michelle asks.

The afternoon sun has just begun to reach into the classroom, so Dusty suggests the first word that comes into her mind. "Sunlight."

"I like it," Michelle says thoughtfully, then to Will, in an elementary teacher's voice, "It only needs to be a *reference* to sunlight, nothing too obvious."

Will gives her a thumbs up and opens his school-issue laptop.

He still hasn't said a word.

Dusty opens her own laptop, but before she can even begin to think about writing, Will's pheromones, or whatever they are, have reached her. His energy is like a force of calm, and she can feel all of the chaos inside her reaching out toward him, needing him as an antidote.

The feeling is stronger than gravity.

A message pops up on her screen via the school's messenger.

WVolkov: you all good?

As Dusty tries to focus on the words, she realizes that the ball of her foot is bouncing her leg up and down and that she has bitten down on her own lip. A drop of blood pools there and she licks it away, noticing its taste. It's almost buttery.

She looks back at the message, and the first initial of the name.

DSilver: Will?

WVolkov: hey

Dusty realizes she didn't even know his last name until now.

DSilver: Your name . . . Russian?

WVolkov: ukrainian. moms side

Her foot continues to bounce, her whole body on edge as she tries to think of something to say.

WVolkov: so ur all good?

Dusty lets herself look up at him, but he's focused on his screen.

DSilver: Yeah, thanks. All good.

Dusty hopes for more, but there's nothing.

She looks up again. Will is typing, his tongue twisted between his teeth as he concentrates. He types slowly and hesitantly. As she watches, Dusty feels her foot begin to bounce against the floor again.

I know it must have looked bad, the other night, she begins to type, then deletes it, knowing that whatever she says, she can't really explain it. And there's no point anyway.

As she tries to peer at his screen to see if his messenger is still open, Dusty is taken aback by how sharp her eyesight is. She's been so focused on blocking everything out that she hasn't fully flexed her senses in the daylight. She can see that his messenger is closed and that he's actually doing the assignment now. As he types, misspelled words are corrected automatically, and Dusty begins to read.

Through the trees and down into the water it kisses her as it kisses him. But at night all he has is a shimmering memory disguised as moonlight. She wondered about consciousness and the stars but it doesn't matter. Because she's the one who let the light creep in.

Dusty's breath catches, then she watches as Will highlights the entire paragraph and presses delete.

He leans back into his chair and sweeps his hair off his face with both hands. They come to rest at the back of his neck, his fingers intertwined, and he slowly exhales.

There's something about his arms being up like that, the smell of him more exposed, that draws Dusty's attention to his veins. They wrap and weave around his muscles, swollen from the warmth of the sun that's been heating up the room.

She feels like flames are licking under her skin, and as if to quench them, her thoughts are drawn back under the waterfall. She imagines if she'd kissed him, what he might have tasted like, the firmness of his kiss, the softness of his lips, the tease of his tongue.

Desire dances up her spine and she has to fight to stop herself from going to him, breathing in every part of him, tasting him . . .

They say there's no harm in daydreaming. But there is.

For the first time since she fed from the stranger, Dusty is ravenous. Her teeth begin to throb, her mouth waters. Through a haze of the deepest need Dusty has ever endured, she knows she's a danger to every single person around her, and to Will most of all.

The sound of his heartbeat, calm and steady, pushes Dusty to her feet.

The door feels like it's a million miles away, and just as she's about to reach it Mr. Martin steps in front of her, confused and concerned. But Dusty doesn't hesitate as she plows straight past her teacher, bumping him sideways into his desk.

"Dusty!" he calls after her, but she doesn't turn back.

Rushing out into the parking lot, her hunger begins to subside the further away she gets from Will. She imagines driving straight to the highway and going somewhere far, far away. But the idea of causing her family, or Mali, any more pain clamps onto her like an iron ball and chain.

She waits in the car for Opi, begging her senses to settle—to even remotely resemble those of a human being. Her mind's eye fills with the deer from last night. She can't believe how stupid she'd been not to drink from it.

But she hadn't been hungry yet. She hadn't known how much time the man had bought her.

Five days.

She needs a plan.

Opening her laptop, she's relieved to find that she's still connected to the school Wi-Fi. Desperate, she throws her caution out the window, opens her browser and searches every word she can think of that might connect the dots—*vampire, scorched trees, levitation, seeing colors, telepathic bond, other people's memories*. The screen fills with everything and nothing as she feverishly reads but finds nothing that stands out.

Slamming her laptop shut, she wants to scream, but hearing students trickle out through the main entrance, she clamps her jaw shut.

Hunger still bubbles beneath the surface of every emotion.

As the air conditioning pumps cool air over her skin, she tries to separate what she knows from what she doesn't know, wondering if, in this new reality, there's an intrinsic link between attraction and hunger. She skims the memories of her strong and fast feelings for Will last week, trying to understand if they were brought on by what she was becoming, or if he smells so good because she likes him so much. Is it a heightened experience of pheromones, or a subconscious knowledge that he would somehow taste *better* than anyone else?

It doesn't seem to matter either way, if she's honest with herself. The bottom line is that she needs to be more careful, she needs to find a way to feed more, and she needs to stay away from Will.

She shakes her head and looks up to the roof of her car.

Bloodlust.

What the actual fuck.

The bell trills and the school doors swing open. Students roll out, heading for the bus or their cars in the lot.

The passenger door opens and Opi gets in. Theo climbs into the back. Dusty grits her teeth harder.

Terrified of even thinking about the blood inside their veins, she winds down all four windows, flushing out the smell of them as they drive home.

Later, she knows she should have expected it, but she's still shocked when they pull into their driveway to find a county sheriff's vehicle parked right next to the front steps.

19

Answers

When Dusty, Opi and Theo enter the kitchen of the Silver house, Chris is seated at the table across from a narrowly built man in his mid-thirties with fair skin, unusually long limbs, blond hair and gray eyes that look up to meet Dusty's from under pale eyelashes. A sheriff's hat sits on the table between two cups of black coffee.

"This is Deputy Sheriff Brookes," Chris says, still in his own uniform.

The officer dips his head to greet them.

"He's here to ask Dusty a few questions." Then, seeing Opi and Theo's confused looks, Chris adds, "About her time out near the Millers' property last weekend."

Opi and Theo nod, hovering, until Chris tells them they can get started on their homework. They beeline to the staircase.

Dusty looks fixedly at her dad, and he gives her a subtle but reassuring smile. She puts her bag down and takes a seat at the head of the table, between the two men.

"Bet you're glad it's the weekend," Deputy Sheriff Brookes says with a surprisingly nasal voice. His words are friendly, but his tone is not.

"Yeah." Dusty nods, trying to remember what it was like to feel calm.

"I won't take up much of your time," he says. "Just have a few questions."

"Okay," Dusty says, attempting to sound cheerful as she feels her mouth force itself into an innocent smile. "What's this about, sorry?"

Brookes stares at her, expressionless, before he finally speaks. "Your dad tells me you camped out last weekend, after a bonfire on the Miller property?"

Dusty nods. "I did."

Brookes takes out a small notebook from one of the pockets of his uniform shirt as he says, "And can you tell me where this campsite is exactly?"

"Not exactly. Sorry."

His eyes are cold, fixed on hers. "Roundabouts?"

"I can point it out to you," her dad interjects.

Brookes ignores him, keeping his eyes on Dusty. "You would've given your father quite a scare, I imagine. He reported you missing on Sunday afternoon, you know?"

Dusty gulps. She doesn't have to feign guilt on this point. "I know," she says in a voice so quiet she can barely hear herself. "I did message him to tell him I was okay, but I should've known how worried he'd be."

Brookes finally looks to Chris, who nods, adding, "She's very competent outdoors." He shoots Dusty a chiding look. "But she's not normally so spur-of-the-moment."

Brookes gives a single nod, as if he understands, or remembers. *Teenagers.*

"I'm asking you these questions because a man has been reported missing."

Dusty gulps again, feeling the panic twisting and tightening in her chest.

"He was staying at a cabin, a new, luxury-type one out on Canal Road, around eight miles south-east of the Miller property."

There's a long silence. Dusty isn't sure what the deputy wants her to say.

"He was reported missing on Tuesday, after he didn't sign into a meeting he was due to attend remotely on Monday, and no one could contact him. He was supposed to be working from the cabin all week."

Another silence.

"The reason I'm telling you this is because you were also reported missing in the same area, just a few days before. We thought you might have seen something during your . . . camping trip."

"Sorry, sir," Dusty manages, hoping the tremor in her voice sounds sympathetic, not scared. "We didn't see anyone else while we were out there."

"What about any predators? Bears, wolves?"

Dusty shakes her head.

He turns his attention to Chris. "And what time and day did you . . . collect your daughter?"

Dusty can tell that her dad has picked up on the deputy's judgmental tone, and that he doesn't like it one bit. "I told you last night, Barry. Monday. Mid-morning."

Brookes scribbles something into his little notebook. "A school day?" he asks.

Chris nods.

"We found a significant amount of blood in the carport of the cabin, as you know," he says to Chris. Turning to Dusty, he adds, "It led into the woods. It appears the victim had been working on his car when something happened."

Dusty tries not to flinch at the word "victim" as she feels her father tensing. His colors shift around him, flickering with fresh worry.

"Did your dad tell you about the cattle that were found?" Brookes asks.

Dusty shakes her head. "No, but I heard about it at school."

Brookes glances at Chris, his expression distinctly judgmental.

Dusty grips her knees, pushing down on her swirling panic.

"The campsite," Brookes says, pulling out his phone and placing it on the table in front of Chris.

The screen displays a map, and Dusty watches as her dad zooms in on the Millers' property, then moves the map slightly east.

"Here," Chris says, placing a pin on top of a dense green canopy.

Dusty isn't sure what's there, but she knows it's not even half as far as the real clearing. She glances at her dad, who is looking at Brookes, calm and composed. She knows she should be grateful, but she can't help wondering why he lied, and what he knows.

Stranger, she thinks, before looking back at Brookes, who's studying the map, zooming in and out from the pin to see the greater area.

"Appreciate it," Brookes finally says, putting his phone away as he stands. He looks down at Dusty. "If you think of anything at all, give me call." He has a sip of his coffee then gathers his hat before he drops his card onto the table. "I'll show myself out." He smiles flatly, then nods at Chris, who nods back.

Dusty stands. "What's his name?" she calls, a little too loudly. "The man's . . ." She hadn't planned on it, but as the words tumble out she realizes she's been wondering since that night.

"Andrew Everett." Brookes fixes his eyes on her before he turns and makes his way to the front door.

"Brookes!" her dad calls as he stands. "I'll be right back," he says to Dusty, then jogs into the living area and through the archway that leads to the house's main entrance.

Dusty's heart is racing.

Andrew Everett.

The sound of murmuring voices forces her to concentrate, and she listens, focusing on the hushed conversation between her dad and the Deputy.

"—autopsy came back," Brookes is saying. "You know those two cows that looked sort of deflated? Well, their bones were all broken inside. Shattered. Like they'd fallen from a great height."

"But—"

"I know, it's the flattest farmland in the area."

Dusty grimaces at the image of crushed bones, but she's glad, at least, that they're not talking about her.

"Keep an eye out, will you?" Brookes asks.

"Don't worry, if I see anything out of the ordinary, you'll be the first to know."

As Dusty listens to their goodbyes, her thoughts drift upstairs, to her room, to her mother's memory, then up to her dad's room. Their room. She hopes it holds the answers she's looking for.

It takes a total of forty seconds for Dusty to decide she needs to google Andrew Everett.

She looks around her bedroom for her schoolbag, but it's downstairs.

Unable to face her dad again, she only has one choice. She finds her phone in her bedside drawer, plugs it into the charger, then sits down on the floor beside it, waiting for it to turn on.

Staring at the black screen, she realizes that she needs to warn Eli about the deputy sheriff. She's certain Brookes will soon be at the Blake house. Or maybe he went there first. But, eyes fixed on the screen, she remembers that she doesn't have Eli's phone number.

She closes her eyes, trying to tap into their strange connection, when a clear image of Eli fills her mind. He's walking through a big house, a woman in front of him, and Deputy Sheriff Brookes behind him. She can hear his thoughts which are going over his story, and it's the same as hers. He even knows to describe the clearing as much closer to Matt's property.

But just as momentary relief sweeps the crown of her head, her phone lights up.

Ding. Ding. Ding. Ding. Ding.

Messages flash on the screen. One after another.

Dusty groans.

She looks down at the phone to see the final tally. Thirty-two new messages.

As she could have guessed, the majority are from her dad, Opi and Mali. But there's another one she opens first.

Will

hope ur okay

He'd sent it on Sunday night at ten forty-five pm.

Ugh. Her whole body shudders.

She lets out a self-loathing sigh before diving into Mali's. Lots of similar check-ins, dotted with questions like, *Are you srsly w Eli?* and *Wtf pls tell me pls pls!!!*

Her dad's are a rollercoaster of worry, fear and anger, all of which she lets join the tally inside her body.

Finally, she opens Opi's. After several iterations of *Where are you* and *Are you okay*, there is one that absolutely crushes her.

Opi

Are you looking for mom?

Dusty feels a flutter from within her chest. Like a thousand moths are trapped there.

Before she can think, she's scrambling up from the floor and striding to her sister's room. She slows, peeking around the open doorway. Opi is lying on her stomach on her bed, leaning toward Theo, who's sitting on the floor with his phone held up to them. She remembers when Theo barely took up any space at all—a shy little boy with long limbs and soft pale blond hair. Now it's like his body takes up half the room, but he still keeps his presence close to him. Dusty has never been more grateful that he's in her sister's life. Their lives. Opi snorts with laughter, imitating whatever they've just seen. She's completely unrestrained. Unselfconscious.

When Dusty steps inside, they look up at her, and Opi's face becomes guarded. She stares at Dusty with her big, round brown eyes. "What?" she asks, apprehensive.

"Op. I'm so sorry."

Theo reads the room and removes himself from it so quickly it would be comical in any other moment.

Opi hesitates, then speaks in a whisper. "We were so worried about you." Her eyes begin to well with tears. "I thought you'd left us too."

Dusty goes to her sister, kneeling before her, right where Theo had been. She takes Opi's hands, squeezing them tightly. Her emotions are the only thing distracting her from the smell of blood, so close beneath Opi's skin, and with just the idea of that, her own tears begin to flow.

"Dust, are you okay?"

"You're everything. You know that right? I would never, *ever* leave you."

Opi plays with Dusty's hair, twisting the strands between her fingers. "The way we found you . . ." Opi pauses. "And how distant you've been . . . You're not eating . . . I can tell Dad is still worried. So am I . . ."

Dusty looks up into Opi's eyes. "I'm gonna be okay," she reassures her. And for almost a millisecond she believes herself. "I'm just a bit messed up right now."

"And what about Eli?" Opi asks.

"It's not what you think. He's actually surprisingly . . . supportive."

Opi looks skeptical.

"Maybe it's my hormones," Dusty offers, knowing Opi's language.

Opi looks thoughtful for a moment, then jumps into action. "Oh my god, totally! Wait here," she calls as she disappears out of the room, hurrying downstairs.

Left alone again, Dusty decides to punish herself well and good. She slips back into her room, picks up her phone and searches "Andrew Everett".

A few articles come up from local papers and websites.

Manhattan Man Reported Missing From Secluded Getaway

New York City Hedge Fund Manager Disappears From Luxury Cabin

Tourist Missing: Presumed Injured or Dead

Beyond the headlines, Dusty doesn't learn much more about Andrew Everett. There doesn't seem to be enough to the story for it to make its way up the big city news cycle yet. But there is a photo of him in one of the articles. He's standing beside a bicycle on a pretty road with the mountains behind him. A helmet is covering his dark, wavy hair but his face is visible. Dusty zooms in, trying to liken it to the face she last saw at the bottom of Black River.

"There you are," Opi says from the doorway.

Dusty drops her phone and turns to her sister.

"Here." Opi hands her a large glass flask with a tea strainer in the center. "Red raspberry leaf. And I threw in some ashwagandha, because, you know, adaptogens.'"

Dusty looks at Opi quizzically.

"For your hormones."

"Ohhh, right." She smiles.

Opi waits as Dusty braces herself and takes a sip.

The infusion of plants tastes bitter and rotten. She pushes her tongue to her palate to force it down. The taste, which she remembers as refreshing and cleansing, is like decay, as if she's sipping from a stagnant pond. But, as the liquid runs down her throat and into her body, she begins to feel glimmers of the plants themselves, like memories. Where they grew, what season it was, the way it felt to exist in one place, bobbing with the breeze, soaking up the sun from above, and everything else from the soil below.

It's like an echo of a life she never paid attention to. *Before*, when she was never present. Always in her head. And now it's too late.

Her stomach lurches and she has the urge to throw up, but Opi still watches expectantly, and Dusty clenches her stomach to hold it down.

"It's all about consistency," Opi says. "I'll make one for you every day, supporting your cycle. And you can let me know how you're feeling!"

Dusty smiles, struggling to cope with her sister's sweetness.

"What?" Opi asks, defensive. "Just because I don't have my period yet, it doesn't mean I don't know that it will be a huge part of my life. And that herbs are one of the best ways to help nurture and balance."

"Op, that's not why I was smiling." Dusty knows it's a sore point for the sixteen-year-old who has been expecting her period every month for the past three years. Dusty's had come relatively late too, at fourteen, which she knows doesn't make Opi feel any better.

"Oh, sorry," Opi says, embarrassed.

Dusty didn't know it was possible to love her sister more.

But, she reminds herself, feelings this big are going to be hard to manage, and that thought alone is enough to let fear resume its place.

Opi waltzes back to her room, where Dusty hears Theo asking her how it went.

"I think she's going to be okay," Opi replies hopefully.

And with the pain that induces, Dusty's resolve is strengthened—she has to find a way to cure herself.

Until then, she needs a better way to feed.

20

This Changes Everything

The bag that hangs across Dusty's back is heavy for its size, but as she scales the side of the large house, she's still reeling from the insanity of what she's done.

She reaches from a drainpipe to an awning to a windowsill with strong, flexible limbs, barely needing half an inch for her feet or fingers to hold on to. The night sky is dark behind her, full of big gray clouds that muffle the sounds of the forest. There's a TV bellowing from a room below, its fast-changing light spilling into the shadows outside. Water flows from a tap as someone washes up in the kitchen.

Skirting the second floor with only windowsills to hold onto, Dusty passes a room with the curtains drawn and the lights out, sensing someone small asleep inside. She moves slowly and quietly, aware of how terrifying her presence would be if she awoke the child within.

A monster in the darkness.

She looks across to the room she wants, feeling him inside, their bond pulling her like a magnet.

When she reaches the window she gently taps her knuckles on the glass.

The modern window glides open silently. Icy, air-conditioned air rushes out and a hand grabs hold of Dusty's forearm, pulling her up and inside.

She's face-to-face with Eli, grinning in surprise.

"You must have some experience sneaking into boys' rooms at night. You're good at it."

"It's not *sneaking* if you knew I was coming," Dusty says dryly.

"I only knew, like, thirty seconds ago when I could feel you were close."

Dusty takes a step around Eli, into the room. It's almost exactly what she would have pictured. The space is big and boxy with a beige, gray and blue color palette. The tall windows are topped by navy linen curtains, while lamps add some needed warmth. There's a desk covered in trophies, magazines and schoolbooks, and a large, comfortable-looking sofa against the wall opposite the four-poster bed. There are clothes, screens, gaming devices and balls strewn across every surface. Dusty has to look away before her urge to tidy becomes uncontrollable.

Almost every inch of free wall space is covered in BMX posters—figures doing flips high in the air, and even some dirt-splattered women in bikinis on bikes.

As Dusty takes it all in, she thinks that the only things missing from the stereotypical room are the remnants of food or snacks, which she imagines would've piled up daily. Before everything.

She slings the duffel bag she's been carrying onto his bed. "Is your door locked?"

"Yeah," he answers, intrigued.

Dusty zips open the bag and dumps the contents onto the unmade sheets.

"What the fuck, Dusty."

They look down at a pile of plastic medical bags, each full of exactly 450 milliliters of dark red liquid.

"Are they real?" Eli asks, picking one up and squelching its contents between his fingers.

"No, I robbed a Halloween supply store. Of course they're real." She picks one up, inspecting it closely for the first time. It's still cold. She can feel that pressure in her teeth responding to what's inside.

Eli looks up at her with shock, and a little bit of awe. "Human?"

"You'd hope so." She sits down on the edge of the bed. "They're from a medical blood bank."

Eli is speechless.

"I almost lost it at school this afternoon," she explains. "I wasn't hungry, at all, then suddenly, I was." She doesn't mention what exactly set her off. "I can't believe I stopped you from catching that deer," she says, shaking her head. "But I'm still worried about what we would do with a whole deer if we . . ."

Eli lets out a long, deep breath. "You don't think we could stop ourselves from killing it."

"I don't know," Dusty admits. "But I figured *this* is worth a try until we know for sure." She tosses the blood bag back onto the pile.

"How did you . . . get them?"

"I remembered that there's a blood collection center outside of Lowville. My dad donated there once when there was a big drive. And after this afternoon at school, and Sheriff Brookes . . ." She pauses and they exchange a look, acknowledging that they still have to speak about *that*. "I thought this could be an easy solution," she shrugs.

"Robbing a blood bank is an easy solution?"

"Surprisingly, yeah. It's a pretty low-key setup."

"What about cameras?" Eli asks, clearly floored.

"There were only three that I could see, and I avoided them the best I could. If they ever check them, they shouldn't be able to identify me. I wore a hoodie and a baseball cap."

"Who are you?"

"It wasn't hard to smell out where they kept the blood," she continues. "Then I only took two bags from each fridge."

Eli looks down at the bed, counting the eight bags.

"I left through the staff bathroom window. It was locked from the inside, but I figure someone will just assume they left it open a crack, especially if they don't notice the blood is missing for a while."

Eli's brow furrows. "And you thought that the day we were questioned by a cop was the best day to do this?"

"I thought the day I found out *his* name," she snaps back defensively, "which is Andrew Everett, by the way, was a good day to gain better control of myself, yes." She can hear both of their heart rates quickening and feels their tempers awakening.

"I know what his name is," Eli says darkly.

Dusty glares, aware deep down that their anger is misdirected.

"What if Brookes followed you? Or put a tracker on your car?" Eli pushes.

Her resolution falters for a second, but she digs her heels in. "This isn't *Mission Impossible*, Eli." Then, thinking of the photo of Andrew Everett, still alive and well, her voice softens. "Besides, I think they think an animal took him. Some predator."

"I know," Eli says, solemnly. "I had . . . flashes . . . of what you said to him."

"Yeah. Me too. Of you."

"If only that was the weirdest thing happening to us . . ."

"Yeah, if only."

"Why did your dad lie for us? About the clearing?"

Dusty hesitates, still unable to talk about her mother's memory, and what it could mean. "He was probably just trying to keep us out of the crossfire. Trying to keep Brookes from barking up the wrong tree."

"So, you don't think he actually thinks we did anything?"

"Murdered someone?" She sighs. "No. They don't even know he's dead. Not for sure."

The reality of their situation sinks in again, and their focus shifts back to the blood.

Eli plucks a bag from the pile and inspects the tabs and tube that sticks out of the main compartment. "How do we . . .?"

Dusty shrugs. "We could just bite it?"

"Huh. On three?"

Dusty nods.

"One, two . . ."

They bite down and their teeth pierce the thick plastic simultaneously. Cool, salty, metallic-tasting liquid spurts into Dusty's mouth, slowly enough for her to take it all in.

The sensation is anticlimactic.

They both pull away once it's safe that nothing will spill out, and swallow what's left in their mouths reluctantly.

Dusty wipes her lips with the back of her hand. "What a waste."

"It was kind of like that first pine marten," Eli says. "The dead one. But not even, because at least that was warm." Eli scrunches his nose in distaste. "We could microwave it?"

Dusty shakes her head. "I should have known. I just thought . . . because it's human . . ."

"We could return them?" Eli suggests.

"I'm pretty sure they've gone bad out of the fridge."

Eli tosses the bag to the other side of the bed. "Out of sight, out of mind."

Dusty feels defeated. She falls back onto the bed, looking up at the wrought iron rectangle above. She wonders what the point of it is, without a net or fabric over it to block out the rest of the world. The dark blue sheets beneath her are drenched with the smell of Eli. Not just Eli now, she realizes, but Eli as he used to be. Younger. Different.

She rubs her eyes. "How the fuck are we going to reverse this? Find a way back?"

Eli looks down at her. "Do you really think that's possible?"

Dusty feels her throat constrict. "No," she sighs. "But even if it's just wishful thinking, we have to try. I *need* us to try."

"Okay," Eli says. "Well, I'm obviously useless, but if anyone can figure it out, it's you."

"You're not useless," she says. "I don't know how I would have gotten through this week, with school and hunting at night and everything else, without you."

He crashes down onto the bed beside her. "We do make a pretty good team," he says.

Dusty smiles, but without a plan ahead of her anymore, she's again too aware of the aching emotions coursing through her. "All I know," she says, "is that I can't let myself feel hungry for *someone* ever again."

"But we need to feed from something living," Eli says, thoughtful. "Maybe we could find a donor?" he jokes, but it's clear from the way he swallows after that it's not the first time he's thought about it.

"Don't," Dusty says.

"You know it's what we're meant to have," he adds. "And it would keep us fuller for longer. It's safer for everyone."

"There needs to be a line, Eli. That's just one we can't cross."

"Why not?"

"Because it's what makes us monsters," she snaps, sitting up. "Once was a mistake. A horrible, horrible accident. But to do it again?" Her face contorts in disgust.

"Okay, okay," Eli soothes. He sits up beside her, their shoulders side by side.

The proximity awakens a thought Dusty came close to reaching this afternoon. "Have you ever wondered . . ." She hesitates, not sure she wants to say it out loud.

"What?"

"If we . . ." She tucks some loose hair behind one ear. "If we could feed on each other?"

The question hovers between them, threatening to spark whoever dares to speak or move first.

Eli slowly turns toward Dusty, trying to conceal a smile. "Wouldn't that make us monsters?"

She sighs.

"No. You're right," he says, his face serious. "It's different between us." He lowers his voice. "I'm game if you are."

Dusty feels her skin prickle on her neck, right on the spot she knows he'd want to bite down on her. It's the place she'd found herself picturing when she was looking at Will.

Eli swallows as Dusty hears his heartbeat quicken. In his green eyes she can see something wild. Hunger.

"I'm game," she says steadily, feeling a distinctly unsteady rush of excitement inside of her. "You first."

"Are you sure?" Eli asks.

Dusty nods.

He reaches up to her hair and pushes it off her shoulder, so it falls down her back.

Dusty gulps, more visibly nervous now. "Wait," she says. "Somewhere less obvious."

"Shit," Eli says, then his tongue darts out of his tense lips, licking them.

Dusty suppresses a laugh. "Did you just lick your lips?"

"Fuck, Dusty, I'm hungry!" His frustration is palpable. His body rigid.

"Okay, okay, relax," she says, then she takes a deep breath in and blows it out.

Eli does the same.

His eyes scan her body, hovering over places that make his colors shift to a specific pinky red. She's learning it's his tell for desire.

"Where then?" he asks, his voice low.

She looks down at herself, thinking. "Here?" she asks, raising her arm as she rolls up the sleeve of her t-shirt and reveals her inner bicep.

Eli nods, swallowing again.

Dusty lets herself feel the trust that's been building between them, and that closeness she's been craving since this afternoon. Eli bends toward her and she tenses in anticipation. When his lips land softly on the skin of her arm, she giggles, pulling it away.

Eli stares in shock.

"I'm sorry!" she says. "It tickled!"

He lets out a slow breath, and she shakes her head, trying to embody the seriousness of what they're about to do.

"Ready?" he asks.

She nods.

Eli reaches for her wrist, then slowly lifts her arm. When his mouth touches the sensitive skin of her inner arm, she breathes through it, letting a shiver spread over her.

Eli inhales as his tongue brushes against her, and Dusty's own teeth throb from the sensation.

She's just about to tell him to do it when he bites down.

Dusty's eyes dart open at the feeling of her own blood flowing into him. It hurts at first, but there's something satisfying in the sensitivity, like pressure is being released. Eli's mouth remains in place for several moments, tasting her. But as quickly as it started, it ends.

He pulls away and falls back onto the bed.

Dusty is stunned. She doesn't notice the blood still trickling out of the puncture wounds as she lies down beside him. She turns to look at him, waiting for him to say something. But he just shakes his head.

"No good?" she manages.

Eli brings his hands to his face and groans in frustration.

"Is it because . . ." she starts, not quite knowing how to articulate her feelings. "Maybe it's because you're not that attracted to me? Like, if we hadn't been through so much together . . ."

Eli turns to her, his eyes full of disbelief. "Dusty . . . we fed from a squirrel. Not to mention the stranger . . ."

She sighs. "I know, but we were starving then."

"What? And we're not now?" He shakes his head.

Dusty is thoughtful, deciding she has something she needs to tell him. "You know how you asked if that guy smells different?" she asks. "The one who was in the hall this morning?"

Eli nods.

"Well, he does. He was what set off my hunger this afternoon."

Eli looks up at the ceiling, thoughtful.

"I think there's a link," Dusty says. "Between attraction and hunger."

Eli's still thinking and Dusty doesn't speak, allowing him to process what she's saying. After a long pause, he turns to her. "I know what you're saying, but Dusty, I am attracted to you. *Very*."

Dusty gulps, unable to control how vulnerable she feels.

He shakes his head. "But whatever we are now, we're not meant to feed from each other. It was like . . . every instinct told me to stop. That you're untouchable. Because we're the same."

She nods. After another pause, she lets out a soft laugh as she says, "I guess that would've been too easy."

"Tell me about it."

Dusty sits up.

"Oh shit!" Eli says, getting up to grab a tissue from his bedside table. He holds it down on her arm, where a trickle of blood runs from the puncture wound.

"Oh," Dusty says, slightly awkwardly, as if she wasn't feeling vulnerable enough.

Eli is looking at the tissue when he pulls it away from her. "Hold on," he says quietly. He leans in close to her again and begins to lick the wound.

Dusty is so shocked she doesn't stop him.

When he comes back up to face her, he can see her confusion.

"Look," he says.

She stares in disbelief. There's still a trickle mark running down her arm, but the puncture from his bite is almost entirely gone. "How did you . . .? Did that only heal when you . . . licked me?"

"Yeah," Eli says, his face slack with disbelief. "And I don't know. I just had this instinct, I guess?"

"Eli, this changes everything!" She stands then spins to face him, and they stare at each other as they both process the implications.

Out of the corner of her eye, Dusty notices a small pool of blood on his dark sheets where she'd been lying. "Shit!" she says.

Eli looks down at the almost-black patch. "Don't worry about it," he says casually. "Mom will just think you lost your virginity or something." He smirks.

Dusty stares at him, blinking. "And just as I was starting to think you're not a complete idiot."

Crouching beside an oak tree, Dusty can feel the predator in her taking over. The night is still and stars glimmer beyond the clouds. When the moon is visible it's bright enough to cast shadows. She feels a twitch in her fingers and on the tip of her tongue.

She's ready.

Sprinting through the forest with a gasp of wind in her wake, her bare feet spring silently from the moss and leaf-laden ground, launching her gracefully to the side of the deer. A buck. She grabs his antlers, holding him in place as he catches up with what's happening and tries to flee.

He pulls away, twisting his head back and forth, but her arms remain strong and steady. He can't go anywhere.

She can smell his fear. She needs to act.

"Shhhh," she whispers. "I don't want to hurt you."

Dusty remains still, steady, and the deer's tension relaxes just a little. She closes her eyes and very slowly, she lets go of one antler, running her free hand down his long, soft neck. She lets her instincts guide her. Somehow, her need to calm the deer allows her to slow down the chaos inside her too, organizing it into a calm and steady rhythm. She doesn't know how she knows the rhythm, but it's familiar.

The buck's breath and heartbeat settle into sync with hers.

He's ready.

Dusty bites.

Warmth floods her mouth.

Her mind drifts, glimpsing that ethereal beauty she'd felt when she'd fed from the man, whose name she can't quite recall right now. She tries to hold onto it, but then she feels Eli, tethering her to the present where she needs to prove there's a world in which she can still exist.

She almost misses the point of no return, distracted by fragments of the buck's life—the plush grove of mountain maple it browsed on at twilight, the feeling of rubbing his antlers on rough bark. But holding onto that rhythm, she opens her eyes.

Her surroundings instantly fasten her to her purpose. She releases the buck from her mouth, hesitating only for a second before she licks the wound through his silky hair. She watches it heal, listening to the deer's fatigued but steady heartbeat, then lets go of his antler.

He stumbles away, shaking his head, and disappears into the thick forest.

Dusty drops to her knees, which fold her to the ground. Her hands drop to her sides, palms facing upward.

"That was insane," Eli says from behind her.

Dusty turns to see him, only a few feet away, his hands on top of his head in disbelief.

"How did you do that?" he laughs, but his face is pure astonishment.

"I don't know," she murmurs in a daze. "I just wanted him to feel calm."

"Yeah, well, whatever that was, it worked. Dusty, you didn't kill him."

She looks up at Eli, her eyes shifting back into focus. "I didn't kill him," she says, as a smile spreads over her face.

"Are we sure it isn't a virus?" Eli says.

They're walking uphill, toward Dusty's house, taking their time.

It hadn't taken long for them to track another deer. Dusty had stood back as Eli took his turn. She watched as his instincts kicked in, overtaking his thoughts and fears, allowing him to do what he needed to do.

The deer had struggled more than Dusty's had. And from ten feet away, where she stood and watched, she could see and feel Eli's energy reaching out to hers for help. She focused, thinking of the rhythm she had found to soothe her deer, then felt the shift as he somehow harnessed it and the deer had settled.

"It would explain the fever and headaches in the beginning," he continues. "Even the sleepwalking."

"Maybe. But it doesn't explain what happened before that, when I got lost with Opi."

"I thought you said that might not be related."

"I guess," she says. But she's still not sure. It's too much of a coincidence. "It also doesn't explain why neither of our siblings are like us," she says. "Or our parents."

"Maybe it's transmitted sexually," Eli offers, only half joking.

Dusty looks at him like he was born yesterday.

"What?! How else could we have caught it if it isn't, like, from sneezing or something our families would get too?"

"Firstly, what makes you think your parents don't have sex? Secondly . . ." Dusty shakes her head, smiling knowingly.

Eli stops walking.

Dusty looks back at him to watch his face as he realizes.

"You're a virgin," he says.

"Please, enough with that word."

Eli jogs to catch up with her. "What word? Virgin? What's wrong with that?"

"It's not the nineteen-fifties. Virginity is a social construct. Not to mention it implies that there's only one type of sex that counts, which is ridiculous."

"Huh," Eli says, nodding thoughtfully. "That makes sense."

Dusty tries to hide her smile as she keeps walking.

"I can't believe I made that stupid comment about you bleeding in my bed."

"I know, right?"

"Ha. So you've never . . ."

"Nope."

Eli nods. "Cool."

"I was pretty . . . shut off from my body before all of this," she says.

"Oh yeah?" he asks.

"Yeah." There's something about the bond between them that makes Dusty feel comfortable opening up to Eli. And from what she's learning about him, there isn't much he'd shy away from either. "I guess I had a lot of head noise, and I was sort of scared of feeling *anything*. Emotionally or physically. So I tried not to think about . . ."

"Sex?"

She nods.

"And now?"

"Well, there's the whole bloodlust thing, which is obviously scary. And confusing. And then the whole *feeling* thing is so much worse now." She tries to laugh it off, but from Eli's expression it's clear he's taking her seriously. "Now," she continues, "feelings are, like, constantly screaming at me. My body. My thoughts. My emotions. And everyone else's too."

"You mean the colors?"

She nods. "I miss being . . . numb. I miss being able to shut people out. But also . . . in hindsight, I can see that I wasn't very happy. *Before*. That maybe being more present, and in my body, would be good for me."

"I'm sorry," Eli says. "But I know what you mean. I think riding helped me get out of my head a lot. And even though I've had a lot of bad falls, broken bones, it's all worth it, because it makes me feel . . . *alive*. Stupid, maybe. But alive."

"I get that now," Dusty says. "The only thing I kind of . . . love . . . about all of this, is when I'm running. *Being* in the forest. Like we're part of it."

Eli nods and they let their words settle over them for a few moments.

"So this guy," Eli says as they near Dusty's house. "The one who set off your hunger. His name's Will, right?"

She slowly nods.

"And he *is* someone you're into? Besides the bloodlust."

She thinks about lying, but she just can't juggle any more of them, and she doesn't want that with Eli. "Yeah," she says. "At least, I thought I might be, before everything happened at the bonfire. But I only got to know him after I . . . started to change. So I don't really know what's real or what came first . . . attraction or hunger."

"But you are attracted to him, right?"

Dusty looks at him. "Why? Is there someone like that for you?"

Eli hesitates as his colors start to streak with ripples of murky green. He shakes his head. "No."

Dusty knows he's lying as his colors shroud around him, retreating from her, shutting her out.

She decides not to press him, allowing what little privacy that exists between them to remain.

The night is warmer than it has been all week and summer break feels so close she can literally taste it in the air. The sounds of the night are so familiar to her now. She takes comfort in them. The sheer volume of blood they drank is enough to ignite their bodies, firing microscopic charges in repetitive waves. Their cells hum at a different frequency than before. But neither Dusty nor Eli acknowledge that no matter how much they've drunk, the deer's blood doesn't come close to a human's.

The word "more" whirls in a seemingly infinite spiral between them.

There's a loud screech somewhere above and they look up just in time to see the silhouette of a bat as it flashes across the moon.

They look at each other, incredulous, and laughter starts to quake in their chests.

"You've got to be kidding me," Dusty exhales.

"Spooky." Eli chuckles.

Dusty laughs as their heads tilt back, watching the sky for more. But there aren't any.

Clouds glide over, covering the moon.

"So, hear me out," Eli says, breaking the silence. "What if we were bitten by vampire bats?"

Dusty looks down to see if he's joking. His smile tells her that he is. But as she watches his face in the moonlight, she remembers something.

"Vampire bats," she says absently.

"I was—"

"Joking, I know. But we studied them last year in biology. They're unique because unlike other bloodsuckers—"

"You mean ticks, mosquitoes, leeches?"

She nods. "Unlike them, there are also bats that are omnivorous." She starts to walk as she combs through her memories from class. Eli follows, interested.

"So, in the way that everyone else in the world is omnivorous," she continues, "maybe the differences in bat species is the key to why *we're* able to survive off of blood alone."

"Okay," Eli says. "Nerd Girl. I love this."

"Blood isn't the most nutritious food source," Dusty explains, "but I guess the bacteria in a vampire bat's microbiome is what helps them synthesize vitamins by breaking down proteins."

"And?" Eli asks.

"Well, feeding specialization like that also causes morphological and physiological adaptations—"

"You mean better hearing, eyesight, stronger, faster?" Eli asks.

"Mmhmm." Dusty nods. "And their saliva has anticoagulants that keep the blood they're drinking from clotting. They also release a chemical that numbs the animal's skin. Maybe our saliva does something like that, but to heal?"

Eli stops, making Dusty stop too.

Their eyes meet, both brimming with excitement from the first taste of anything that makes sense.

"But . . ." Eli starts. "Wouldn't the bats have evolved to be like that over millions of years?"

Dusty sighs, the fleeting excitement already dissipating. "Yep. But we changed almost instantly."

"Well, it's something," Eli says. "Our microbiomes? That makes sense. That's what could have changed. That might be *how* we're like this."

"But it doesn't explain why," Dusty adds. She turns and they continue walking until Dusty's house appears through the trees.

"There was a part of me that just wanted to confess today," she says softly. "So the sheriff would just arrest me and put me where I deserve to be."

"You? I'm the one who pushed him."

"I'm the one who called out. You were just protecting me."

They're quiet for another moment. Remembering.

"But then there's the rest of me," Dusty continues. "Who just wants to survive. Pretty spineless if you think about it."

Eli hesitates before he speaks. "It's not spineless. It's human."

"But are we human now?"

The question rings in their ears.

21

Trust Me

The smell of coffee and melting butter wafts through the house. Dusty looks up at the pitched ceiling above her bed, watching the room brighten. A drawer thuds shut downstairs, rattling cutlery. A ceramic cup clinks as it's placed on a saucer. Her stomach churns at the smell of food cooking in the kitchen.

Feeling movement beside her, she turns her head. "Morning," she smiles.

"I think I slept," Eli says, rubbing his eyes.

His hair, growing longer every day, is flecked with gold in the morning sunlight.

Dusty nods. "You drifted off at around five-thirty."

He rolls onto his stomach to look out the window. Blue sky soars above green mountains. Painfully perfect.

"I think it's around seven now," Dusty adds, aware again of the familiar sounds from below.

"An hour and a half," Eli says with a satisfied expression. "I'll take it. Did you sleep too?"

"No. I still haven't since I . . . levitated."

"Oh right. *That*."

Their eyes meet, acknowledging the secrets they carry for each other.

"I can feel myself getting more tired every day," Dusty says. "It's not normal tired, like sleepy. More of a heaviness. Fatigue. But my brain and body can't switch off." She can already feel that she'll need to feed again tonight, but she doesn't bother saying it out loud.

"I need your help," she says, standing, serious.

"Okay," Eli says, unfazed.

"I need you to distract my dad. When I say I'm going to shower, keep him down there, okay?"

Eli looks at her flatly. "Down there? What do you mean down there?"

"Downstairs. When we go downstairs."

"Ugh," he groans. "Do we have to? Your sister is scary as hell and your dad, uh . . . hates me."

"She's not. And he doesn't. Or, he won't."

"And *why* do I need to distract your dad?"

"Just trust me?" Dusty asks softly, using the bond between them to express the weight of what she's asking. "Please?"

He studies her, softening, then heads toward the door.

"What are you doing?" she whispers.

Eli turns, confused.

"Out the window," she chuckles. "You'll have to knock on the front door like a normal person."

Eli scratches his head. "Doesn't your dad think we're together?"

"Yeah, but that doesn't mean he'd be cool with you sleeping over. Especially after, you know, how weird everything was at the clearing."

Eli blows his breath out. "Okay. But just so you know, you're the first girl I've ever done this for."

"Wow, I feel so special," she says, deadpan. "You're the best fake boyfriend ever."

Eli winks before climbing back onto the bed.

"Give me ten," she says.

Then he slips out the window.

Dusty changes into her boxers and sleep t-shirt, then goes downstairs. Her dad is at the dining table with his breakfast, a black coffee, and a well-thumbed crossword puzzle book. He looks up at her, and immediately begins looking her over, like he's trying to understand what it is about her that's different. Changed. When their eyes meet he hides his uncertainty with a smile.

Dusty wonders what else he's hiding.

"Morning," Chris says, relieved to see Dusty in the kitchen at breakfast for the first time in a week.

Opi looks up from the stove and beams at her older sister, propelling Chris's relief even further. The fight between his daughters must be over.

"Breakfast?" Opi asks, hopeful. "I just picked the first perfect tomatoes of the season."

"Oh," Dusty says, hesitant. "Eli and I are actually going for an early hike. He's packing a picnic."

Chris raises his eyebrows and Opi's smile drops. He isn't sure what he's supposed to say to that as Dusty sits down at the table. It's not like she's saying that Eli will be sleeping over from now on. *Or is that just around the corner?* he wonders.

He tries not to let dread overshadow his morning off, with both of his daughters safe at home. Unlike last weekend.

Still taken aback by the shift in her, he tries to pinpoint what it is exactly that's different about Dusty. *Has she grown?* he wonders. *Has she been working out? Or does she just look older?* The healthy flush of her cheeks when they found her in that clearing has faded a little. It was the one thing that had convinced him she was okay. There's a faint wash of purple under her eyes again, and her smile feels a little like she's putting it on for show. There's also something about her eyes that wasn't there before she ran off to do who-knows-what with that boy.

Whatever has changed, her resemblance to her mom, Sarah, still takes his breath away.

He takes another bite of his pancake just as the doorbell rings.

Choking down the food, he bangs his fist on his chest to clear his throat and appear as neutral as possible.

"I'll get it," Opi says, already walking to the front door.

Chris listens as the door opens and a confident voice says, "Morning, Ophelia."

Opi doesn't reply.

"Is Dusty home?" the boy asks.

"She's in the kitchen," Opi answers, obviously annoyed. Chris doesn't blame her.

Footsteps sound before Opi reappears, steely, followed by Eli.

Eli glances at Dusty, then walks straight up to Chris, his hand outstretched. "Morning, sir. It's nice to see you again."

Chris clears his throat. "Morning." He tries not to let the shock of how firm Eli's handshake is show.

Eli hovers, glancing around the room.

"Breakfast?" Chris asks, trying his hardest to sound like the offer is genuine.

"Oh, no thank you, sir," Eli says. "We're going on a hike soon, and I've organized something for us to have while we're out." He flashes another smile, which is nothing short of dazzling, and when their eyes meet, Eli's gaze unflinching, Chris finds himself smiling back for a second, forgetting.

As soon as Eli looks away, Chris is able to remind himself that this kid has no right to be this confident. Not at seventeen. Not in this house.

"Where are you hiking to?" Opi asks, her tone pricklier than Chris is used to.

"The peak," Eli and Dusty say in unison. They glance at each other, before looking around the room awkwardly.

"That's not very far," Opi says, her brows pulled together.

Eli shrugs. "We might go down to Angel Lake, later." He turns to Chris. "If that's okay with you, sir?"

Chris nods slowly. He doesn't think he likes this kid, but he does think he could get used to being addressed as "sir" in his own house and decides he's in no rush to tell Eli he can call him Chris.

Dusty starts to arrange the napkins, cutlery and vase on the table. She glances up at Chris to find him watching her and tucks her hands into her lap. Her mother used to do something similar when she was anxious.

"I'm going to go up and shower," Dusty says, standing.

Eli smiles and sits down opposite Chris as Dusty disappears upstairs.

Without Dusty in the room, it's even more apparent how little Chris knows about this boy. What he does know is that whatever their relationship is, it didn't start off on the right foot. He wants to trust his daughter, but what happened last weekend doesn't make it easy. And trust is difficult enough for Chris already.

Treading lightly up the small staircase, Dusty's mother's memory throbs in her mind. She tries not to let the fear she'd felt pool in her chest. She needs to focus, and find something that will explain why her mom had been so scared of her dad.

Over the shower she left running, she can hear fragments of the strained conversation in the kitchen. As Eli explains to Chris what being a professional BMX rider entails, Opi doesn't say a word, but from the aggressive clatter of pots and pans it's clear she's still in there.

Reaching the top of the third-floor stairs, Dusty crosses the threshold of her father's room. She looks up at the peaked ceiling, trying to remember the last time she was in here. She can't.

This is where she would come in the middle of the night and nestle between her parents, Opi too, and it felt like her entire world was in that one bed. Then they'd wake together, drenched in warmth and sunshine. There had been such certainty. Dusty's place was there, with her family.

A knot twists in her stomach and her whole body responds with a clammy sweat.

Focus, she tells herself.

Looking around, she's struck by the lack of femininity in the space, and wonders when exactly it was eradicated—was it the instant her mom was gone? Or more gradual, over the years? Either way, the room has a distinctly masculine feel and smell.

Sunlight strikes through the big bay windows, stark against huge, dark, ancient-looking wood furniture. There's a row of boots beside an immovable closet, but other than that, the only trace of anything personal is a framed photo of Dusty and Opi on the dresser, and a comb placed beside it. The room is tidy but stuffy, and she has to stop herself from opening the window to let fresh air in.

Carefully sifting through the drawers, she finds only the obvious clothes and personal items. From under the bed, she pulls out boxes covered in dust that reveal decorative knickknacks that had belonged to her grandparents.

Nothing.

She's praying she'll know what she's looking for when she sees it. Something. Anything to shed light on what had happened between her mom and dad.

She turns to the closet. The heavy door creaks as she tries to pull it open, and her heartbeat quickens. She knows she doesn't have much time left. She pulls it again, slowly, but the creak groans louder. Holding her breath, she tugs at it, fast like she's pulling off a band-aid.

She stops to listen.

Eli is asking her dad about his work.

Her body relaxes.

At the bottom of the closet are two more boxes. She shuffles through the first, mostly paperwork, but there's nothing mentioning her mom. She's just about to open the second when she hears footsteps on the stairs to the second floor, followed by a knock, then Opi's voice.

"Dusty? Can I come in?"

Shit. The bathroom door isn't locked, and all it would take is her sister barging in to discover that Dusty isn't in there.

Another knock. "Dustyyyy."

More footsteps below.

"What're you doing up here?" Opi snaps.

"I was . . ." Eli starts, "I was wondering if you could show me your garden. Dusty says you . . . grow things?"

Dusty opens the box. More paperwork. She begins leafing through, moving as quickly as she can.

After a long pause Opi responds, "Why?"

"Because no one at my house has ever grown a thing," Eli says.

There's another pause as Dusty continues scanning the documents.

"Maybe later," Opi says slowly. "I need something in the bathroom now."

"Wait!" Eli says, a little too loudly.

"What is your problem?" Opi asks, anger pulsing in her voice.

"Please," Eli says softly.

"Let go of me."

Dusty hurries, rushing through the last of the papers. When she gets to the very bottom, there's a photo, rumpled by time. Dusty holds it close, shocked by the resemblance. The girl staring back is around her age, with Dusty's heart-shaped face and hazel eyes, but her sister's light brown hair. Her mom.

And she's not alone. Beside her are a man and a woman, their features more vaguely familiar, and behind them is a small, pretty suburban house. Dusty never met them, but she assumes they're her mom's parents. Her own maternal grandparents.

"I'm sorry," Eli is saying.

"What's wrong with you?" Opi demands.

Dusty closes the box, then the closet. Quickly stuffing the photo into the band of her boxers, she darts down the stairs.

Eli and Opi are at the other end of the landing, standing off face-to-face.

"Eli, cool it," Dusty says. They both whip to face her, confusion all over Opi's face. "Sorry, Op," she says.

"What're you doing over there?" Opi asks. "What's going on?"

"Nothing." Dusty tries to shift her voice into an easy tone. "I just went to look for a t-shirt to wear after I shower. I couldn't find the one I was looking for—I thought it might be up with Dad's laundry."

"And you left the water running?" Opi asks, horrified.

"I was distracted, sorry."

Opi turns to glare at Eli again.

Dusty can hear Eli's heart beating fast, but his colors are shifting, slowing, now she's here.

They both turn to stare at Dusty, waiting.

"Bathroom's all yours, I can shower later," she says to Opi, then to Eli, "Let's go. I'm starving. Just give me one minute."

She slips into her bedroom and changes into denim shorts and a cotton top, then packs a bag with her notebook inside of it. She reaches for her phone but decides not to bring it, placing the photo inside instead.

Back on the landing, Eli is hovering, anxious. In the bathroom, Opi has turned off the shower.

"Ready?" she asks. But as they walk downstairs and stop in the entranceway so she can make a show of putting on her hiking boots,

Dusty decides that she doesn't want to spend the day with him, or anyone.

She needs to be alone.

Mali checks her phone. Again.

She's sitting at a booth in Bernie's Diner with her parents, breakfast on the table between them.

"Phone away," her mom warns, sipping on her iced coffee.

"Eat up," her dad adds. "God knows you're not going to stop training over summer. My baby's gotta stay *strong*." He winks, making Mali smile.

She tucks into her scrambled eggs, trying not be annoyed that it's been an hour since she messaged Dusty to see when she should come over, like they'd planned. She knows Dusty would've been up early, like always, but still, she hasn't heard back.

As much as she wants to give Dusty space to be with Eli, she's starting to think that her best friend should have picked up on the fact that something happened with Kristen at the bonfire, something bad, and that Mali might need her.

The waitress, a strikingly beautiful woman with shoulder-length, straight brown hair and big, dark eyes comes up to the table. "Refill?" she asks, smiling broadly as she holds up a fresh pot of coffee.

"Yes please," Mali's dad says, putting his cup down on the table.

"Are you . . . Will's mom?" Mali asks the woman. If she didn't know he was an only child, she would have asked if she was his sister. The resemblance is uncanny, but she looks too young to have a teenager.

"Yes!" the woman says. "Alina."

They all exchange introductions.

"I'm so glad to meet you," Alina says. "Will doesn't give much away, as I'm sure you've noticed, so I never know who he's hanging around with."

The bell on the entry door chimes.

"Oh, it's the Riveras," Mali's mom says.

Alina excuses herself and goes over to seat them on the other side of the diner.

"I wonder where Amber is," Mali's mom adds.

Mali wonders what's up with her friends suddenly getting boyfriends and deciding it's okay to ignore her. She'd messaged Amber last night, asking if she'd watched the latest episode of *Below Deck*. It had been next-level drama, which Amber would usually have loved dissecting in detail with Mali.

She knows she shouldn't be surprised that she never heard back—not after spending the last three lunches outside with Will, leaving Amber and JD on their own for the remainder of the week.

Still, *it's weird*, she thinks. *Everything is.*

22

Beyond

"Did you hear what your dad said?" Eli asks as they ascend the mountain behind Dusty's house.

She glances at him, waiting for him to elaborate.

"When you were up in his room . . . about the search today . . ." he says.

Dusty stops in her tracks.

"It was kind of crazy. I could tell he didn't want to talk much, but the more I asked him, it was like he couldn't help telling me things. I know you think I'm joking, but I swear people are like . . . more receptive to me or something. Well, everyone other than your sister. Anyway, I hope he didn't notice that I almost spewed when he told me."

"Told you what, Eli?" Dusty urges, frustrated.

"I was asking about his work, asking if he does many search and rescues . . ."

Dusty can feel her heart pounding in her throat. She must have been more distracted when she was up in her dad's room than she realized.

"He told me he doesn't go on all of them, that it depends on the jurisdiction—"

"Eli, spit it out."

He sighs. "*Anyway*, he said that some people in town and some from the properties out near the cabin that . . . the man had been staying at, they're forming a volunteer search party today. Your dad said that it doesn't look good for him to be missing so long, but that even if he's dead they'll need to find his body. So they can find out what happened to him."

Dusty doesn't know what to say. Luckily, with Eli, she doesn't need to say a word for him to know how she feels.

"I know," he says. "I'm freaking out too." They begin to walk again, when he adds, "Do you think we should join them?"

"What? Why?"

"I don't know, to throw them off track or something?"

"No," she says, seething with frustration. "We definitely should *not* do that. Do you know how weird it would look? If we just showed up? Two random teenagers . . .?"

"Right," he says, scratching his head. "I guess we'll just wait and see, then."

She sighs. "I'm sorry. I'm just . . ."

"I know," he says.

Dusty had thought she wanted to be alone before this unsettling piece of information. Now, she needs it more than ever. She looks up the mountain, feeling the photo of her teenage mom burning through her bag. The dappled light is beautiful through the dark green pines. The rocks and boulders that scatter down from the peak bounce sunshine through the understory as it quivers in the breeze.

"Well at least after what you said last night," Eli adds, his tone more upbeat, almost positive, "the microbiome stuff, I think we can figure this out. Maybe find a cure." He pauses, slowing his pace. "But until then . . . Even though I slept a little, I feel . . . *fatigued* today too."

Dusty stops again to look at him.

"I'm worried that the deer wasn't enough," he adds.

Dusty wants to agree with him, to tell him she knows, but instead she says, "I think we just need to clear our heads today. Maybe you could try riding your bike?"

Eli studies her. "Are you trying to get rid of me?"

She sighs. "Aren't you going to ask me again why I needed to sneak into my dad's room?"

"I wasn't planning on it. Figured you'd tell me when you're ready."

Dusty lets herself smile, and she can feel Eli's tension dissipate instantly. "You're cooler than I thought you'd be, you know?" she says.

"I thought I was an idiot," he says, flashing her a mischievous smile.

"I was looking for information about my mom," she says, rolling a rock under her hiking boot. "I had a memory, the other night. It wasn't my own though—it was hers. Kind of like how you and I can see and feel what the other sees and feels, except this was definitely from the past because my mom was there, in the spare room, which is now *my* room, and I was remembering through her eyes."

"Woah," Eli says. "Dusty, that must have been . . . I don't even know. I can't imagine."

"You haven't experienced anything like that yet?"

He shakes his head.

"Lucky," she says, thoughtful. "Anyway, it made me wonder about the reason she . . . left. I thought I could find some answers in my dad's room."

"And did you?"

"No," she says. "Not really. But I think today, I'd like to be alone."

Eli lets out a breath as he nods slowly. "Of course. Yeah."

"Sorry," she says.

"Don't be. It's not like we have to play boyfriend and girlfriend all the time. Especially when we're not in front of anyone. Like your terrifying sister."

Dusty laughs. "I don't think anyone has ever described Opi as terrifying."

"Well, she is." He hesitates before tapping two fingers to his forehead in salute. "Let me know if you need me."

"I will."

His green eyes meet hers for a moment too long, revealing his hesitation to leave. But he turns anyway, and she watches as he begins his descent through the trees, realizing that it's been a while since she had one of the violent, intrusive thoughts that almost always come when someone she cares about leaves. It makes her wonder again what she and Eli are to each other now. Is he flirtatious with her? Yes, but he is with everyone. Is she attracted to him? Yes, because he's beautiful, charming and surprisingly funny. Is he the only person who knows her darkest secret? Yes, the only one. Last night she'd even let him drink her blood, which is by far the most intimate thing she has ever done with another person. But still, their relationship remains unclear.

It's different to the closeness she'd felt with Will, who she'd shared just as much about herself with in a day as she has with Eli in a week. Whose presence pulls at her, louder and stronger than anything else.

Either way, neither of them knows her fully. No one does.

She wonders if it's like that for everyone. If everyone is a stranger, even family. If living is just pretending, all the time, even with the people closest to us.

As she gets closer to White Mountain's peak, feeling increasingly fatigued as she tries not to think about the search party out there looking for Andrew Everett, she pauses to take in the view around her. She's facing the same direction her bedroom window faces, but from up here she can see so much further, so much more. The sky meets the mountains that lead down to the lake and river below, reflecting bright blue and the occasional cloud. Warm air rises up from the valley below, skimming the canopy until it crashes over her like a soft wave.

The faint sound of footsteps somewhere behind her makes Dusty spin around.

She waits, wondering if Eli has come up after all. But she can't imagine why he'd have gone around to the other side of the mountain.

The footsteps grow nearer and Dusty listens as they transition from trampling over a bed of pine needles to scuffing across ancient rock. Her heart thuds in her chest as she stands there, frozen.

Then, his scent hits her, and seconds later, Will appears, strolling across a smooth outcrop, looking out at the view.

When he finally notices Dusty, his expression is just as shocked as hers.

"Will."

He'd convinced himself she wouldn't be up here so early, if at all. *Didn't she say she doesn't go outside much anymore?* Either way, given how clear she's been that she wants nothing to do with him, he loathes himself for being so stupid. This is her mountain, after all.

"I'm sorry," he says. "I'll go." He begins to walk away.

"Wait!" she calls.

Stopping in his tracks, he uses every ounce of courage he has to turn around.

She's backlit by the morning sun, the mountains, forest and sky behind her, standing so still that if it weren't for her hair moving in the breeze, she'd look like a statue. When she finally moves, taking one step up onto the outcrop toward him, he feels it again—that sense of time suspending itself when she's near.

She waits.

He begins to retrace his steps back toward her, trying to ignore his thundering heart.

They're around twelve feet or so from the highest boulder of the summit, exposed in every sense of the word. When he's finally close enough to see her properly, he has to force himself not to look away. She's so beautiful, out here in the wild, it almost hurts.

"I can explain," he starts, not sure there's any excuse for overstepping her already clear boundaries like this. "Ever since I was here . . . well, down there, last weekend, at your house, with Mali . . . I couldn't stop thinking about seeing the summit. The view, I mean. I hike a lot—" He stops himself, shaking his head at the way the words tumbled out, fast and uncontrolled.

Dusty is watching him, making him increasingly aware of how much he's sweating.

He needs to regain a semblance of calm. "Anyway," he says, slower now. "I've seen it. The view. So I'll go."

"No," she says. She looks around, then nods to a small pine tree at the edge of the outcrop. There's a patch of shade on the rock beneath it. "Stay?" she asks. Her eyes flick to his throat, hovering there for a moment, before she begins to walk toward the tree, turning back to make sure he's following. As if he wouldn't do whatever she asked of him.

In the shade, she slides her bag off her shoulder and sits. Will breathes deep, collecting himself, then sits beside her.

"Are you . . ." He pauses. "The way you left class yesterday . . . Are you okay?" He hopes his voice doesn't betray how whiplashed he'd felt in her wake, or how before she'd fled, he could feel her watching him. His logical mind had been irritated by it, wishing she'd just leave him be—let him move on. But every other part of him, starting at the space within his chest that's felt hollow for so long, basked in her gaze. Just like it does now.

When she'd run, even after everything, he'd wanted to run after her. The only thing that stopped him was knowing that she was probably running to Eli.

"Yeah," she says. "Sorry, I know that was weird. I'm just still a bit . . . off. I needed some air."

He nods, chancing a look at her. Their eyes meet and his chest tightens. He watches her lips part as she hesitates over what to say next.

"So you really do spend your spare time outside," she says, turning to look out toward the view.

"What? You thought I just said that to impress you?"

She laughs.

Breathe, he reminds himself. "It's hard to feel lonely when you're surrounded by . . . all this."

She nods. "It must be hard, though. Moving around like you do?"

"I'm used to it. Usually, friends aren't worth the effort. But here, I don't know. It's different. We've been in Black River for six months, which is normally the time it takes to know somewhere isn't right. That we'll be moving on soon."

"And it doesn't feel like that now?"

He shakes his head. "No. It doesn't. Not for me, at least."

Dusty's hair blows around in the warm breeze. She gathers it, twisting it around her fingers before dropping it down her back. "So you've been talking to Mali," she says. "Have you been hanging out, or whatever?"

"She's been coming out to sit with me at lunch," he says, looking at her to gauge how she might feel about that. She gives nothing away. "She's kind of the last person I ever expected to make friends with."

"Why's that?"

"I don't know. She's outgoing, popular. She's *your* best friend."

"Ouch."

"No, I just mean . . . I always wanted to talk to you, but you two seemed kind of intimidating . . ." He sweeps a hand over his face. "Anyway. I hope it's not weird . . . for you, I mean."

"Why would it be weird?" she asks, then she lets herself smile. "It makes sense, really. I can see why you'd get along."

They're quiet for a moment before Will asks, "What're you doing up here, anyway? You sort of gave me the impression that you don't spend much time outside when you're at home. That's more your sister's thing?"

"It was," she says, relaxing a little. "But lately I've been reminded how much I used to love it out here."

"It's . . . amazing," he says, then inhales the fresh mountain air. "And your house. It's like out of a book or something."

She laughs. "It's a bit run down . . . but yeah. I'm lucky. I *was* lucky—" She stops herself, shaking her head. "I actually came up here because I just found a photo of my mom. One I've never seen." She reaches for her bag and pulls out the notebook he'd watched her drawing in the first time they spoke, then, an old photo. She hesitates, then hands the photo to him. "I needed somewhere quiet to think about it."

"Wow," he says, holding it close. "She looks just like you. Your sister too."

Dusty nods.

"And are those . . .?"

"Her parents, I think. I never met them and I didn't even know she had any photos of them. She never spoke about them. Ever. She grew up in Georgia, so I'm assuming this was their house there."

"Do you think . . . when she left . . . that she went back there? To Georgia?"

"I don't know."

Will traces the edge of the glossy, crumpled photo with his finger. "Your name," he says. "Did she name you after the singer?" When he looks up at Dusty there's a gentle smile on her face, as if she's remembering something.

"I was named after the singer, yes, but my mom didn't name me. Or at least, she wasn't the one who loved her. It was actually my grandpa, my dad's dad. He was obsessed with Dusty Springfield. My grandma used to tease him and say how hard it was to live in the shadow of the love of his life. He wouldn't hear a word of it, of course. He loved my grandma more than anything. He'd say that he only loved Dusty so much because she could capture the tune of his love for Grandma. That she put how he felt for her into words and melodies."

Will smiles, trying to imagine what it would feel like to love like that, spanning years and years. Dusty sniffs, and when he looks at her, a tear rolls down her cheek.

"I'm sorry," she says, wiping it away. "I don't know why I keep feeling the need to tell you every little detail about my life."

A loose strand of her hair blows up and it takes every bit of Will's self-restraint not to reach out and tuck it behind her ear. "No, I'm sorry," he says instead. "Losing them, especially when you lived with them, here . . . it must have been so hard when they were gone."

"It was," she says, then blows the strand of hair out of her face. "But I know I was lucky, to be able to know them like that. I know not everyone gets to be around their family."

Will nods. "Still, having that, and then not having it . . . It's almost worse than never having it at all."

"Yeah, maybe," she says, her eyes searching his. Then she looks away. "It's just all so . . . raw again."

"Finding this must've been a surprise." He holds out the photo.

"Right," she says.

When she reaches for the photo, her fingers graze his. Her warmth seeps into his skin.

She quickly pulls her hand back, turning back to face the sun. "In the weeks after my mom left, there were still photos all over the house of us as a family, just sitting there in frames like the worst thing I could have imagined hadn't just happened. So one morning, I woke up and took them all down. My dad found me stuffing them into the trash. He stopped me. Said he'd put them somewhere safe in case I wanted them one day. He didn't say it, but I knew he was thinking *in case she comes back*. I told him I didn't want them. That I never would. But after finding this, it makes me wonder where they are."

Will tries to think of something to say, anything that could help her navigate whatever it is she's going through. And as the silence spreads between them, he thinks about how if things had played out differently, he could try to comfort her without saying a word.

He looks down to the ground, noticing a small wildflower growing among fallen needles gathered in a crack of the outcrop. Delicate purple petals on a tall, thin stalk. He reaches for it, hesitating as he thinks of leaving it for the bees. But there's something about it, like it was meant for her, in this moment, and he plucks it from the crack.

Dusty forgets to breathe as Will, surrounded by the most beautiful blues, holds out the small purple flower.

She goes to take it, careful not to let her fingers touch his again. Her body is still recovering from the last time. "Thank you," she says, certain he has no idea how much it means to her. She opens up her notebook and places the flower on a blank page. She looks at it for another moment, admiring it, before closing the notebook and pressing the flower inside. "That's the first thing that's ever gone in here other than black ink," she says.

Will considers this. "Maybe it's not a bad place to keep that too." He nods to the photo of her mom.

She isn't sure, but as she picks up the photo and slips it inside the back cover, it feels right. "You're a good listener," she says.

Will smiles. It's crooked and perfect, dimple and all, and for a second, she forgets why she's been avoiding him. His colors have slowly begun to coil around her, and her fingers tingle with the urge to touch him. To trace them over his lips, or rake them through his hair. To know what it feels like to hold his hand.

He tilts his head to the side, as if he's trying to figure out what's happening between them. It exposes his neck to the sunlight.

Suddenly, Dusty is awash with a need so strong she almost lunges for him. She doesn't know what she wants more—to kiss him or taste him.

"You should go," she says quickly. She knows how cold her voice sounds, but that's the point. She needs it to cut through him like a blade. "Eli will be here soon," she adds, twisting her words into the wound.

"Oh," Will says, clearly jarred by the shift. He sweeps his hair back with one hand. "Got it."

He stands and she watches his blues darken and retreat from her.

"See you at school," he says.

Dusty turns to fix her gaze on the view beyond them, and listens as he walks away, back down the mountain. Her whole body aches with every step, the air around her still thick with his presence.

Monster, she reminds herself.

When he's gone, she starts to sweep away the few stray pine needles from the outcrop beneath her, clinging to control, breathing deep. A small metal object scatters across the stone from where Will had been sitting. She leans to pick it up, turning it over to find that it's a compass, its needle spinning from the movement. She feels a rush of warmth. *Of course he carries a compass.*

But when the warmth begins to hurt, like it's pulling too hard at her heart strings, she shoves the compass into her bag and opens her notebook again, plucking the photo from inside the back cover. She stares at her mother, at the faces on either side of her, at the house behind them, until at last, she feels that tug again, strong, as she's taken back in time.

Blocking her ears, the sound of the fire alarm raises her adrenaline as she runs through the house. She can already smell smoke, but she knows where it's coming from. It's always the same place.

Down the stairs, through the hall, into the living room.

The TV is on, but no one's watching, and the iron rests flat on a shirt on the board, smoke curling up from the fabric beneath it. Quickly, she pulls the plug out from the wall then lifts the iron up, revealing the black scorch that's burned all the way through to the board. It smells like toasted marshmallows.

"Sarah!" a woman's voice calls, then a second later, she appears. It's the woman from the photo. "Where is he?" she asks, yelling over the blaring alarm.

Sarah pulls out a chair and grabs the wooden spoon they keep handy. She climbs up and presses the wooden handle into the button, stopping the alarm.

"Where's your father?" the woman asks.

"I don't know, Mom. You were supposed to be watching him."

Frustrated and scared, she sighs, then runs outside.

The mountains come into view, pulling Dusty back, but the sensation of seeing through her own mother's eyes remains like a filmy residue, distorting her vision. Distinctly unnatural.

Her heart thuds, her mom's adrenaline still flooding her veins.

Trying to gather her thoughts, she wonders if it was always like that for her mom—the panicked pressure of being in a state of fight or flight—or if Dusty is somehow just glimpsing the worst. She can't help but feel like it was a punishment for being so harsh with Will. And for everything else.

Slowly slipping back into herself, the mountains become crisp and clear again. She places the photo back inside her notebook, clutching it to her chest, and lays back on the cool granite, staring up at the blue sky.

When Will's phone chimes in the afternoon, he tries not to let his first thought be *Dusty*.

When he left her up on the mountain, he'd felt a wild combination confusion, anger and embarrassment, and by the time he reached the bottom, he'd resolved himself—he has too much self-respect to indulge his feelings for her.

She's made herself clear. Whatever was between them, it was over before it began.

She's with someone else.

He picks up his phone.

Unknown number
You're not on any social media.
Weird. Got any plans tonight?
🔘 Mali

He smiles.

Later, he's walking through town with her. They're on their way to a party not far from Mali's place. Will hadn't felt like going at first, but looking down the barrel of another night at home, Mali hadn't had to twist his arm too hard.

"It doesn't make sense," she's saying. "It's one thing to want to spend all your time together as a new couple, but to ignore your friends *completely*?" She shakes her head, incredulous.

"Wait, are we talking about Dusty or Amber?"

"Both! It's weird, right? That both of them would suddenly hook up with people they've barely shown any interest in before, and now suddenly *no one else* exists? I mean, maybe Dusty had a *little* crush on Eli, and yes, she's never been great with replying to messages. But we made a plan, and she just ignored me. All day."

Will has been trying to tell Mali that he saw Dusty this morning, but Mali's ranting, combined with his residual embarrassment, has him clamming up. Not to mention the fact that she'd be suspicious if he tried to explain why he went to White Mountain in the first place. If all he'd wanted was to go for a hike and take in a nice view, there are literally dozens of other mountains to choose from.

"Maybe they'll be there," Mali adds.

Will's stomach drops, and Mali apparently notices.

"Amber and JD," she clarifies.

"Maybe," Will echoes, desperate to change the subject. "What about you?" he asks. "I didn't think you wanted to be around 'the drama'?"

"Ehh, I couldn't face another night at home watching reality reruns. It's like, I know they're toxic for my brain, but I can't stop myself."

"I think that's called addiction."

Mali laughs, making Will wonder again about last weekend, when he'd found her on the edge of the road, shivering and upset. He wants to ask about it, but he's not sure it's his place, and it might be something she's trying to leave behind her.

"Oh my god," Mali says. "I forgot to tell you. I met your mom this morning!"

"Oh yeah?"

"Yeah. She's *stunning*. How is she so young?"

"I mean, she had me when she was seventeen, so . . ." He never knows how to respond to comments about his mom's appearance.

"Wow. Our age," Mali says.

They turn onto a quiet street. The houses are big, surrounded by big yards full of big trees. The contrast in scale to Will's own street is striking. He could swear that the streetlights are dimmer here too, warmer, in the nicer part of town.

As they walk, he starts to hear noises from a house at the end of the street. Music and voices, glass bottles being dropped into the trash.

"So whose party is this anyway?" he asks.

"Good question."

Will starts to smile. He's used to not knowing what he's walking into, and as they walk up the steps to the front door—the point when he'd usually feel his apprehension spike, slick and unsteady—Mali's presence fortifies him, making the whole thing entirely less daunting.

It's the first time he's shown up to a party with someone else.

Mali opens the door and the noise of the party leaks out into the still night. Will reaches into his pocket, his hand searching for his compass, but it isn't there. He checks the other pocket, but it's empty, and before he has a chance to wonder where he could have lost it, they're moving inside where there are more people than Will had expected. A lot of seniors from the look of it. As Mali scans the crowd, he notices she's less confident than she'd seemed just moments before.

"Looking for someone?" he asks, leaning close so she can hear.

She shakes her head. "No."

They make their way to the kitchen and find a spot by an island littered with Solo cups and booze. Mali seems to relax a little.

"Drink?" she asks.

"Sure."

She pours them vodkas that she mixes with lime soda.

"To new friends," she says, holding the cup up.

"Cheers," Will says, hoping she doesn't notice the warmth flushing his cheeks.

"You know," Mali says as she sips her drink, "I think there are almost as many girls looking at you as there are looking at me."

Will takes a swig, assuming she's joking. The sickly sweet soda isn't sweet enough to cover how much vodka she poured. He coughs it down, but as he looks around, he can't help but notice that there are a few girls glancing their way.

"You came!" one of them says, walking over to pull Mali into a hug.

Will vaguely recognizes her from a few of his classes.

"Hey, girl," Mali says. "Will, this is Josie. Josie, Will. We're on the track-and-field team together."

"Hey," Will offers, taking another sip of his drink.

"Where has your group been hiding out this week?" Josie asks Mali. "I mean, everyone knows about Dusty and Eli, but your whole table was empty yesterday."

Mali's smile drops a little. "Well, I've been with Will in his super secret spot—"

"It's not secret. It's literally right outside the fire exit."

"But I don't know about JD and Amber," Mali continues. "They weren't in the cafeteria?"

"Not yesterday," Josie says. "I saw them in the morning, but Amber wasn't in chem last period."

"Josie!" Someone beckons, and the girl promises to find Mali and Will later before she disappears into the crowd.

Mali scoffs. "I mean, none of this is really surprising with JD. He sometimes disappears at lunch or blows off class to do something music-y. But Amber? Her mom had to force her to stay home when she was sick last winter. She's so obsessive about not missing anything, not letting her grades slip . . ." She shakes her head. "No. This is too weird."

She downs her drink then quickly pours herself another. Mostly vodka this time.

"You okay?" Will asks quietly.

She looks at him like he's crazy. "I'm fine."

His eyebrows pull together, still questioning her.

She sighs. "It just doesn't make sense," she whispers.

"What doesn't?"

"Amber. JD. Dusty. Something just . . . isn't right." She takes a large sip of her drink as something catches her eye. "Oh my god, maybe she's here!"

Will follows Mali's line of sight to the front door. Eli is standing there, surveying the sea of faces.

It feels like they're both holding their breath, waiting for Dusty to appear.

When she doesn't, Mali turns away. "At least some things don't change," she says, pouring herself another drink.

Will is still looking when Eli's eyes land on his.

A million emotions course through Eli as he stares at Will. There's jealousy, going off like an alarm, and it isn't just linked to Dusty. It's also the fact that Will, like everyone else here, remains unchanged, untouched, untampered with.

The longer he stares, Will stares back, and Eli can't help but respect how unphased he seems. Unintimidated when everyone else in the school seems to try to bend to Eli's will. It reminds him of Dusty, and he's almost amused by it, making that jealousy twist into something more like empathy. It must have sucked, having a chance with someone like her, only for it to end so suddenly, with no explanation.

When Mali pulls Will away, all Eli can think is *I shouldn't be here.*

He hadn't wanted to come, but with his mom and dad hosting a "game night"—a.k.a. his dad's friends ribbing each other over poker, and their wives in a separate room grazing on cheeseboards, getting louder and louder with every bottle of wine—he couldn't stay at home.

And he wanted to give Dusty the space she needed on the mountain.

He's frozen in the doorway, overstimulation stopping him from going inside, when he smells it. The scent that's been torturing him all week.

"Bro, I didn't think you'd come," Jesse says, holding up a clenched hand to bump fists.

"You said it was just a few people," Eli says, trying to block any air from coming in through his nose.

"News travels fast," Jesse says. "Come on."

He leads Eli through a crowd that parts for them. People nod at Eli and pat him on the back as if they go way back. It's his own fault, Eli knows, from sharing so much of his life online, inviting people in. Letting them think they know him. But he could swear that it's been worse this past week. Heightened, like everything else, even though he hasn't posted one thing.

Every interaction sets him more and more on edge—hugs lasting a fraction too long, handshakes that send shivers down his spine—making him more aware of thudding heartbeats everywhere. The soft, swishing flow of blood within their veins. He pictures the deer he fed from last night, and that moment he was able to stop himself. That moment before he took too much.

When they reach the lounge where Matt and their other friends are hanging, they all cheer when they see Eli. He's offered beers and a joint, but he holds his hands up in defeat, and says "I drove tonight."

From the surprise on their faces, he wishes he'd just pretended to drink something.

For the next hour or so, Eli observes everything around him through new eyes, letting it distract him from a feeling that's been there, under the surface, unnerving him all week. A feeling he's kept buried. Deep, deep down. So far even Dusty hasn't noticed it.

When he'd first seen Jesse tonight, he'd been able to let the millions of other smells in the house distract him. But the longer he's near him, he's harder and harder to ignore.

Jesse is almost as tall as Eli, and arguably just as strong. Or he was, before last week. Jesse has a thick head of dark hair, and dark eyes and eyebrows that dominate his finer features. As Jesse speaks, Eli can see from the way that girls look at him that they find him attractive. Eli supposes that Jesse is objectively good-looking, but is immediately uncomfortable with the thought.

The more he watches him, though, Eli can no longer deny it—Jesse does smell different. Better than anyone else in the room.

Just acknowledging the thought makes the house feel claustrophobic. Without a word, Eli turns and walks to the front door.

Outside, he takes in the night air, trying to do that thing that Dusty does, when she calms herself by feeling the trees or whatever.

It doesn't work.

He's becoming too aware of his own heart, beating out of control, and can't seem to manage to catch his breath no matter how much cool air he sucks in. He starts to gasp, his panic surging, then turns to kick the wheel of his own car. The whole thing buckles.

"You okay, man?" someone asks.

"Shit," Eli curses, realizing Jesse followed him outside.

"Come on. What's up? You've been weird all week."

Eli doesn't look back. Instead, he gazes up at the sky. "It's nothing. I'm just . . . I don't know . . ." He shakes his head.

Jesse moves closer.

"Don't," Eli snaps, turning to face his friend. The word Dusty used spins in his head, confusing and disorienting—*bloodlust*.

"Bro, I—"

Eli cuts him off by grabbing the collar of Jesse's t-shirt, glaring at him, warning him. But as their eyes lock on to one another's, Eli feels a shift, distinct, like he's tapping into something. Gaining control. "Give me your arm," he says.

Jesse's eyes remain locked on Eli's as his arm rises beside him, then he holds it up to Eli.

Eli frowns. Had he actually expected Jesse to comply? Confused, he's about to look at Jesse's raised arm but something inside him makes him stop. Something tells him that if he breaks eye contact, it'll break whatever control he has over his friend.

Instead, Eli grabs Jesse's wrist with his free hand, and as he draws it close, toward his mouth, Jesse doesn't flinch. He doesn't question it.

"Don't be scared," Eli says.

"I'm not scared," Jesse replies, his voice distant.

With Jesse's forearm so close to his face, Eli can hear the blood within. He can smell it. He feels his teeth pulse and he leans in a little closer.

Jesse doesn't move a muscle. It's like he's no longer inside himself, and instead, Eli has taken the reigns. Jesse has no choice anymore. He is Eli's, and he will do whatever Eli tells him to do.

Eli draws Jesse's wrist to his nose and his lips graze Jesse's skin. The world around them starts to fade to black. He can feel the pulse in Jesse's wrist beating, thudding, and his other hand moves from Jesse's collar to his neck, muscular and strong, like Andrew Everett's.

A sudden sound sends a jolt of awareness through Eli, and he flinches, breaking eye contact with Jesse. He feels the shift again, like something's been unlocked, shattered. He looks up to the doorway of the house, where Will is standing, looking down at them.

"What the fuck!" Jesse curses, pushing Eli in the chest. "How did you . . . What *was* that?"

Dazed, Eli turns back to Jesse, trying to understand himself. "I—" he starts, but he shakes his head, unsure of what to say.

"You just . . . What's your problem?" Jesse asks, anger and confusion burning in his eyes.

Will walks down the steps, then along the path beside them, heading down the road. "Assholes," he mumbles to himself.

"Eli?" Jesse says, demanding an answer.

"Fuck this," Eli says. He turns and gets into his car, slamming the door behind him. His hands shake as he tries to turn the key, and the second the ignition rumbles he tears away, his foot heavy on the accelerator.

He speeds past Will then looks in the rear-view mirror to see Jesse staring after him.

Eli hits himself in the head, once, twice, three times.

"What the fuck!" he screams.

His vision blurs for a second, and an unfamiliar sensation washes through him. Like he's being pulled somewhere else, outside of his own body.

Light flashes so bright it's blinding. Then, there's nothing but a blurry haze, indistinct, like fog has swallowed up the world around her. She feels her body rising as her eyes close. Images flood her mind, fast and indecipherable. It's like they're trying to tell her something, but it's too much at once.

Dusty awakes with a gasp.

She's still looking up at the sky, but it's no longer blue. Black surrounds her, sparkling with stars and a waning moon.

She can't believe she slept, and here, of all places. At the top of White Mountain.

She scrambles to remember what she'd been dreaming, but it's already gone. All she can recall is that light, because when she blinks, she can still see it.

She sits up and her notebook falls from her chest, spilling the photo and flower from its pages. She tucks them back in and packs her bag to make her way back down to the house.

Celestial light limns the rocky outcrops as she descends, the glimpse into her mom's life playing on repeat. But before she enters the cover of pine trees, she looks back up to the peak. Something lingers at the front of her mind, close, yet out of reach. She looks back up to the moon, and before she can tear her eyes away from its silver gleam, a dizzy sensation swarms her head, taking her somewhere else.

It's the same waning moon above but she's standing on the roof of a house. Pewter gray shingles crunch under her shifting weight. There's a stone chimney to her left. The sounds all around are familiar, but the house is not.

She looks out to the forest, dark and still, but in the distance there's a dim, golden glow. Her first thought is that it's the town of Black River, but she can't be certain. Dusty tries to get a better sense of where she is, or who she is, but she's not the one in control of where she looks, or how she moves, and all she can feel is hunger. Overwhelming hunger. Dusty knows that hunger all too well. It's specific, reserved for blood.

Just like her dream, she grasps for more, but it's too late. Dusty is back within herself.

She looks around then back up to the moon. The shift is confounding as she realizes that whatever that was, it wasn't a memory, like her mother's had been. It was right now, in this present moment, the moon exactly the same, the night exactly the same. *Tonight.*

It felt different too—that sensation of spiraling pressure going up into her brain, not unpleasant, like a whirlwind of sparkles, tingling as they rose up and circled her crown.

For a second she wonders if it was Eli's eyes she'd seen through, some kind of evolution of their connection. But she knows it wasn't. It didn't feel like him. Which means that, here on the mountain, there is someone else like them.

23
Definitely Not Flawless

Despite having slept for most of the day. Dusty is already tired. She's also ravenous.

After checking in at home, where she'd had to stop herself from interrogating her dad about her mom, or what he knew about the search today, she pretended to eat some leftovers from the fridge, then went up to her room, locked her door, and climbed straight back out the window.

Running through the forest, her legs ache a little, less powerful than they had been just days ago. She follows the scent of a deer, and when she finds it, it isn't alone.

Eli is standing beside it, one hand gripping its antler, the other over its back as he feeds. His eyes are closed, and there's an intensity to it that hadn't been there when he'd fed last night.

An urgency.

She listens as the deer's heart rate starts to slow.

"Eli," she whispers.

He doesn't stop.

"Eli," she says louder.

A low growl sounds from the back of his throat. She moves closer, and when it's clear he isn't going to slow down, she reaches out for his arm. His hand is gripping her wrist before she can even register that he'd moved. The deer's knees buckle, but freed from Eli's grasp, it trots away.

Dusty and Eli stare at each other, their breath and hearts loud against the sound of night. Finally, Eli lets go of her wrist.

"Sorry," he says, shaking his head. "I had a weird night. I needed to feed."

"It's okay. I get it. I'm hungry too."

They continue to stare at each other, letting the implications of their hunger sink in, until Dusty says, "Come on. Let me hunt, then I have something to tell you."

Dusty feeds from a doe, feeling satiated, for now, and they begin to wander down the mountain.

"I have something to tell you too," Eli says.

"Yeah?"

Eli nods. "You first."

Dusty takes in a deep breath then blows it out. "I had another vision."

Eli stops. "Of your mom?"

She shakes her head. "No. I mean, yeah, I did, earlier today, but there was something else, tonight. It wasn't a memory. It wasn't the same. I could tell it was, like, right now. Everything about the night, the moon . . ." She looks up at the sky. "I was standing on someone's roof. I think I was looking out toward town. From somewhere on the mountain."

"*This* mountain?"

She nods. "And whoever I was . . . I was hungry. Blood hungry."

"Shit." Eli clasps his hands behind his head, taking in what she said before he speaks again. "I went out tonight. To a party."

Dusty is surprised by the change in subject. "You did?" She can't think of anything worse right now. "How was it?"

"Well . . . not great," he says. "I felt pretty . . . sketchy."

"Did anything happen?"

He hesitates, then nods.

"What?"

"Well . . . I was talking to my friend Jesse, outside. It was just the two of us. He was asking what was wrong, why I've been acting weird, and I sort of . . . locked on to his mind. It was like . . . I could control him."

Dusty's eyes widen. "What do you mean, control him?"

"I mean . . . literally. I told him what to do, and he did it. I could make him do and feel what I wanted. But as soon as I broke eye contact, it was over. And he was pissed. Like he knew something weird had happened, but he couldn't understand why he had done what I told him to do."

Dusty shakes her head, trying to process.

"You know how I've told you that people are more . . . receptive to me?" Eli asks. "Like your dad, this morning, when I was asking him about his work. And people giving me things for free. Girls flirting with me, more intense than usual?"

She nods.

"Well, it was kind of like that, but more focused. I think . . . I think I could have told him to let me feed from him, and he would have."

"Holy shit," Dusty says. "Hence the ravenous feeding just now?"

He closes his eyes for a beat, self-conscious. "But that wasn't it. There's something else I wanted to tell you."

"You're kidding," Dusty says, feeling like she's hit her limit for new information.

"I'm not," he says, serious. "When I was driving home, I think I had a vision too."

"What? What of?"

"It was weird," he says. "It was like I was seeing through someone else's eyes. I almost fucking crashed. I was driving one second, and the next I was walking down a driveway toward this huge house. It was all modern and high-tech-looking."

"Do you know where you were?"

"No. But maybe it was somewhere around here? The trees and the sounds were the same."

"The house, did it have a shingled roof, and a chimney?" she asks, recalling her vision.

He shakes his head. "No. But it was crazy nice, all concrete and glass, and there was this indoor pool next to it, with the same glass walls and a concrete roof that had plants growing on top. The pool was all lit up, blue, and . . . I don't know . . . I felt really weird. Really . . . powerful."

"Shit," Dusty says. "Give me your phone."

He pulls it out of his back pocket, unlocks it, and hands it to her.

Dusty frantically scrolls, then holds up the screen. "Was this it?"

It's a video of a boy wearing sunglasses and a beanie over dyed blond hair that sticks out the bottom. He's DJing in front of an indoor pool encased by glass.

"That's JD, right?" Eli asks, grabbing the phone to look more closely. "God it's annoying how he thinks he's better than everyone because he grew up in the city."

"Yeah," she says. "And that's his house, here on the mountain."

By the time the sun has risen, Dusty is on her bedroom floor, dressed and waiting for her dad and Opi to get up and head downstairs, when she feels warmth in her underpants.

She runs to the bathroom and sits on the toilet.

"Cool," she mutters. "Happy Sunday." Looking down at the blood, she realizes that she hadn't been sure she'd still be able to get her period.

As she changes into some leak-proof underpants, she wonders what this means for her, if anything at all. She doesn't know why she'd doubted her cycle in the first place, but supposes it's from only having fiction as a point of reference. If she was going off that, she'd be frozen in time, flawless, unable to age or have children of her own one day. "Guess that answers that," she mumbles, as a glimmer of relief tingles somewhere inside her.

It makes her feel more human.

She glances up at the mirror and notices the purple hue under her eyes is a little worse than it was yesterday.

Nope, definitely not flawless.

She picks up her phone and sends Mali another message—a GIF of a cat looking up with the world's saddest, most apologetic eyes. It's the tenth message she's sent since she checked her phone last night and realized she'd forgotten they'd made plans. Mali has yet to respond to one.

Dusty knows she deserves it.

Eli had gone home shortly after the revelation about JD, and they'd exchanged numbers finally, agreeing to meet up in the morning. She could tell from his colors that he wasn't telling her everything about what happened with Jesse, but she tucked that thought underneath the pile of other things she's worried about, including Mali, as she tried to think about what the JD vision means. Because *if* JD is like them, the common denominator really is the mountain.

She'd searched online for viruses with vampire-like symptoms, ticks that might spread any of these non-existent viruses to humans, cases of human bite wounds on people or animals and reasons one's microbiome might change. The internet is a deep, dark place, and she saw things she wishes she could unsee, but none of it sheds any light on her reality.

She needs answers. Today.

Meeting Eli on the road between their houses, they could continue along it, guided by the winding asphalt spiral of White Mountain Road, all the way to JD's big, modern front gate like anyone else would. But they agree that it might be best to approach from the back. Where they can remain hidden.

The morning is hot. Dusty is in cut-off denim shorts and a fine, blue t-shirt. Her feet are bare and her hair is up, but she can already feel sweat trickling down her neck.

"I used to love the heat," she groans as they walk. "We should've waited 'til night."

Eli looks equally uncomfortable. He's in gray gym shorts and a white cotton tank top, but unlike Dusty, he's still committed to socks and sneakers. Sweat drips down his neck and arms.

"You okay?" she asks. "With what happened, last night?"

"Huh? Oh, yeah, great," he says sarcastically. "Mind control. Love that for me."

"Hey, at least it's more useful than being a walking mood ring."

"Ha," he says, but he's clearly still distracted.

"So I was thinking," she says, trying to help him out of his own head. "Amber and JD's sudden relationship. It has to be linked with his transformation."

"*His* transformation? What about her? You don't think she's like us too?"

"Well, Amber's from town, not the mountain . . . So going off what we thought before, that *our* link is the mountain . . ."

"You think he's feeding from her?"

Reluctantly, she nods. "I should have known something was up when I saw him at school. He was acting weird, but I was so caught up in my own head . . ."

"All the more reason to pay him a visit," he says. "See if he's really like us, and what he knows." His eyes meet hers, gentle and sincere.

Dusty nods, grateful to be with him as they continue through the forest.

There's a fallen tree ahead, cracked at the trunk's base. Dusty climbs over it first and she can hear Eli inhale, taking in the air around him.

"You smell different," he says abruptly.

Dusty clams up, mortified. "Do I?" she asks casually.

"Yeah." Sunlight hits the angles of his face as he inhales again, and when he opens his eyes she can see that they're slightly bloodshot. He smiles. "I like it."

Dusty covers her mouth, trying to stop herself from laughing.

"What?" he asks, confused.

She lowers her hands, grinning. "I got my period."

Eli's face flushes all over, but his expression gives nothing away. "Oh," he nods frankly. "Cool."

Dusty looks at him, expecting more. "What? Nothing gross to say?"

Eli is the picture of innocence. "There is nothing gross about a woman's cycle."

"Ha!" Dusty laughs, delighted. "You really are full of surprises."

"Speaking of blood," Eli says, "I'm already hungry."

Dusty's smile falls from her face. "I know. Me too. The deer don't last long, do they?"

"Nope."

They keep walking.

Dusty ducks under a branch before climbing over a small boulder. The mountains in the distance are clear and bright through breaks in the trees, and she wonders which ones Will has explored. As if punishing herself for even thinking of him, she pictures Andrew Everett, wondering which mountains he had planned on cycling, if that's why he was in the area.

"Hey, you know how Will is . . ." Eli starts. He follows Dusty into a dense grove of trees then catches up to her side. "The one you're . . . hungry for."

Dusty glances at him, apprehensive. "Yeah?"

"Well, I think . . . I—" A warbler bursts out of the leaves, startling him. "Shit." Eli sighs. "That almost—" He's cut short again, this time by a tall, black-coated steel fence in front of them. It had been camouflaged by the trees.

The joists rise at least ten feet high into sharp tips.

"Here we are," Dusty says. "I knew it was high security out front, but I always thought it was just for show."

"What the hell?" Eli says, gripping the fence. "You'd think it's quiet enough out here. Why would you need a fence like this?"

"I don't know."

"What does his dad do?" Eli asks.

"Or his mom," Dusty corrects automatically. "I'm not sure. They used to live in the city, but I don't know much else."

"Maybe they're drug dealers. Or in the military or something?"

"Maybe."

They peer through gaps in the fence and the crammed trees that continue beyond it, which eventually stop and give way to an expansive, freshly cut lawn. At the top of the rolling green, they can glimpse a portion of the ultra-modern house and the indoor pool from Eli's vision.

Movement stirs the leaves on the other side of the fence, their rustling followed by the steady thud of a heartbeat.

Dusty scans the trees until she sees colors emanating from behind one just in front of where they stand. Red, purple and dark gray.

"What's up, guys?" a voice says.

Dusty flinches, even though she should have expected it. "JD?" she asks.

The colors continue to shift, shrouding the leaves closest to them. A second later, JD emerges.

"No shit," he says. "This is my house."

Dusty studies him, trying to pinpoint what's different. She hadn't been paying attention the few times she saw him at school.

Wearing a red t-shirt, shorts and sneakers, his hair is messy, like usual, peroxided ends giving way to dark roots. His brown eyes are clear, the whites almost startlingly bright, making him look healthier than he used to. He seems taller too, somehow, like his head is held higher, his shoulders more squared. Instinctively, Dusty takes in the smell of him.

Under that subtle difference that confirms that he has definitely changed, there's a sweet, metallic trace of blood. Purely human.

A shiver purrs through Dusty's body.

JD steps closer to the fence, his head tilted. "So?" he asks. "I'm assuming you aren't here to hang. You're far too cool for us, aren't you Eli?" He looks Eli up and down like it's a challenge.

"Easy, dude," Eli says dismissively.

"We just want to talk," Dusty adds. "I'm assuming you can tell—"

"Tell what?" JD says innocently.

"Tell that we're like you," she says, her expression imploring him to drop the act.

"Like me?" he smirks, looking between them, smug.

"Look, we're just trying to figure out what happened to us," Dusty says. "Thought we could help each other. Get to the truth."

"The truth," he says, grinning. "Oh, you mean the truth that Sherriff Brookes was sniffing around for?"

Dusty and Eli exchange a look of surprise. "How did you—?"

"What, you think you're the only ones who get to see through other people's eyes?"

Dusty can feel Eli's anger prickling beside her. Frustrated, anxious, she cuts to the chase. "We just want some answers, JD. We need to figure out a way to reverse this."

"Reverse this?! Why the fuck would you want to do that?"

Dusty stares in shock. From Eli's stillness beside her, he must be doing the same.

A smile returns to JD's face, hard to read. "You two don't look so hot today," he says.

"Is he always this annoying?" Eli asks.

JD chuckles, but from the way his colors darken, Dusty can tell Eli hit a nerve.

"Where's Amber?" Dusty asks, her voice firmer now.

JD looks her up and down. "Why do you care?"

"Where is she?" Dusty probes, holding her ground. She forces herself to breathe, slow, because if Amber's in trouble, she'll need to think before she acts. Every one of her instincts is telling her that JD is stronger than they are.

She thinks back to how she felt, in the days after Andrew Everett, trying to imagine what more human blood, consistent and frequent, would do to her body.

A broad smile transforms JD's face. "She's never been better."

"Is she here?" Dusty asks, looking toward the house. She tries to picture when she'd seen them at school last week. Amber hadn't looked like she was in trouble, but then again, it wouldn't be the first time someone was being abused in plain sight. Still, Dusty wonders how Amber could let him feed from her then just go to school like nothing was wrong, how he could have fed from her without killing her in the first place, how it had all played out the night of the bonfire.

JD huffs a laugh. "You barely give anyone but Mali the time of day for years, and *now* you care?" His eyes bore into Dusty's, challenging and indifferent all at once.

Dusty breathes again, trying to ignore Eli's rising anger beside her. Her hands go up, sending a clear message of submission. If Amber does need their help, they'll need to be smart, and looking at the bigger picture, they need to know what JD knows. It might lead them to the truth.

"We just thought we should get on the same page," she says. "Seeing as we share the same secret. Do you know what happened to us?"

Before he answers, Dusty sees a figure appear on the lawn, around fifty yards behind JD, peering through the trees at them.

"Amber!" Dusty yells.

She doesn't react, doesn't move a muscle. Her long, dark curly hair and her summer dress flap in the breeze.

JD laughs. It's a forced, jarring sound.

"Let's go," Eli says through gritted teeth. "This is pointless."

"Pointless?" Dusty asks, floored.

But Eli's eyes tell her to trust him, and she realizes that she does, implicitly.

She sighs, but as Eli turns to go, Dusty can't help but ask again, "Do you know what happened? Do you know what did this to us?"

JD's smile remains plastered to his face, but for a second Dusty thinks she sees a flash of hesitation in his eyes.

"Is there a way back?" she pushes. "We need to talk about it. We can help each other. We can hunt together. You don't need to feed from *people*."

Her desperation only fortifies JD's indifference. "What, like, start a blood cult?" he sneers condescendingly.

Dusty can feel Eli's desperation to leave, pulling at their bond as clearly as if he were pulling at her arm. They begin to walk away, aware of JD's eyes on them with every step. And before they're out of earshot, Eli can't help adding, "That kid is creepy as fuck."

Dusty agrees, but something makes her wish Eli hadn't said it.

"So what do we do about Amber?"

Dusty's question rings in Eli's ears as they walk back through the forest, the heat of the day rising, making it hard to think. "I know we have to do something," he finally answers. "But you felt it right? How much stronger he is than us?"

Dusty doesn't respond, but he knows she sensed it too.

"You know Amber," he says. "What do you think?"

Dusty shakes her head. "There's always been a sort of . . . thing between us. You heard what JD said. I'm not very good at . . . letting people in. I mean, I know that Amber's smart, nice, she works hard, she's close to her family. But other than that, she's always been a bit competitive with me. I think my friendship with Mali annoys her a little. They're pretty close. They have a lot in common. But Mali would still consider me her best friend. And the fact that I do well at school—I think she thinks that I don't have to try hard. That everything is easy for me."

"What happened to women supporting women?"

Dusty looks at Eli flatly then rolls her eyes. "I just can't see why she would go along with this. I mean, I did notice something brewing between her and JD at the bonfire. But even if she did like him, why would she let him feed from her so quickly? It just doesn't make sense. She was at school last week, she had opportunities to tell someone . . ."

"Maybe she likes it," Eli says.

Dusty stops walking and Eli remembers how upset she'd been at the idea of feeding from anything but an animal. At the implication of it being anything but a bad thing.

"I'm sorry," he says. "I just . . . You didn't *hate* it when I fed from you." He recalls the moment right before, when his lips had been on her skin. How he'd wanted to kiss her as much as he'd wanted to bite.

"That was different," she says. "I'm like you."

Eli shrugs, not wanting to push it, even though it's almost all he's been able to think about—that what he really needs is human blood.

It's like ever since they fed from the deer without killing it, the option has just been there, on the table, begging him to consider it. And after seeing Jesse last night, as confusing as that was for a whole lot of other reasons he's not letting himself unpack, just the idea of tasting Jesse's blood has been coursing through his veins, like his body is begging for it.

"You're right," he says. "I don't get it either. She could have said something."

"Unless . . ." she starts, thoughtful.

"What?"

"Well, maybe we're getting ahead of ourselves. Maybe he's *not* feeding from her, and she's like us too?"

Eli lets that sink in. "But the mountain . . ."

"I know. It would mean that one of our few theories is out the window, and we're back to square one."

Eli sighs.

"I guess we'll have to wait and see at school tomorrow. Get close. Figure it out."

The thought of facing school again makes Eli feel sick. He wonders what it'll be like after the summer, if they're still like this when they're seniors, then after, when they're supposed to be out in the world, functioning adults.

He rolls his neck, trying to clear his mind. He needs to feel something other than stress and hunger.

They're almost at the point between their houses when he realizes what he needs to do. "I'm gonna ride again today," he says.

"In this heat?"

"It's not ideal, but I . . . I just need to. I need to keep moving."

"I'm starting to understand what you mean."

"Wanna come? I found a trail that would make a good track a little further down, on the north side of the mountain. I might build some jumps down it."

Dusty shakes her head. "I need to cool off. And I still have to figure out some things at home. See you tonight?"

"See you tonight."

Sitting on the porch swing, bare feet perched up in front of her, Dusty watches as her sister moves around the garden below. A wide, shallow basket that belonged to their grandfather sits at the edge of the garden, already filled with freshly harvested spinach, asparagus, radishes and the first ripe strawberries.

A breeze washes up the mountain, and Dusty sighs with relief. The day has felt like it's gone on forever, so hot it's like she's living in a fever dream.

"I can feel you watching me!" Opi calls out. She kneels down beside a bed of flowers—yarrow, coneflower, lavender and salvia. The bright afternoon sun amplifies their blooms, and Dusty is fascinated by the way Opi's colors react to the living world around her.

"Just making sure you're not slacking off!" Dusty calls backs. She shifts and the swing groans under her, swaying with movement.

Opi takes some scissors out of the back pocket of her shorts and begins to prune. Dusty has barely left her side since she returned from confronting JD this morning. Unsure of what to make of his animosity, or the fact that he's feeding on human blood, she's been overcome by an urge to watch over her sister. It makes her hope, selfishly, that Amber is letting him feed from her. It might be what's keeping other people safe.

Their dad has been in town running errands, leaving Dusty's mind still trapped on a loop of her mother's first memory. The more she replays it, the harder it is to fathom that her mom had really been that scared of her dad, or that the memory was real at all.

Gravel crunches in the driveway, and a minute later her dad appears from the side of the house, carrying two large trash bags.

"I come bearing gifts!" he calls.

Opi stands, brushing her hands on her cotton blouse. "Mulch?!"

He nods, grinning at her obvious excitement. "There was a big pile just outside town. Only five bucks a bag."

She runs over, opening one of the bags in a hurry to inspect what's inside. She scoops up a handful of small wood chips and sniffs. "Hardwood," she says. "I'll mix it with compost in case it rains. Last year I used too much and half of it ran down the mountain in that storm." She rolls her eyes and Dusty watches as their dad beams with pride. He hasn't noticed Dusty up in the shadows of the porch.

His phone trills. He pulls it out of his pocket, glancing at the screen before he lifts it to his ear. "Brookes?" he says.

Dusty's stomach drops.

Chris wanders over to the bottom of the steps, away from Opi, as he listens.

Dusty puts her feet down on the ground to stop the swing from swaying. She strains her hearing, turning down the sounds of the afternoon so she can pinpoint the voice on the other end of the line.

Cicadas, birds, the wind in the leaves. Dusty lets them fade away until Brookes' voice is clear.

". . . a shoe," he's saying. "One of those special ones for cyclists. It washed up on the bank of Black River a few miles north-east of the cabin."

Dusty swallows as the blood drains from her face.

"It might not be his," Brookes continues, "but it's the first lead we've had. There was some . . . flesh inside it. I think. We sent it off for testing. That'll get us an ID at least. But given that he's been missing almost a week, it doesn't bode well for the state of his body, if the shoe was his."

Dusty's stomach lurches as she gags.

"How can I help?" Chris asks. He looks up to the porch, noticing Dusty for the first time.

She tries her best at a smile, but when their eyes meet she looks away, trying to seem nonchalant, and continues to listen.

"We're going to need to take the dogs out again. They're on their way now."

"Okay," Chris says. "I'll meet you out there?"

"Yep. I'll wait at the cabin. We'll head out from there."

"Gotcha, see you soon."

Dusty looks back at her dad as he puts his phone back in his pocket. He looks at her for a long moment, his gaze making the surging panic inside her reach new, sickening heights. "Going somewhere?" she asks, her voice a pitch too high.

"Yeah," he says. "Sorry. I was looking forward to finally having a meal together tonight."

She lets out a shaky breath then tries on another smile. "All good," she says. "Is it to do with that missing man? What's his name again?"

"Andrew Everett. Yeah." He glances at his watch, then hovers, looking like he wants to say something. But instead he jogs up the steps, past Dusty, inside to change. By the time he leaves Dusty feels faint, her body riddled with nauseating anxiety.

24

Hunger Pains

Two weeks to go until summer vacation. This is what Dusty keeps telling herself on Monday morning, like a broken record, as she faces another week of high school as someone who is living on blood.

Scanning the students around her for Mali, who never responded to her messages, she doesn't make it inside the building before being met with her first obstacle. And it's arguably the biggest of them all.

Will is getting off the bus, just ahead of her. His headphones are on, and he looks deep in thought. Just the sight of him makes her breath hitch in her throat, and then his scent hits her.

"Dusty?" Opi says from beside her.

When she doesn't move or respond, Opi waves a hand in front of her face.

"Is she okay?" Theo asks.

Eyes still on Will, waiting for him to reach a safe distance ahead, breathing through her hunger pains, she can feel their concern rippling toward her, their changing colors lighting up her periphery. She can't believe there had been a time when all she had to worry about was not thinking about her mom. She'd welcome that pain in exchange for *this*—feeling so hungry for someone it hurts.

And it's not just his blood that she craves. She feels the memory of his eyes on hers on top of the mountain, the way they lingered on her lips, the way his voice, soft like the breeze, sent shivers over her skin. It had been so easy to open up to him, even though she knows she shouldn't have.

When he's finally inside, Dusty turns to Opi, forcing a smile. "I was just looking for Mali."

Opi's eyes narrow on her sister.

Still feeling protective of Opi, Dusty hadn't even wanted to go out to feed last night, but when Eli had made the point that *she* would be the danger to Opi if she didn't, Dusty had relented, but returned home within half an hour. She'd lain on her bed, feeling Opi's presence through the walls, then listened as her dad returned home from the search and went to bed.

He was still asleep this morning when it was time for his daughters to leave.

"Ready?" Opi asks, still eyeing Dusty.

Dusty nods and together with Theo, they continue inside.

The hallway of Black River High is crowded, an excited energy palpable in anticipation of summer.

"Hey!" Eli calls from where he stands by the lockers with Jesse and Matt. Despite his broad smile, his colors move with an anxious edge, flitting and twitching, restless.

"That's our cue," Opi says to Theo as she drags him away.

Dusty looks back at her sister, wanting to stay close, wanting to warn her about JD, but she's knows she can't be with her all day.

As Eli heads toward Dusty, Matt calls out, "What, no intro?"

"She's too good for you losers!" Eli calls back.

Dusty holds her hand up in an awkward wave.

Matt laughs and gives Dusty a mischievous smile, while Jesse's eyes remain on Eli, a curious look on his face.

When Eli reaches Dusty, he drapes his heavy arm over her shoulder.

"Why *don't* you want me to meet your friends?" she asks, looking up at him.

"Because you're my excuse to get away from them. And if they meet you, they'll like you, and then we'll be stuck with them, which is beside the point, remember?"

"Right," she says, noticing the strange way his colors still move, and how heavy his heartbeat thuds. "How was it with Jesse?"

"Fine," he says. "I think he convinced himself that he imagined things or was drunk or whatever. He even apologized."

Dusty glances sideways at him, the feeling that he's keeping something from her still niggling.

Eli pulls her closer and she rolls her eyes.

But he has a point, she thinks. Together, like this, she feels like she's in a bubble that safeguards them from the outside world. From everything they no longer are.

She's about to ask if he's seen JD or Amber yet, when someone bumps against her shoulder, hard.

"Hey!" she snaps, turning to see who it was.

Mali is striding away from her, purposefully not looking back. "I guess I deserved that," she mumbles. "I've gotta go," she says to Eli. "Cafeteria at lunch?" she calls, already moving to catch up with her friend.

"Mali, wait up!"

She doesn't stop.

"Mali!"

Dusty follows, and just before Mali reaches their homeroom she spins around. "What?" she asks, cold and expressionless.

It takes Dusty a second to adjust. She has never once experienced this side of Mali, and the feeling is completely surreal. "I'm so sorry I was M.I.A. on Saturday," she says. "I know we made plans, and I was a dick for forgetting. I've just been—"

"Shit, Dusty," Mali snaps, cutting Dusty off. "Not everything is about you. Do you always have to be so selfish?" She turns on her heel and walks into the classroom.

Through the doorway Dusty can see over a dozen faces staring at her, including a smirking JD, who has shaved his hair down to a buzz cut since yesterday, natural brown regrowing like a shadow, and Amber, her expression unreadable. The only person not looking up at Dusty is Will.

Slowly, she makes her way to her desk.

Between staring at JD, Amber and Mali's backs because they all refused to look at her, and trying to pretend that Will doesn't exist at all, Dusty's anxious head noise has trickled through her every limb all morning. She's been half expecting Deputy Sheriff Brookes to burst into the school at any moment, having found the body that the dogs have managed to link to her, and although Dusty is aware that police investigations, or forensics, don't work like that, her fear is real, justified, and she feels it everywhere.

As she makes her way to the cafeteria at lunch, she checks her phone, refreshing the *Adirondack Daily Enterprise* website over and over to see if there are any updates. There aren't, but it doesn't make her feel any better.

Inside the busy room, the smell of food thick and heavy, Dusty sees Mali at their usual table. Will is there too. Dusty can't help but think how out of place he looks, his colors, still mostly blues, remain close to him, the texture of the haze smoother than anyone else's in the room as he talks to Mali.

Dusty focuses her hearing through the clatter of trays, cutlery and people.

"Remind me why we aren't outside?" Will asks.

"What the fuck?" someone says loudly on the other side of the room, drawing Dusty's attention.

She looks over. It's Eli's table, where Eli is standing, slinging his bag over one shoulder.

"Don't mind us," Matt adds, "we weren't in the middle of a conversation or anything."

Jesse watches, that curious look still on his face as Eli walks away from his friends and makes his way toward Dusty. He nods to a half-empty table where they sit down, ignoring the eyes on them.

"Where's your food?" Eli jokes.

"Good one," she says dryly, unable to muster even an ounce of humor.

"Seriously though, do you think anyone will notice we're not eating?"

"Like who?" she says. "All my friends?"

Eli shrugs. "Your sister's over there."

Dusty glances over at Opi's table, where she's laughing with Theo and another friend, happily eating a veggie burger.

"I'm guessing it didn't go so well with Mali?" Eli adds.

Dusty shakes her head, then slumps her face into her hands as a wave of exhaustion hits her.

"JD's over there," he says, his voice low.

Dusty looks up, scanning the room.

"He shaved his head since yesterday," Eli adds. "It took me a while to find him. I'm assuming that's Amber with him?"

Dusty sees them at a table at the far side of the room, whispering close. Between them, there's an open textbook which JD tears a sliver of paper from, then scrunches it in a tiny ball, handing it to Amber. Looking around, JD's gaze lands on a table of freshmen on the far side of the room, then he whispers something to Amber.

Dusty filters through the sounds of the room to listen.

"Which one?" Amber asks.

"Hmm," JD says. "The girl in the pink top."

Amber smiles, then positions the tiny ball of paper on her right thumb before flicking it in the direction of the girl.

To Dusty's amazement, it lands directly on top of the girl's head, caught in her curls.

"What the fuck," Eli says.

Then they watch as JD and Amber repeat the game, taking turns, the little balls landing directly on their target each time.

"And I thought my friends were immature," Eli adds.

Just then, JD and Amber both turn and stare directly at Dusty and Eli.

Dusty's defenses awaken with a shiver, and she can feel Eli's right there with her.

JD smiles, then tears another strip of paper, balls it up and flicks it. The ball lands in Opi's hair.

Opi's hand reaches up to the spot the ball hit her, looking around, confused.

"You're fucking kidding me," Eli says, moving to stand, but Dusty reaches for his arm, stopping him as she notices Mali approaching JD and Amber's table.

"Amber?" Mali says cautiously.

Amber glances at JD, who smiles at Mali, relaxed.

Mali looks between the new couple, curious, then turns directly to Amber. "Can we talk for a minute?"

Amber looks at JD again, who raises his eyebrows. She looks back at Mali. "What's up?"

"I meant in private?" Mali says.

"Don't mind me," JD cuts in. "We're all friends." His voice has the same edge it had yesterday, and from Mali's expression, it's clearly as unrecognizable to her as it had been to Dusty.

"Just wanted to check in," Mali says awkwardly. "See how you're doing . . . I'm sorry I wasn't around much last week. I didn't mean to upset you, or to make you feel like we couldn't sit together anymore . . ."

She waits, giving Amber a chance to say something.

JD and Amber look at each other again, then burst into laughter.

"What's so funny?" Mali frowns.

"Sorry," JD says, still chuckling. "That was rude. We've just been . . . busy getting to know each other, that's all."

"Is that why you haven't replied to any of my messages?" Mali asks Amber.

Amber doesn't answer. She just sits there, biting down on a smile.

Mali looks between them, brows furrowed. When it's clear the conversation is going nowhere, she turns to go back to Will.

Dusty watches as JD rips a clump of pages out of the textbook, scrunches them up into a tight, fist-sized ball, then pegs it.

The paper flies fast, hitting the back of Mali's head with precision.

As Mali turns to look back, Dusty stands, her chair skidding back across the shiny floor. She hadn't wanted to make a scene, but her caution has evaporated, her temper too hot for her to think clearly.

The room goes quiet as she walks straight up to JD, glaring at him as he looks up at her with a sly grin. Dusty doesn't have to look to know that Eli is beside her.

"What the fuck, JD?" she hisses. "Drop the villain act or—"

"Or what?" He smirks.

"Not here," Eli says quietly. From the sound of his voice, Dusty can tell his jaw is clenched.

"Eli Blake," JD says. "Who died and made you notice anyone other than your own reflection?" He leans back in his chair, smug, baiting Eli.

"What is wrong with you?" Eli whispers. "It's like you want everyone to know—"

"Oh so this *is* about you," JD says loudly. "For a second I thought something was different. That you'd changed." He smiles, staring Eli directly in the eyes.

The room has gone completely still and quiet, the tension so visceral Dusty can feel it crackling against her skin. She finally lets herself glance around, noticing that Matt and Jesse have stood up at their table, ready to come over if Eli needs them. Opi, Theo and their friends are silently watching, and Mali is still standing where she'd been hit, Will by her side.

"We were just having some fun," JD adds. "Testing out some of our new-found skills."

"Not here," Eli repeats.

"Or what?" JD asks with amused condescension. "Who made you the authority on what we can and can't do? You, more than anyone, should know that popularity doesn't make you powerful. Not anymore."

Dusty can feel Eli's anger soaring, his colors red and hot, swarming down around JD as he stares at him. Then, she watches as Eli's colors appear to penetrate JD's head, sinking inside him. JD's own colors disappear completely.

"I said, not here," Eli repeats firmly, calmer now.

JD's eyes are glazed and unfocused. "Not here," he echoes quietly.

Amber turns to look at JD, then gently shakes his shoulder. "JD?" she says, concern creeping into her voice.

Dusty reaches for Eli's hand. "Let's go," she whispers, then pulls, coaxing him away.

Eli's colors begin to retreat from JD, greens, blues and oranges overtaking the reds, as he finally breaks eye contact.

"What *was* that?" JD whispers, amazed.

Eli huffs a laugh, then flashes JD a knowing smile.

Dusty pulls at Eli once more. "Let's go," she whispers.

Finally, he turns to walk away.

Dusty looks back at Mali, who is staring at Dusty exactly like her dad does now—like she's a stranger.

"That little shit," Eli growls as Dusty follows him into the empty hall. "He was baiting us."

"And we almost took it," Dusty says, a heady cocktail of adrenaline, exhaustion and shock pounding at her temples. "But you . . . you really did it. You had control over him."

"Yeah. And everyone was watching." Eli's fists clench in a fresh wave of frustration and he grunts as he kicks a low locker with full force, just as the cafeteria door swings open.

Mali stands there, her brow knotted in confusion as she stares down at the locker, its metal door crumpled inward.

Dusty scrambles to think of excuses, but when Mali finally looks up at her, it's as if she knows Dusty is about to tell her another lie.

"Don't," Mali says. Her eyes are full of emotion, like she's holding back tears. "There is something going on with everyone on your mountain, and you're going to tell me what it is. Right now."

Dusty's eyes widen as an image fills her mind—Mali and Kristen King, who lives on White Mountain too, walking away from the bonfire together, into the darkness.

"What happened with Kristen?"

"Uh uh," Mali says, shaking her head. "You first. And start from the beginning."

Dusty looks ahead through her windscreen at their boxy high school. They're sitting in her car, the only place they could be guaranteed total privacy. But she's already starting to regret such a confined space, her hunger as present as her anxiety, clawing under her skin.

Dusty takes a moment to breathe before she begins. "It all started the Tuesday before the bonfire, that day I was late for school . . ."

She tells Mali about the presence, the sleepwalking, why they left the bonfire, how they fed from animals, the fact that her relationship with Eli is just a cover story, that they hunt at night. She tells her everything, except two things—what they did to Andrew Everett, and the fact that all the animal blood in the world can't stop her from craving Will.

Dusty doesn't look at her best friend once, until she's finished talking. Slowly, she turns to Mali, whose drained face is wet with silent tears. Her colors—dark reds, greens and purples—are coiled around her like a protective shield.

There's a long silence as Dusty's story hangs between them.

Mali plays with the hem of her top, her eyes blinking in thought. "I wouldn't believe you if it didn't explain so much," she finally says. "Kristen . . . JD and Amber . . . You . . ."

Dusty reaches out and takes Mali's hand in her own. "What happened with Kristen?" she asks again.

Mali's eyes don't meet Dusty's, but she doesn't pull her hand away, and Dusty feels a glimmer of hope.

"It was so fucked up," Mali starts, her voice shaky. "We were dancing. Close. I could tell she was into me. Like, really into me. Everything was moving fast, in a good way, so I led her somewhere we could be alone. There was a field nearby. Out of sight. The grass was taller. And there were some trees just beyond. We could still hear the music, but we were alone." She sniffles, hesitating over the memory. "So we started kissing. It was amazing, it felt . . . right, you know? But then her kisses became . . . harder. She pulled at my lip . . . with her teeth and . . . fuck, Dust, she *bit* me."

Dusty swallows, consciously trying to push away her own feelings to be present for her friend. She doesn't have to feign the look of shock that's on her face. "Mali . . ." she whispers. "Are you okay?"

Mali looks up at her, and her eyes say it all. *No.*

She continues, "At first, I thought she was just . . . really into it. But it hurt. It really hurt. I tried to push her away and she let go of my lip. I thought it was over. But then she grabbed my face and started to . . . *lick* my lip. I think I was bleeding. I didn't know what to do, so I slapped her in the face. Hard. She was so shocked that she stopped. Her whole body was trembling. I put my hand on her shoulder to see if she was okay, but when I touched her, she started sobbing." Mali shakes her head. "She just looked up at the sky crying, telling me to get away from her. She was hysterical. It was so scary, I can't even . . ." She sighs, lost for words.

"So what did you do?" Dusty asks.

"I ran. I ran into the trees and by the time I stopped, I was lost. Eventually, I found the road, but I was way out of town and it took me all night to get back. Will found me the next morning. That's when I found out you were missing."

"I'm so sorry I wasn't there for you."

Mali pulls her hand away and looks up to meet Dusty's gaze. Her eyes are unreadable. "Were you ever going to tell me? If JD hadn't forced your hand today, would you have just kept me in the dark?"

"I don't . . . I didn't know how to," she says frantically. "I didn't want you to look at me like you're looking at me now. And I didn't know about Kristen. If I had, I would have told you right away. I'm so sorry you had to go through that on your own."

Mali sighs. "Honestly, you being missing the next night was a good distraction, if that makes sense? If I hadn't been worried about you, I think I would have lost it. I even almost convinced myself I'd imagined it. There wasn't even a bite mark on my lip. It didn't make sense."

Dusty nods. "Yeah, it's weird. If we lick a wound, it heals."

Mali doesn't bother to hide the disgust on her face. "So, you really . . . don't know what happened to you? Or why?"

"No," she says, but her head is spinning, wondering how Kristen managed to pull away from Mali, on what sounds like her first time, when Dusty hadn't been able to stop herself. Mali doesn't know how close she'd been to dying. Noticing some dust on the dashboard, she swipes it away. "We're trying to figure it out," she says. "It's been hard. Our . . . hunger is distracting, and that came first for a few days. And even though we knew the mountain was the most likely link between me and Eli, our families didn't change, so it wasn't until Eli had a vision from JD's point of view, and I had one of someone else—"

"Kristen?" Mali asks.

"I mean, now you've told me what happened, I think it must have been her." Dusty's brow furrows as a thought occurs to her. "Have you seen her? Since the bonfire?"

Mali shakes her head. "No. Not at all. But she's a senior, we don't have any classes together. And I just assumed she was avoiding me."

"Have you told anyone else what happened?"

"Told them what? That the girl I was making out with bit me aggressively? Oh, but there's no actual wound to prove it? Will's the only one who asked, anyway . . ." She looks up at the school through the window. "What about Amber? Do you think . . . is JD *feeding* from her?" She shudders. "Fuck, I can't believe I just asked that."

Dusty is quiet for a long moment, letting her own self-loathing simmer down as she tries to think. Finally, she says, "That's what made the most sense—that JD was feeding from her, and it was just a few people who live on the mountain who had changed. But after watching her today . . ." She shakes her head. "I think she's changed too."

"Jesus," Mali says. "So does that mean it could happen to *anyone*?"

Dusty doesn't answer.

"And you?" Mali asks. "You said you left the bonfire because you realized *you* wanted human blood?"

Dusty nods.

"But you've been feeding from animals instead?"

Dusty nods again. *It's not a total lie*, she tells herself.

"And you don't . . . want it from people now?"

Shit. She shakes her head. *Liar. Monster.*

"Okay," Mali says, considering. "So what are we going to do about Amber?"

To Dusty's relief, the school bell goes off. Lunch is over. "Leave it to me," she says.

"What do you m—"

"Mali, promise me you will leave this, for now?"

"*Leave* this? Are you serious?"

"JD is dangerous. I can feel it. They both might be. And I don't think they're hunting animals. Or at least JD isn't, which means—"

"That people deserve to know."

Dusty shoots Mali a look that makes Mali recoil.

Dusty breathes. "I'm sorry," she whispers. "Please. Please don't tell anyone. Not until we know what we're really dealing with."

Mali slowly nods, but Dusty can smell the fear and confusion on her. "I'm sorry this happened to you," Mali says. "Believe me, I am. But you have to understand how crazy this is."

"I do."

"What about Opi? Does she know?"

"No," Dusty says, her panic rising. "Please. We just need some time to figure it all out. Maybe we can reverse it."

"How? What could you find out that you don't already know?"

Dusty's pulse is pounding in her ears and her skin is slick with clammy sweat. She wipes her hands on her jeans. "I don't know," she whispers.

"And we're just supposed to get out of this car and pretend that everything's normal?"

Hot tears begin to fall from Dusty's eyes.

"Oh my babe," Mali says, her shoulders dropping. "Come here." She leans over the center console, hesitating only for a second before she pulls Dusty close.

But with her face buried in Mali's neck, Dusty's teeth begin to ache. She can smell it, coursing through her best friend. Blood. So much blood. She pushes Mali away. "I just need some answers," she says, wiping her wet cheeks. "Something. Anything."

PART IV

25

Gravity

Looking up at the gray shingled roof and stone chimney, Dusty is now certain that it was Kristen's eyes she'd seen through.

She's standing outside the picture-perfect mountain home with dusky-blue panel siding and white trim around the windows and beams. The paved driveway runs downhill from the road, then broadens to meet the house and the matching double garage beside it. The house itself is two stories from the front, but positioned on a steep slope so that it continues down into a third story. Below that, Dusty can tell from the rippling light hitting the surrounding trees that there's a pool.

Out of the corner of her eye she sees a curtain move from one of the second story windows. Someone is home.

Dusty approaches the front door, grateful that Eli is hanging back, hidden by the forest. When they'd met up on the road, Eli's energy was more anxious than usual, wound up from their confrontation with JD. He'd wanted to come too, but Dusty thought she might have better luck talking to Kristen if it didn't feel like an ambush. Besides, Dusty could smell animal blood on him, and he was covered in dirt and sweat.

She presses the doorbell.

As she waits, the house remains silent. She rings again but there's still no answer. She can vaguely sense the presence of one person inside, and Dusty is pretty sure Kristen is an only child, but just to make sure, she walks over to the garage and peers through a small pane of glass. There are no cars inside.

"Kristen!" Dusty calls out, taking a bet that it's her hiding out. "Kristen!" she calls again. "My name is Dusty, I'm a friend of Mali's."

Dusty scans the windows of the house, dark facing the light outside. There's no movement.

"We need to talk," she says, quietly, knowing that if it is Kristen inside, only she will be able to hear her. "I know what you are, because I've changed too."

She waits another moment before she hears footsteps, followed by the front door creaking open, just a crack. Dusty moves closer.

The door opens a little more, until Kristen is revealed in full view.

Dusty tries to keep a neutral expression, but she is looking at a very different Kristen King to the one she'd seen the night of the bonfire.

The valedictorian, star athlete with the outward appearance of a Barbie doll, who is always, always perfectly polished, is a complete mess. Her blonde hair is a disheveled, greasy heap tied up in a messy bun. She's wearing track shorts with a baggy Harvard t-shirt tucked into them, no bra underneath. Her bare feet are filthy, but not just with mud or things you'd pick up in the forest—they're coated in the grime and build-up of someone who's been walking barefoot outdoors and hasn't showered in weeks. There are scratches on her tanned legs that haven't been cleaned or tended to, and her face, which is normally made up with skillfully discreet makeup, is bare other than the black remnants of old mascara under her eyes.

Kristen is also looking Dusty up and down, clearly intrigued by what she sees. She scans Dusty's face, her expression shifting as she notices one thing and another.

"I'm sorry to come here like this," Dusty starts. "But Mali only just told me what happened."

Kristen's heart rate accelerates instantly.

"It's okay," Dusty puts up her hands. "*She's* okay. And honestly, I'm just amazed you were . . . that you didn't—"

"Prove it," Kristen says softly. "Prove what you are."

"I don't . . . How?"

Kristen shrugs, waiting.

"Okay," Dusty says reluctantly, then she lifts her own forearm up to her mouth and bites.

Kristen's eyes widen as she watches blood trickle down Dusty's arm, then stop as Dusty licks the wound, sealing it. Kristen gulps and her words come out in a shaky whisper. "I didn't mean it . . . With Mali. I didn't know."

"I know." The heat of the afternoon, combined with her stress and growing hunger, are making Dusty nauseous and lightheaded. She notices steps that lead down onto a stone terrace beside the house, with a firepit surrounded by chairs. She nods toward it. "Can we sit down?"

Kristen hesitates, then nods her head slowly. As Dusty leads her down the steps, she looks back and notices Kristen is squinting her eyes so tight they're almost closed. Dusty wonders when she last left the house in the daylight.

Finally seated, Dusty says, "There are others like us, here on White Mountain."

Kristen looks dazed, like she's struggling to compute what she's hearing.

"You know Eli?" Dusty explains. "At the bonfire, I realized he was like me. That he was changing too. So we ran away together. We stayed away, hunting animals for a few days. Now we hunt here on the mountain."

"Animals?" Kristen asks, confused.

Dusty nods. "For their blood. Deer, mostly. They're big enough that we don't kill them."

Kristen nods, slowly understanding. "Who else?"

"Do you know JD?"

It's clear that Kristen doesn't.

"He's a junior, like me and Eli. He lives a little further up the mountain."

Kristen is thoughtful, and as Dusty watches her, she realizes that although she's unkempt, her complexion is glowing. And the more her eyes get used to the light, they open to reveal that they're clear and bright, the whites almost pure white. There isn't a trace of discoloration under them, no signs of fatigue, and her cheeks are flushed with rosy warmth.

"Are you . . . How have you been feeding?" Dusty asks, tentative.

Kristen looks up, cagey and scared.

Dusty decides to take a different approach. "I was pretty amazed when Mali told me what happened. How did you stop yourself?"

Kristen inhales, like she wants to swallow up the memory and trap it inside her. But instead, she sighs. "I don't know. I didn't know what was happening or what I was doing." Her eyes fill with pain as she speaks. "When Mali slapped me there was this moment when I knew that if I tasted her again, I wouldn't be able to stop. So I focused everything I had on letting her get away. I liked her so much . . . And then, when I knew she was gone, I just ran in the other direction. Away from the party . . ." She's lost in her thoughts for a moment, then finally says, "Until I came home."

"And you've been here ever since?"

"Sort of. I go out, sometimes, at night. To . . . hunt, like you. But not in the day." She shakes her head as if the idea of being outside in the daylight is insane.

"Is that because of the heat?" Dusty asks.

"I guess. And just, people . . ." She looks Dusty up and down suspiciously. "How are you wearing that? Aren't you hot?"

Dusty looks down at her sneakers, jeans and white tank top. She's already decided it's the last time she'll wear jeans until fall, at least. "Yeah. Insanely. What about school?"

Kristen laughs. It's bordering on frantic and more than a little unhinged. "Why would I go to school?"

"Well . . . I still do."

The look on Kristen's face makes it clear that to her, this is the most bizarre thing about their conversation.

"If I didn't, my dad and my sister would know something is wrong," Dusty explains.

Kristen takes this in.

"What about you? What have you told your parents?"

"Oh, they think I've had a nervous breakdown," she says, matter-of-fact. "Which I guess I have. They make me have these Zoom appointments with a psychiatrist. They tried to make me go in person but I lost it. Zoom was the compromise. I refuse to speak, which is probably more convincing. She wants to medicate me. My parents think it's because I was too focused on school. That I've burned out. And I've already been accepted to Harvard, so as long as I sit for finals . . ." She shrugs.

Dusty doesn't know what to say. She doesn't really know this girl, and other than the fact that she has always seemed like a nice person, she has no idea what her version of normal is. But it's clear that she's struggling. She's been alone in this. Reaching out with her senses,

Dusty finds Eli close by. He feels panicked, chaotic, and Dusty has a sudden urge to get back to him. She's never been more grateful that she's had Eli, no matter how horrible this has been, or what they've done.

"You're not alone, you know?" Dusty says. "I don't know much about what's happened to us, but as of today, what I do know is that a few of us from the mountain started to change at the same time—you, me, Eli and JD. My little sister, and Eli's little brother are fine."

"So the older teens?" Kristen asks.

Dusty hadn't thought of it like that until now, but she slowly nods. "I guess. My sister's a sophomore, and Eli's brother's only eleven. Can you think of any other teens that live here?"

Kristen shakes her head. "Not that I know of."

"There's one other girl from town," Dusty adds. "Amber, who's been spending a lot of time with JD. But other than her, whatever has happened seems to be isolated to this mountain. I haven't been able to find anything similar online, and everyone at school seems the same. But somehow, we're connected. Have you had any visions?"

"Visions?"

"Yeah, like glimpses into someone's mind?"

She shakes her head. "I don't think so."

"That's okay. It's only happened once or twice for me and Eli . . . other than the ones I'm having of my mom."

"Your mom?" Kristen asks, confused.

"Sorry. This is a lot, I know. All I'm trying to say is that we're in this together, and if there's anything you need or want to talk about, I'm here."

Kristen's face is scrunched up in a frown.

"In the week before the bonfire," Dusty presses, "did anything weird happen to you?"

Kristen thinks, as if she's looking back years into the past. Finally, her eyes meet Dusty's. "When I woke up that Wednesday morning and I felt like I was getting sick, it was so weird—I was sunburned."

Dusty tilts her head, questioning.

"Like, the whole front of my body, not the back," Kristen continues. "Which is crazy, because I'd been at school all Tuesday and then I was planning this fundraiser in my room all afternoon. And I swear when I went to bed, I looked normal. But then the next day I got that fever and needed to sleep and by the time I was feeling better the sunburn had faded away."

"Do you think you could've left the house that night? Eli and I both think we went outside, but we don't remember it. Like we were sleepwalking."

Her eyes become vacant, lost somewhere else, before she nods slowly. "Yeah. I keep having these memories. Like dreams, except I haven't slept so they couldn't be, and in them I'm walking through the forest in the middle of the night."

"You haven't slept at all?" Dusty asks. She's only had scattered moments of rest herself, but no sleep at all seems unfathomable.

"Why would I?" Kristen asks, confused. "I don't feel like I need to."

"You're not tired, at all?"

Kristen shakes her head, and Dusty wonders again what, or who, she's feeding from.

"So I'm assuming that means you haven't levitated?" Dusty asks.

From Kristen's expression it's clear that she has no idea what Dusty's talking about.

"What about any other . . . abilities?"

"Abilities?"

"Yeah, other than your senses, or feeling stronger and faster?"

Kristen considers, then shakes her head. "Why?"

Dusty considers telling her, but decides baby steps might be best for now. She doesn't want to overwhelm her, and she doesn't need another enemy.

They'll need to work together if they want answers.

Feeling Eli's anxiety increasing, Dusty stands. "I've got to go, I'm sorry." Moving closer to Kristen, she squats down in front of her, trying to catch her glazed stare. "I can't imagine what you've been through, Kristen, going through this alone." She takes her hand, which is hot like her own. "I'll give you my number," Dusty says. It's clear that Kristen doesn't have her phone, so Dusty takes a pen out of her backpack and writes her number on Kristen's forearm. "Message me if you need anything. Or you might even be able to reach out in other ways. I meant it when I said we're all connected somehow." She squeezes Kristen's hand before she walks back up to the driveway.

Dusty finds Eli pacing through the shadows of trees. The rich scent of earth, rising in the heat, surrounds him like a fog.

"I've gotta blow off some steam," he says.

Dusty can hear his heart racing.

"Is it what happened, with JD?" Dusty asks.

"He was throwing paper balls at people's heads. What is he, ten? Who the fuck does that?" Eli reaches up and puts his hands on the top of his head as he continues to pace, his t-shirt clinging to his sweat-soaked body.

"Eli," Dusty says softly.

He doesn't stop moving. Back and forth, red and orange surrounding him, uncontrolled, reaching out in every direction.

"Eli," she says, louder this time. "What's going on? Is this about the mind control? And what happened with Jesse?"

He squats down to the ground, his knees bent low as he runs his hands over his hair and face.

Dusty runs to his side, bending down and placing her arm around him. "You can tell me anything," she whispers. "I mean it."

He looks up, his green eyes meeting hers, the whites marked with tiny red veins, purple darkening the skin around them.

"You won't understand," he says. "It's different for you."

"What's different?"

He lets himself fall back, so he's sitting on the leaf-covered forest floor.

Dusty moves so she's facing him. She sits, legs crossed, waiting for him to say more.

"I'm so fucked up," he says, his face crumpling with worry.

"What, Eli? Please, tell me. I can't help if I don't know."

He lets out a sigh, trying to steady his rapid breathing. "It's Jesse," he says.

"Eli, you didn't know what you were doing. You didn't—"

"It's not the mind control. It's . . . he's . . . He's the person I want to feed from the *most*."

Dusty lets out a breath, finally understanding. "Do you . . . just want to feed from him?" she asks, cautiously. "Or is it more than that?"

"I don't know," he says, shaking his head. "I mean, it's like you said, with Will. He definitely smells better than everyone else. *Different*. But Dusty, I swear, I'm *not* into guys that way." He picks up a leaf and begins to rip it. Over and over until the pieces are so small there's nothing left.

"Eli, we don't know anything about this. We don't know how this works. Just because he's your . . . taste . . . it doesn't mean you want him in other ways."

"But with Will . . . you called it *bloodlust*. It's so confusing. I swear I've only ever been into girls. But now . . . I don't know who I am anymore. What if more of me has changed than I realized?"

"Well, maybe it has. And I understand that that might feel scary, but we can deal with that, eventually."

"But why Jesse?" Eli sighs. "Why does it have to be my friend? When I'm around him I don't know how to act. It's making me feel crazy."

Dusty considers what he's saying, remembering how her hunger for Will goes hand in hand with wanting to kiss him. With wanting *him*. "When you're around him," she asks, "Do you think about him in other ways? Aside from your hunger?"

Eli groans. "I don't know. No? I don't think so. When you see Will, what's it like?"

Dusty closes her eyes, and Will is instantly there. His stormy blue eyes tracing her face, the feeling of him, the urge to taste his lips on hers.

"Fuck," Eli says.

Dusty opens her eyes, feeling herself blushing. "What?"

"You're right, maybe it isn't the same," he says, eyebrows raised.

"You felt that?"

He nods, letting his mouth twist into a cheeky grin.

Dusty buries her head in her hands, her voice muffled as she asks, "What're we going to do?"

"You know we can't keep going with the animals, don't you?" His voice is deep and serious.

She whips her head up to face him. "What do you mean?"

He levels his eyes with hers. "Dusty . . ."

"No," she says, shaking her head. "No. No. No."

"If JD can do it, and he's clearly some kind of psychopath, we can too. We *can* feed without killing."

"So you *want* to be like JD?"

"No! Of course not. But, just like normal people, people like *us* don't have to be all the same. You know it's not like that. Like you with the colors. I bet you've always been good at reading people. Don't they call that something? Emotional intelligence?"

Dusty hasn't thought about it this way, but of course he's right.

"And Kristen," he continues. "She's like, an insane combination of being really nice and really fucking disciplined. She's always thrived off that shit. That's probably how she stopped herself with Mali. Plus, girls just have better impulse control."

"Not me," Dusty says, her stomach sinking like a stone as she pictures Andrew Everett, the life gone from his body.

"There were two of us, Dusty. He was gone before we knew what was happening."

She can't speak. The hum of crickets sounds louder with every passing second.

"Dusty, *you* stopped with the deer. I wouldn't have been able to if you weren't there. I know you can do it." He reaches out and puts his hand on her leg. "We're fading away. Can't you feel it? We need to feed. We need human blood."

"No," she finally repeats, standing so his hand drops away from her.

"Wait," Eli says, standing so they're face-to-face again, breathless.

Slowly, his colors begin to shift, reacting to their proximity, and he slips his arm around her waist to pull her closer, his forehead pressed against hers, their lips a breath apart.

"Eli," she says softly. "I can't . . . I don't know how I feel—"

"I know," he says, sighing against her. "I don't know either."

They remain there like that for a moment, so close it feels like they're one, until Eli steps back. "I've gotta go," he says. "I need to move."

Dusty nods. "Okay."

"Thanks for hearing me out," he says.

"Any time."

"Come find me, if you need me?"

She nods again, before turning, uncertain as ever, and heading into the forest. Alone.

26

I Shouldn't Be Here

By the end of the week, as the sun sets on another Friday of this new reality, Dusty is wondering what excuse she might use for not eating dinner at home. Trying to keep up her school grades, she's spent every night trying to focus on final assignments, pretending to eat meals in her bedroom as her unabating hunger, fatigue and anxiety swarm within.

She hasn't heard anything new about Andrew Everett, nothing about the search efforts, and she hasn't gotten any closer to figuring out what's happened to her or what happened to her mom. The seclusion has made her dad feel more like a stranger than ever. A mysterious presence who lurks on the other side of the wall.

But he's home now, and the dread of having to face him coats her.

She looks at her reflection in the mirror, trying to conjure another of her mother's memories for the thousandth time. But nothing comes. Instead, the smell of food from the kitchen rises up to her room and makes her stomach churn, even with the window wide open.

She and Eli have taken turns hunting every night, keeping an eye on each other's houses, worried about what JD and Amber might try next. But by Thursday it had felt pointless. There'd been no trace of

JD or Amber anywhere on the mountain outside of JD's property, and they haven't caused any more trouble at school that Dusty knows of. She wonders if what Eli did, taking control of JD's mind like that, had rattled them enough to keep them in check.

Not being out there hunting together has only added to the distance she feels between herself and Eli. He hasn't been back to school since Monday. He's been focused on riding, and Dusty hasn't gone to see him on his track.

So, when she heads downstairs to tell Opi and her dad that she's meeting Eli for dinner, she'll be dishing out a double lie. She places her hand on the doorknob, but a tingle pulls at her brain.

She stands among the trees, blinking, wondering how she got here.

Her mind twists with confusion, searching for answers. She had been walking up to the summit to watch the sunrise, but now, the sun is high in the sky.

Breathless, she starts to run downhill, until she sees home through the trees.

She rushes inside, up the stairs, ignoring the voices from somewhere behind her. When she gets to the spare room she turns the old key, making sure the door is locked.

A moment later, the muffled voice of a child calls out, "Mom!"

"Mommy!" yells another. "Where are you?"

She covers her mouth with a shaking hand. Terrified.

There's a gentle knock, right on the other side of the door. She hadn't known he was there.

"Sarah," her husband's voice says softly. "The girls have made something for you. Do you think you could come out so they can show you?"

She can hear the pain in his voice, but she remains silent.

"I know you need your space, honey, but they need you. I need you."

There's a long pause. She doesn't breathe.

His footsteps trail away, and she crumples down onto the floor. Terrified of everyone.

Dusty's own hand trembles against the doorknob, her mind processing what she just experienced.

Her mother had been as scared of her own daughters as she had been of her husband. Not only that, she'd been scared of herself.

Had she been delusional? Dusty wonders. *Had her mind been playing tricks on her? Was she unwell? Is she still unwell?*

And then it dawns on her—her mom had been lost, confused in the forest, confused about how time had passed and how she'd gotten there. Like what had happened to Dusty and Opi when they went foraging.

Dusty breathes, reeling, trying to connect the dots.

If her mom was terrified of her children, could it have been because she was terrified of what she might do to them? Could she have changed, just like Dusty has? Could that be the reason she left?

Her head spins with memories. The way her mom retreated and pushed her loved ones away, just like she has. The way, before she left, she wouldn't come down for meals, and how she couldn't even look at them most days.

Distant. Distracted. Detached.

Trembling, Dusty thinks of her father. What he's gone through, and the gentle care she'd heard in his voice, trying his best to hold his family together.

She feels like her heart is in a billion pieces, shattered by guilt. *How could I have ever doubted him?*

Suddenly, all she wants is to be in her dad's arms. Her chest heaves with sobs that never make it out her mouth. She's drowning in the heartbreak of it all. All over again. His, her own, Opi's, and her mother's.

Her feet tread quickly down the stairs. Her dad and Opi are sitting at the dining table, as if they've been waiting for her. There's something formal in the way that they're positioned, serious, and there's a stack of leaflets in front of them.

Dusty is more than a little taken aback. The contrast to her heightened emotions jarring.

She glances at the title of the leaflet on top—"Understanding Eating Disorders."

Shit. Here we go.

Dusty sits down opposite them, tremors of her feelings still flowing through her. She lets out a sigh as she picks up the leaflets and starts flicking through them.

Her dad and Opi let her take in what's happening as Dusty tries to think about what she can possibly say to this. When she looks up, their faces are so full of love and concern, but from their heartbeats and the colors that drift like clouds around them—gray and yellow with bursts of pink from Opi—Dusty knows that they're anxious.

Tears pool on the rims of her eyes, more present these past few weeks than any other time in her life.

"Dad . . . Op," she begins, looking between them, digging into her deepest stores of energy to face this. "I love you so much, and I am so grateful for the way you love me. I've been . . . distant, I know, and you're right, I haven't been eating as much as I usually do. I've been stressed and distracted. But I can assure you, I *do not* have an eating disorder."

Her dad clears his throat to speak but Opi cuts in. "You haven't been in the cafeteria since Monday. I know you're not eating at school."

Dusty feels like she can't breathe. She closes her eyes, trying to will this conversation to magically end.

"Dust," Opi pleads. "You look terrible. Your eyes—"

Dusty looks at her sister. "I've been crying a lot, okay?" It's not a lie, at least. "And I haven't been in the cafeteria because I don't want another weird confrontation with JD."

"What confrontation with JD?" her dad asks, but his daughters ignore him.

"And it's still all this mom stuff," Dusty admits. Again, not a lie. "Do you . . . Dad, are you worried about me not eating, because she hadn't been eating too?"

Her dad frowns. "Your mom?"

Dusty nods.

"No, sweetheart. I mean, sure, when she was . . . withdrawn . . . toward the end . . ."

The words *the end* feel like a punch in the guts. So final. "What about sleep? Was she sleeping?" Dusty asks.

"Honestly, kiddo, I don't know. She was mostly staying in the spare room, which is your room now. Are you wondering if she left because she was hiding some sort of illness?"

"I don't know, maybe."

"I don't think so, Dust."

"I'm just . . . I'm trying to understand. What do you know about her childhood?"

Her dad leans back in his seat. "You know everything I know, honey. She never spoke about it. Just that she grew up in Georgia, and that her parents died when she was eighteen. But . . ."

"What?" Opi asks.

"Well, she never told me *how* they died. Which made me think . . . it must have been terrible. I asked, lots of times, but she couldn't speak about it. It was only a few years before we met. I could tell she carried the sadness with her, but it didn't stop her from feeling joy too. It didn't stop her from being able to love. But over time, it was like it all came back to the surface again. And it ate her up. Sometimes it was like she'd hit an off switch just to cope. To be around other people. Even us."

The familiarity of his description churns Dusty up from the inside.

"But life kept going, you know?" He leans forward, his elbows on the table. "When you're married, it's easy to believe that time heals all wounds. That what you've built together can bury the past. You forget your partner had a life before you, and it's hard to understand how it still affects them. Especially when they won't talk to you about it. And it wasn't until your grandparents were gone, my parents, and the house wasn't as full . . . it kind of showed how much she'd relied on them, especially with you girls and the day-to-day, and she started to slip further and further away from us. I was so busy trying to hold what was left here together that by the time I noticed how bad it was, it was too late. She'd shut us out. And then she was gone."

Gone. Another punch, but this time directly to the heart.

"But you're not her, honey," her dad says. "Sometimes I do worry that you keep things too close to your chest. That you don't open up—"

"I can't do this," Dusty says, standing. She feels like she's inside a furnace, her emotions running so hot she's afraid she'll combust. Her eyes meet her dad's and the love she sees is all she needs to be rushing around the table, falling into his lap and wrapping her arms around his shoulders.

A hand brushes the hair out of her face, and she looks up to see Opi beside them, reaching out, still riddled with concern.

Dusty meets her eyes and mouths, "I'm okay."

"Okay," Opi mouths back.

Dusty remains there for a moment, wondering how much longer she can lie. Wondering if it will play out exactly like it did with her mom. If she'll have to leave them in the end, to keep them safe from whatever she is.

"Honey," her dad says, leaning back so he can see Dusty properly. "We just wanted to make sure you're okay, and for you to know that we're here to support you, whatever it is you're going through. At first, I thought it was drugs, but—"

"Dad," Dusty cuts in. She tries to take in a deep breath, but it's more like a gasp. She swallows it. "Thank you," she manages. "I'm sorry that you're so worried about me. But I promise, I *am* eating. And I have never done any drugs. It's just . . . I'm going to go see Eli now. Okay?"

Opi and Chris look at each other, then back at Dusty.

"Are you sure about him, Dust?" he asks. "I'm sorry if we upset you—"

"No, it's okay Dad. *I'm* okay. And Eli is amazing. Really. You should give him a chance." Then, letting go of her dad, she stands. "Thank you," she says. "I mean it. And I love you."

Before she has a chance to unravel again, she turns to leave.

It doesn't fully hit her that she has nowhere to go until she's in her car with the ignition on.

She calls Mali.

"I'm with some of the girls from the team!" Mali shouts. "We're on our way to that party at North Lake!"

Dusty had forgotten. Mali had offered to come be with her tonight, but, naively, Dusty had said she wanted to be alone.

All week she'd felt like Mali was walking on eggshells around her—studying Dusty when she thought she wasn't looking, Mali's colors revealing her hesitation and fear. So Dusty had made herself scarce. She'd tried sitting outside, noticing tiny bees fly in and out of the house Will had made, smiling at the growth of the seedlings beneath as they sprouted closer to the sun each day. But when she'd heard Will and Mali approaching the fire exit, she'd fled.

So now, Dusty tries her best impression of "normal", saying, "Oh, that's right! You guys have fun!"

"Want me to come to you?" Mali yells over music. "Josie, pull over!"

"No, no," Dusty says. "You have fun! I'll see you tomorrow?"

Mali agrees and Dusty puts the phone down.

Immediately, she indulges an urge to straighten all of the air vents in the car and shove any rubbish left by Opi into the center console. She scans, looking for something else to neaten, but there's nothing. Her bag is on the passenger-side floor, and she reaches for it, hoping to find something to throw out or sort through. Instead, her fingers brush against a small, cool object. She pulls Will's compass out of the bag, thumbing the grooved edge as she turns it so the arrow aligns with north.

Through the closed windows the sounds of the night call to her. She wants to get out, to kick her shoes off and run through the forest, grasping at that feeling of being *alive*. But she's too tired, and she has all night to hunt.

Instead, she rolls down all the windows and puts the car into drive.

The town of Black River is buzzing. With summer vacation almost here, there's an air of lightness infecting the locals who would be looking forward to months of swimming in lakes and meals grilled outside in the sunshine.

Dusty can feel this energy everywhere. She's been driving for a few hours, trying to let the blur of her surroundings keep her mind clear and closed off. But every so often, thoughts arise from the murky swell, seducing her into daydreams of what her summer might have looked like if everything hadn't changed. Days spent reading in her bed, basking in the sunshine pouring through her open window. Maybe the occasional swim in the lake or Black River. Maybe with Will.

She glances at the time. Nine forty-five. Just about long enough to cover her imaginary date with Eli.

She'd thought about calling him and telling him about her mom and the fact that she, too, had found herself somewhere, unable to understand where the time had gone. But every time she and Eli have spoken lately it's like they're talking in circles, always leading back to *blood* and the fact that Eli is becoming increasingly tempted by the thought of feeding from *someone*.

Will's compass glints in the streetlight from where it sits on the seat beside her, reminding Dusty who she actually wants to talk to about her mom. She knows she can't, not without telling him what she's going through. Still, she finds herself veering to the north side of town, to an intersection she'd stopped at weeks ago. Where she'd dropped him after the waterfall.

He's probably been looking for his compass all week, she realizes, and suddenly she feels terrible for not returning it to him sooner. She wonders if she can put her new abilities to the test and figure out where he lives. Then, she can leave it on his doorstep, unburdening herself from yet another reminder of him.

The intersection is quiet, so Dusty closes her eyes.

A slow and easy rhythm reaches out to her—she sees it in blue waves, sparkling across her blackened vision. Her heart begins to beat faster and her eyes blink open.

He's close.

She follows the blues, turning down a street of small, identical houses framed by metal fencing that lines the sidewalks. She inhales the night air and the scent of wildflowers draws her to one house in particular. She sees them, bursting from the yard in place of a lawn. There's a small beehouse too, placed in a nook on the front windowsill.

Stopping a few houses down, she turns off the ignition.

The sounds here are different from the mountain. Speakers boom as an action movie plays somewhere across the street, someone empties their recycling, a baby cries out for its mother who rushes in with hushed, soothing coos. But the natural world is here too. Crickets chirp, a robin cucks its last note for the day, and fireflies rise from overgrown weeds and grasses in a narrow alley across the street.

She knows she needs to be quick, that she can't risk seeing him, but just knowing he's near, the feeling of him close all over her, makes her ache with need.

"What am I doing?" she whispers, then snatches the compass from the seat and gets out of the car.

The front gate creaks as she opens it. She looks up to the house, checking for movement within, but all she can see is the calm haze of blues. Slipping inside the boundary, slowly, quietly, she walks up the path to the front door.

Dusty bends to place the compass on the front step, but then realizes it could easily be stepped on there. She looks around, searching for the right spot, somewhere it will be safe but noticeable. Finally, she sees a small hook at the center of the front door. She pictures the wreath that might have hung there when they'd first moved here at Christmas. It's perfect.

But as she lifts the compass to hang it on the hook, she hears footsteps. Then the front door opens.

At first, all Dusty can see is the blue and indigo that radiates from inside. She focuses, letting Will's figure come into view, backlit by the glow of a hall light.

"Dusty," he says, and her hairs stand on end as she feels his voice all the way down to her toes. "Where did you . . ." he starts, noticing the compass she's still holding up, as if she's frozen in place.

Her heart races. "You left it . . . on the mountain," she manages.

Will takes a step closer, reaching out to take the compass from her hand. When their fingers touch she feels lit up from the inside.

The indigo starts to flicker among his blues, dissolving into streams of pink that reach for her. "Why didn't you . . . have you had this all week? You could have just given it to me at school."

Her throat bobs as she tries to think of what to say.

"I mean, thank you," he adds. "Do you"—he glances back down his hallway—"want to come in?"

"Oh," she says, flustered. "No. I can't."

He studies her, assessing her in that way that makes her feel like he can see right through her. "Sit for a bit?" he asks, nodding to the front step.

"Okay," she says, even though she knows she shouldn't.

Her heart starts to slow as they look out toward the street, the night hard to see beyond the streetlights. For a second she wants to tell him how much he'd love the view of the stars from the mountain, but instead, she asks, "Is it important to you?"

"Huh?" he says, turning to face her.

When she looks at him it's clear that he's in his own daze. "The compass," she clarifies.

"Oh. Yeah. I mean, it's probably worthless, but I've had it for a few years." He lifts the compass up, inspecting it closely. The movement brings his arm an inch closer to Dusty's, making her inhale a deep breath. "I used to think I wanted to travel after school," he continues. "And for some reason this compass always felt like my ticket out of wherever I was. Like a reminder that there's always somewhere to go, a different path, if you want it."

"You don't want to travel anymore?" she asks.

"I mean, sure, I guess. Here and there. But after moving here, to Black River, I've been thinking more and more about something more permanent. I like the idea of watching the trees grow around me, you know?"

She nods, and a laugh escapes from her mouth.

"What?" he asks, his eyes narrowing as he watches her sideways.

"No, it's just . . . Yeah, I know exactly what you mean. When you were at my house, did you notice the giant beech tree?"

He nods. "Yeah, I did."

"That's been there since before my ancestors settled there. The story is that my great-great-grandfather was going to fell the tree to help build the house, but my great-great-grandmother had already fallen in love with the tree, so they built the house beside it. I've always thought of the house and the tree as companions . . . that the house was like an offering to the tree, built to honor it."

When Will doesn't say anything she glances at him, noticing now that his heart has started beating a little faster. His midnight eyes lock onto hers, holding her there, making her shiver. "What?" she manages, her voice suddenly husky.

"Nothing," he says, and he looks away.

She clears her throat. "Do you know what you want to do . . . work-wise?" she asks.

He shakes his head. "Not for sure. But I can see myself setting up a workshop, maybe. Making things."

"Like beehouses?"

His face shifts into a broad smile. "Yeah, like beehouses. But I'd probably need to expand my skillset to other, slightly more useful things."

She chuckles. "Yeah, I guess beehouses aren't the most lucrative trade."

His smile deepens, but when their eyes meet again, the smile fades. "What're you really doing here, Dusty?"

"I—" She stops herself.

His eyes move down to her mouth, which is still open, as if the words still might come out to explain. Her lips tingle under his gaze. The feeling trickles along her tongue, down her throat, and somehow they're suddenly even closer, as if they've both leaned in, just a fraction.

She watches as he draws his bottom lip under his top teeth, as if he can feel it too. The energy between them.

Dusty's teeth respond with an ache, sending fear tearing through her.

She stands, saying, "Sorry. I just wanted to give you your compass back."

Will shakes his head, sighing as he slides both hands over his face then up through his hair. Dusty walks away, certain she's the worst person on earth.

Eli hears a car in the driveway and his stomach drops. It's late. *The sheriff. It has to be the sheriff.* Seconds later, the doorbell rings and Eli freezes in place, listening, paralyzed by fear.

"Sorry it's so late, Mrs. Blake. I was out but wanted to see how he's doing before I went home."

The familiar voice doesn't make Eli feel any better.

"Jesse! It's so sweet of you to check in on him! He's been sick *again* this week," his mom says. Eli can picture her expression exactly, her eyebrows curving down in drooping sympathy. "Head on up, he'll be happy to see you."

Eli still can't move, even when there's a knock on his bedroom door.

The handle turns, but the door doesn't open. He's never been so glad he keeps his room locked.

"Eli?" Jesse says, his voice muffled.

Even through the closed door, Eli can smell him. It's like doing a shot of liquor, invigorating and dizzying at the same time. Eli has imagined this smell all week, or more accurately, he's tried to forget it.

He's thrown himself into building his track, clearing trees and heaving dirt to make jumps with his bare hands, his body fighting hard against the heat, fighting to keep his thoughts at bay.

The door handle jiggles again.

"Jesus, dude," Eli mumbles. "Can't you take a hint?" He flicks the lock and the door swings open as Jesse stumbles in.

He looks up at Eli and chuckles, clearly amused by his friend's annoyed face. Then he looks down at Eli's boxers and sweaty white t-shirt. "Are you alright man?" Jesse asks in disbelief. "It's freezing in here." He rubs the cold from his arms.

"I wasn't expecting company," Eli grunts as he walks over to the sofa and sits. He scoops up a ball that had been on the floor beside him and begins to toss it between his hands.

"Yeah, well, when one of your best friends isn't at school for days, dodging everyone's messages . . ." He walks over to Eli's desk and sits in the swivel chair, facing it toward Eli. He leans forward, his elbows resting on his knees. "So?"

"So what?"

"What's going on with you? I know I was drunk last weekend, but I swear . . . did something happen? When we were outside?"

Eli keeps throwing and catching the ball, his focus intense.

"Alright," Jesse says. "You're gonna be cagey, I get it."

"That's the thing, you don't get it."

"Alright," he repeats. "So tell me."

Eli blows a breath through his lips, then catches the ball for the final time before he closes his eyes. But the break in concentration lets Jesse's presence flood him, and he imagines locking eyes with him, taking over, and—

He sits up, burying his face in his hands, trying to push what he's feeling away, because he still doesn't know what it means.

Jesse has been his friend since elementary school. They've grown up together. So it makes sense that he'd be here, checking in on him. *Why does it feel like more, then?* Eli wonders. He meets Jesse's gaze, for just a second, and there's something in his eyes, in the way they crinkle, that makes Eli wonder if he's missed something all along. Missed that it's Jesse who has feelings for him.

Jesse leans back in the chair, unafraid. His head tilts, and the lamplight hits a vein in his neck. Illuminated. Pulsing. His Adam's apple bobs, and when Eli looks away, down to Jesse's arms, his veins are visible. Full.

Eli swallows. "You gotta go, man."

Jesse raises his eyebrows.

Eli's teeth pulse. He stands and walks to the window opposite Jesse. For a second he thinks he can feel Dusty out there, somewhere in the darkness, but he's pulled away from the thought by Jesse's reflection. It's not just concern on Jesse's face, there's longing there too.

"Go," Eli repeats, his voice heavy with sadness. Not because he now knows how Jesse feels, but because even without using his control over him, he's tempted to use those feelings in exchange for the thing he wants more than anything—blood.

Dusty was right, he thinks. *We're monsters.*

Dusty runs through the forest, a creature of the night. Her bare feet are heavy against the ground, fatigue weighing down her limbs and her every breath, but she doesn't stop. She can't. She has to feed.

Surrendering to the predator she's become, she lets herself take pleasure in the chase. A deer. A doe in her prime. Just a moment of distraction, a moment to focus on one thing alone.

But when she's done, it all comes back. Everything that hurts. And she wonders if her mom had changed too, if whatever caused it was attracted to that broken part of her, like Dusty, and if it shattered her until she couldn't take it anymore. Like Dusty.

Maybe it's the broken ones who fall prey. Maybe that's why Opi and Dad didn't change.

She turns in the direction of Eli's, knowing she's let the uncertainty between them go on too long, knowing she had no right to make him feel bad for considering satiating this unending hunger. For being just as confused as she is. She's the one who just went to Will's house, after all.

The back of Eli's house comes into view, his bedroom light still on. She's about to reach out to let him know she's here when he appears in the window.

He's not alone. Jesse's behind him.

Eli is struggling. His self-control at the end of its tether, just like her own. So she waits, watching to make sure that Eli's okay. That Jesse doesn't get hurt.

But just watching them, *feeling* them, makes her mouth water. The hot liquid cries out for a real taste. She's dizzy with the craving, desperate for it to stop.

To her relief, Jesse leaves, and she turns to walk home, too tired to run.

A flicker of light ahead grabs her attention. She wonders if it's a car, Jesse's maybe, but she doesn't think the road is there, and there's no sound coming from that direction.

The light moves, pale blue, shimmering through the trees. She follows like a moth to a flame. It stops, hovering for a moment, seeming to react to her movements. Dusty squints, disoriented, trying to figure out if the light is near or far, small or large.

It moves again, faster up the mountain. She gives chase, running now. She loses it for a moment but catches another glimpse through a break in the trees. Leaves and twigs snag in her loose hair as she tries to keep up. She's so distracted that she doesn't see the fence rising up in front of her until she's slamming into cold metal, its dull strength reverberating into her.

Wincing, Dusty peers through the fence to JD's property, wondering why she's here. She can't tell if anyone's inside or not, it's too far, but she does have a feeling, hard to place. She wonders if it's the pull of what they are, and what the light has to do with it—leading them to each other, like it led her to Eli the night they found Andrew Everett.

No, she thinks. *It's more than that.*

Her hand skims the fence as she begins to walk the perimeter. It's almost easier to see the house at night, lit up through the trees beyond the fence. It's mostly just glimpses of concrete and glass, and the surrounding lawn lit up like a sports field. A breeze gushes through the trees, flooding Dusty with a scent she's all too aware of. Blood.

She spins around, searching in the dark for its origin, following her nose. She stops when her bare foot lands on something soft. Fabric.

She bends to pick it up, recognizing it immediately—JD's beanie. Gripping it in her hands, she inhales again. The smell of blood is faint, just a trace, but within seconds she's pulled into a vision.

The woman waits for him at the table, her arms resting on the wooden surface in front of her, palms up. The sleeves of her pale pink shirt are rolled up, and he's awash with a feeling of relief and comfort as he approaches her. She looks up at him, and he tries not to notice the meekness in the soft smile she offers him, or how his appetite is tiring her.

He sits down in the chair beside her, and she nods, just once, before he takes her arm in his hands and bends toward it, ready to feed.

Dusty gasps, her body recoiling, sickened, while at the same time reinvigorated with hunger and thirst.

His mom, she thinks, still reeling. *JD has been feeding from his mom.*

She knows she doesn't have the right to judge after what she's done, but still, there was something about it that felt . . . wrong.

She waits there a few more minutes, unsure of what to do with what she's seen. His mom had offered herself willingly, and it means JD doesn't need to be out here, harming anyone else. But she still doesn't know how Amber's feeding, or how much JD's mom and dad actually know.

A fresh wave of exhaustion hits her, and slowly, she returns home.

Back in her room, she checks her phone. There's a message from Will, but she can't bring herself to read it. She looks around her room, her fingers itching for something to tidy, but everything is perfect. She resists the urge to sweep her arms across the surfaces so her belongings crash to the ground, wishing she could escape into a book and be anywhere but here. But just the thought of the visceral overstimulation she experienced last time she tried to read has her muscles clenching. Desperate for an outlet, she opens her notebook, avoiding the photo and the flower inside, and on a fresh white page she presses the inky tip of a pen into the paper. This is when it usually just starts moving, gliding across the page in lines or swirls, giving her the release she needs. But the pen doesn't move. It remains in place, digging into the paper, the pressure building.

27

Blessing

"I think I need to see Kristen," says Mali.

Dusty looks up from her phone.

She'd been reading the message Will had sent late last night for the hundredth time.

Will
you've got to stop dusty
stop running away from me
stop giving me hope make
up your mind please

Mali is sitting on Dusty's bed, looking down at Dusty on the floor, waiting. "Can you come with me?" she asks.

"Of course," Dusty says, only just registering what Mali said.

"Thanks. I just . . . I think it will help. I haven't been sleeping great, after what happened. It still feels like a nightmare. Maybe if I see her, in daylight, I'll be able to see that she's just like you."

Dusty nods, wondering if she should warn Mali that Kristen isn't exactly like her. That Dusty suspects she's feeding from someone. "I think that's a good idea," she says.

"Good, let's go." Mali stands, heading for the door.

"Mali, wait," she says. "It's just . . . Kristen . . . she . . . she's—"

"Spit it out, girl."

"I think she's feeding from someone."

Mali is quiet for a long moment. "Who?"

"I don't know."

"Okay," she says, considering. "Maybe it's her mom, like JD?"

Dusty had told Mali about what she'd seen last night as soon as she'd arrived. She'd had to explain the other visions in more detail too. "I don't know," Dusty answers.

"Well, is she acting . . . different, like JD? Obnoxious? Dangerous?"

"No, not that I—"

"Okay then, let's go."

"How are you so cool with this?" Dusty asks, exasperated.

"I've watched every vampire movie there is, *remember*? You made me."

"You know that's not what this is."

"Sure. But still . . . I've become desensitized to weird shit. We all have, at this point."

Dusty sighs, knowing that Mali wouldn't be so relaxed if she knew what Dusty had really done. That Dusty is a murderer. "Fine," she finally says. "But I'm staying close."

Outside, Dusty starts toward the garden, ready to take the trail through the forest.

"Uh-uh," Mali says from behind her. "If you think I'm setting one foot into these woods after what's happened to y'all, you're grossly mistaken."

Dusty looks back as Mali gets into Dusty's car and waits.

"I'm cool," Mali says when Dusty climbs in. "But I'm not that cool."

It takes less than two minutes for them to get to Kristen's. As they pull into the drive, the front door opens and Kristen is already walking toward them, cautious.

She stops as soon as she sees who Dusty is with. She's in athletic-wear—shorts and a tank top—with clean bare feet, and her blonde hair has been washed and brushed and pulled back into a glossy ponytail.

"You didn't tell me she'd look even *better*," Mali groans.

Kristen raises her eyebrows.

"She can hear you," Dusty whispers, unable to stop her growing smile.

Mali flashes her a look, her eyes wide.

Dusty gets out first. "Hope you don't mind," she says, approaching Kristen, "but someone wanted to see you."

Kristen hesitates, then nods.

Mali gets out of the car, her eyes on Dusty.

"This way," Kristen says, leading them to a wooden glider swing in a clearing on the other side of the driveway. She ducks under the awning as she climbs onto one of the two benches that face each other. Dusty and Mali follow, sitting on the bench across from her.

"Sorry," she says. "I don't think I've been on this in years. But my mom and dad are home."

There's a long silence that amplifies how nervous both Mali and Kristen are. Dusty watches as Mali's colors change every second, reaching out to Dusty for support, while Kristen's are fretful and guarded.

Kristen is the first to break the silence. "I'm so sorry, Mali," she says, her voice soft.

Mali looks up at her, meeting her eyes for the first time. "I didn't hear from you . . . after . . ."

"I didn't think you'd want to. I didn't know what to say."

"You look good," Mali says to Kristen.

Sheepish, Kristen runs her hand over her smooth hair and down her ponytail. "I'm doing better," she says, "since I saw Dusty."

"Good," Dusty says, meaning it.

"Dusty said you're feeding from someone?" Mali asks, matter-of-fact, like she's asking about the weather.

Both Dusty and Kristen's heartbeats quicken. Mali shifts in her seat, making the glider sway.

"It's not what you think," Kristen says.

"So tell me then," Mali answers coolly.

Kristen nods as she blows out a long breath. "After the bonfire. After I . . . tasted you." She looks down at her hands which are clasped together. "I knew what my body needed. It was all I could think about. A life-or-death craving. And I knew I couldn't go home to my parents. I couldn't be a danger to them, like I had been to you. So I went into town. I didn't want anyone to see me so I stuck to backstreets and alleys. There was a woman smoking out back of that grimy bar. A guy came out too. He was trying to talk to the woman but she wanted to be alone. He was pretty sloppy and when he went too close to her she kicked him in the nuts. It was pretty badass actually." She smiles. "The woman went back inside, leaving him out there, alone. He smelled disgusting. He was like, the opposite of you, in every way." She looks up at Mali, who's frowning as she listens. "I found him as revolting as I found myself. Like we deserved each other. So I fed from him. He struggled a little, but I guess I was already stronger than him, and he was so drunk he barely knew what was happening. Then, looking back, it was almost like he . . . liked it? I don't know if I would have kept going or not if the alcohol in his blood hadn't tasted so gross. But I guess it was a blessing, because when I'd had as much as I could stomach, I stopped. He was weak by then. He couldn't stand. But I could tell from his heartbeat that he was okay, so I sat him down and . . ." She stops, looking between Mali and Dusty, her hands still clasped tightly together.

"Go on," Dusty urges, needing to hear more.

Kristen swallows before she continues. "Blood was running from where I'd bitten him, and I didn't know what to do so I licked it and . . .

the bleeding just stopped. He healed before my eyes." She lets out a long, deep breath. "So that's what I've been doing. Going into town and waiting for someone so drunk they can barely stand, so drunk they'll barely remember, and pinning them from behind so they won't see me. I hate myself, obviously, but physically, I feel amazing, for four or five days, and then I'm all edgy and jumpy and . . . thirsty. So I go back to the alley and wait. I don't know if it's the alcohol that helps me control myself, and I don't really want to find out otherwise." She looks down to her hands, twisting her fingers together.

Dusty's head is spinning, but it's Mali who speaks first. "So you're basically Carey Mulligan in *Promising Young Woman*."

Kristen looks up, horrified. "These men don't deserve it. No one does."

"I'm sorry," Mali says, shaking her head. "I just . . . You didn't choose any of this. You're just . . . surviving."

When Dusty and Kristen's eyes meet, Kristen's are glassy with tears. "I've had visions since you came over last week," she says. "Two. The first one was you."

Dusty's stomach lurches, wondering if Kristen somehow knows what she did.

But a smile spreads over Kristen's face. "You were hunting a deer," she says. "And I know that it's not enough for you. That your body wants more."

Dusty can feel Mali looking at her, but she can't meet her gaze.

"You may look a little . . . anemic," Kristen continues, "but at least you're not a psychopath."

"You're not—"

"Don't bother. I have so much respect for what you're trying to do. For your restraint. It's not . . . easy. *Taking* the way I do. It feels . . . dirty. It's so intimate, doing *that* with strangers—" She stops what she's saying when Mali looks away.

Dusty tries to imagine what they went through that night. How confusing it must have been for both of them. "Eli thinks it's all circumstantial," she says. "That we're just playing the cards we've been dealt. Like you controlled yourself with Mali because you've always been so disciplined. And because girls have better self-control."

All three of them manage to huff a laugh, knowing how far from the truth that is.

"What was your other vision?" Mali asks.

"It was your friend, JD. At least, I think it was, because when I looked him up later, I recognized the house. He was with some girl, she looked familiar . . . You mentioned someone. Amber? Long curly hair? Olive skin?"

Mali and Dusty nod quickly.

"Anyway, they were inside his house, and they were . . ." She shakes her head. "They were cutting each other."

Mali and Dusty are both quiet for a moment, before Dusty asks, "What do you mean *cutting* each other?"

"Well, they had a sharp knife, and they were taking it and pressing it into each other's skin, then licking the wounds to see if they would heal. It was like they were testing their own limits or something."

"And then what?" Mali asks, the discomfort in her voice as clear to Dusty as the colors around her.

"I don't know. Then I was back in my body, and I couldn't see them anymore. But there was something weird about their dynamic . . . It was like he was . . . proud of her? And somehow it made him feel stronger."

"You should know," Dusty says. "I had another vision last night too. JD was feeding from his mom."

As Mali and Kristen exchange equally repulsed looks, a thought begins to occur to Dusty. She feels a rush as a piece of the puzzle suddenly clicks into place.

"It was daylight though," she says out loud. "The vision. So it wasn't happening at the same time I was seeing it. It must have been a memory."

Both Kristen and Mali look confused.

"When you had your vision, Kristen, did it feel like it was the same time of day?"

Kristen thinks, then nods. "Yeah, I think it was. Somehow I knew it was happening at that moment, at the same time I was seeing it."

"Right," Dusty says. "Just like when I had a vision of you. And Eli said the same thing when he saw JD."

"What are you getting at?" Mali asks.

"Well, I think what I saw last night was a memory, like the ones I've been having of my mom."

"Maybe it has something to do with the colors you see," Mali says, thinking. "You said Eli can . . . control minds? Persuade people to do things? Maybe if you can see how people are feeling, you can also experience what they've felt in the past?"

"Wait," Kristen says. "Eli can control minds?"

Dusty nods, and Kristen seems to accept it. It's just another insane part of their new reality.

"It needs a trigger," Dusty says, processing the revelation out loud. "Every time I've had a memory, as opposed to a vision, I've been touching something that directly links me to the person or the moment. My room at home, where my mom spent a lot of time. The old photo of her. And last night, JD's beanie. Maybe he'd been wearing it when he fed from his mom."

Mali blows a long, slow breath out her mouth. "Shit, guys. I officially can't keep up anymore."

They look at each other, silently acknowledging that they all feel the same.

"So what should we do?" Mali finally asks. "About JD and Amber . . . and, like, everything?"

"Well, we can't exactly call the police," Kristen says.

Dusty senses movement in her periphery and turns toward the house.

There are two faces peering through one of the lower windows. Realizing they've been caught out, they pretend to inspect the drapes.

"My parents," Kristen says. "I better get back inside. They'll be so excited that I have friends here, they might come out and try to rope you into a meal, which would be awkward, obviously."

Mali smiles, then turns back to Kristen. "I'm glad you're okay," she says. "I mean . . . As okay as you could be right now. But I still think we need to do something about JD and Amber."

Both Kristen and Dusty nod.

"I'm going to talk to Eli," Dusty says. "At least there's three of us now, we can figure something out. Try to talk to them again."

"What about me?" Mali says, offended.

"No," Dusty and Kristen say at once.

"You need to stay away from them, okay?" Dusty warns. "We don't know what's going on with them . . . or with any of us, really."

Mali frowns.

"I'm serious, Mali," Dusty says.

Reluctantly, she nods.

Dusty catches a familiar scent through the trees.

Her phone is in her hands, poised to type the message she's been avoiding sending all weekend. But it's Sunday afternoon now, and she knows she has to reply to Will before school tomorrow.

Dusty
I'm sorry. Please ignore me?
I won't bother you again.

She stuffs her phone into the back pocket of her denim shorts, doubting that he'll reply.

Following the scent she'd been tracking, she heads down the mountain until she hears a heavy thud, then the sound of snapping wood and rustling leaves. There's a strained groan, then a yell of release and another loud thud.

As she steps into the freshly cleared forest corridor, the sun beats down on upturned soil and exposed roots, drawing up their rich smell like hot breath. From about forty feet further up the slope, the soil has been packed down into mounds, one after another, going down as far as her eyes can see.

Eli is standing in the center of the cleared path, shirtless, covered in dirt and sweat.

"'Sup?" he says casually, nodding at Dusty before going over to a small, but not insignificant tree. He pulls it from the ground like it's a tough weed then dumps it on a heap of others.

"Aren't you exhausted?" Dusty asks.

"Yup."

She watches him do the same thing to several more before he starts packing down the next stretch of loose earth with his bare hands.

"Are you okay, Eli?" she asks.

He doesn't turn around. "Yeah, I'm great," he answers, his tone contradicting his words.

Dusty moves closer. He swivels around to face her, taking a step back. He takes out two AirPods that Dusty hadn't noticed, looking at her expectantly, as if she should hurry up and get on with whatever she's come to say.

"I just saw Kristen again," she says. "She had a vision of JD and Amber . . ."

He tilts his head, waiting.

"They were cutting each other. Like, literally cutting their skin with a knife, and licking the wounds to watch them heal."

"What the fuck. Why?"

Dusty shrugs. "To see how fast we heal? Kristen thinks they were testing their limits."

He's thoughtful, his jaw tense.

"I had a vision too," Dusty adds. "Or . . . a memory."

It occurs to Dusty that with Eli, she seems to be able to tell him things without saying them out loud, or even without touching him. She closes her eyes and pictures JD feeding from his mom, along with the conversation she had with Kristen and Mali, about the difference between visions and memories.

"No shit," Eli says as he visibly shivers. "Dusty, you have an ability too. It's not just colors."

"I guess not," she says, not sure if she feels proud or horrified by it. "Do you think . . . that we can communicate like that because of our bond? Or because of my ability?"

"I have no idea," he says. "Or it could really be a trauma bond. Because of what we did. Because we fed from him at the same time."

"Maybe," Dusty says, overwhelmed. "Anyway, I do think we need to do something about JD and Amber, or at least find out more about them."

"They're not here."

"What do you mean?"

"They left. Yesterday morning, I think."

"How do you know?"

"They were on foot. They steered clear of here, but I could smell them. I started to follow for a bit, just to see. But I lost them at Black River, and I didn't exactly feel like being down there. There hasn't been a trace of them out here since."

"Okay," Dusty says slowly. "Well, let me know if you do . . . smell them?"

Eli nods as he runs his fingers through his hair, which is still growing out, thick and coppery, longer on top than on the sides. He's avoiding Dusty's eyes and pushes his hands into the pockets of his shorts. A rivulet of sweat runs down his neck, tracing a line through the dirt.

Dusty is so sweaty she feels like her tank top and denim shorts were painted onto her.

"I went to see you last night," she says. "Jesse was there. Everything . . . okay with that?"

Eli's whole body tenses up. "I didn't kill him, if that's what you're asking?"

"You know it's not," she says, feeling like her heart is breaking all over again. For a while there, Eli had been the only one helping to hold it together.

He sighs and his shoulders drop. "I'm sorry." He steps toward her. "And I'm sorry for the way I acted the other day. I shouldn't have . . . I didn't mean to make you uncomfortable. I just . . . I don't think I'm going to last much longer. It's making me feel crazy. I want to be like you, I do. I wish it was possible, living off animals. But Dusty, I don't think it is. Not for me, at least. Maybe that makes me a monster, but maybe it's time to accept that that's what we are."

Dusty fights to hold back tears.

"Fuck. Come here," he says, striding over to fold her into his arms.

The heat of their two bodies is almost unbearable, but she leans closer anyway. "It's okay," she whispers. "You do what you have to do. Don't worry about me."

Eli doesn't respond.

When their sweat and the heat is too much to bear, they step back.

Dusty wipes her face. "So I take it this has something to do with bikes?" She looks up and down the track.

Eli laughs. "No shit, Sherlock."

"Impressive."

"I was good before. But you should see me now." He grins.

"I love this for you," she says. "But I need to get out of the heat."

"Swim?" he asks, but from his face she can see that he knows—she can't bring herself to swim. Not anymore.

She shakes her head.

"I'll come find you tonight," he says.

She nods, then turns to leave. As she walks home, Dusty can't help but feel like she just gave Eli her blessing to drink human blood.

The last week of school is a blur, spinning chaotically under Dusty's mask of indifference. The gnaw of the multiplying questions she asks herself on a loop, layered on top of needing more and more blood just to have the energy to go to school and pretend she's still herself, feels like a nightmarish marathon. And the last day of school is the finish line.

Will never did reply to her message. But he has ignored her, like she asked, and she's continued to make herself scarce, avoiding any chance of an interaction.

JD and Amber haven't been seen. It would be one less thing to worry about, except their absence was replaced by a new billboard on the road into town. Every morning Dusty has had to speed past the words "Missing: If you have any information on this man, please contact . . ." alongside Andrew Everett's photo.

When she asked her dad about it, he said that the search party has been combing the river, but they haven't found anything yet. Dusty assumes they've been making their way upstream from where they found the shoe, but when she pressed her dad for more, he said that he didn't know how far they'd gotten, and that underwater searches were a long, tedious process.

So there's that, at least.

She still can't decide if the fact that he misled the sheriff about the location of the clearing is significant, or just a father being protective.

Eli hasn't been at school either. He's stayed on his track, all day every day.

The few times they've hunted together at night, he's been distracted, grappling with the very thoughts Dusty is trying to ignore.

There is no longer solace in being in this together. There isn't any solace at all.

And now that the last day of school has arrived, Dusty is realizing that it doesn't mean anything. It won't provide any relief. She's still facing a long summer with none of her questions answered and her thirst unquenched. This is her life now. This is who she is.

The atmosphere at school is electric. When the final bell rings, ecstatic excitement erupts from every room and hallway. Dusty is swept along the current of bodies, trying not to breathe them in, trying not to crumble. A big group of seniors chant up ahead, and Dusty's sadness deepens as she wonders if she'll be able to make it to this time next year.

Next to her, one boy jumps, pushing himself up from another boy's shoulders. They topple down, laughing, knocking into Dusty's legs.

"Watch it," she snaps.

"Touchy," one of them says. The other laughs.

She's about to say or do something she will most definitely regret when the door beside her opens, letting another twenty or so students out into the flood.

Shoulders nudge her, sending defensive shudders all over her body, each touch making her more agitated. One girl squeals with delight right beside her ear and Dusty's teeth pulse. Her top lip pulls up and she has to force her mouth shut as she backs away. She doesn't stop until she can feel the cold, hard surface of a locker against her back.

She closes her eyes.

"Dusty?" a voice says, but she's so overwhelmed she can't pinpoint it.

It isn't until the soft, cool touch of a finger grazes her own that she realizes who is next to her. Her protest melts on her tongue, then down through her body. Without looking, she links her pinky finger with Will's.

The red that she sees through her tightly shut eyes becomes marbled with shades of blue, slowly taking over until she begins to drift on a calm, sparkling sea.

She can feel his heart beating faster the longer they touch, but his calm is unwavering, and it's infectious.

She doesn't open her eyes until the hallway is quiet and empty.

She turns her head just enough to check that he's really there. He is, pressed up against the lockers with his head leaning back, his face tilted, watching her.

"Are you okay?" he asks. His voice is like cool water.

"No," she answers honestly. "I hate crowds."

"Me too."

She scans his face, taking in every detail. It makes her heart feel too big for her chest. As she lets her eyes meet his again, she realizes that their fingers are still linked.

"Sorry," she says, letting go.

"Don't be," he says. "Thought I could break the rules just this once."

"The rules?"

"Yeah, I'm supposed to be ignoring you, aren't I?"

Dusty cringes, her body feeling like it's folding in on itself.

Will pushes himself away from the lockers. "Have a good summer," he says, then turns and walks outside.

28

Truly, Finally Broken

The sun doesn't set over the mountain until after eight-thirty now. Dusty tries to wait until darkness falls, but she can't. She has to hunt.

The forest is covered in shimmering, golden light. It seems to sparkle in time with the hum of cicadas and birds chiming like bells. Dusty still can't believe all of this had been at her fingertips, all along, and she chose to stay inside and shut it out. Despite her fatigue, every step, every breath out here helps to hold her upright. The stretch of her legs as she climbs over a boulder, the bend in her back when she ducks under a tree. It keeps the torrent of emotions flowing inside her, alive.

It's only when she stops that it threatens to drown her.

The scent of a deer reaches her on the breeze, but before she can move toward it, she begins to feel that pull taking hold of her, drawing her into someone else's mind. She clings to the physical world in front of her, afraid of what she might see, but she can't stop it.

He stares down the track, but something else holds his attention. He lifts his t-shirt up to wipe the sweat from his face. He knows he's being watched but he resists turning around.

"I'm not gonna lie," Jesse says. "This track is insane. Did your dad help build it or something?"

Eli huffs a laugh. "Nah, man. I did it myself."

"How?" Jesse asks, incredulous.

Eli doesn't feel as scared as he has, because if Jesse lets him, he's already decided what he's going to do. He clenches his jaw at the thought and breathes in through his nose, letting Jesse's scent in. Then finally, lets himself look. "That's kind of what I wanted to talk to you about," he says. He puts his bike down so there's nothing between them.

"Finally, bro—"

"This is going to freak you out, okay?"

Jesse cocks his head, looking directly into Eli's eyes. "Yeah?"

"Yeah."

Jesse takes a step closer, crossing an invisible line. "So tell me."

"It's not what you think," Eli warns, seeing it so clearly now—the way Jesse feels about him. Even though he wants to be as transparent as possible, he knows he's manipulating him, using Jesse's trust, his friendship and attraction. But those are the cards Eli's been dealt, and he's ready to play them. "I can't give you what you want," Eli says. "But I can tell you what's happened to me."

"Eli, what're you—"

"I'm telling you this because I trust you, because I've known you forever, but also, for whatever reason, it's like I don't have a choice. Like you're meant to know."

"Okay," Jesse says, his voice wary.

"After I tell you, I'm going to ask something of you, and I need you to know that you can walk away at any moment. You can say no, okay?"

Jesse's eyes search Eli's as he listens, confusion and understanding interchangeable with every breath.

"I don't know how it happened," Eli begins, "but I've changed. Like, physically changed. And it's not just me. Dusty too. That's why we left the bonfire together. That's why we've been pretending to date—"

"What—"

"Just let me finish, okay?"

Jesse nods.

"We didn't know until I got into that fight with Sam. When I hit him and saw the blood. I knew something was off before that. I felt this energy inside me, this strength, and like, I couldn't eat anymore. Not food, at least." *He tries to ignore Jesse's quickening heartbeat as he continues.* "Jess, since then, I've been surviving on blood. Animal blood. But it's not enough."

Jesse just stares for a long moment, then he bursts into laughter.

"I know," *Eli says.* "It sounds insane, but—"

"Wait. So, you're saying you're like . . . a vampire?" *He laughs again.*

"No. Well, not exactly. But . . . I crave blood. I'm stronger, faster, my senses are like, insane and . . . you know a few weeks ago, when we had that weird moment outside the party?"

Jesse's nods once.

"Well, you were right. I did do something. I can sort of . . . make people do things."

Jesse looks at him flatly, like he doesn't have the energy to humor him any longer.

"I know," *Eli says.* "It sounds crazy, and I've only tried it twice. But here, look." *He places his hands on Jesse's shoulders. Jesse scoffs, but relents. Eli looks into his eyes.*

Within seconds he can feel that click, like he's latched on. He drops his hands from Jesse's shoulders and steps back slowly, eyes still focused, unblinking.

"Cross your arms," *Eli says.*

Jesse does it.

"Jump twice."

Jesse does it.

"Tell me the last time you jerked off."

"This morning."

Eli blinks, releasing him.

"What the fuck!" *Jesse hisses.* "I wasn't . . . How did . . . What's wrong with you?" *The color has drained from his face.*

"Hey, I played nice," Eli says. "I could have asked you to tell me your deepest secret."

Jesse swallows. Then shakes his head in disbelief.

"I'm not messing with you," Eli says, stepping closer again. "And there's no easy way to put this, so I'm just going to come right out with it, okay?"

Jesse's eyes are scanning Eli, trying to understand.

"I'm not joking, Jess. What I want, what I need, is your blood."

Jesse sighs. "Dude, enough."

"I'm serious. I'm telling you the truth. You keep asking me what's wrong. I'm telling you. Listen to me, okay?"

Jesse keeps looking at Eli, trying to think.

"I can bite myself if you want? To prove it?" Eli says. He lifts his own arm to his face.

Jesse rolls his eyes, then pulls Eli's arm down. He snaps his hand away almost instantly. "What the . . . You're on fire."

"You have no idea," Eli says quietly, the thudding pulse in his teeth starting to spread rhythmically through his body. "I'm not going to hurt you," he says. "I've tried it once, on Dusty, but it didn't work because she's like me, and you . . . you smell different to everyone else. I don't know why, but I'm starting to wonder if it's your pheromones or something. If maybe . . . you feel something for me, on top of just friendship?"

Jesse's heartbeat is pounding, fear flashing in his eyes.

"I want to be honest with you," Eli says. "I don't think . . . I don't think I feel the same way. I know I don't. So I'm asking you as a friend. A friend who is just as freaked out as you are right now, who's well aware that I might be manipulating you by asking this."

Jesse doesn't say anything for what feels like a lifetime. A part of Eli wants Jesse to run. To punch him. To laugh again. But he doesn't. Instead, he says, "You're fucking serious, aren't you? You want to bite me . . . and drink my blood?"

Eli nods.

Jesse sighs, then looks up at the sky. When he looks back down, he holds out his own arm and says, "Do it."

Eli is so shocked he doesn't react.

"Do it," Jesse urges. "Hopefully you're messing with me. If you're not, you better get it over with before I freak out and change my mind."

Eli nods, stepping closer to his friend. He takes Jesse's arm, pulling him close to him. "Is this okay?" he asks.

Jesse nods again, then swallows.

Eli knows there's no going back now. He leans in close, then, placing his mouth on Jesse's wrist, he bites.

As Dusty comes back into herself her heart is pounding. Her body is feeling everything Eli had felt. She's swollen with it. Every cell hums with want and need.

He did it.

She pictures Jesse's face, the way he'd looked at Eli, his feelings for him undeniable. And as much as Dusty understands why Eli needed to do it, it only confirmed her worst fears about what it makes them.

Another breeze brings the scent of deer, and she clings to it.

The smell of cooking emanates from the house, but Dusty still avoids the kitchen like the plague. It's one thing to smell it, but another to witness the life she's missing out on. She's halfway through her bedroom window when she notices something on her bed. It's a shoebox, pale pink and scuffed at the edges. She crawls across her bed to turn on her bedside lamp, her feet shedding leaves and dirt onto the sheets.

Crossing her legs, she sits beside the box and runs her hands over the smooth surface. Slowly, she opens the lid.

It's full of photos, all of her mother. Leafing through them, Dusty sees her mother as a young child for the first time, then a girl, then a teen, over the decades until her early thirties. Which is when she left.

Dusty can't discern how she feels. Not anymore. All she knows is that her mother left these behind. Every trace of her past. Proof of her life.

Closing the lid, Dusty picks up the box and carries it downstairs. Her dad is still seated at the dining table while Opi is elbow-deep in soapy water, doing the dishes.

"We just finished up, but there's more in the fridge," Chris says, hopeful.

"I already ate," Dusty says, placing the box on the table.

Chris looks between Dusty and the box.

"Why did you . . . I don't . . ." Dusty starts, struggling to find the words.

Chris watches her, confused.

"It was me," Opi says from the kitchen. "I left them for you."

Dusty turns, surprised, waiting as Opi dries her hands on a flower-print tea towel.

"What is it?" Chris asks.

"I know how much you've been struggling," Opi says, her eyes on Dusty. "I didn't know if showing you these would make it better or worse. I'm sorry."

Opi moves to the table as Chris opens the box. "How . . ." he says, his face pure astonishment. "I thought they were gone."

"I found the box," Opi explains. "Under Dad's bed. A few months after she left."

Chris nods. "I put every photo of her I could find in here." He looks to Dusty. "After I found you trying to throw the framed ones away. I wanted to save them, in case you ever wanted them back.

When the box disappeared, I assumed you'd found it and thrown them out after all."

They both turn to Opi.

She looks down at the box as she speaks. "I heard you guys, when Dusty wanted to throw out the frames. It kept me up at night, worrying they'd be gone, that I'd never see her face again. So I took them." She glances up at her dad, then Dusty, then back to the box. "I still look at them almost every day. I didn't want to tell you. I didn't want to make you sad." She exhales as if the secret has been choking her, the confession making it easier to breathe.

"I'm so sorry, Op," Dusty says. "I knew how much you missed her the first few years. But the last few . . . You're so happy . . . so confident . . . so *you*. I just assumed you'd put her behind you. That you were too young to be broken by her."

"She didn't break me," Opi says with an earnest smile.

"Is that how you feel?" Chris asks Dusty, his face crinkled with worry. "Broken?"

Dusty's shoulders droop and her eyes begin to water.

"It's not too late, Dust," Opi says, her big brown eyes wet with tears of her own. "I still remember what you were like, before she left."

Dusty nods, looking between her dad and sister, reassuring them. Lying to them. Because it *is* too late. They don't know what she's become. They don't know that she is truly, finally broken.

Sitting on the roof just outside her bedroom window, Dusty stares up at the starlit sky. The leaves of the ancient beech tree whisper in the night air, telling Dusty that the world is much bigger, and much older, than her problems.

As the stars twinkle in agreement, she feels Eli moving through the forest toward her.

She listens as he approaches, then bounds up the tree. In a breath of movement he's sitting beside her, his shoulder leaning against hers.

"We don't have to talk about it, if you don't want," he says. "Just wanted to make sure you're okay."

"With what?" she asks. "The fact that I'm the last one not feeding from people? Or that my visceral anxiety is as heightened as everything else and I'm constantly being forced to think about my mom?"

Eli shrugs. "Both?"

She manages to chuckle, turning to face him. Even in the dark, she can see the way Jesse's blood has changed him. How clear and bright his eyes are and the way his colors move in a constant flow around him, more vibrant than before, steadier, calmer even.

She rests her head on his shoulder.

"Speaking of visceral anxiety . . ." Eli says. "Any news from the sheriff? About the search?"

"No. Not yet."

Eli nods, then they watch the sky for a while, saying nothing.

But the longer they're silent, the more apparent it is—things have changed between them. Without school, or fake dating, or needing to hunt together because Eli is doing the very thing Dusty is fighting with every last ounce of energy she has left.

They don't bother to mention searching for more answers, or dare to hope for a way back. Not anymore.

29
The Fire Tower

> **Mali**
> I know this might not seem relevant
> to you rn, and I totally understand if
> it's the last thing you feel like doing,
> but tomorrow is July 4th. Come to the
> old fire tower with us? It'll just be me
> and Will. Company might not be
> the worst thing ♡

Dusty looks up at her ceiling that's been overtaken by the bright lights of the projector. It's been almost a week since school broke for summer, and she and Opi have spent almost every night like this, watching their favorite movies from the pillow-laden bedroom floor. Tonight, it's *Far From the Madding Crowd*.

"What're you doing for the fourth?" she asks.

Opi rolls her head toward her sister, but her eyes remain on the screen. "Huh?"

"Tomorrow," Dusty says. "The fourth."

"Oh. There's a party in town. I think more than half the sophomores—"

"Technically you're juniors now."

"Oh yeah," she says, grinning. "Anyway, it's going to be big. We'll watch the fireworks. Why? Want to come?"

It isn't until she's asked that she decides. "I think I'm going to the old fire tower," she says.

"You and Eli?"

Dusty shakes her head. "No. Mali." She can barely admit to herself that Will will be there, or that the idea of seeing him makes her heart skip a beat.

"Nice," Opi smiles, barely hiding how happy she is that Eli hasn't been around. Dusty hasn't seen much of him since he came to her on the roof.

"Oooh," Opi coos. "This is my favorite part!" She sits up, her head tipped back, staring up at the ceiling where Bathsheba and Gabriel finally seem to be on the same page.

Dusty had waited until almost dawn to hunt. She wanted to be full, as full as she can be, ready for the day ahead.

The old fire tower is halfway up Mount Grace, a ten-minute drive from Dusty's house, but she drops Opi and their dad into town first.

As they pass house after house with giant flags in pride of place, she tries to ignore the smell of barbecued meat rising from backyard cookouts. But being one of the few days of the year their dad socializes, it's nice for Dusty to see his slightly excited, slightly anxious energy hovering around him as they approach the center of town.

She drops them as close as she can get. With the central streets closed for pedestrians, and people from all over setting up chairs and tables for the fireworks later tonight, it's the busiest day of the year for Black River by far.

The collective anticipation for the day ahead is palpable to the point of overwhelming Dusty, so it's a relief to be headed back into the wilderness.

Unlike White Mountain, there are no residents on Mount Grace. Instead, there's a parking lot at the northern base that branches off into trails of varying difficulty that lead up to the peak. Once used to scan for forest fires, the old fire tower is no longer in use thanks to a newer, taller structure across the valley. The plan is to meet in the parking lot and hike up to the fire tower which has streams beneath it that flow into a natural pool. Hopefully they'll have the place to themselves.

When Dusty's Jeep pulls up, the only other car is Mali's dad's four-by-four. A good sign. Mali and Will are already unloading their bags, and when Mali looks up, she tries to play it cool and not make a big deal about Dusty actually showing up. But from the swell of red and pink emotions surrounding her, and Mali's beaming smile, it's obvious to Dusty that her friend is thrilled. She can't help grinning back at her.

Dusty checks her concealer in the mirror, making sure the purple circles around her eyes aren't too visible, then grabs her bag containing a towel, change of clothes and a bottle of icy water and gets out.

Walking over to them, Dusty tries not to feel self-conscious about her white sundress, and how her black bikini might be visible through the fine fabric. Even though she knows it doesn't exactly go with her hiking boots, she's glad she wore it, because she feels hotter and heavier every second in the heat.

"There she is," Mali says, still grinning. She looks between Dusty and Will, who haven't made eye contact, then asks, "Ready to go?"

Dusty nods.

When Will doesn't say a word, Dusty chances a glance at him. Slinging a bag over his shoulder, he's outwardly calm, cloaked in blue, but beneath there are pulsing flickers of violet and pink.

As they set out on the trail, Dusty leads the way, grateful for the breeze rolling up the mountain, cool in the shade of the lush canopy of green hardwoods. Giant, slow-moving cumulonimbus clouds hover high above in the blue sky, dwarfing the surrounding mountain range.

"Not sure if you know, Will," Mali calls out from the middle, "but it's a rare privilege to get Dusty's head out of her books and her ass off the mountain. Makes today pretty special."

"I've heard," Will calls from the back.

Dusty wishes his voice didn't purr in her ears.

"She actually knows a lot about nature and stuff, though," Mali adds. "Because of her dad. And where they live. Will is like, Mr. Nature, Dust. He hikes everywhere. Even before school."

Dusty glances back at her friend, offering a nod and smile of recognition. Behind Mali, Dusty catches Will looking directly at her. She expects him to look away, but he doesn't. Instead, his gaze feels like a challenge.

Flustered, Dusty turns back to face the path.

There's a long beat of silence before Mali adds, "Cool, cool. I'll just talk to myself. I didn't realize JD and Amber were such a key part of, you know, having conversations."

Dusty hears Will's soft chuckle from the back, and she can't help but smile too.

As the trail steepens, the forest seems to vibrate in the sunshine. Even though she isn't running like she does at night, the vibration is echoed within Dusty's own body, her cells firing glimmers of that feeling that's becoming more and more familiar to her. It takes her a moment to pinpoint it, then the word thrums into her mind. *Alive.*

"Slow down," Mali whispers, so only Dusty can hear.

Dusty abides, focusing on the sounds around her as she tries to keep her new physicality in check. She can hear the chatter of mountain wildlife layered with Will and Mali's familiar footfall, breath and heartbeats. The beginning-of-summer energy they carry with them is surprisingly heartening, even if Dusty knows she can't really be a part of it. It has her wondering if Mali was right. Maybe company isn't so bad after all.

A loud, piercing whistle cuts through the chorus of cicadas. They stop, and as they look up, there's another screech, closer now.

"What *was* that?" Mali asks.

"A broad-winged hawk," Dusty and Will answer in unison, still looking up as the small raptor appears high above through the trees, circling for prey.

Mali chuckles and when Dusty and Will look down, their eyes meet again. Dusty is hit with a river of his colors. They swirl and reach out and wrap around her.

"Umm, guys?"

The colors evaporate, revealing Mali, looking between Dusty and Will. Dusty turns to keep walking. She doesn't slow down until the sound of running water is trickling in her ears. She looks up to see the sheltered top platform of the fire tower through the trees, and moments later they're standing at the edge of a sun-drenched, rock-covered clearing.

The stream runs through the middle of a tumble of rocks, its water weaving down the slope between cracks and stone hollows, then feeding into a deep natural pool. The crystal-clear water fades into a heavenly blue at the center, sunshine sparkling on the surface. Towering above it all is the sixty-foot-tall, rusty steel fire tower, rising from the boulders in the middle of the clearing. The place is completely empty.

"Yes!" Mali yells as she runs toward the natural pool, leaving Dusty and Will behind.

For a moment, Dusty just marvels at the sun-kissed oasis, but then the flowing water reminds her again of what Will had said to her. That all water runs to Black River. And suddenly all she can see is Andrew Everett in his watery grave.

"I wasn't sure you'd be here," Will says, slowly moving to join Mali who is already laying down a blanket, covering it with food and drinks.

"Yeah, sorry," she says, joining him, not entirely sure why she apologized.

Will looks at her from under his squinting, furrowed brow. He closes one eye to block out the sun. "Don't be," he says.

While Mali and Will jump right in, Dusty dips her toes into the cool mountain water, welcoming the icy jolt. She's surprised to see Will looking up at her, a curious smile on his face. He doesn't seem to care if Mali notices him watching her anymore. Dusty can't help but smile back, and is about to take her dress off to swim when she senses a familiar presence somewhere behind her.

Dusty turns just as Eli and Jesse emerge from the trees.

"Told you it was nice," Eli says to Jesse, then walks straight toward Dusty, wearing his most charming grin.

Dusty is speechless. She can feel Mali and Will watching.

"Hey," Eli says, stopping a foot away from Dusty.

She takes in the sight of him. It's the first time she's seen him in daylight since he fed from Jesse. He looks noticeably stronger, and his colors flow freely around him, arising from the crown of his head then cascading downward to loop back inside of him through his core. There's a subtle layer of purplish gray underneath it all, exposing his tension.

"Hey," she manages. "I didn't know you were coming."

He hesitates, then turns to Mali and Will. "Hope you don't mind if we join you?"

Mali welcomes them with warmth, but with one eyebrow raised, Dusty can see that her best friend knows something's up. Will nods, acknowledging them, but doesn't speak.

Jesse glances between Dusty and Eli, hesitant, before taking off his shoes and t-shirt, then sitting down on the edge of the water.

Eli drapes his arm around Dusty, squeezing her close to him as he whispers into her ear. "Sorry, I didn't mean to make this weird."

"What're you doing here?" she whispers.

"Matt was going to hang with us at my place, but he bailed to go to a party in town and I didn't really . . ." he sighs, then lowers his voice even more. "It's weird when it's just me and Jesse now. We had to do *something*. I couldn't just be alone with him all day. Now that I'm . . ."

"Feeding from him?" Dusty says flatly. She glances back at the others, who are already making small talk. "But why *here*?" she asks.

"I don't know," he says, defensive. "I was panicking, then I felt pulled to you, and it seemed like good idea. I'm still so confused . . ." He looks back at the others, then at Will, who is now sitting on a rock with his feet in the water, the sun beaming down on his shoulders as he looks directly at Eli. "This must be hard for you," Eli says.

Dusty sighs. "It is. Which is why you being here, with Jesse here too, is . . . complicated. And I really don't know if I can take anything more right now."

Eli nods, understanding. "Will does smell good," he says.

Dusty knows he's joking, trying to lighten the mood, but her face remains stony and cold. "I'm sorry," Eli says. "I just . . ."

"What?"

"I missed you," he says, then shakes his head. "You're like, my best friend now. More than that. We're—" He stops, turning his head to the tree line.

A moment later Dusty smells it. *Them.* She turns, and the others, who'd been pretending not to be fascinated by their conversation, follow her gaze.

JD and Amber appear from between the trees on the clearing's edge. JD is grinning, while Amber stands slightly behind him.

"'Sup motherfuckers!" JD yells. He strides to the pool's edge, then kicks off his shoes, pulls off his t-shirt, and jumps into the water with a bomb that drenches everyone.

Amber approaches more slowly. Her eyes, a rich chocolate brown, glow in that way that Dusty understands. Amber is well-fed.

"Shit," Dusty mutters.

"Hey, guys," Mali says cautiously.

"What's up?" Amber responds, nonchalant. Her eyes move over everyone's bodies in a way that makes Dusty and Eli feel the need to immediately rejoin the group.

"Where have you two been?" Mali asks.

"Oh, we just went on a little trip," JD says. "We've been . . . hungry for *more*, if you know what I mean?"

Dusty watches as Mali and Jesse become increasingly uneasy. Will gives nothing away.

"I'm going to check out the view," Amber says to JD. She jumps over the stream, then over the rocky ground to the base of the fire tower, and begins to ascend the rickety, open-air staircase.

"Okay . . ." Mali says slowly, then turns to Dusty and Eli with wide eyes.

Jesse looks at Eli, and although Dusty doesn't know how much he knows, it's clear that he's putting the pieces together. He can see what JD and Amber are.

"What do we do?" she whispers to Eli.

"Don't worry," Eli says. "Remember, I'm stronger now and I can always do that . . . thing, with my eyes."

JD starts to chat away like everything's normal, but the more he speaks, the quieter the others become. It only seems to add fuel to his fire. He starts to show off, flipping into the water in somersaults then pushing himself out with ease. It's obvious that his body has transformed, with tight muscles that knot over his once-skinny frame. But no one says anything, and after several more flips and bombs, JD walks over to the tower.

Turning back to Eli, he says, "Want to see who's game to do the highest jump?"

"I think I'm good, bro," Eli answers cooly.

Amber is sitting at the top of the fire tower, looking down at everyone, her legs dangling over the sixty-foot drop. Instead of taking the stairs like she had, JD starts to ascend the frame, pulling himself up using only his arms and upper body strength.

"What're you doing, JD?" Mali yells. "Maybe chill on the whole daredevil act."

"What's this guy's problem?" Jesse asks.

Will watches, characteristically quiet.

When JD is about halfway up the tower, he turns himself around and in a swift movement he swings away from the tower and lets go.

Everyone draws in a breath, then holds it.

The deepest part of the natural pool, which is at least fifteen feet away from the tower, is only around ten feet deep. JD hits the center of the water with so much speed that his legs, possibly more, would be crushed against the solid rock bottom. As the group look down at the shadow of his body under the water, Dusty can feel the chills of their fear and dread.

But a few seconds later, bubbles arise, followed by JD, who can't contain his own laughter. "You should see your faces!" He swims to the edge, ready to pull himself out, but he is met by Eli, who holds out his hand to help him up. JD takes it and is pulled out and onto his feet like he doesn't weigh a thing. "Cheers, bro," he says, a sharp edge on the words, but Dusty notices how he avoids making eye contact.

Eli flashes a smile, then pulls him away, his arm around JD's shoulders. "Time to take it somewhere else," he says.

"So touchy!" JD smiles. "And last I checked, it's a free country. Happy Independence Day, y'all!" he calls back to the others.

Dusty is listening from the edge of the water, trying to steady her pounding heart.

"You think you're pretty funny," Eli says, "fucking with your friends?"

"I'm not fucking with them. I'm fucking with *you*." He looks back at Dusty. "Did your girlfriend have any good squirrels today?" he asks a little too loudly.

Dusty can feel Eli's rising temper, and how hard he's trying to hold it back. "I'll tell you one more time. Take it somewhere else."

"You think you're so much better than me, don't you? But we're the same." He smiles. "Maybe I should ask your boy Jesse how he's doing? How it felt to have your teeth sinking into him."

Dusty has been watching Eli's fists clench into tight balls that radiate red, and before JD sees it coming, Eli slams one into JD's cheek, sending him falling backwards.

JD brings his hand to the place he was hit, then grins, and looks back to Dusty.

There's suddenly movement in her periphery, and when Dusty turns to look, Will and Jesse are walking toward them. They stand beside Eli, facing JD.

JD's grin twists so his top lip curls up, his teeth slightly bared. Dusty is moving before she can think, stepping between JD and Will, cautioning JD with a single shake of her head.

A loud clang echoes through the air making Dusty flinch. She turns to see Mali climbing the stairs of the fire tower, picking up the phone she just dropped onto the metal steps. She continues up. Amber is still sitting at the top, quietly watching from high above.

"Mali!" Dusty calls, frustrated.

"I just need to talk to her!" she calls back, continuing up the fire tower.

Heart still pounding, Dusty is barely holding herself together.

"You should go," Eli says to Jesse. "Take him with you," he adds, nodding to Will.

"I'm not going anywhere," Will says, his voice firm.

Jesse doesn't move either.

JD laughs out loud. "What're you even doing here, Will, is it? I thought you were like, special needs or something?"

A wave of rage sweeps through Dusty and her body takes over once again. She lunges at JD, grabbing his arm and twisting it behind his back so he's facing the other way. He's still laughing, but it doesn't matter because the second she's touching him, she's gone.

A large man sits at a desk, hunched over a laptop. It's the only thing on the clean, sterile stone surface. Floating shelves flank the walls on either side of him, almost completely empty apart from the odd book or object. Behind him is a wall of glass. It bounces a reflection back—JD approaching slowly, cautiously.

"What?" the man says without looking up. His voice is cold.

JD's heart is pounding, but not from the usual fear of his father. It's been replaced with something dark. Loathing.

"What do you want?" his dad says, looking up at his son. His eyes appear black in the dimly lit room.

"I wondered if you've had a chance to think about those decks I showed you?" JD asks. He's aware of a hot flutter rising up his body, the same feeling that's been lingering there all week.

"Decks?" His father sits back in his chair, a look of repugnance on his face.

"Yeah . . . with the Maschine MK3 . . . for music production. I'm going to a party tomorrow night, a bonfire. I wanted to bring them. Test them out in front of a crowd."

The man stares at his son with a subtle, amused smile. "God, I thought moving here, to this mountain, would help you become a man. A real man, who isn't interested in crap like DJ decks." He shakes his head. "JD the DJ. Ridiculous."

JD doesn't say anything, but he can feel a foreign sense of bravery settling into his bones. "We all know we moved here because you're paranoid. Because you need to control me, and Mom, like everything else."

The large man stands, pushing the office chair out from underneath him. He's at least a head taller than his son, and a few dozen pounds heavier. "You little prick. Your mother has ruined you, you know that? Obsessing over you. Spoiling you. And what does she have to show for it? A loser. A nobody." He walks toward JD, his weight and aggression looming over him, then he raises his hand and cracks it over the back of JD's head.

The feeling inside JD flutters again, running up his spine, spreading. "Fuck you," JD spits.

"What did you say to me?" his father asks sharply.

"Fuck. You." JD pushes his dad in the chest, surprised as his dad falls down onto the solid, polished concrete floor.

JD can sense the adrenaline rushing through his father's body, causing his arteries to flood his muscles with blood, raising his blood pressure. His black pupils grow even larger, and his skin oozes a sickly-sweet sheen of sweat. JD crouches over him, hesitating only for a second before his lip curls up, drawn to the beating pulse on his father's neck, and he plunges his teeth into him. The rushing blood transcends everything JD has ever known, and when he returns back into himself, JD knows strength for the first time in his life. The sensation is so seductive that he barely notices his father is dead.

"What's wrong with her?" Will asks, panic lacing his low voice.

JD yanks his arm away from Dusty, turning to laugh in her face. "Cute," he says. "You think you can overpower me."

Eli is at Dusty's side, and she looks back to Will who is studying her, his brow furrowed.

"Why are you fighting it?" JD taunts Dusty. "Come on, give in to your upgrade."

Voices draw everyone's attention upward. At the top of the fire tower, Amber and Mali are arguing, their pitches steadily rising.

"Amber, please!" Mali yells. "You don't have to act like this. Dusty's still the same, for the most part . . . Why are you . . . Is it JD? Does he have some kind of control over you? We can help you!"

"You have no idea," Amber says coldly. "He *chose* me. I know it might be hard for you to understand—"

"I'm just worried about you," Mali pleads. "You're my friend, and I know what's happened to you isn't your fault—"

"Shut up!" Amber screams.

There's the sharp, unmistakable sound of a slap and Dusty looks up just in time to see Mali falling over the edge of the tower. There's a loud thud as her shoulder collides with the metal frame, then her body hurtles through the air, plummeting like a brick.

Dusty's instincts take over, and just before Mali hits the ground she's swept up in Dusty's arms. The force sends them both tumbling backwards onto the rocks.

Everyone else is staring, stunned.

A slow clap starts to build from behind them, and no one has to look to know it's JD.

Dusty helps Mali sit up, frantically checking she's okay. Mali is rigid with shock, unable to speak.

The metal tower creaks, and by the time Dusty looks over Amber is at the base, then she and JD are running into the trees beyond. Gone.

A sweet, metallic scent fills the air. Dusty breathes in deep through her nose as she homes in on its origin.

Eli is repeating her name. "Dusty, Dusty." But he can't get her attention, because all she can see is the rich, fresh blood trickling down Mali's arm.

"Run," Eli says, shaking Dusty.

Will is at Mali's side, checking on her. He turns to Dusty to do the same, reaching out to her.

"Run!" Eli repeats.

30

I Am a Predator, and You Are My Prey

Dusty slams the front door behind her, stopping for the first time since she fled the fire tower. The entranceway of her house is still and quiet. Her hands tremble as she clenches them into fists, the rest of her body rigid. There's a rush of air behind her as the door is flung back open.

Eli stands in front of her. He reaches his arms around her, pulling her close. They breathe together, reeling from what just happened.

"Mali, Will . . ." she starts, but she can't find the words to ask.

"They're okay. Will drove Mali home. I tried to follow JD and Amber's scent."

"Where . . . where are they?"

"I lost them along the way, but I think they were headed back here, to the mountain."

Dusty's panic begins to rise, but she's able to breathe when she remembers that her dad and Opi aren't here. They're safe for now.

"Dusty . . ." Eli says, his voice desperate. "You have to feed. I mean *really* feed."

She takes a step back from him, the rhythmic click of cicadas outside throbbing in her head.

"The longer you fight this, the more dangerous you are. The more unpredictable everything is. You *know* you can control yourself. If I can, you can. Why are you still fighting it?"

"Why?" her voice trembles. "Are you seriously asking me *why*? *Again*? We're talking about human blood, Eli! Feeding off human blood!"

He sighs. "Exactly. Human blood. Not human life. We don't have to kill anyone for it. Not again. I think . . . I think if we started out like Kristen, without killing, you wouldn't feel the same way about it. I don't know why the fuck we're like this, but we have to face that it's not going away. The longer you go without it, the more twisted and fucked up you're going to feel."

Dusty doesn't notice the tears streaming down her cheeks. "I can't. I can't do it."

"*Why*, Dusty? What if someone was willing? Like Jesse was. I've been thinking—maybe we crave the people who like us, because *they* might be okay with it? They might *give* themselves to us, so we don't have to take from others."

Dusty shakes her head. "Do you even hear yourself? That is so fucked up, Eli. That's called using someone. Taking advantage of *their* feelings so *you* can enact the most messed up part of yourself on them. Do you want to know what I saw, when I touched JD?"

Eli waits.

"I saw him kill his own dad. And you know how that made him feel? Strong. Not guilty. *Powerful*. And you saw him today, it's like the more he feeds, the stronger he gets and the more superior that makes him feel. It's like he's slipping further and further away from who he used to be. Is that what you want? Is that what you see for us?"

Eli shakes his head. "No, Dusty. That's not who we are. It doesn't have to be like that. Look at Kristen."

"We're murderers, Eli," she says, her voice flat now. "Just like JD. That's who we are. But by all means, go, do whatever you want." She steps aside, the open doorway behind her. "I just want to be alone."

Eli shakes his head, running his hands over his hair. "Dusty—"

"Go. Please. Just leave me alone."

He opens his mouth like he's going to say more, but he doesn't. Instead, he turns and leaves.

Dusty is facing the mirror that hangs beside the coatrack, her own reflection now visible in Eli's wake. The sight of herself is enough to shatter her.

Her knees crumple beneath her, and she lies down on the Persian rug that's been on the floor of this entranceway for generations. The old wool pile bristles against her bare arms and legs, and just as she's thinking she can't take one more moment of this life, she is pulled away, into the mind of a stranger. A stranger she's now starting to know as her mother.

Sarah had never known what it meant to feel seen, until she'd met Chris. Even though there were parts of herself she kept hidden, the version of herself that she was through his eyes felt good. Special. A version she wanted to remain. It was like she had a witness, who made her existence real and meaningful. She was no longer the girl with a father with dementia. Dementia that killed him and her mother, burned and buried them under the ash-cloaked rubble of her family home.

That girl was gone, and the one Chris saw was born. And everything that he came with—his home, his family, his kindness, his strength—was hers.

He offered it all freely, just like his love.

Little things about her, that before him had lived in the shadow of illness, the shadow of fire, were being noticed and cherished. The feeling filled her up to the brim. Looking back, she was so swept away by the perfection of it all that she forgot to look within. She forgot that she didn't know how to love herself, without him.

When she was carrying their first child, a baby girl, her heart had soared. Her changing body, giving life, giving love, and that man, right by her side.

She had expected there to be lows that equaled the highs. But what she didn't expect was how much it would take to give. No matter how hard he tried, he would never be able to fathom it.

And then there were two. Two girls depending on her love. But she was no longer the version of herself that he knew so completely. No longer the version of herself that he could fully see. Roles were divided, out of necessity, and they could no longer share the same perspective. She could no longer see the version of herself that she'd loved through his eyes. And as life continued and the years went by, she did her very best, but she was lost, untethered again.

Buried by this new person she was, her past inescapable. Wandering in the forest, lost and confused, missing time—her father's illness had come to claim her, hiding inside her all along.

She looks down at the rug in the entranceway, terrified. She can feel what she's about to do before she articulates the thought. She knows the pain she's about to cause. She knows she's going to leave. She knows it's the best way to keep her girls safe.

She has no love left to give, because she has no love for herself.

The ceiling comes back into focus, and with it, Dusty's first glimpse at some sort of truth: her mother had known unimaginable loss, yes, but she hadn't changed like she has. Dusty feels cracked open, too exhausted to process any of it, too exhausted to stop herself from feeling it all.

She lies there, listening to the world through the open front door as her emotions drain onto the floor beneath her, lulled by the cicadas outside.

She's too exhausted to notice that the house isn't empty after all.

That her sister is at home, upstairs, and she heard every word Dusty and Eli said.

Hidden in the tree, Eli waits for the sun to set before he treads along the sturdy branch, passing over the high fence of JD's property.

When his feet hit the ground he pauses, waiting, listening. But no one's around.

He sprints over the lawn, the rolling green lit up with bright lights shining from around the house as he tries to decide what he's willing to do. All he knows is that JD and Amber are getting out of control, and that more people will be hurt if he doesn't stop them.

Dusty won't survive unless she feeds, and she won't do that until she sees that this doesn't make them monsters. He just needs to get into JD and Amber's heads and convince them that there's another way.

When he reaches the house he knows they're there. He can smell them. But he can't see them. The lights from outside bounce off the glass walls of the house, mingling with the light inside, the reflection disorienting as he quietly moves around the perimeter.

As he reaches the first concrete wall, he stops to listen. There's a faint shuffle of movement, somewhere, then nothing.

He begins to move again, slowly approaching a corner of the house. He waits, listening, then peers around the corner just as his legs are knocked out from under him.

Eli scrambles to get up, but JD grabs at his arms, pulling him down. With a free leg, Eli kicks, hard, his foot landing on JD's stomach, knocking the wind out of him.

Standing, Eli bends down and grabs JD by the throat, dragging him up the wall, pinning him to it. JD's eyes are closed so tight that Eli almost laughs, but instead, he asks, "Why are you doing this? Why are you so determined to be an absolute psychopath?"

"Me?" JD asks. "You're the one sneaking around my house." His eyes flash open, and Eli scans them, hurrying, ready to lock on and take control, but the air around him shifts and suddenly everything is dark.

He gasps for air, choking on the fabric over his face as his arms reach out for something to hold onto. Someone to fight.

Hands clamp down on his wrists, pulling his arms behind him. He struggles, but there's no point. He never stood a chance.

"Got him," Amber says.

JD chuckles as Eli's feet start to move beneath him, propelled forward by the pair holding him up. "We didn't know which one of you would come first," JD says. "I was kind of hoping it would be Dusty, now you're feeding and all." He laughs. "And you thought *I* was gay just because I hang out with girls . . ."

Eli struggles, thrashing his arms to free himself as they begin to move downstairs. His feet trip and stumble underneath him as he gasps, every breath through the fabric hot and stale.

"Here we go," JD says. "Nice and private. The perfect place to find out what we're made of. It was becoming a little tedious, doing it on ourselves, right babe?"

Amber doesn't answer as the air grows cold, and the little light that had been penetrating the fabric over Eli's face turns to black.

Dusty doesn't notice that it's dark outside until the sound of a car on the gravel driveway reconnects her to reality. She'd stopped thinking a long while ago, her brain trapped in a fog of exhaustion that rendered time irrelevant. But as soon as headlights glow through the front door's windowpanes, she gets up from the rug and rejoins the present, ready to meet her needs—to be alone, and to feed.

Slipping out the back door and down through the garden, she walks toward the tree line. The sun's warmth still lingers under the canopy, thick and sweet. She breathes it in, about to run, to seek the hunt, to cling to the only part of life that's true, when a heart-stopping smell drifts to her on the breeze, bolting her in place.

She listens to footsteps in the grassy garden begin to crunch on forest leaves.

"Dusty?" he calls through the dimness.

Her entire body tingles in response, surging her into action. In a movement so fast that she barely registers it herself, she's in front of him.

His name escapes from her mouth without permission. "Will," she whispers.

The warm light from the porch reaches his face, exposing the tension she can already feel. His eyes are locked onto hers, questioning.

"Why are you here?" she asks, her voice deep and thready, like a warning.

"Why do you think?"

She studies him, trying to understand.

"I brought back your car . . ." he says, his voice slow and steady, a contradiction to his colors and racing heart. "But that's not why I came. I . . ." He shakes his head, his eyes still firmly on hers. "Dusty, you caught her. You caught her from a six-story drop. The way you moved . . . the way you've been acting . . ." He steps closer, closing the space between them. "What *are* you?"

In the haze of blues around him, one is muddier, a hue Dusty recognizes as fear, primal, but present. "You should listen to your instincts, Will," she says softly. "They're telling you to run."

He steps closer again. "What *are* you, Dusty?"

The full force of his scent, his energy and his colors, seeps in through her pores. Intoxicating. Her teeth ache so much she has to push her tongue against them, trying to relieve the pressure. She closes her eyes, seeking control. "You have to leave," she says, breathless. "Now."

"I'm not leaving until you tell me the truth."

Her eyes flash open.

"JD and Amber," he pushes. "*They're* obviously fucking dangerous. And you're telling me you are too." His heart rate continues to rise as he speaks, his colors now reaching out to her. "Mali almost died today, Dusty, so this isn't just about you. You might not feel anything for me, but you do owe me the truth. I have the right to know."

The air between them is filled with static, almost unbearable, and through it Dusty realizes that she's been so afraid of her own power, her own strength, that she hasn't noticed Will's. His power to dissolve her self-control. His strength that unravels her.

As he waits for her answer his eyes search hers, and it's as if he begins to see past her mask, see how scared she is. He reaches up and places a hand on the side of her face, his cool palm cradling her neck and jaw, his fingers combing into her hair.

Unable to breathe, Dusty roots herself in place, at war with her every urge. To hold him. To kiss him. To tell him her every thought. To grab him by his hair and tilt his head to the side and plunge her teeth into his neck. Taking it all.

A loud boom reverberates through the forest, making them both flinch. Will's hand falls from her face as the sky is illuminated by a sudden flash of light and color, followed by another, then another.

It takes Dusty longer than it should to remember it's the fourth of July. Fireworks.

It's the jolt she needed. A warning shot. And he needs a warning shot too.

She thrusts him back against a tree with the full force of her speed, her skin aching where his hand had touched her. Aching for him to touch her again. Will tries to move, winded, pinned against rough bark, his t-shirt twisted in her grip, but he shakes against the pressure of her, like she's made of stone.

Fortified by the shift in power, her eyes scan his face then move down to his neck where his pulse is throbbing. "You really want to know what I am?" she asks.

He nods, unflinching as she lingers, hesitating over every inch of him.

The booming fireworks are her only tether to what remains of her self-control, and for a moment it's so clear—what she's most afraid of isn't being like her mother. It's of showing herself to the ones she loves, and them still finding a reason to leave her. Again.

The leaves above them shiver as they're met with the first drops of rain.

Will's eyes are still on hers, waiting.

"Don't you understand?" she asks. "I am a predator. And you are my prey."

The fireworks slow, then stop, and the sky is dark once again.

There's nothing but the sound of rain and their breath, until a desperate plea calls to Dusty down a now-familiar bond.

She gasps as panic takes the reins of her body, and another name slips from her mouth. "Eli," she whispers, then louder, to Will, "Go home. Leave the mountain. Now."

Will is shaking his head, but before he can speak, she's gone.

31
The River

Seated on a chair, his wrists and ankles bound in tight straps, Eli blinks as the fabric is removed from his face.

He tries to turn around to see his captors, but they're just out of sight, whispering behind him.

Scanning the dark room around him, he tries to listen to what they're saying, picking up pieces of an argument.

". . . just use a knife."

"We've done that. We should try burning him first."

His eyes search for something, anything, that might help him get out of here as he calls down the bond to Dusty. But the room is empty. No furniture, just concrete. Like some kind of bunker.

"Shit," JD curses. "She's already here."

A second later, a heavy door closes and they're gone.

Dusty's dress is soaked through by the time she reaches JD's property. Another wave of panic surges as Eli calls to her, but this time he's warning her away.

In that moment it's clear what their once-confusing relationship is. How their initial attraction evolved into friendship, then something so much more. It's familial. Their bond comes with the feeling that she would do anything to save him, just like Opi, driving her beyond the chaos inside her.

My brother, she thinks. *My sister*, she feels him whisper back.

Grasping the fence, she looks through the gaps, through the trees on the other side, to the house a few hundred feet away from her. Bright lights spotlight the surrounding grass, their glow reaching the forest around Dusty. She looks up, trying to figure out the best way over.

She can smell that Eli was right here, not long ago.

A few yards to her left, there's a tree with a branch that reaches over the fence like a bridge. She spins to move toward it, but there's a breath of breeze around her, a haze of interconnected colors, and suddenly JD is blocking her way, Amber by his side.

They reek of Eli.

"What are you doing to him?" Dusty asks, trying to ignore the fact that she's so exhausted she can barely speak.

"You guys," he says, amused. "So self-righteous, so easy to rile up."

"Cut the shit, JD," Dusty snaps, then turns to Amber. "Where is he? Please. Just let him go."

Amber says nothing as JD just smiles, and Dusty wonders how who they were *before* determined who they are now. And what, if any, enhanced powers they might be developing.

JD looks Dusty up and down as her legs sway from fatigue. "Aww," he says with a pout. "You're not doing so well, are you? And you clearly can't do . . . whatever the fuck it is that Mr. Alpha in there does with his eyes . . ." He nods in the direction of the house. "We thought getting him alone would make it easier, but *shit* he is strong. Ever since he fed from Jesse, we knew you two would become a problem for us. Did you really think we came to your little gathering today just for fun?" He shakes his head. "Lucky for us, you're both so predictable."

"What're you talking about?" Dusty pleads. "What do you want from him?"

"We want answers, just like you. We're just a little more proactive about it. So we thought we'd create an opportunity to test some things out on you guys. Find out more about what we're capable of. What our limits are, and of course, the million-dollar question."

Dusty grips onto the fence to hold herself upright.

JD smiles, then looks at Amber. "You want to tell her?"

"You're supposed to be the smart one," she says to Dusty. "Surely you're wondering too?"

"What? Wondering what?" Dusty doesn't know how long she can stand here listening to them.

"Are we immortal?" Amber asks, matter-of-fact.

Dusty's stomach drops, remembering Kristen's vision of them cutting themselves as the question lingers in the air. She supposes it's possible, like anything at this point, but it reveals that like Dusty, they too are blind. They know nothing about what they are, and they have nothing but fiction and legends to guide them.

"Or more specifically," JD adds. "What would it take for us to die? If we don't feed would we starve to death? Could we survive a gunshot to the head? And now we have *you* . . ." He turns to Amber, who hesitates, her colors shifting, unreadable, but before Dusty knows what's happening, they're lunging for her, restraining her by her arms.

Dusty stumbles as they begin to drag her through the forest, quickly and purposefully, like they know exactly where they're going. She struggles to free herself, but she knows there's no point. Their power is immeasurably greater than her own.

"Where are you taking me?" she groans, her feet tripping as they hold her up, forcing her forward.

"We know what you did," Amber says.

"You talk about it enough," JD adds. "You didn't really think you'd get away with it, did you? That all that animal blood could change what you really are?"

In Dusty's ear, Amber whispers, "You're a killer."

She shudders as she stumbles down, and they heave her along, descending the mountain, all the way down to Black River.

Will holds his phone out in front of him, its flashlight illuminating Dusty's tracks.

He'd followed, the second she'd run, without hesitation. If he hadn't just seen how scared she was, how hard she was trying to push him away, he may not have thought she needed his help. But after today, it's even more clear that whatever is going on, she's in danger.

He's guided by her more obvious bare footprints, sunken into wet dirt, leading him to muddy tracks where the forest floor is leaf-littered and rocky. With the rain, it'll all be gone in minutes. He has to hurry.

As he moves over fallen trees, up and down boulders, scrambling to keep his phone from slipping from his wet hand, he wonders if he'd imagined when she'd whispered Eli's name, or if his jealousy is getting the better of him. It was like she was answering a call, although Will hadn't heard a sound.

Her tracks get fainter as the rain intensifies, the muddy traces over leaves almost completely washed away. The distance between them growing.

Panic begins to creep inside him.

Reaching the perimeter of an ancient sugar maple, any trace of Dusty disappears on the thick layer of leaves below. He searches with the flashlight, spinning, fumbling for a sign, anything to guide him. To take him to her.

There's nothing.

He stands there, his heart thudding in his chest, in his ears, everywhere, until he hears a voice call out, "Who's there?"

Will spins, the growing feeling that something terrible is at play more present than ever.

"I'm not going to hurt you."

Will holds his phone up in the direction of the voice, its light just reaching a rain-soaked woman.

Kristen King.

Dusty's hair is plastered across her face, wet with rain and tears, when she hears the surging flow of the river.

"Amber thought the pool would do," JD says, their pace swift as he and Amber continue to drag her through the night. "But I don't want my mom to have to see you in there every day. Besides, what if we need to cool off? Or the sheriff sniffs around? And then I remembered your little secret. It would be more poetic if we brought you to the body. Buried you alive right beside him, for comparison's sake. See how long it would take you to rot like him. That is, if you rotted at all. But I'm afraid the sheriff's too close now. They'll find him any day."

Dusty listens, but Amber's words still linger in her mind. *You're a killer.* Why would she say that, like JD isn't one too? Then, through the haze of her own guilt and everything else she's carrying inside her, Dusty realises. "You don't know, do you?" she asks, turning her head in Amber's direction. "You don't know what he did to his dad."

Through the wet strands of hair over her eyes she can see their interconnected colors react, different enough now that she can see whose belong to one or the other. JD's darkening, sparkling. Amber's slowing, tentative.

"How did you—" JD starts.

"What's she talking about?" Amber asks.

"You think Eli's the only one who developed an ability?" Dusty pushes.

"I *know* he's not," JD snaps, pulling them along.

"Yeah?" Dusty asks, breathless. "What's yours?"

JD chuckles.

"Because mine is being able to see things," Dusty says. "Other people's memories."

Amber slows beside her, while JD tries to continue forward, to the river.

"He killed him," Dusty continues. "His own dad. The night before the bonfire."

Amber is quiet, but Dusty can feel her grip falter. She shakes her arm free, just long enough to wipe the hair out of her eyes before Amber takes hold of her again.

"Fuck this," JD mumbles. "Don't—"

"This isn't about testing your limits," Dusty pushes again, her eyes landing on JD's through the darkness. "Or finding out what we are. It's not even about the blood. You're addicted to the power. You felt small all your life until the moment you killed him. Now you're just chasing that feeling."

As Dusty speaks, Amber's colors begin to spiral, whirling slowly around her, detangling from JD's as his reach out, darker still, flecks of light sparking in them like tiny stars.

JD tuts. "You always thought you were so much better than everyone. But you're not, you know that, right? No matter how hard you try, we're the same."

Dusty wonders if he's right. If she deserves whatever is about to happen to her. "Maybe," she says, turning to Amber. "But I don't think you're the same as us. You haven't killed anyone, have you? You don't actually want me to die."

"Enough!" JD commands, his voice sending a cold shiver through

Dusty's core. The effect on Amber must be similar, because she picks up her pace as they continue toward the river.

Dusty's bare feet squelch through mud and wet leaves, and for the first time since the day she started to feel different, she realizes she's cold. Her sodden dress clings to her aching body.

As they reach the water's edge the rain begins to slow.

"Are you really going to do this?" Dusty asks Amber.

"She will do whatever I say," JD says, unbuckling his belt. He slips it off and fastens it tight around Dusty's wrists where Amber still holds them against Dusty's back. Then, he steps down into the river.

Amber does the same, and together they tug Dusty into the water.

The current is strong and the cold cuts a sliver through her exhaustion, giving her a glimpse of Eli, trapped somewhere dark, and a fresh wave of panic churns in her stomach. There's a glimmer on the surface of the water, and Dusty looks up to see the clouds above her parting, revealing the black eternity beyond, glistening with stars and a bright moon.

"You obviously know you can hold your breath for a long time," JD says, looking down into the deepest part of the river. "Let's hope, for your sake, it's forever."

"Eli will kill—"

They pull her under.

At first there's only cold and complete darkness, but as Dusty's eyes adjust, moonlight reaches down, all the way to the river's bed. For a second she sees Andrew Everett down there, the last sight of him ingrained in her mind forever, then there's nothing but rocks and shadows.

She's pulled down, thrashing as she's dragged all the way to the bottom, but they're too strong, and she's too weak. JD lets go, while Amber, who grips her bound arms hard, pins her down to the riverbed. They watch as JD swims to a rock as big as his torso, and begins to roll it toward them. He grabs hold of Dusty's ankles with one hand, then rolls the rock with the other, straining until it thuds onto Dusty's legs.

The weight of it crashes onto her knees and shins, sending sharp pain wincing through her. Reflexively, she gasps, taking in a mouthful of cold water. She feels like she's choking, but she doesn't. *Maybe they're right*, she thinks, and she'll be trapped down here forever. Not dead, but not living.

JD lets go of her ankles and swims a little further this time, to a rock heavy enough that she could never push it off, not with the little strength she has left.

Unable to move her buried legs in front of her, Dusty sits there, watching, Amber still beside her, gripping Dusty's arms bound at her back, as JD begins rolling the giant rock in her direction.

She knows this is her last chance.

With all the strength she has left, she jerks forward. Amber's hands slip from her arms as she pivots them to the side, just enough for her hands to clasp onto Amber's. Amber looks down, confused, then up to meet Dusty's pleading stare.

But while Dusty had hoped to implore Amber to free her, what she gets is her mind being pulled beyond itself, into a memory of Amber's.

She looks down at the white sheets strewn around her. She can feel the wound in her neck, burning as blood trickles down her shoulder and onto the bed.

There's a neon sign in the shape of a slice of pizza on the wall above her, its glow surreal. As a hand sweeps the hair off her face, she tingles with fear. He's ready to feed again. She doesn't know how much more she can take. How much more she can give.

She looks up at him, wondering how it got to this. There'd been something so alluring about JD at the bonfire. A surprising confidence that struck a chord deep within her. The way he'd watched her, so unexpectedly, it made her feel special. When he'd asked if she wanted to see his house, it only enhanced that high. No one else had been here, only her.

He grabs hold of her face and she groans. He leans in, his ear to her chest, listening. She wonders if he can feel her heart, because she can barely feel it beating.

He has taken almost all her blood. She's worried he won't stop before it's too late.

He looks up, his face shifting as if something is dawning on him. Without a word, he picks her up and carries her through the cold, quiet house, then outside, across the manicured lawn to the trees beyond. He doesn't stop until they're away from the bright lights, where it's dark and peaceful. He puts Amber down, crumpled on the earth, and with his bare hands he begins to dig.

She watches as he breaks through fallen leaves, soil, then roots, turned up and tossed aside. Then he gathers her up and lays her down in the hole. She doesn't have the energy to say a word.

He gets down into the hole beside her, wrapping her in his arms as she fades in and out of consciousness. His wrist is suddenly on her mouth, warm, salty liquid making its way between her lips.

"Drink," he whispers.

She does what he says because it feels like a lifeline, and the more she tastes the greedier she gets, until he takes his wrist away from her and holds her close once more. They remain in the ground all the way through the night, her heartbeat returning, growing stronger, matching the rhythm of his.

Dusty lets go of Amber's hands.

Amber's eyes are searching hers, trying to figure out where Dusty went. But Dusty is processing what she saw.

He can turn people. Change them. Make them like him. Like us. That's his power.

The water moves beside her, snapping her back into the present. JD has reached them, the giant rock in position as he gestures to Amber to pin Dusty down. Amber complies, pulling at Dusty so she's lying on the rocky riverbed, her arms tied up beneath her. She watches, helpless, as JD pushes the rock one more time, rolling it on top of her torso, crushing her, pinning her, her face pressed down to one side.

Her arms, her back, her hips, her neck, her jaw all feel like they're cracking under the weight of it. She gasps again, choking down more cold water. She tries to move, tries to look around, but she can't. All she can see are the ripples of moonlight on the riverbed.

JD and Amber are gone.

My sister, Eli thinks again, repeating the word that had come to him as he called for Dusty down their bond. It has filled his head since the moment JD and Amber left him in the dark.

Since this all began, he's wondered how to feel about Dusty, confused by their connection and his growing admiration for her. Now, it's so clear. She's family. And he can't help her, not from in here.

His throat constricts as another sensation of choking washes over him. She's running out of time.

He struggles against the straps around his wrists and ankles, thrashing, the metal chair buckling beneath him. He jerks his ankles hard and the chair gives way, crashing to the cold concrete floor, taking Eli along with it.

With his face pressed into the ground, his heart clenches, aching, helpless.

His breath starts to slow, the floor beneath him cooling him down, and he begins to notice a breeze. As if air is flowing from somewhere in the room, being pulled through the crack under the door behind him. He's trying to figure out where it's coming from when he hears the faint sound of footsteps on the other side of the door. Two people coming down the stairs, fast.

Dread pulses through him as the door groans open and light glows in. He braces himself.

But then he smells the last person he could have expected, along with someone else, someone like him.

"Will?" Eli asks.

"How'd he know?" Will whispers.

"Our sense of smell is . . . enhanced too," says a female voice.

Footsteps hurry toward him, then hands are on the straps around his wrists and ankles, ripping them apart.

"Kristen," Eli says as she comes into view.

She reaches out and offers her hand to him, pulling him up.

"Where's Dusty?" Will asks.

"They have her," Eli says as he begins to run out the door and up the steps. "Quick. We have to be quick. I can feel it."

None of this feels real. Nothing has since the morning she insisted on going out foraging. And now, after everything she heard Dusty and Eli say, Opi wonders if it's somehow her fault. If she set off the series of events that has led to this moment—running down the mountain in the middle of the night with Eli, Will, Kristen and Mali. Running to save Dusty.

Mali had arrived at the house not long after Dusty had left. She was looking for Dusty and Will, saying she needed to explain something to him.

"Are you talking about the fact that my sister is living on animal blood?" Opi had asked.

From there, Opi had demanded answers. And as Mali gave them to her, everything started to make sense. The bonfire. The clearing. Dusty's behaviour. Everything.

But as the time passed and they became increasingly worried about where Dusty was, Will too, Mali had expressed her theory that Dusty was in need of human blood, like the others.

They'd been halfway down the mountain, searching the forest in the rain, when they ran into Eli, Will and Kristen.

Opi's skin still prickled at the sight of Eli, but the panic in his eyes, laced with determination, had propelled her to follow him. She knew he was their best shot at finding her sister.

And now, as they get closer to the bottom, the sound of Black River raging just beyond the trees, Eli and Kristen are at the lead, getting further and further ahead as they use some kind of bond, along with their senses, to find her. To save Dusty.

Even Mali, a track star, is breathless as they try to keep up.

Eli and Kristen disappear from sight, but Opi, Will and Mali keep pushing forward until they burst through the tree line, coming to a stop at the river's edge.

The bright moon above illuminates the scene. JD and Amber are there, between Eli and Kristen and the river, blocking their way.

"Where is she?!" Opi screams, the rage in her voice startling everyone.

JD and Amber look at her. They're outnumbered now, and Opi feels nothing but determination. No fear. No panic. Just the certainty that she cannot and will not leave this place without her sister.

"She's in the water," Amber says.

JD turns, staring at Amber in shock as Eli and Will burst past them, diving into the water.

JD moves to follow, but Mali lunges for him, screaming as her arms circle his neck, trying to pull him away from the water. He jerks his head, knocking her in the nose with a crack, and her arms give way as her body falls back onto the rocks.

He turns, and his head tilts, his face twisting into a smile as he stares down at Mali's face. Opi can't see the blood, but from the way Mali winces and covers her nose, she can tell it's there.

JD takes a step toward Mali, but Opi's attention is drawn to Kristen, just to her right. She's staring at a rock hovering in the air, as if it's suspended. Opi peers through the night, the moon revealing that the rock *is* untethered. It just floats there, mid-air.

Opi's brain tries to compute what she's seeing as Kristen's eyes move, and the rock moves with them. As if she's in control. Only seconds have passed since Eli and Will went underwater, but it feels like a lifetime, everything moving in slow motion as Opi tries desperately to keep up.

"JD," Amber pleads from the riverbank. "No."

But he ignores her, and springs toward Mali.

The rock flies through the air, fast, then lands with a crack against the side of JD's head.

Kristen stares in shock as JD turns to Opi, assuming she was the one to throw it.

He launches swiftly toward Opi, but Kristen steps between them, saying, "It was me."

JD looks at her, his expression pure rage, and without hesitating he grabs her face in his hands and there's a loud, horrific snap.

Movement in the water stirs Dusty from what felt like a trance. The two large rocks pinning her down ache against her chilled bones, her skin raw like it's on fire. But then, the crushing weight is gone and she's being pulled up off the riverbed, gliding up to the surface. Air fills her lungs like pins and needles as she's dragged to the rocks, the smell of Will flooding her as he helps her scramble over them, Eli by his side.

She coughs, still spluttering water as she looks beyond them, where Opi, Mali and Amber are standing, looking down at someone lying on the ground.

"Kristen," Mali says, her voice shaking as she kneels next to the still figure.

"Where is he?" Eli asks, running over to them.

"He left," Amber says with disbelief.

"He ran," Opi says almost at the same time. "That way," she says, pointing into the forest.

Eli turns his head to look, but his vision snags on Kristen. "What happened?"

"JD, he . . ." Opi gulps. "She . . ."

Eli bends and places his ear to her chest.

He lifts his head, looking up at Mali when he says, "She's dead."

"Dead?" Amber says, her hand reaching up to cover her mouth.

"No," Mali whispers, brushing her hand over Kristen's hair.

Dusty watches from the rocks, unable to move, as Mali's tears glide down her cheeks, glistening in the moonlight.

A strange sound gurgles from Dusty's throat as she tries to speak. She looks down at her white dress, now covered in blood that drips from her chin, as she slowly lays her head down on the rocks, giving in to the aching fatigue.

Her body rises and, at first, she feels like she's levitating again, but Will's arms are beneath her, scooping her up and carrying her further into the forest. He places her down on a patch of soft, leaf-laden grass, then props her head on his knees.

A soft wave of calm spreads over Dusty and she feels like she's inside a blue flower, surrounded by gentle warmth.

"What do I do?" he asks.

Even now, Dusty feels his voice as a tingle down her spine.

Eli is suddenly beside them. "Dusty, you need to feed," he says, his voice deep and quiet. "You will either die or hurt someone you love if you don't. Will knows what we are, and he wants to help you."

"It's okay," Will urges. "Please." His pounding heart is almost deafening.

Dusty's brow furrows as she tries to hold on to her thoughts. *No. He can't see me like this.*

"Eli's right," Will adds. "Enough."

But then what's happening sinks in. She shakes her head. "No. No. No."

"I can't imagine how scared you must be," Will says. "But I'm not. You're the strongest person I know, and just the fact that you've fought this all these weeks, when everyone else gave in, is proof of that."

"I don't know me," she whispers. She tries to get up, but she can't, and she doesn't remember what she was trying to say.

"You're *you*, Dusty," Opi whispers, suddenly close to them.

Dusty's eyes flutter as she tries to keep them open.

"You told me to listen to my instincts," Will says. "Now you need to listen to yours. You need to feed, Dusty. You need—"

"What I need . . ." she says slowly, barely able to speak. "It got someone killed."

He bends down close to her, and she wonders if he didn't hear her.

"I killed a man," she whispers, her heart in her throat. She braces herself for him to look at her like a stranger. To run. To leave her.

"When?" he says calmly, his eyes scanning her face.

"After the bonfire . . . We . . . It was an acciden—"

"Hurry up," Eli urges from somewhere beside her.

"You didn't choose this, Dusty," Opi says. "You didn't know what you were doing. But now you do."

"Eli knows you won't hurt me," Will continues. "*I* know you won't hurt me, so you have to choose between life, and whatever form of starvation you've been putting yourself through."

She closes her eyes.

He didn't run, she thinks. *He's still here.*

"What do I do?" Will repeats.

"Here," Eli says. "Give me your wrist."

Dusty shakes her head, peering through drooping eyelids as Will holds out his arm to Eli, and Eli bites down.

"No," she gurgles. But the most beautiful scent washes over her.

As the light continues to fade, Dusty's fear, her grief and her love begin to coil within her. Spinning faster and faster, they move like a tornado, drawing out the oldest, stickiest, most stubborn thoughts from the dark places they hide. Her muscles resist at first, but she wills them to soften, lulled by Will's blue embrace. In the spiral's wake, she feels lit up, as if she's made of sunshine.

Will holds his wrist just in front of her and she reaches up, grabbing his forearm and bringing it toward her face as a drop of his blood lands on her lips.

She licks, and her mouth floods with water, the sunshine inside her shimmering, and she lets go of any hesitation, moving her mouth over Eli's bite, letting Will's blood fill her.

It's slow at first, running down her throat, then she sucks more urgently.

His blue calm enveloping her, she pictures the deer, the first one she fed from, and realizes that the rhythm that had calmed it was Will's. He had given it to her, in the brief time they'd spent together, like a seed he had planted.

She feels her own energy begin to rise as his life force pumps inside her, and she knows that she can't go back from here.

A quiet moan sounds from his throat, making her pull from him even harder. He is everywhere and everything is a blur as she soars through the stars.

"Dusty!" Eli's voice warns, firm.

She feels a hand shaking her shoulder.

Her mouth loosens from Will's wrist, just slightly, and she begins to come back from wherever it is she goes when she's feeding.

Slowly, she releases her teeth from Will's skin, and still dazed, she licks his wrist, nursing his wound.

When she opens her eyes, Will is staring down at her, awestruck.

"Are you okay?" she asks. She tries to sit up beside him, but her body is still sluggish.

"Easy," he whispers. "I'm okay."

She can feel her wounds healing, her fractured bones mending, his blood weaving her back together. She sweeps back the hair that's fallen over his face to see him fully.

He's the most beautiful person she's ever seen.

But movement behind him snaps her out of her daze. Dusty gasps as she remembers where they are, and what's happened. She pushes herself up, seeing that Eli and Opi are there. For a second, a knowing smile pulls at Eli's face, while Opi studies Dusty, her eyes straining against the dark of night. Both of their colors reveal a clash of relief, love and sorrow. Dark and slowly swirling, with fretful, sketchy edges.

Just beyond them are three figures.

"Kristen," Dusty whispers.

Ignoring her wobbling legs, she goes to them.

"She's dead," Mali says, still kneeling beside Kristen's body. She turns to Dusty. "She's dead."

"She's dead," Amber repeats from above them. "And he just left me."

The memory of being pinned to the riverbed strikes Dusty like a flash of lightning. She doesn't know what to say to Amber. She doesn't know how to feel.

"What do we do?" Mali asks. "Should we call the police?" She looks down at Kristen, a sob escaping her as she repeats, "What do we do?"

"We can't," Eli says gently, now standing above them.

"But—" Mali starts.

"We *can't*," Eli repeats, more firmly.

"He's right," Opi says.

Dusty glances back at her sister, who's helping Will stand up, steadying him.

"Not if we want to protect Dusty," Opi adds.

Mali looks up at Dusty, and for a moment that look returns to her face, like she doesn't know her anymore. But she wipes her eyes, still wet with tears, and the look is gone. "What about JD?" she asks.

"Let's get home safe," Eli says. "Then I'll go out looking for him."

Amber opens her mouth to say something but before she can, Eli cuts in. "Don't even think about running."

She closes her mouth.

"It'll be morning soon," Opi says.

"But what . . . what about Kristen?" Mali asks, turning to look down at the limp figure, her neck and head at an unnatural angle, her ponytail splayed among dirt and leaves.

"If we leave her here, someone will find her," Eli says. "Eventually."

"And if they do an autopsy," Dusty says, still finding her voice, "they might be able to tell that she's . . . different."

"Does that matter now?" Mali asks.

"It does if we don't want anyone looking around for more people like her," Eli says. "If we don't want anyone looking for *us*. We'd become science experiments."

"We have to bury her," Dusty says. She's still aware of Will's blood inside her, and the way it allows her emotions to flow freely, already feeling less overwhelmed than before, despite everything.

Mali shakes her head as fresh tears fall. Everyone waits, quiet, until she wipes them away again. Then finally, she nods, understanding.

32

Because of You

Dusty watches as Eli carries Kristen's body in his arms. He makes it look like it's nothing, like she's barely there. Which, Dusty supposes, is true.

Absorbing the sadness of this loss, she follows Eli into the forest, Mali, Opi, Will and Amber close behind them.

When they find a quiet spot under an ancient sugar maple, a little further up the mountain, away from any houses or trails, Eli places Kristen on the earth. Then, together, they all begin to dig a shallow grave with their bare hands.

As they bury her, heaping soil on top of blonde hair and cold skin as the sky slowly lightens above the canopy, Dusty watches their individual colors reach down, saying heartfelt, wordless prayers.

Opi, who must have collected whatever flowers they passed on their way, goes to place them on top of the upturned soil. Dusty has to stop her, shaking her head as the others sprinkle leaves and rocks over the grave instead, camouflaging it.

Back at the river, they step down into the water to wash themselves clean. The surface of the flowing water begins to reflect the pinks and oranges of sunrise—a mask atop the depths of the river's secrets—and Dusty says another silent prayer for Andrew Everett, grief and remorse gliding through her, as, she imagines, they always will.

As they approach the tree line just below her house, the sound of a crackling radio stops Dusty in her tracks.

Eli and Amber have stilled too, while Will, Mali and Opi glance around uncertainly. Dusty holds a finger up to her mouth, signaling everyone to stay quiet.

When they're close enough to see, they peer through the dense trees to the sheriff's vehicle parked in the driveway, with Deputy Brookes, another officer and Chris standing beside the front steps.

"We're going to prison," Amber declares.

"Shhh," Eli says, straining to listen.

Dusty listens too.

"Thanks for your help on this one, Chris," Deputy Brookes is saying. "Hope the all-nighter doesn't throw you off too much."

"I'm just relieved we finally found him," Chris answers.

"Or what's left of him," the other officer says.

Dusty's stomach drops, and when she looks at Eli, his face is a ghostly white.

Brookes glares at the officer before turning back to Chris. "Anyway, hopefully we get some answers from the coroner. But even if the state of him makes it hard to determine a cause of death, the fact that he was buried like that means that there's a killer on the loose."

"But do you think . . ." Chris starts. "Could one person have moved those rocks onto him like that? It took four of you to roll them off."

Brookes turns to the other officer. "Wait in the car?"

The younger man hesitates, then slinks down the steps, out of earshot.

"It's like those cows," Brookes says to Chris, his voice lowered.

Dusty has to work to listen, but she can already feel the effects of Will's blood in her system, and she can hear what he says next as if he were beside her.

"Something feels . . . strange about this. You know another cow was found the other day? Just one."

"Oh yeah?" Chris asks, his colors shifting.

"It was about a mile away from its paddock, but same as last time, no broken fences, no open gates. And . . . Well, like that other one, it appears to have been dropped from a great height. Its bones were all shattered inside its skin."

Dusty shivers as she wonders if it's possible that the incident with the cows could have anything to do with what's happened here, on the mountain.

"I'm telling you this," Brookes continues, "because I need you to tell me that you know of an animal that could have done that. Some sort of predator, maybe airborne, because like last time, there were no tracks."

Chris considers for a moment before shaking his head. "Sorry, Brookes. I wish I knew. But nothing, no man, machine, or animal, could lift a cow and drop it without leaving tracks. It's impossible."

Brookes nods. "That's the thing. Everyone else at the station is trying to convince me it *is* possible. That it's some cult, like they said last time. And honestly, I don't blame them. Because I'd rather think that there's a satanic cult out there than have to wonder about the alternatives."

Shaking his head, Brookes turns and walks back down the steps.

Dusty's heart is pounding as Eli finally repeats what they've heard to the others, leaving everyone gaping.

Dusty watches her dad, his brow pulled together in a frown as he waits for the officers to leave. She doesn't turn around to face the others until Chris is inside.

"What do we do?" Opi whispers. "Do you think . . . is there any way they'll find out it was you?"

Dusty can't bring herself to meet anyone's eyes but Eli's as fresh waves of guilt and anxiety crash over her. It's disorienting, because even though she's barely spared a thought for it, she feels stronger. Better than she's felt in weeks. Better than ever, really. A hand slips into hers, Will's, and the waves soften slightly.

"Don't worry," Eli says, turning to Opi. "One thing at a time."

She flashes him a glare, as if it's automatic. But when he dips his chin, a subtle gesture of reassurance, and says, "Ophelia," her head tilts slightly to study him, as if she's recontextualizing all of her assumptions.

"Okay," Eli continues. "Amber, you're coming with me."

She doesn't protest, still barely able to speak since JD fled, and Dusty still isn't sure what to make of it. After seeing how she was changed, that JD *infected* her, Dusty wonders how strong their bond is, and how similar or different it might be to Dusty and Eli's. Whatever it is, Amber was shocked to know what JD had done to his own father, and had hesitated enough to make Dusty think she might still be Amber, somewhere in there, after all.

"I'll come too," Mali says to Eli. "Help you look after her, or whatever. She can't go home. Not yet. Not after what happened."

Dusty frowns, worried that the real reason Mali wants to go is because she can't look at her anymore. But it's clear that the tone of blue dominating Mali's colors is sadness, so Dusty lets go of her own worry, knowing Mali will need time.

"I know we have a lot to talk about," Dusty says. "All of us." She looks around at everyone, still wondering how they all got down to the river and how everything else transpired as it did. "But let's leave it until later? I think we all need to process last night, in our own time."

Everyone nods.

"But thank you," Dusty says. "All of you. For coming for me."

She hugs Mali, then Eli too, before they head down the trail to Eli's, Amber in tow.

Dusty turns to Will and Opi. "Dad's in the shower," she says. "If we go in now, he might not even know we were out."

Will hesitates as he looks between the sisters.

"You should come in," Opi says to him. "Rest. Clean up properly. It's been a long night."

He looks to Dusty, unsure.

"Come in," she repeats.

They go in through Dusty's window and wait for Chris to head downstairs in silence. Dusty's room is warm and quiet, sunlight streaming through the windows, lighting up the old furniture with a soft glow. All that remains unsaid feels thick between the three of them.

Then, they shower and change, Will throwing on a pair of Dusty's sweatpants and a baggy t-shirt that's slightly tight on him, before Opi suggests they go downstairs and make an appearance.

"It wouldn't hurt if you ate something, either," she says to Will.

"Go back out the window," Dusty says. "Wait ten minutes, then knock on the front door?"

"I can just go," he says.

"Don't?" she asks. "If you don't want to. Don't?"

He smiles before heading outside.

When she turns to her sister, Opi's eyes are already welling with tears.

"Are you okay?" Dusty asks, pulling Opi into a hug.

Opi nods into her shoulder, quietly sobbing. "I shouldn't be," she says, her breath quaking. "But I am. I'm just so relieved you're okay . . . that it wasn't you." She leans back to look at Dusty. "You look so much better," she says, her eyes scanning every part of her sister. "Already. I can't believe it. Dust, I thought you were going to die."

"So you're . . . okay . . . with what you saw me do to Will?"

Opi nods. "I would have told you to do anything, whatever it was going to take, to make you better."

Dusty huffs a laugh of relief, disbelief, and everything else she's feeling all rolled into one. When she looks back up at her sister, she cups her face and begins to wipe the flowing tears from her cheeks.

"So . . . how did you find out?" Dusty asks.

Opi breathes deeply before she answers. "I overheard you and Eli talking yesterday and then Mali filled in the gaps."

Dusty's confusion is obvious. "Wait. You were home yesterday? Why? I thought you were in town for the fireworks?" But before Opi can answer, Dusty's eyes widen. She smiles, her senses confirming the shift in her sister. "You finally got your first period."

"Is it that obvious?!"

"No." Dusty laughs. "I mean, to me, yeah. Heightened senses, remember?"

"Oh my god. Does that mean Eli knew too?" Opi cringes.

"Who cares?" Dusty says, shrugging it off.

"I had to leave the party," Opi explains. "I tried to call you. I wasn't exactly prepared."

Dusty squeezes Opi's hand, remembering what it felt like, without a mom to call. "I'm sorry I wasn't there for you," Dusty says.

"You had a pretty good excuse, I guess."

"So you heard *everything*? Everything Eli and I said?"

Opi nods.

"I don't . . . You must have so many quest—"

"I was relieved, if I'm honest," Opi interrupts. "I knew you'd been lying to me. I mean, I'm used to you being private, keeping things close to your chest, but it never felt like you were purposefully keeping things from *me* until recently. I knew you weren't eating much, you weren't reading. You were sneaking out most nights and you started to look so tired because of it. I wanted to kill Eli. I thought you were doing it all for him."

"You thought I'd lose my shit over a boy?" Dusty asks, eyebrows raised.

Opi laughs, nodding.

"Please," Dusty says, rolling her eyes. "At least, well . . . I guess I kind of did, just a different boy."

"Will?" Opi asks.

Dusty nods.

"So does it really mean you can't eat anything at all?" Opi asks.

"Nothing," Dusty says.

"I can't even imagine," she says. "I'm so sorry."

"I'm sorry too."

"You sounded so hopeless when you were arguing with Eli yesterday, so adamant that you didn't want . . . what you need. He sounded so worried about you. I was scared that even if you didn't want to, you might leave—"

"Never," Dusty says firmly. "I will *never* leave you, okay?"

Opi nods again.

"I have some things to tell you," Dusty says. "About mom. Things I've learned through my new . . . abilities. But is it okay if I tell you later? I'm just not . . . I just need to catch my breath."

Opi looks at her, curious, but says, "Okay."

Dusty stands, mentally preparing to face her dad. "Come on," she says.

"Wait." Opi stands, hesitating.

"What is it?"

"Well . . . I'm not sure if it's related, but now I know what's been going on, maybe it is . . ."

"What is?"

"Well, a few weeks ago, I woke up and there was someone in my room, standing at the foot of my bed."

Dusty's whole body reacts instantly, fired up with a panic that's so intense she breaks into a sweat. "What do you mean?" she asks, her jaw tight.

"They pulled off my sheet," Opi explains. "And started to pull me toward them. I couldn't see who it was, but I know I was awake because they left when they heard you and Eli come in through your window. And I had this feeling . . . that they'd be back for me."

"Jesus!" Dusty says, beginning to pace. "Why didn't you tell me?! Or if not me, Dad?!'

"He's been just as worried about you as I have. Probably more! But also, I can't explain it, it's like I wanted to keep it a secret. Like every cell in my body was telling me not to tell anyone."

Dusty's head is spinning, wondering if it could have been JD.

She goes to her bedside table where her phone is charging, picks it up and messages Eli to ask if there's been any sign of JD. He replies right away, telling her there's been nothing, then down their bond she gets a sense of things at his house. Amber on the floor of his room, staring into space, Mali and Eli talking, debriefing on the night that passed.

"I'm going to fix this," Dusty says to Opi. "I don't know how, but now we know a bit more, I can look for a way to reverse this. I've accepted what I need right now. What I am. But it doesn't mean I'm going to give up."

Opi gives her a reassuring smile, then together, they head downstairs.

"Morning, girls," Chris says, looking up from his crossword.

They both go straight over to their father, slipping their arms around him.

He chuckles, hearty and warm. "Everything okay?" he asks.

Opi slips away to the stove to turn the kettle on, giving Chris a chance to pull back and look at Dusty.

"You look . . . better, kiddo," he says, his eyes scanning her face.

"Thanks," she says.

"Where were you last night?" Opi asks casually.

"Another search," he says. "We found the poor guy. Rest his soul."

Dusty gulps, then manages, "That's terrible."

Chris nods, his colors shifting with his thoughts.

Then the doorbell rings.

Dusty runs to get it, her heartbeat quickening as she flings the door open. The sight of Will on her front doorstep makes her draw in a deep breath. "Are you okay?" she asks again.

"I'm hungry," he says, then gives her a gentle, crooked smile, dimple and all.

In the kitchen, Chris tries to hide his confusion at Will's arrival. Dusty isn't sure if it's because he's relieved Eli might be out of the picture, but he's his usual warm self, and offers to cook them all breakfast.

Dusty opens all the windows, letting the sun and fresh air in, and the smell of food out. When it's ready, Will devours a big breakfast of eggs, sausages, and mushrooms coated in Opi's herbs.

Chris laughs, mumbling something about teenage boys and their appetites.

Will asks Opi a million questions about her garden, before Opi offers to take him outside and show him.

Dusty goes upstairs, the promise of a moment alone luring her like a magnet. As she climbs the last step, she notices the hall runner is slightly askew. It happens from time to time, and out of habit, she bends to straighten it. Sun bounces into the landing from her room, hitting the floor at an angle she rarely sees. It's in just the right place to catch on something glimmering between the floorboards.

She bends down, looking at what seems to be a tiny diamond nestled in the narrow crack, its angles catching the light from outside.

She finds a hair pin in a bathroom drawer and plucks it out.

It isn't just a diamond. It's a diamond attached to a fine, silver chain, and she can instantly picture it around her mother's neck. Dusty always assumed that her mother had been wearing it when she left.

She goes into her room and looks in the mirror as she puts it on.

A small hand reaches up and touches the diamond.

"Is it a star?" Opi asks.

"No, sweetheart. It's a diamond. It was formed deep in the earth over millions, maybe even billions of years." She watches her daughters staring in awe at the necklace as she speaks. As if it's magic.

"Woah," they say with wonder.

They're lying in the grass on the southern slope of the garden, the big old house behind them, the branches of the beech tree above. Sunshine catches in the girls' hair, bringing out the rich darkness of Dusty's and the golden highlights of Opi's.

Sarah is thinking that like the diamond, they are miracles—her girls with perfect little toes and beating hearts and big, beautiful smiles—and she can't believe that she played a part in making them.

There's a loud honking sound above them and she squints to look up, seeing the arrowhead formation of Canada geese as they fly north. Their enormous wings carry them far and fast on a mission they'll never question. Their path is laid out before them, their migration in their DNA. It's what they're born to do.

Sarah thinks of the distance the geese cover and how big the world is, and she's reminded once more that there's a world outside of these mountains, a world she often pretends doesn't exist at all. But she's not going to think about that today. Not on a perfect day, when every year, there are more and more bad days than good.

Dusty laughs at a beetle that's landed on her arm, its tiny legs tickling her skin, and Sarah feels nothing but pure, absolute love.

Grief tears through Dusty as she rolls her finger over the diamond, feeling the pressure of it pushing into her skin. The grief is just as painful as the day her mom left, but instead of it demolishing her, terrifying her, she lets it roam.

"I'm going to find you," she whispers out loud, like it's a promise.

And for the first time since she left, Dusty can feel her mother's love in her bones.

She reaches for her notebook and opens it, then, with pen to paper, her hand moves freely, swirling in spirals, drawing lines that over a full page look like the shifting knots in a tree.

She's just about to put her pen down, giving in to this fleeting moment of stillness, when footsteps ascend the old, creaking staircase.

"So," Will says, looking around. "This is Dusty Silver's room."

She smiles.

The hunger that overwhelmed her every time she was near him has faded. Not gone completely, but it's now overshadowed by what she feels for him.

"Come in," she says.

He steps inside, scanning all the little things that at some point in her life, Dusty has counted as special.

"How are you feeling?" she asks, her cheeks flushing when she thinks of what he let her do to him.

"A little tired," he admits.

"Are you sure you're okay—"

"Yeah," Will says, smiling shyly. "It was . . . sharp, at first," he continues, more serious. "Then cold. Like, ice cold. But then the sharpness softened. And it was . . . surprising."

Dusty feels a flicker of embarrassment, but she doesn't try to restrain it as she waits for him to say more.

He smiles with his eyes as his cheeks flush. "It was good. It felt good."

"Good," she says softly.

He hovers, unsure of what to do. He looks up at the half-vaulted ceiling and his Adam's apple juts out from his throat.

Dusty swallows.

The hunger is definitely still present.

"Can I ask you something?" he says, looking back down at her.

"Anything."

"What's it like? Being you."

Dusty thinks. But it's impossible to know where to begin.

"Not the blood," he tries to clarify. "I mean . . . the rest of it."

She nods, and he sits down beside her on the bed.

"Imagine everything is intensified. Sounds, smells, light. I can feel other people's emotions, even see them in colors that flow around them. And when I hurt, I *really* hurt. When I want, I *really* want. When I love . . ." She glances up at him, then reaches for the diamond necklace around her neck, rolling it between her thumb and fingers. "It's been hard. Brutal, really. At first all I wanted was answers. I thought that if I knew why I was like this, how it happened, that somehow everything would be okay again. But I can see now that things weren't okay before either. So even though so many awful things have happened, things I will never recover from, and even though I don't have any answers, or know if this is forever, I feel like I've made it to the other side of something. And what's on the other side is me. *I* am still here. More here than I was before."

Will looks into her eyes and smiles. "Have I told you how much I like listening to you speak?"

Dusty feels herself flush, but holds his gaze.

"And Eli?" Will asks. "I don't want to come between . . . whatever you are to each oth—"

"We're family," she says. "We've been to hell and back together."

"Yeah. I can't imagine."

"But as far as our relationship goes . . . he's like a brother to me. Everything else was just for show."

Will nods, letting the implications sink in.

"But, Will?" Dusty says. "Just in case it isn't clear . . . I haven't stopped thinking about you since the moment I crashed into you outside the cafeteria. Before I knew what I was, and even after everything that's happened . . ." She hesitates but decides to give him the full truth. "You overwhelmed me. Everything about you. I wanted you . . . your blood . . . so badly. But also, I just wanted to be around you. To hold your hand."

His eyes move back and forth between hers as she speaks, clinging to every one of her words. When she slips her hand into his, his colors light up, brighter than ever before.

"I meant it when I said that I didn't trust myself around you," she goes on. "I was so hungry, so in denial, that all I knew was that I had to push you away. But it was never just about your blood. I know, now, it's because of you." She thinks about Eli and Jesse, and how despite Eli's hunger, the emotions behind it are different. Unclear.

And her feelings for Will are as clear as water.

"I just thought you should know," she says softly.

With his free hand, he sweeps his hair off his face as he looks into Dusty's eyes. "I've been thinking about you since the first time I saw you, Dusty."

She can feel herself beginning to smile. "You have?"

"Yeah, I have."

Her energy pulses through her, steady and strong, and she can feel his reaching out, tiny sparks bursting when his colors collide with what she thinks might be her own. They're faint, softer than others, but they're definitely there.

Will lets go of her hand and starts to trace his fingers along her arm. Goosebumps rise from her skin. She reaches up and places a hand on his cool cheek, her eyes moving from his, down over his mouth.

There's only a moment before they collide in a kiss that melts the world away.

Their lips part as they taste each other, their tongues softly exploring, becoming feverish as their kiss deepens.

His hands feel like they're everywhere. Imprinting glimmers so that Dusty doesn't know if he's touching her there *now*, or if it was moments ago. Her face, her neck, her waist, her hips, all at once. As her own hands trace his arms, lean and strong, his scent feels like dew on her skin. She inhales, letting it soak her.

Eventually, Will pulls back slightly, leaning his forehead against Dusty's, hugging her close.

Dusty smiles softly. She is in her body completely, aware of every sensation, and for once, feeling it all doesn't hurt at all.

33

White Mountain

There's a loud noise ringing in Dusty's head. She opens her eyes, unsure if the sound came from within a dream, or somewhere inside the house.

It's the middle of the night. Sleep and darkness cloud her vision, but she remembers the sensation of kissing Will, how he'd left, saying he'd come over tomorrow.

She looks around her dark room, feeling a pull that makes her stand, drawing her out into the hall.

She looks in Opi's room.

Her sister is not in her bed.

It's as if she's in a trance. She's calm as the pull tugs her downstairs, then out of the house like she's connected to a string.

The night is still and uncommonly quiet, as if the mountain is holding its breath. She looks up at the sky, a canvas covered by brilliant stars, and a moon so close Dusty feels like it's watching her. The Milky Way flows like a luminous river through the darkness. Leaves crumple under her bare feet as she walks around to the north side of the house. She begins the ascent up the mountain, hesitant, her body telling her to brace herself—something momentous is about to happen.

Through the trees, she can see a strange light glowing from somewhere higher up. She wonders if she could still be dreaming. But the sound of her own footsteps and the texture of the earth beneath her tell her she's wide awake.

A twig snaps up ahead and Dusty pivots.

Through the eerie glow she catches a glimpse of white fabric, then long hair glistening in the moonlight. She follows.

As the light intensifies and trees give way to rocky outcrops, she sees the figure. It's her sister.

"Opi!" she calls out. The sound of her own voice is muffled, making Dusty feel like she's disturbed something she shouldn't have.

But Opi doesn't turn around.

It's like she's sleepwalking.

Dusty follows, pushing through the night air, thick with anticipation.

The glow of light up ahead is neither natural nor artificial, neither warm nor cold, but it's getting brighter, casting otherworldly shadows on the landscape.

Dusty wants to call out again, but that feeling tells her she shouldn't.

A prickle spreads across the back of her neck then cascades down her limbs. Then, like a switch has been flipped, the light disappears.

Dusty looks around, searching, until she finally sees Opi, even further ahead now, lit by the moonlight.

She's almost at the summit.

Dusty moves faster, climbing up and over rocks that become steeper with every step. A small fir tree blocks her path and as she steps around it her breath catches in the back of her throat.

Low, scattered clouds glide above as if they're being drawn to the mountain, veiling the moonlight.

Opi is at the mountain's peak. Motionless.

A flicker in the sky draws Dusty's attention up. At first she thinks it's a star, but white wisps begin to flow from it, creating a glowing, ethereal pattern directly above the mountain's summit. It's almost geometric, but there are no words to describe what she's seeing.

Then, very slowly, a dark shadow begins to rise from the other side of the peak, perfectly round, its blackness like a void absorbing all the light around it, featureless against the starry, cloud-cloaked sky.

It continues to rise until it hovers—an immense black orb suspended between the luminescent pattern above and the mountain below.

Despite its lack of discernible features, the presence of the orb is palpable. Dusty feels like it could swallow her whole.

Every cell in her body begins to tremble, and as she gazes into the black void, she's awash with unease, as if she's staring into an abyss. But at the same time, it beckons, an invitation to understand the truth while warning of dangers that lie within.

The wispy pattern of light above the orb begins to dim, then disappears completely. At the same moment, the orb becomes solid. Metal, maybe, reflecting the world around it like a mirror before it shivers into solid matte. Soundless.

As Dusty watches, unable to move, Opi is drawn up into the air, weightless, her eyes closed. Her limbs and head fall back as if strings are pulling at her torso.

A scattering of rocks rise with her, caught in the pull.

Opi stops, thirty feet above the ground, levitating just beneath the hovering orb.

Everything is still.

There's a faint glimmer of light over the orb's surface, then a ripple of air courses outwards like a breath, invisible if not for the movement in Opi's hair and clothes.

Dusty's mind goes silent, and it's as if the presence has taken over. Another consciousness, penetrating her mind, beginning to communicate with her. Showing her.

She's flooded with images and emotions, abstract at first, then clear and familiar. Like her mind and body are translating them into a language she can understand.

An ancient intelligence planting seeds across worlds, changing life's trajectory.
Cattle scattered across a field, useful parts plucked to be studied. To experiment. To perfect.
The presence in the forest, hovering, watching the young people who live here, close enough to scorch the trees.
Two girls forage. What's hidden in the mountain lingers in their bones, making them special. One's body is ready, but the other's isn't.
She sleepwalks up the mountain, answering the call, rising up with the three others. The ripple runs through them, changing them.
Watching their progress through the trees, fascinated by the different ways they respond to their new needs. How unique they each are. Waiting for them all to accept their fate.
Dusty, the last one, giving in.
The younger girl's body is ready now. It's time.
A distant place. A point of origin. Still and perfect. Where life creates life, spiralling out into the infinite, connecting it all.

Looking up at her sister, Dusty can see an outpouring of colors around her, like rainbows that spring from the crown of her head, then weave back down inside her, shimmering with the light of a billion stars.

With the consciousness still attached to her, communicating, Dusty understands what she's seeing. Opi's non-coding DNA communicating what to enhance and what to repress, her microbiome responding, changing.

She was right.

As Opi's body slowly descends, Dusty's mind begins to regain control of itself. When her sister's feet touch the ground, the orb transforms into a small ball of light. *That* light. It lingers for another moment, then ascends into the night, out of sight.

Dusty spins around, sensing movement behind her. Eli is there, called to the presence just as she was. And beyond him stands JD, gazing up at the point the light disappeared.

Turning out to face the expanse of wilderness around them, the rolling, jutting mountains dotted with lakes, bound by rivers full of life and death, Dusty knows that this world is changing, and that she is right here in the thick of it.

Something vast is at play, and each and every one of us is a part of it.

Author's Note

I've come to believe that our bodies are vessels that contain entire worlds. Like Mary Poppins's carpet bag or Hermione's beaded purse, our outward appearance does not reflect the scale of what lies within. We are deep, dark, beautiful and eternally complex. We also live, breathe and age, constantly responding to the physical world around us. So it's only natural to let some of what exists within us out.

Everyone has their tics or ways in which these internal facets manifest. Some are obvious to other people, some more subtle. Either way, I didn't feel like I could bring the characters in this book to life without exploring this part of existence. Like me, when an internal storm is raging inside Dusty, she weathers it outwardly by giving in to an urge to control what's in front of her—neatening up a surface or drawing line after line and dot after dot in a book. And when that's not enough, because some storms are simply too mighty, the storm creates physical aches and pains in her body—finding it hard to breathe, her chest clenching around her heart, her muscles chronically tense. She's also no stranger, as none of us are, to an intrusive thought—fear or anxiety taking shape in a daydream you never asked for.

It's easy to feel ashamed of the ways in which we find an outlet, especially when they interfere with our lives and feel harmful and toxic. But I think it's important to remember that it's really just a very clever, very creative way that our bodies communicate with us. They're telling us that we're not okay, that we need to slow down or self-soothe or find a different sort of outlet. So rather than hating the tics, I've started to feel grateful for them. They remind me to connect to my breath, to stretch my body, to eat what makes me feel best, and to get outside and reconnect with the natural world. These things help my inner storms dissipate.

All this is to say, there is no such thing as normal. And I think that's the best thing about being human.

Acknowledgments

It's hard to find the words to describe the feeling of putting this book out into the world. Back in 2023, the year I started writing it, it had been seventeen years since I'd written anything creative. What has unfolded since my fingers first began tapping at the keyboard is nothing short of surreal.

Firstly, I would like to thank you, the reader, for giving this book your precious time. I hope it found a way to give you a little something in return.

Secondly, I'd like to acknowledge that I count myself profoundly lucky. Every person who has read this and given their feedback has collectively taught me how to be a writer, and every person in my life has made seeing this through possible.

Throughout the process of writing this—and before and after—I've had the unwavering love and support of my husband, Tim, whose belief, care and optimism have helped keep me afloat. Your early feedback had a profound impact on where this story went, and I can't thank you enough for wrangling our noisy boys in rain, hail and shine so I could focus. Our love and gratitude for you know no bounds.

Ted and Jimmy—the lights of our life: my love for you is infinite and eternal, and I hope you feel that every day of your lives.

Thank you to my mum, Joan Sauers, who forged my love of storytelling from day one. The fact that you wrote your first novel at the age of seventy is what inspired me to try to do this, and your unconditional love is the foundation of who I am.

Thank you to my dad, Gary Heery, who is always himself no matter where he is or who he's with. You normalised creativity and individuality for me from such a young age—traits that were a big part of me finding the courage to write this.

My sisters, in blood and in friendship—Aurelie, Billie, Amelia, Ginger, Sunday, Brooke, Anna, Lily, Caitlin, Edie, Jo, and so many more—your energy recharges me always and I'm endlessly grateful for you, even if sometimes our time together is fleeting. To the rest of my family, old and new, near and far, passed and present, I love you all so, so much. I'm sorry it took me so long to reply or call back sometimes, and I'm sorry for what I missed while I had my head down trying to make this book happen.

To Edie Lauer and Anthony O'Neill, who read the first draft alongside my mum and husband: your feedback gave me the first glimmer of hope that there might be something here people would want to read.

My agents, Lou Johnson, Belinda Bolliger and the team at Key People—being able to navigate this journey with you means everything to me. If someone had told me two years ago that I'd have a team of the smartest, most inspiring women backing me, I'd never have believed them.

A very special thank you to my publisher and editor, Anthea Bariamis, who took a chance on a first-time novelist and helped draw these characters out of the cobwebs of my mind. I trust you completely. Thank you for trusting me right back. You are the best book fairy a girl could ask for.

To the rest of the team at Simon & Schuster and Atria Australia

(I still have to pinch myself when I say that) and the freelancers they worked with—I feel so privileged to be in your hands. Rosie Outred, you are an absolute dream to work with. Thank you for keeping a close eye on every word in here, and for everything else you do, every step of the way. Emily Wilson, Jasmine Aird, Josie O'Malley and Hannah Janzen—thank you so much for all your hard work in the lead-up to publication. To Coco McGrath, the book's copy editor, and its proofreader, Celia Killen: I clung to your every comment and was so grateful for each one, big and small. Thank you for making this as clean and sparkling as it is today.

Arub Ahmed and Lucy Pearse at Simon & Schuster UK—I'm so grateful for your notes, time and care.

To Carolina Rodríguez Fuenmayor, the incredible artist who illustrated the Australian cover—thank you for your beautiful vision and for, arguably most importantly, giving Dusty bangs. Thank you to Tara Phillips, the extraordinarily talented artist who created the character illustration of Dusty and Will. It is such a pleasure to see these characters imagined by you.

I would like to acknowledge that this book was written on both Cammeraygal and Dharawal land, far across the world from where the story takes place. There, the Adirondack Mountains are the land of the Mohawk, Kanyengehaga, Keepers of the Eastern Door; the Seneca, Onondewagaono, Keepers of the Western Door; the Onondaga, Onontaga, Fire Keepers on the Mountain; and later custodians, the Younger Brothers—the Oneida, Oneyotdehaga, People of the Standing Stone; the Cayuga, Gayokwehonu, People of the Great Swamp; and the Tuscarora, the Hemp Gatherers—who, over generations, witnessed the rise and fall of the Champlain Sea, a prehistoric inlet of the Atlantic Ocean that once covered much of the Adirondack Mountains. This earth is ancient, and invaluable is the knowledge of those who had the opportunity to live with it, stewarding it and adapting to it as it inevitably changed and evolved. The world has a lot to learn—and remember—from you.

I am especially grateful for Adirondacks Forever Wild (wildadirondacks.org), which proved to be my most invaluable and frequently consulted resource throughout writing this. Whoever put so much care into compiling such detailed information on every imaginable habitat and species in the Adirondack Mountains—I am in awe of you.

Finally—and maybe oddly, but here it is—I'd like to thank my endometriosis. A constant companion since my early teens, my fateful foe, you have taught me more about myself and the world I live in than almost anything or anyone else ever could. Even when I didn't know what you were for so long, you taught me strength and resilience. You taught me to trust my instincts, and to advocate for myself when so many tried to steer me toward doubt. Because of you, I had to find a way to be in my body, listen to it, and give it what it needs. Enemies to lovers—we are one. And I am eternally grateful for you.